MEGAN'S SONG

H. LEE PRATT

FIVE STAR
A part of Gale, a Cengage Company

GALE
A Cengage Company

Farmington Hills, Mich • San Francisco • New York • Waterville, Maine
Meriden, Conn • Mason, Ohio • Chicago

LIBRARY OF CONGRESS CATALOGING-IN-PUBLICATION DATA

Names: Pratt, H. Lee, 1930-2016, author.
Title: Megan's song / H. Lee Pratt.
Description: First edition. | Farmington Hills, Mich. : Five Star, [2018]
Identifiers: LCCN 2018014453| ISBN 9781432847067 (hardcover) | ISBN 9781432847470 (ebook) | 9781432847487 (ebook)
Classification: LCC PS3616.R3836 M44 2018 | DDC 813/.6—dc23 LC record available at https://lccn.loc.gov/2018014453

First Edition. First Printing: December 2018
Find us on Facebook—https://www.facebook.com/FiveStarCengage
Visit our website—http://www.gale.cengage.com/fivestar/
Contact Five Star Publishing at FiveStar@cengage.com

Printed in Mexico
1 2 3 4 5 6 7 22 21 20 19 18

MEGAN'S SONG

MEGAN'S SONG

PROLOGUE

From the front page of the *Wyoming State Tribune*, Thursday, June 25, 1925:

AVALANCHE IN GROS VENTRE RIVER VALLEY
HUGE LAKE FORMED BY LANDSLIDE NEAR JACKSON

JACKSON, Wyo., June 25.—Twenty miles northeast of Jackson, several cattle ranchers narrowly escaped death on Tuesday when a mountain side suddenly crumbled and hurled an avalanche of rocks and earth into the Gros Ventre River valley below.

Only by some swift riding did one rancher escape the avalanche to reach higher ground, where he watched the flood of earth and rocks sweep by at the speed of a fast-moving railroad train, razing everything in its path. In the Teton National Forest, huge trees in the path of the landslide splintered into pieces, according to reports from the local telephone company.

The extent of the damage has not yet been fully ascertained, but the meager accounts reaching this newspaper state that the landslide destroyed at least three ranches and buried alive several herds of livestock.

It was also reliably reported that Parley Frampton and a party of movie people had embarked on a filming trip beyond the area of the slide. The fate of the party is as yet unknown.

CHAPTER 1

Thursday Afternoon, June 4

The paddle fans dangling from the ceiling of the Clubhouse did little to move the air, much less disperse the odor of human sweat, popcorn, and cow shit. This mattered little to the good folks sitting in the dark on hard-backed chairs, for they were all entranced by the images flickering soot and silver on the movie screen—all, that is, except Megan Foxworth.

She was seated in the middle of the middle row next to Gertie, the telephone switchboard operator. She wrang her handkerchief between strong, blunt-tipped fingers. She needed to get back to the Rocking Lazy F Ranch before her husband, Terry, arrived from the railway station with the new herd of dudes, but she had refused to deny herself her one pleasure.

The lights came up. While the projectionist was changing the reel, Gertie sat quietly, staring at her lap. It had been a long show, starting with three reels of news and comics. This was the last of the six reels of the feature starring Megan's sister, Luella, now known as Daphne Devine. In ten minutes Megan's respite would be over.

The lights went down for the last time, and the audience stopped gabbing and catcalling to each other. The images started flickering on the screen, and Gertie plucked at Megan's sleeve and whispered something to her.

This annoyed her. Megan was studying Luella's every move, fascinated by the long, white trail of her wedding gown as she swept up the aisle. She was wondering if she would ever get used to Luella's bleached blonde hair when Gertie's agitated voice finally got her attention.

"What is it, Gertie?"

"I don't think you've heard a word I've said." Gertie sniffed softly. "I told you. They are going to kill you."

"What are you talking about, Gertie?" Megan realized her voice was rising and quickly modulated it back to a whisper. "Who is?"

Gertie huddled in her chair. "I don't know, Megan. I just . . . overheard people, . . . uh, well, someone is coming to town to . . . ah, take care of you—well, not just you. All of you."

Megan sighed. She was used to Gertie's exaggeration of the snippets of the private calls she overheard. "Just because you can, doesn't mean you're supposed to listen in on folks' conversation, Gertie. It's against the law, isn't it?"

Gertie nodded, head down. "I know. I just . . . well, anyway." She shifted in her chair with a note of injured dignity in her voice. "I thought you might like to know."

"Well, shush. The movie is almost over." The Thursday afternoon matinee was her only chance to escape from—No, that was a selfish thought, but she did have a right to some time for herself, and she didn't want Gertie spoiling it.

Maxwell, the pianist, was doing a wonderful job of accompanying the film. He'd even been whacking a leather pillow with a cane to create the sound of gunshots. Now the piano music modulated to the wedding march as the heroine and her father swept up the aisle to join the hero at the altar. Megan unwound the handkerchief from her fingers. The end was coming soon, and she was going to cry.

But her eyes stayed dry. Maybe it was because this was the third time she'd seen it, or maybe it was because she was jealous of Luella, who played the role of the heroine. But the ending had already been spoiled by Gertie's gossip. Which was ridiculous, of course. No one would want to kill her or her family. *Well,* she thought, *maybe. Possibly. If.*

Last week the movie had been about gangsters and Prohibition and rumrunners, and a lot of the characters had been killed. Of course everybody knew whiskey was available at the ranch, but why would anyone want to kill them for that? Terry and her in-laws only bought a few bottles at a time for the guests. Of course her Terry drank, but then so did his pa and a lot of the other men in town. That didn't make them gangsters. Men needed to relax, and, besides, the government was being foolish about Prohibition.

The lights went on, washing away the last of her fantasy. As she rose to leave, she felt the familiar agony of jealousy again boiling up inside. Her sister couldn't act; all she ever did was flounce around in fancy clothes looking gorgeous. Megan knew she was at least as pretty as Luella. Besides, she could sing and accompany herself on the autoharp, unlike her sister.

Now all she had to do was get Gertie to drive her to the ranch before Terry got back from the railroad station at Victor with the new herd of dudes. She shuffled out hip to hip with the crowd, nodding and howdying to her friends and neighbors. The cool, pine-scented air scoured the bouquet of theater odors from her nostrils. The sun, still high in the afternoon sky, glared off the white siding of the two-story, wood-frame building.

She blinked her eyes until they adjusted and was immediately overwhelmed with despair. Her mother-in-law, Fiona, was barreling toward Gertie and her. Fiona was pushing her husband, TT, in his wheelchair, using it as a battering ram to herd lesser mortals out of her way.

Guilt sliced into Megan's soul. Fiona had told her she was going to stay at the ranch and take care of her husband. Fiona and TT had obviously left after Megan had and crept into the theater once the lights went down. Now she had been caught.

Fiona had gained weight since Megan first met her. Her two-piece, olive-tan riding suit bulged in places. Megan thought of her sturdy, brown, lace-up oxfords as "bug crushers."

Fiona halted two feet from Megan and peered down on her, a pleased smirk on her face. "Well, you certainly enjoy going to the movies, don't you, Megan dear? Now that your dear sister Luella is such a big star. Oh, I forget; she calls herself Daphne these days, doesn't she? Daphne Divine." The sneer in her voice told Megan what Fiona thought about Luella's stage name. "Hello, Gertie. Did you enjoy the movie?"

Megan sensed Gertie cringing under Fiona's sarcasm and answered for her. "Of course she did, Mother Foxworth." Her mother-in-law insisted on this old-fashioned form of address. "But I thought you were going to visit the Wilsons this afternoon?" Megan hoped her voice sounded calm and collected. "How are you feeling, TT?" He needed a shave, his dark stubble a shadow across his face.

"Me? I'm fine. That movie was a bunch of poppycock. Life ain't like that." Something behind Megan drew his attention. "Excuse me, gotta go talk to John." He wheeled away with a furious burst of energy.

"Anyway," Fiona said, "We were going to visit the Wilsons, but TT wasn't feeling well, so we came to the pictures instead."

Megan nodded. "I see."

Indeed she did see. The reason TT wasn't feeling well was probably related to a bottle, but then Megan didn't blame him too much. His old wound gave him a lot of pain; besides, it must be hell for him to be trapped in that wheelchair. None of that excused her mother-in-law lying to her, however. "Did you enjoy it, Mother Foxworth?"

"Your sister was certainly convincing as the flapper, wasn't she? Shimmying and shaking like all get out, and all that skimpy clothing she wore. How could anyone do a decent day's work dressed like that?" Her gaze traveled down Megan and back up. "I'm so glad you dress like a decent woman, Megan dear."

Her mother-in-law's caustic remark ripped into Megan like the big iron blade down at the sawmill. Back when Terry was courting her, he'd been really pleased that she wore frocks in the latest style. Yet as soon as she said her vows, Fiona insisted that she dress like an old frump, "to look decent for your husband, dear."

To Fiona, "decent" meant a one-piece, gingham housedress in blue check. It had been advertised as "easy to launder." It was. She'd doused it in suds a dozen times since she'd bought it three years ago, and the cotton fabric was faded and beginning to go threadbare. Fiona, of course, had her hair and nails done in a beauty salon. She always dressed in the latest New York fashions in the evening to impress the dudes and dudines. But then, she and TT had once lived in New York. In a moment of sympathy, Megan realized that Fiona missed her home and family.

At the time, she hadn't noticed that Fiona disapproved of her hair, her makeup, and her clothes. She'd been so busy fighting her own mother, who had been anxious to cover up for her father's impropriety that she'd sold her daughter to the highest bidder. If only her father hadn't agreed. Now there was nothing she could do about it. Was there? No, there wasn't. Two years ago she'd said her vows in front of Reverend Swanson; she was married, and that was it. If she could just keep on going to the movies, life would be bearable.

Stop whining, Megan. You made your bed, now lie in it.

Fiona was staring at her. Megan realized she'd been woolgathering. "Oh! Thank you, Mother Foxworth. Well, it turned out all right at the end, didn't it?" She stopped partying and drinking and married the right man. She looked around, feigning innocent curiosity. "Would you excuse me, Mother Foxworth? Gertie is going to drive me back to the ranch now."

"Megan! Wait!" Someone was pushing toward her through the half-dozen moviegoers who still stood around gabbing. It was Steve Leek, the man who brought the movies into town and projected them.

He came to a stop and nodded to Fiona. "Afternoon, Mrs. Foxworth." He turned to Megan. "Wanted to ask you, Megan, if you'd sing and play your autoharp next week?" He turned aside and spat a stream of dark-brown chewing tobacco juice onto the ground. "It's about time more folks heard your lovely voice. I could put you on before the show starts."

A small glow of surprise and pleasure worked its way out of the darkness that had infected Megan. Singing in public one time would do no harm.

She was about to say yes when Fiona interrupted. "Why, that's a charming idea, Mr. Leek. I'm sure Megan would love to consider it. But she's far too busy at the ranch, aren't you, Megan dear?"

Megan slammed the lid on the pot of misery that threatened to scald her. She nodded mutely. "Maybe some other time, Steve."

"Okay, any time you say, Megan. You all have a good evening now."

Megan lifted her head. "I'll be getting on back to the ranch now, Mother Foxworth. Come on, Gertie."

Fiona shifted the focus of her attack. "And what about you, Gertie?"

"Oh, I thought the movie was just wonderful, Mrs. Fox-worth," Gertie said. "Megan's sister is such a magnificent actress. Everyone in town is so proud of her and the director, Mr. Daniels. He's from Wyoming too, you know, down south somewhere. Wouldn't it be great if they'd both come to town so we could actually meet them?" She snapped her chewing gum in rhythm with her words.

Megan's anxiety was ratcheting upward toward panic. She had to leave, now. She put on her most reasonable, business-like voice. "I really need to go, Mother Foxworth, or the dudes will go hungry tonight. Gertie has offered to drive me. Where did you park, Gertie?"

The approach of a familiar rattling sound told Megan it was too late. With a squeak of brakes and a final flapping of its canvas top, Terry's big touring car pulled to a stop behind Fiona. Megan saw a smug look of triumph flicker across her face and realized Fiona had known all along that Terry was coming here and not going directly back to the Rocking Lazy F. He was late, by at least fifteen minutes, so that was why Fiona had been delaying. Megan felt like screaming with despair but smiled brightly, as if this was the most natural thing in the world.

Terry looked at her with the special smile that meant now that he'd caught her out, he'd be demanding "special attention" tonight.

The frustration and humiliation she'd hog-tied for the last half hour broke loose and demanded her attention. The idea of divorce whined through her thoughts like a mosquito. She swatted at it. Divorce wasn't honorable. Nice people, good people, didn't get divorced. Only lower-class people and movie stars did such a thing.

Of course, she would honor her marriage vows. She had promised to love, honor, and obey, and she would. She intended to have babies; that was what all women did. She was puzzled why Fiona nagged her constantly about being a good and faithful wife. She did understand that there were, quite simply, obligations a woman fulfilled, and she didn't need to be reminded constantly. She wondered too what the big deal was about making babies. Heck yes, she had tried—and tried and tried and tried.

Terry climbed down from behind the wheel of the open, eight-passenger car and turned to the dudes, sweeping his new, black Stetson from his head. "Sorry 'bout the delay, folks, but you know how it is with flat tires." On the seats beside and behind him, a mixed herd of wind-battered and mud-spattered dudes was coming slowly alive. It was a long, bone-rattling ride from the railroad station in Victor, Idaho, over the Teton Pass and down into Jackson. Megan was sorry for them, but she knew they'd all be good as new after a day or two at the Rocking Lazy F.

"Now listen up, everyone," Terry said. When the dudes continued to chatter, he stuck two fingers in his mouth and whistled piercingly. "I need to make a quick stop here, but my wife"—Terry made a mocking bow in her direction—"is going back to the ranch right now and will whomp up the biggest, best dinner you've ever had in your life. Right, Megan?"

Time to play the game. Megan put on her best cheerleader face. "You bet, folks. We'll have dinner for you in just about one hour."

"In the meantime," Terry continued, "you all go into the Clubhouse there and get some, ah, refreshments. They're on us, seeing as how we had that little delay back there in the pass. I've got to pick up a few supplies before we go on out. It'll take me 'bout a half hour." Terry was really quite appealing, with his curly, dark hair and infectious grin.

Megan linked arms with Gertie. "I'll head on back now, Terry. Gertie is going to drive me."

"You do that, Megan. These dudes are going to be real hungry."

The setting sun, glowing off the snowfields atop the Tetons, frosted the mountain's rim with golden light. Megan was half aware of the vast open spaces around her. Gertie's old Ford rattled and bucked and jounced over the potholes, which was just as well, as it saved Megan the need to talk. She could savor her misery in peace. Yes, she'd made a bad bargain, and, yes, she would honor her commitment. All she wanted in return was an occasional few hours to herself to nourish her hopes and dreams. She could be a star like Luella; she just knew she could. Then she would be famous and make a lot of money, Terry would be proud of her, and Fiona would have no excuse for humiliating her in front of everybody the way she had two nights ago.

One of the guests had asked, and she'd started to sing and play. Then along came Fiona with her nasty crack about, "I'm sure the guests would rather hear good music, Megan," at which point Fiona had wound up the Victrola and put on some of her fancy-schmancy classical music. The sound it produced was tinny and scratchy and hard to hear. Besides that, the guests had started to applaud until Fiona interrupted.

The heck with Fiona, Megan thought. Megan would sing and play for the dudes tonight. They would like it. Maybe one of them would turn out to be a music producer, and he'd offer her a big contract, Terry would praise her and . . . *oh, to blazes with it.* It was time to bake that gooseberry pie.

CHAPTER 2

Thursday Evening, June 4

Terry had waited beside his mother, watching Megan as she scurried across the town square and got into Gertie's car. Her tight little bottom waggled enticingly under her dress, and the urge began to rise in him—but he quickly suppressed it when he glanced at his mother. If she guessed what he was thinking, she'd bring up "that subject."

She did anyway. "Well, son, has she been to Doctor Byrne?" Terry sighed. "And stop sighing like that."

"Yes, Ma. She went yesterday."

"And?"

"Same old story. Doc can't find anything physically wrong. Just says try to get her to relax and don't push her."

"I surely don't see how any more relaxation would help. Every time I look, she's sitting reading one of those movie magazines or coming into town to watch a movie. Are you sure you're doing your part of the job?"

Terry blushed. "Put away your spurs, Ma. We'll make a grandson for you yet."

"And stop calling me 'Ma.' Your language has become frightfully common since we moved West."

"Yes, Mother. Now I'd best round up the dudes and get them out to the ranch."

A squeaking sound made him turn. TT wheeled his chair up to him and asked, "Aren't you forgetting something?" Terry shook his head with a puzzled frown. "The sheriff?" TT prompted.

"Oh come on, Pa. Sheriff Goodman can wait until tomorrow."

His pa seized his arm in a firm, almost painful grip and drew his head closer so he could talk without being overheard by any of the few stragglers still moving through the square. "Son, you know how your mother and I rely on you to make our old age comfortable. At this moment I'm feeling quite unwell."

His pa, "Terrible Terrence" Foxworth, better known as TT, was "feeling quite unwell" not because of any germ. Terry allowed himself to admit that his pa had been hitting the bottle a bit heavily of late. He'd talk to him later and get him to ease up on the hooch.

"Now, Pa, the sheriff will understand. He knows you have troubles with your wound. He'll understand if I see him tomorrow."

Behind him, his ma sniffed heartily and cleared her throat. "Terry, you know it's important for us to maintain good relations with Sheriff Goodman. If we don't . . . I hate to think of what could happen to your father and me."

Terry wrapped his arms around her and patted her awkwardly on the back. Come to think of it, she did feel rather frail. "Okay, Ma, baby-making can wait a while."

She sniffed and wiped her eyes. "That's my real son talking." She smiled a quick, hesitant smile. "Just as long as it doesn't wait too long. I'm not at all sure your father and I have that much longer to live. Sure would be nice to have a grandson to dandle on my knee."

Terry pushed his pa to their car, hoisted him into his seat, and put the wheelchair in the back seat. Pa handed him a carefully folded copy of the *Wyoming State Tribune*. "You give our best regards to Sheriff Goodman, all right?"

After Ma settled into the driver's seat, Terry waited until the car started. She got real fussed if it did not, but it had damned well better start. The damned thing cost as much as their new Electrolux D refrigerator. He headed back across the square toward the sheriff's office, holding the paper tightly under his arm. His ma's talk about being ill, and the thought that she and Pa might die soon, had left him feeling weak and depressed. She was right: they had done everything for him, and the least he could do was to see that their life was comfortable.

As he hurried across the new town square, he gave a moment's thought to how nice it looked: the city had done a good job of hauling in fill dirt and leveling the site. It was going to look quite nice when it was finished, especially with the new elk-antler arches.

The creak of wooden wheels and the rapid *clop, clop, clop* of horse hooves made him look up. The four-horse mail and passenger stage from Victor was just pulling in from its run over the Teton Pass. Terry waved to Bob, Clay, and Ray atop the front seat. He wondered how much longer they could be in business. The stage mostly carried commercial travelers now, for dudes insisted on motor vehicles.

"Hey, boss!"

Terry yanked himself out of his worries. Junior Frampton was strutting toward him, his face set in its usual cocksure grin. He looked like a younger version of his father, slim-hipped and bowlegged, with lanky, blond hair. He had worked for the Rocking Lazy F for two years now, and Terry had rarely seen him anything but self satisfied.

Junior halted beside him. They exchanged the usual bullshit and shoulder punches for a moment, but as Terry tried to move on, Junior kept gassing about nothing in particular.

"Look, Junior, I need to move on, so excuse me, okay?"

"Going to see the sheriff?"

Terry gave him a warning look. Junior glanced away, turned back with a shit-eating grin. "Well hey, I just saw Megan riding home with Gertie," he said. "She was at the matinee, I reckon? She enjoy it?"

Terry's warning look was more pointed this time, but Junior seemed armored against it. "You sure are good to that wife of yours, boss. Letting her go to the movies all the time. Hell, I even saw her in town the other day. She was wearing a dress that looked a lot like them flapper dresses them movie stars wear, like her sister. Sure nice you can afford to buy her fancy clothes like that."

Terry squeezed hard on the edges of his turquoise and gold belt buckle. The pain reminded him to stay calm. They both knew Junior meant that Megan looked like a whore. Hell, he thought so, too, but he had to pretend he approved. If he lost his temper, he'd lose the battle. He had to keep Junior under a tight rein.

The bigger the lie, the better. "I'm proud of her, Junior. She looks so much smarter than the other women in town. Now, don't you have chores to do?"

Junior's sly grin returned. "Saw Sheriff Goodman with a fancy new saddle the other day, all covered with silver *conchos* and shit like that."

Terry felt anger boiling up from his balls but only nodded slightly.

"Saddle like that would make me a real happy man, you know? I could just go riding off into the sunset and never have to say a word to anyone."

Anger rose to Terry's guts. He'd need a glass of milk when this was over. "And damn fools who go riding off into the sunset like that, sometimes they have an accident and never come back."

For just a moment Junior's gaze lashed him like a cold

norther. Terry felt a stab of worry, but Junior's look was quickly replaced by his normal shit-eating grin. "Aw, now, boss, you know I was just making a little joke, is all."

Terry smiled to show he wasn't going to make a case of it. "Right. Now you get on back to the ranch. And see if Mrs. Foxworth needs any firewood or anything, hear me?"

Junior nodded and ambled off.

Damn it to hell! Terry got himself headed in the direction of the sheriff's office again and allowed his mind to chew its cud for a while. He could always handle Junior, even if he was getting to be a problem.

But Megan . . . well, that was something else. Megan worried the shit out of him. She'd gotten so damned uppity lately, so fucking independent. She always had been ambitious; he knew that when he married her. She was always plunking on that damned autoharp and singing, pretending she was going to be a big movie star one day—even after he'd all but rescued her from poverty, for chrissake.

If she'd just get pregnant! That would put an end to all that nonsense, and, besides, it would keep her nose out of the family business—a long way out. He hated it that Ma and Pa paid her for her work. It gave her money of her own, but it did keep her from asking too damned many questions about—

"Afternoon, Terry."

Well, damn, he'd walked right into the sheriff's office without realizing it. "Sheriff. How's it going?"

"Things are going just fine, Terry. Now that you're *finally* here."

Terry swallowed his annoyance and slapped the *Wyoming State Tribune* down on the roll-top desk. Sheriff Goodman was cylindrical from chin to crotch; he was built like a cast-iron boiler and just as hard.

Terry glanced around cautiously. No one else was in the office or in the street outside. He slid an envelope from the folds of the newspaper to where the sheriff could see it. He quickly scooped it into a drawer and locked it.

"You got a calendar, Terry?" Terry nodded. "And a watch?" Terry nodded again.

"Well, maybe you oughta pay a little closer attention to them, you know what I mean?"

The hard look on Sheriff Goodman's face made Terry damned uncomfortable. "Yeah, you're right, Sheriff. I'll do that from now on."

The sheriff finally let a very small smile touch his lips. "Glad to hear that. So tell me, how're things going? You haven't seen anybody snooping around, have you?"

Terry shook his head vigorously. "We keep the hay covered. Haven't seen any stray cows munching on it. Gotta go. I left some dudes at the Clubhouse. Expect they're getting pretty hungry by now."

After Gertie dropped her off, Megan had hurried into the kitchen and helped the cook prepare the promised dinner. The living room of the Rocking Lazy F Ranch was filled with happy noise, which suited Megan just fine. Terry had deposited the new herd of dudes and dudines and then gone out again on some vague errand. That was good, too, because she didn't have to think too much.

Now the long-term guests were making sure the newcomers realized the distinction between them and that the long-termers were entitled to special status. From mainline Philadelphia, from Long Island, and from "cottages" in Rhode Island, they were scions of America's wealthiest families. While they spent a month or more at the ranch, playing at being cowboys, underlings back East were running the family businesses.

The stuffed and mounted heads of elk, deer, and moose gazed

down on the activities with glassy-eyed indifference. Someone had once tossed an old hat onto the prize rack of elk antlers. It had been there five years ago when the Foxworths bought the ranch and converted it into a dude ranch. Megan suspected it would remain there forever.

She spotted six dudes playing five-card stud at the round table, their groomed and perfumed wives gossiping and knitting near the fire. Several children played some mysterious childhood game that involved a lot of whispering and covert glances at their parents. A pair of teenage girls banged out "Chopsticks" on the shiny new upright piano. When they realized Megan was watching, they smiled at her. She turned away and resumed wrangling the vast herd of dirty dishes off the table. The girl's smiles reawakened all the depressing feelings she had buried since Fiona humiliated her this afternoon.

What in the devil had gone wrong with her parents' life? Megan thought. It was only seven years ago that she was seventeen, blissfully happy and looking forward to attending trade school. Then, suddenly her father landed in jail, there was no more hope for school, and her mother was pushing her at every eligible lout in town.

She was nineteen when the Foxworths arrived from New York and stunned everyone by buying the old Wilkerson spread. They spent a ton of money refurbishing the place and on advertising; now the Rocking Lazy F was one of the best-known, most popular dude ranches in five states. Terry courted her for two years, and when she was twenty-one, she reluctantly agreed to marry him. Now, at twenty-three, look where she was.

The noise level was rising, which probably meant Fiona had brought in a couple of bottles. Gertie's urgent warning in the theater that afternoon came back to her—but who would want to kill her? Who would want to kill any of them over a few bottles of Irish whiskey?

Gertie had probably not overheard the conversation correctly. The new telephone service in town was just wonderful, but the quality of the sound was not—especially on long-distance calls, when the voice of a caller would fade in and out, and crackles and hisses interrupted.

She was carrying the last of the dishes into the kitchen when she noticed the teenage girls, Sissy and Susie, hunched over her copy of *Photoplay,* the one with Luella's picture on the cover.

Sissy looked up at her as she went past. "Oh, Mrs. Foxworth, somebody told me Daphne Devine is your sister!"

Megan put down the pile of filthy dishes. She ducked her head and nodded. "That's true, she is."

"Gosh, that's thrilling," Susie gushed. "Why aren't you a star? You're just as pretty as she is."

Megan looked around to make sure Fiona wasn't watching, then sat between the girls as they bombarded her with questions about the movies and Hollywood. Susie would turn a page, and Sissy would point to a photo and ask if Megan knew that person.

Sissy stabbed a finger at a photograph Megan knew all too well. "Golly, he's so good looking!" Sissy said with a great intake of breath. "It says he directed your sister in her latest movie. Do you know him?"

"Oh, no!" Megan realized her answer was probably more emphatic than necessary and bent closer to the page to conceal her face. "I haven't met him. That's Steamer Daniels."

Susie said, "He's handsome enough to be a star, too."

"He was an actor," Megan said, "before he became a director. Wouldn't you just love to work for such a dreamy man?"

"Gosh, are you sure you don't know him?"

"Oh, no. No such luck. I've just read about him in the movie magazines."

"Megan dear?" Megan's heart shriveled. When Fiona

sounded like a dove cooing, you knew you were in trouble. "I think you might want to finish washing the dishes," Fiona burbled. "Terry will be home soon, you know."

"Yes, Mother Foxworth." Megan stood. "It won't take me long to finish."

The kitchen maids happened to have this afternoon and evening off. Fiona had long ago decided Megan was as strong as a horse and could easily manage the huge pile of crockery and silver. Megan set to work.

An hour later she was drying her hands when Charity Palmerson entered the kitchen trailed by her son, Bertie. She had relaxed a bit since arriving at the ranch a day ago, but Megan wondered why she was so worried about her son. Bertie looked perfectly healthy to her. Yet Mrs. Palmerson was constantly after him about his health, frequently saying, "Button up; you'll catch a cold. Don't exert yourself so much, Bertie; you know it's not good for you."

Megan tucked her long, brown hair behind her ears. She wiped her hands on her apron. Despite all the dishwashing she did, her hands were not red and raw. She smoothed Bag Balm on them regularly.

Mrs. Palmerson said, "Mrs. Foxworth, I've just been told you sing beautifully and accompany yourself on . . . what do you call it? An autoharp?"

Megan put on her best "be charming to the guests" face as she struggled to finish drying her hands with the soggy dishtowel. "Uh, yes, I do. And, please, call me Megan."

"Oh, yes. All you people here in the West call each other by your first names, don't you?" Mrs. Palmerson reminded her of a bottle of champagne that was about to pop its cork with happiness. "Then you must call me Charity. You will play for us, won't you? One of your cowboy songs, perhaps?"

Megan glanced around to see if Fiona was in sight. She wasn't. Megan fetched her autoharp and sang "Home on the Range," and the guests applauded and cheered. She went right into "On Top of Old Smokey," and they applauded and cheered even louder. A great sense of peace and contentment spread through her. She was halfway through "San Antonio Rose" when Terry walked in. Or, rather, he staggered in.

He stopped, fixed his gaze on her, shook his head, and looked again. That special smile spread slowly across his face as he nodded slightly. Then he seemed to remember something and walked on through toward the ranch office. Something in his behavior aroused her suspicions.

She quickly finished the song, bowed, and made her way out of the living room. The sight of Fiona glaring at her from the kitchen as the dudes applauded was sweet revenge. Now if Terry would only forget about "special attention" tonight, everything would be all right, at least for today.

She followed Terry, the sounds of her footsteps covered by the jolly noises behind her. He was in the office, standing in front of the four-drawer wooden file cabinet, oblivious to her presence. She hung back and watched as he put a sheaf of papers in the second drawer, then closed and locked it. It took him several tries to drop the key in a small brass pot half hidden behind a pile of books on top of the cabinet.

He started to turn. Megan took a step forward, as if she had just arrived. "Terry, darling! I'm so glad you're home."

He blinked and frowned at her suspiciously. "Hey, Megan. Whaddya want?"

"Why, I just came to say hello, darling!" She might as well admit she'd seen him at the file cabinet; a feeble excuse would be better than none. "I just saw you headed this way and wanted to say hello, that's all. What on earth do you keep in that dusty old cabinet?"

"Just business papers. Nothing for you to worry your pretty little head about."

"Oh, all right. Are you coming to bed now?"

"In a minute."

When he finally did come to bed, he fell asleep almost instantly. Megan's relief was short-lived. Her mind worked over Gertie's warning, but she worried for no more than ten seconds before dismissing it as her need for more drama in her boring life.

CHAPTER 3

Saturday Morning, June 6

The intercom on Alan's desk buzzed like an angry bumblebee. He reached for the switch and pushed it down. "I thought I told you to hold all calls, Miss Dinkins."

"Yes, Mr. Segal, but there is a . . . lady here to see you."

Alan wasn't sure he liked the tone of his secretary's voice, a bit sarcastic and secretly amused. "A lady? Send her down to casting. I'm not interviewing actresses today."

There was a babble of noise from the intercom; seconds later his office door swung open. He could see Miss Dinkins's arms waving frantically to stop the woman, who ignored her and pushed her way through the door. She paused, looked directly at him, and then closed the door behind her with a graceful movement.

"I'm not an actress, Mr. Segal." Her voice carried the lilting rhythms of an Italian accent. "I'm a business woman."

Whoever she was, she had exquisite taste. Her cream-white summer suit looked European. It was probably by the hot new Italian design house of Fendi, which had just opened their doors this year. A blaze of orange at neck and cuffs accented the severe tailoring of the suit. A small hat supported a black veil that tucked under her chin. From what he could see of her face, she was probably quite beautiful. She wore elbow-length, black, kidskin gloves and carried a black bag tucked under one arm.

Alan realized he'd been staring and forced himself to rise and move from behind his desk to greet her. "Perhaps I should be interviewing actresses today." He smiled and shook the hand she proffered. "But you say you are here on business? And what is your name, if I may ask?"

"You may," she said. She moved to the guest chair and perched herself on the edge. "My name is Pia Donatelli."

Alan felt the lethargy he'd experienced all morning beginning to lift. Whatever this lovely creature wanted, it would be most interesting to deal with her. "So, let me guess: you represent an Italian film company, and you are here to negotiate distribution rights for your country."

"A clever guess, Mr. Segal, but no. That's not why I am here."

"Some coffee, perhaps?" Alan leaned toward the intercom, ready to summon Miss Dinkins.

"No, thank you." She drew a breath and exhaled steadily, as if to calm herself. "I'm here about your loan."

Her words sizzled through him like slow-motion lightning, frying his emotional circuits. She couldn't possibly be saying what she was saying, but there she sat, as if they were talking about the price of bread. He sagged back in his chair and stared at her.

"My . . . m-my . . . lo-loan?" He hated it when he stammered.

"I'm sure you understand, Mr. Segal. My . . . ah . . . business associates asked me to stop by, as I was in Los Angeles, and remind you. You are three months behind in your payments. And do stop staring. There are a number of women in our family business. Sometimes we get results where men fail."

Alan tried to tear his gaze away from her. Her voice remained light and pleasant, but he noticed her hands clutched her bag so tightly, the leather creased under her fingers. She sat, quite rigidly upright, a tight smile playing across her mouth. "Are you aware of the rumors about this film you're working on now, Mr. Segal?"

His shock at the incongruity of a woman being an enforcer, as they called them, was beginning to subside. There had been threats on the phone from gravelly male voices with heavy accents. A thickset goon with black hairs sprouting from his hands he might have expected, but this?

"I pay no attention to rumors, Miss Donatelli. It's a waste of time."

"Perhaps you should? The rumors are that, ah, *quel* film *è una cosa schifosa*. How do I say it in English? Ah yes, this picture is a piece of shit. Would you like to know why?"

Alan shrugged. "Only a damn fool listens to rumors."

"Because they say your leading lady is a real lush, that she's running up the cost because your director needs so many takes to get a good one out of her."

Alan controlled his voice with difficulty. "No, I didn't know." He plucked out his breast-pocket handkerchief and wiped his face.

Pia shifted position slightly, turning away from him. "In essence, what we are saying is that you must find some way to make this film into a hit, a big hit, so it makes oodles of money." She breathed in deeply, exhaled slowly. "We would hate to have to, ah, enforce the collection of the loan."

The buzzer of the intercom sounded, startling both of them. "Mr. Segal, I'm sorry to interrupt, but you have an urgent call."

"Thank you, Miss Dinkins. Get their number and tell them I'll call right back." He clicked off.

"Now then, Miss Donatelli." Alan rose and straightened his lapels. "I assure you, everything is under control, and this production is going to be a big hit, a very big hit. You know I've signed Steamer Daniels to direct?" Pia nodded. "And you know his last picture was a big hit, right? Made a ton of money, right?" Another nod. "That's your guarantee. Now go back to your associates and tell them to get off my back and let me finish this picture without any more, ah, pressure."

Pia rose gracefully and stood holding her handbag like a schoolgirl. "I may be able to persuade them to give you an extension of one month. But no more, Mr. Segal."

She opened her bag, drew out a piece of paper, and handed it to him. It was from an Italian newspaper. The black and white photograph was coarse and the subjects poorly lighted, but their faces were quite clear enough. His sons, Dov and Gur, smiled out at him from the wrinkled newsprint. They held the reins of their horses in one hand and trophies in the other. Behind them, another horse and rider soared over a jump.

"Your sons are quite the expert horsemen, Mr. Segal. Their tour of the jumping circuit in Italy has been most successful for them. Of course, the fact that they are on tour makes it so easy to keep track of them." Pia snapped her purse closed. "Jumping is such a dangerous sport, isn't it? Riders are thrown into fences and break their necks. They fall in the path of other horses, and a hoof lands on their face." She held out her hand. "Well, good-bye, Mr. Segal."

Alan felt as if he'd looked the Gorgon in the eye and been turned into stone. At last his mouth melted a bit. "Pl . . . p-please . . . d-don't hurt them," he gasped.

"Oh, we won't. Not if we receive a payment by the end of next month. Good-bye."

As soon as the door was firmly closed, Alan dashed to his private bathroom, dropped his pants, plopped down on the toilet, and gave in to the fear that was weakening his bowels. He remained there for uncounted minutes, fear and anger stampeding through his mind. That kind of terror hadn't gripped him since he was a snot-nosed kid on the docks in Brooklyn. His hands shook as he cleaned himself.

Back then he'd given as good as he got; he'd earned the respect of the other dock hands and a way out of that life to the

West Coast. He'd gotten up at midnight in the face of an oncoming cold front to light smudge pots in the orange groves. He'd hauled crate after crate of fruit into the studio commissary, and then he'd gotten his break, sweeping studio floors. Now he owned his own film studio. Damned if he was going to let them whip him.

He strode to the window in his office and stood staring down at the studio street. Actors and actresses in costume, gaffers pushing 10K Klieg lights, grips shoving carts laden with props, writers and directors—all moved with buoyant energy as they went about their job of translating dreams into celluloid.

Who in that mob down there was spreading rumors? Miss Donatelli's gossip about Daphne was insulting. Daphne was a bit flighty, with a delicate temperament that sometimes made her appear inebriated, but she wasn't a lush. It was Steamer's artsy-fartsy shooting scheme that was causing problems, not Daphne.

His nerves were slowly quieting, his pulse dropping. How dare they threaten him? *Damn it to hell,* he fumed. It wasn't his fault that he had run out of money. Paul Marshal, his production manager, had screwed up the budget to begin with. Well, no, that wasn't right. Alan remembered now how Paul had explained it and apologized profusely. The supplier had raised the price of negative stock but hadn't informed him in a timely manner. On top of that, the lab had raised their prices. That's what had made the budget jump like a bucking bronco.

And he'd hired Steamer, who had turned out to be a nit-picking perfectionist who burned through negative stock as if it were firewood. Then when the bank refused to lend him any more money—well, what the hell was he supposed to do? Thank God TT had introduced him to those people back east. They charged sky-high interest rates, but he'd be able to pay them back.

It was going to be a good film, a genuine, certified hit, all because of Daphne. He sat in his leather chair and projected their last night together on the screen of memory. She was good in bed, damned good.

He felt a small twinge of guilt. If Bettina knew he was cheating on her, she'd—He didn't want to think about what she'd do. She was always so damned busy with her charity balls and lunches and fundraising drives. What else was he supposed to do?

No, Daphne was a hundred-proof star, an A-number-one, first class moneymaking celebrity. The movie magazines couldn't get enough of her. The public couldn't get enough of her. The movie would be a smash, and his money worries would be over.

The intercom buzzed. "Yes, Miss Dinkins?"

"About that phone call, Mr. Segal, I think you—"

"Not now, Miss Dinkins. I'm too busy."

The intercom made fizzing sounds. Alan could almost hear her brain engaging. "Oh, but that really was an urgent call, Mr. Segal. From Miss Devine's sister. You know, Mrs. Foxworth."

"Oh." Alan digested this briefly. "What did she want?"

"She said she's been trying and trying to reach her sister but hasn't been able to. She sounded, well, quite worried about her." Again Alan heard that faintly sarcastic, amused tone to her voice.

A two-frame blip of alarm went through him. Maybe he'd better talk to her. "All right, get her on the phone; let me know when you make a connection."

Ten minutes later the intercom announced that Mrs. Foxworth was on the line.

Alan lifted the heavy, black receiver. "Hello, Megan. And how are you today?"

"I'm well, thank you." The connection was poor with hissing and crackling. "But I'm worried about Luella. I've been trying to reach her for days now, and she doesn't answer. Is something wrong?"

Alan spoke soothingly. "Not that I'm aware of, Megan. Daphne has been working very hard, very hard indeed. We're under a lot of pressure to complete the film. The distributors, you know? They're expecting the film in a year, and we have a lot of work to do yet. Of course, I'll certainly double-check and have Daphne call you. Now then, how is TT?"

"Well, you know, his wound from that automobile accident bothers him, and he hates being in a wheelchair." He could hear the strain in her voice. "But we're taking good care of him, and he'll be all right."

"Tell him I'm thinking of him."

"I will. By the way, I do hope you and Luella and Mr. Daniels could come up here sometime. Our weather is just gorgeous now, and everyone says the scenery here is spectacular. Maybe you could even make a movie here someday."

"Yes, yes, that's a good idea. Well, thank you for your concern about Daphne. I'll have her call you." Alan replaced the receiver and stabbed the intercom switch. "Get hold of Steamer and tell him to get his ass in here immediately, if not sooner."

Five minutes later Miss Dinkins rang back. Mr. Daniels was away from the studio. She'd left a message for him.

The lady's lounge in the lobby of Segal Productions was a whore's dream of heaven, with marble counters, baby-blue and rose-pink satin curtains, and gold-plated fixtures.

Pia was oblivious to the decor. She sat before a gilded mirror, cursing under her breath. Uncle had promised her she'd never again have to do anything for the family—then two days ago he'd called.

She stripped off her long black gloves and glared at the inside of her left forearm. Six round scars forming the shape of a cross stood out against her olive skin. All but the last, at the bottom of the cross, had healed.

She had earned every last one of them, proven her courage and devotion to the family. The first time she disobeyed was the worst. She could still feel the agony of Uncle's cigarette pressing into her arm and could still smell the stench of her own burnt flesh. Later she learned to go elsewhere in her mind and ignore the pain. Afterward, when Uncle took her to bed and comforted her, also got better with time.

And the rewards, ah, the rewards! The magnificent jumping horses Uncle bought her after each incident, the money and the encouragement he lavished on her. They had enabled her to become the jumping champion of Italy. The feel of a powerful stallion between her legs was an aphrodisiac like no other. Who needed men?

Then, after the birth of Tommaso, Uncle had promised she would never again have to work for the family. He'd said that she could go to California and live in peace with her son and not have to do any more jobs.

And then came the phone call. "Another job, Pia, my angel," Uncle said. "A Mr. Alan Segal is behind in his payments to our associates in New York. Since you live so close now, you are the logical one to take care of it. After this, no more. I promise."

She clamped down on the despair rising in her. There had been "one last job" after another. The only way she would ever be free of Uncle was if he died or was killed. The thought thrilled her and terrified her at the same time.

She looked around cautiously. There was no one else in the lounge. She opened her purse, drew out a small silver flask. It contained calvados apple brandy, from the exclusive *pays d'auge* area of France. For medicinal purposes only, of course, but if this wasn't an emergency, what was? A small sip restored her peace of mind. She resisted pulling the chrome-plated .25

caliber pistol from the inside pocket. Someone might walk in unexpectedly.

She rose and pulled on her gloves, adjusted the veil over her face. She'd left Tommaso alone in their hotel room for too long. He'd be frantic with worry about her. And he'd be hungry; fourteen-year-old boys were always hungry. She refused to think about his fifteenth birthday, when Uncle would expect her to send him back to Italy to be raised as a Donatelli male.

CHAPTER 4

Saturday Afternoon, June 6

Steamer slammed the door to Alan's office and stalked across the thick carpeting. "What is so damned important that you have to get me off the set just when we're on a roll?"

"What took you so long? I sent for you this morning." Alan glared back at him for a moment, then gestured to a chair in front of the desk. "Sit down, Steamer. I just want to check up on how things are going. I don't have to tell you we're behind schedule."

"No, you don't." Steamer allowed himself to perch on the edge of the chair. Alan's behavior puzzled Steamer; he was wound up tighter than a two-dollar alarm clock, nervous and twitchy. "Look, boss, I'm doing my best to get stuff in the can as fast as possible."

"All right, keep at it. Now about the rushes yesterday." Alan retrieved a copy of the shooting script from a desk drawer. "I noticed scene twenty-two was a lot different from the script. What's going on?"

Oh shit, here it comes. "Well, look, I'm working with Daphne to, ah, make her look good. I think she's gotten, um, over-tired. She needs a rest. But . . . so, I'm trying to make things a little easier on her, shoot things so she can get more rest." *She's not tired; she just needs to lay off the bathtub gin.* Everyone knew she was Alan's mistress, so how do you tell your boss his girlfriend is hitting the bottle too hard?

"You shot a hell of a lot of takes of that scene."

"Uh, yeah. Well, as I said, I want to make Daphne look as good as possible. She's a big star, and she deserves it."

"Okay, just do your best to keep the expenses down." Alan shoved the script back into a drawer. "By the way, her sister called. She's all worried about her, can't reach her. Tell Daphne to call her, okay?" Steamer nodded and rose to go. "I had a terrible phone connection with Megan. What do they use for telephone wire in that hick town, string?"

Steamer reined in the retort he was about to make. Jackson was a hick town, but he wasn't about to let an outsider know that. "Well, it may not be as sophisticated as Hollywood, but it's got the scenery in this place beat all to hell."

"Really?" Alan perked up. "That's what her sister said. Tell me about it."

"Um . . ." Steamer had made a tactical mistake. "Well, the Grand Teton Mountains, they're rugged, have snowcaps year round. And the Snake River. It's cold and clear and full of trout, runs through meadows of emerald-green grass." Steamer felt a sudden pang of homesickness but dismissed it quickly. He was through with that life forever. It was too backward, too slow. But he'd keep his ranch land there, just in case.

Alan leaned back with a far-away look in his eyes. "So tell me, what do the folks there do for amusement?"

"Oh, there's a big dance every Saturday night. Sometimes the boys get a little out of hand and get into fistfights over the girls. And there's a rodeo every year, with bronco riding and calf roping and that kind of stuff."

The glazed look went out of Alan's eyes. "That's it!"

Steamer felt as if a mule had kicked him in the stomach. "That's it? What does that mean?"

"We're going to shoot up there. All that gorgeous scenery and all. That's what we need to, ah, well, to add production value to this flick."

The bottom dropped from under Steamer. "That's a terrible idea," he blurted. He instantly wished he could suck the words back in. It had been exactly the wrong thing to say. Just as you can't tell your boss his mistress is a lush, you can't tell him his artistic sensibilities come from the comic pages.

"No, it's not!" Alan jumped up and began pacing excitedly. "And we'll take Daphne. The fresh air and sunshine will do her good, make her feel a lot better."

It was the first sensible thing Alan had said. Steamer made a few more objections, but Alan kicked them to pieces like a stubborn mule. As he left the office, Alan was already on the phone calling Paul Marshal.

Steamer walked back to the set in a fog of chagrin. He was sure people smirked after they passed him. It seemed as if everyone on the lot knew about Daphne and Alan, and it was damned humiliating.

And if that weren't enough, Alan had just told him to stop shooting so much film. How the hell was he supposed to make Daphne look good if he couldn't shoot around her constant errors? She was getting worse every day. The movies were going to talk any day now, and when they could record sound as well as pictures, Daphne would be finished. Her high, reedy voice and giggle would doom her.

Now what? If he quit, Alan would blackball him with the other studios. He touched the small white box in his coat pocket. He had bought the ring yesterday afternoon. He was going to ask Allison to marry him. When she said yes, he'd have to start saving for a home for them.

No, all he could do was continue to shoot around Daphne and somehow use less film.

The large stage door was open when he arrived. That meant Clamps Donovan had brought the new set in from the carpenter shop. He heard F-Stop shouting orders to the crew setting the lights for the next scene. F-stop was Lawrence Lentemann, the director of photography

Daphne was reading a lurid romance magazine, her eyes wide and her mouth slightly open. Steamer rapped on the door frame of her dressing room; she looked up.

"Sorry about the delay, Daphne. Alan had some urgent business that couldn't wait. Are you ready to do the next scene?"

"You betcha," she squeaked. "You know I'm always hot to trot, Steamer."

Esse Blankenship, the screenwriter, had done scene thirty-two as a series of unimaginative long shots, medium shots, and close shots. Steamer had planned one continuous take that would be much more interesting. He'd been inspired by *The Last Laugh*, a film by F. W. Murnau. His cinematographer, Karl Freund, had invented what he called "the unchained camera," in which he took the camera off the static tripod and put it on a moving dolly.

Scene thirty-two was to start with a shot "out the window," showing the villain lurking and spying on the heroine. The camera was then to turn to see Daphne approaching the window. The assistant cameraman would then pull focus as she came into a close-up, registering terror at seeing the villain. She was then to turn around and flee from left to right into her bedroom and dive into the closet to hide as the camera tracked after her. The success of the shot depended on Daphne hitting her marks exactly, so that the carefully rehearsed camera moves and lighting would work.

So all right, he should have known better. After four takes, he gave up. Daphne missed her marks, turned left instead of right, and did not complete one good take. He gave up and shot scene thirty-two as written. She didn't have to move. All she had to do was stand in the right place and follow his directions as he talked her through each shot.

Even so, it took three or four takes of each camera setup. When at last he had what he felt were passable takes of each shot, he called a wrap for the day.

Daphne vanished into her chauffeured limousine. The lights died with a clack of heavy switches, and the crew melted away into the dark recesses of the set. As F-Stop departed, he patted Steamer on the shoulder with a sympathetic look and a shrug. Steamer was soon alone with his confused and angry thoughts.

Damn it, he'd come to Hollywood with such high hopes. He'd started with Tom Ince, "The Father of the Western." Ince ran his studio like a factory system, producing movies on a production-line basis. Steamer had worked his way up from sweeping the studio floors to numerous small roles and finally had attracted a lot of attention for his portrayal of a sheriff.

But acting bored him. It was all about exteriors, the human exterior, and the more handsome that was, the better chance one had of making it.

He was, instead, interested in the human interior. He wanted to explore the range of emotions he knew humans went through and had persuaded Ince to let him direct. Then, at a small party celebrating the success of one of his films, Alan Segal had offered him more money and a chance to direct Daphne Devine. Now here he was, stuck with her.

He jumped up. Sitting here whining would not help. Alan worked late; maybe he could still persuade him to stop this crazy plan for a trip to Wyoming.

Miss Dinkins had gone home, but he could hear a masculine voice in Alan's office. He opened the door quietly to find Paul Marshal and Alan circling each other, talking and gesticulating animatedly.

Alan looked up. "Ah, there you are, Steamer. I'm glad you stopped by. Paul has come up with new figures for the cost of shooting in Wyoming."

Steamer felt as if he'd been jabbed with an electric cattle prod. *Oh shit, now what?* He sank into the vast luxury of Alan's sofa. The aroma of the soft leather calmed him. "I see. Tell me about it."

Paul and Alan trotted out facts and figures for a good ten minutes. All they'd need would be a skeleton crew. Douglas Cragmont, the leading man, would not be needed. They'd take Daphne because she was the real star, and, besides, Esse had reworked the script to take advantage of the scenery. They went on, blah blah blah, and the bottom line was that it would cost no more to shoot on location than in the studio.

Why hadn't he kept his mouth shut about the glories of Jackson Hole? "Ah, well, all that sounds great. I'm glad to hear about the cost factor, but . . . well, look, I've developed a great new lighting scheme for shooting Daphne, and there's no way I can do that on location." Hell, it was difficult enough doing it in the studio.

"Steamer, we won't need all that stuff. We won't need to shoot Daphne in close-up. We're going to put her in front of all that spectacular scenery. And Esse has great shots planned of Daphne watching the rodeo, stuff like that. Maybe we can hire some local cowboys to get into a fistfight, and she can react to that. This whole segment is going to have great production values."

Steamer groaned quietly and hoped they hadn't heard. "Damn it, Alan, I explained this to you. I've worked out a complete scheme for shooting using camera moves. Each shot is tied to the next in a way that will give a flow of movement that will—Well, it will add excitement to the story line. I won't be able to do that up there. The camera will be stuck on a tripod, and, well, you see . . ." He realized that Alan and Paul had exchanged covert glances.

When Alan spoke next, his voice sounded as if he were soothing a spoiled child. "Now look, Steamer, you can do all that stuff when we get back in the studio. Besides, you were the one who suggested we shoot up there in the first place."

Steamer bit his tongue to keep from groaning out loud. The smug tone in Alan's voice at this last bit of sophistry was almost more than he could stomach. "Yeah, yeah, okay." Alan was forever bleating about "making meaningful movies," which meant lots of violent action, gunfights, horse chases, and barroom brawls. Esse's scripts somehow always favored scenes like that.

Wait a minute. What had Alan said this morning? "The fresh air and sunshine will do Daphne good." Steamer felt better. Maybe it would, and maybe it would be easier to keep her off the sauce.

Bettina Segal walked slowly around the dining table. Henry, the butler, had done a good job setting the four places, even if he had given her an odd look or two. The silverware and Spode "Stafford White" china gleamed in the light of a dozen yellow candles. A small grease spot on the linen tablecloth drew a disapproving frown. She'd have to speak to the laundress about that.

The clock on the mantel above the fireplace chimed, drawing her attention. Alan was late, as he had been more often than not lately. She would have to speak to him about that. As she moved to the telephone to call him, she heard the front door slam shut, so she walked to the fireplace instead. Even though it was June, and warm, she still liked the sight of the fire—especially tonight.

The door opened, and Alan hurried in. He kissed her on the cheek and turned to sit. "When are the boys returning?" He gestured at two chairs where their sons usually sat when home. In one was a stuffed teddy bear, its dark brown fur worn thin; in the other sat a lion with a missing eye and a well-chewed ear.

Bettina had picked out a stuffed animal at the birth of each son so that they would absorb the character of the animals and grow up to be strong, powerful men. The animals always sat in the seats the boys occupied when home. Dov really was like a bear: gruff and shaggy with a shambling gait. Gur was the lion of the family.

"I miss them terribly," lamented Bettina.

"I do, too."

Alan started spooning vichyssoise into his mouth. "But it's important for their education, seeing all those museums and art galleries and all that stuff. When they're not jumping, that is."

Bettina half-suspected her sons were getting quite a different sort of education. "Yes, I know. But . . . well, anyway."

Henry cleared away the soup bowls. Alan wiped his mouth. "Got something I need to tell you. Change in plans for the production."

The next course, an alligator pear filled with jellied consommé, appeared in front of her. She took a small bite and glanced at the stuffed lion. "I miss Gur so much. Always bouncing around, so full of energy."

Alan said, "I've decided what my film really needs is some shots on location, out in the real wilderness."

"I miss Dov, too."

"Yes, right. So what I've decided is to go up to Wyoming and film up there."

"Do you remember how Gur used to tackle the other player? He was so fast! Nobody could get past him."

"Um." Alan was cutting the roast beef Henry had put in front of him. "Steamer isn't very happy about it, but he just doesn't understand. Paul is getting everything pulled together, and we're leaving on Friday."

Bettina nodded abstractedly. "And Dov, remember how proud he was when his team won that lacrosse championship?"

45

"Sure." Alan drained the red wine from his glass. "Anyway, I just wanted to let you know."

Something in his tone of voice made her glance up. He was looking away. "Thank you. So, who all is going on this expedition?"

Alan rattled off the names of a dozen crewmembers. Bettina nodded politely as she listened. When he finished, she asked, "What about actors? Won't you need Douglas?"

"Uh, no. I'm not planning on using him. I'm just going up to shoot scenery."

Bettina's suspicion meter registered a jump. "Oh, I see. So you won't be taking Daphne either?"

"Well, no, we have to take Daphne along. Esse has planned some shots with her."

Something snapped inside her. Ever since the boys had gone off to college, Alan had been pulling away from her; she was lonely for the warmth and closeness of family. Was he having an affair with Daphne? She had nothing concrete to go on. Yet there had been a few looks from people at the studio, an averted gaze and a small snicker, half-seen and -heard as she passed. She wanted to jump up, storm to Alan's end of the table, and fling accusations in his face—but no, it was too soon. She did not have enough evidence, and she'd make a damned fool of herself if she said anything.

She straightened in her seat. "That sounds like so much fun. Why don't I go along, too?"

"Oh! Why, uh, we're going to be shooting in the backcountry, you know, have to ride horses to get back there, camp out in tents, eat canned food, stuff like that. You wouldn't like it."

"It sounds just like the early years of our marriage, Alan. If you can take it, so can I. I need to get out of the house for a while before I go crazy. I'll need to go shopping for riding clothes, but I've got the rest of the week. We'll be taking our private rail car, won't we?" Alan slowly nodded. "By the way, a letter from the boys came today. It's on the table in the hall."

After dinner Alan retrieved the letter, opened it, and immediately felt faint with fear. It contained several news clippings, all showing his sons with Pia Donatelli.

His father had forbidden his children to speak Italian in the house. "We're Americans now. We speak American" was his constant refrain. Alan still remembered enough to grasp the essence of the clippings: his sons were big stuff in Europe, and it was all thanks to the sponsorship of one Pia Donatelli, champion of this and that and the other.

He ripped the clippings into confetti and flushed them down the toilet. If Bettina saw them, she'd have too many questions.

CHAPTER 5

Monday Morning, June 8

Terry rinsed the sponge and rubbed it over the bar of saddle soap again, building up a good lather. His parents insisted that all the tack used by guests was to be kept clean and in good repair. That was, he agreed, a good idea, but why did he have to be the one to do it? When he owned the ranch, things would be different.

His mind drifted back to his meeting with the sheriff yesterday afternoon. He wished Pa hadn't agreed to pay him a percentage of the value of the booze that came into town. Since Sheriff Goodman had to know when and where the shipments were coming in—in order to "protect" them—there was no way of concealing the quantities from him. And, since the business was growing, his cut was growing. It made Terry feel more than a little uncomfortable, and he hated that feeling.

The door to the tack room squeaked open, and Junior Frampton drifted in. They howdyed, then Junior took the sponge from Terry. "Let me do that," he said with a big grin. He scrubbed the skirting of the saddle vigorously, whistling while he worked. He'd heard a champion whistler on the radio a while back and was determined to do "The Flight of the Bumblebee" as well as the man on the radio.

Terry leaned back against the saddle rack and rolled a cigarette. He was still clumsy at it. Junior could roll one-handed and ride a horse at the same time. He had never said anything directly. Instead, the first time Terry pulled out a pack of factory smokes, Junior had casually pulled out his sack of Bull Durham and done the one-handed roll, whistling all the time as he looked innocently into the distance.

Terry snapped a match alight with his thumbnail. At least he'd mastered that trick. He fired up the cigarette and inhaled deeply. "I don't reckon you came here to help me clean tack," he said.

Junior polished a small spot with great care for a moment. "Well, I thought maybe I'd apologize for that little incident the other night."

That "little incident" had been a minor brawl. Terry didn't remember what it was about other than the fact that a lot of their good Irish whiskey had been involved. They'd traded a few hard punches before they slipped in the mud, fell on their backsides, and called it quits.

"Well, you know, maybe I mighta had something to do with it, too," Terry allowed. "I'd say we're even."

It had taken Terry a long time to get to the point where he felt even. When his parents bought the ranch five years ago and had actually moved here and started dude ranching . . . well, Terry had been trying to learn the ropes, as they said out here. Junior was two years younger than he was, but they quickly had become friends—mostly.

"So, how've things been?"

Junior took another saddle from the rack and attacked it with the saddle soap. "Wages down at the sawmill aren't any great shakes, you know."

Ah, that was why he'd come. Terry often sensed that beneath all their backslapping comradery, Junior was more than a little envious of his life. This would not be the first time he had asked to borrow money.

"That so?" *Make him squirm a little first—pay him back for that punch.* "I heard the X-Bar-C was looking for a good hand. Fifty and found," Terry said.

"Well, fifty bucks a week and found ain't bad, but have you seen their bunkhouse? Wouldn't want my dog to sleep there. And their cook? His chow ain't fit for a dog neither."

"I expect I could find a Lincoln to help you out."

"I'd sure appreciate that."

Terry took a five-dollar bill from his wallet and handed it to Junior.

"Thanks." Junior heaved the clean saddle up on its rack, took down another, and started soaping it. "I expect you're cleaning this tack for all those fancy folks coming next week."

Terry coughed out the lungful of tobacco smoke he'd inhaled. "What folks?"

Junior smirked. It was there and gone so quickly that Terry wasn't sure he'd seen it. "Why, ain't you heard? All those Hollywood people."

Terry stomped the butt of his cigarette into the dirt. "Far as I know, the next batch of dudes isn't coming until next month."

"Oh, not them. Megan's sister, Luella, is coming, along with a bunch of people from that movie studio where she works." Junior ticked off names on his fingers. "Then there's that director guy, Steamer what's his name; and his boss, Alan somebody or other; a guy name of Paul Marshal; and a whole crew—lights, cameras, all that stuff."

Terry shoved his hands into the back pockets of his waist overalls and rocked on the heels of his boots. "How come I haven't heard about this?"

Junior's air of innocence was almost genuine. "Damned if I know. Don't you talk to your wife?"

"My wife? What's she got to do with it?"

"Well now, it was her what arranged everything. Worked with my dad to set up a pack trip into the backcountry. Seems like they want to film some real wilderness."

Terry kicked the saddle rack, hard. He remembered now. He'd heard Megan talking about Luella and the movie people, but she was always talking about them. How was he supposed to know this was for real? She'd said something about Parley and a pack trip, but Parley did all the pack trips for the dudes staying at the ranch. How was he supposed to know this was different? *Damn.*

He felt as if he'd awakened to find a rattlesnake in his bedroll. He'd have to move very carefully. He knew it was time to talk to Ma and find out what Megan had been up to.

Junior was whistling "The Flight of the Bumble Bee" as he hung newly cleaned bridles on their racks. He looked around. "Something wrong?"

"Nah. Just remembered something. Thanks for helping. I need to talk to Ma."

Terry strode through the living room on his way to the office. The anger that had burned through him was dissipating rapidly. The unexpected and unwelcome invasion by the Hollywood people just might provide an opportunity to do something about his situation. He glanced into the dining room, where Megan was serving breakfast. She waved; he waved back.

Ma was in the ranch office, sitting at the rolltop desk. When he entered, she shoved some papers into a pigeonhole and looked up. "Something bothering you?" Terry sank into a comfortable chair and put his feet on the coffee table. "And get your feet off the table. Where do you think you are? In the bunkhouse?"

"Aw, Ma!" He eased his dirty boots off the table anyway. He could feel her getting riled up. He took his Barlow knife from his pocket and scraped dirt from his fingernails. "Hear tell we're expecting some extra guests next Tuesday."

"Welcome to the party, son."

"Aw, Ma!" He snapped the knife closed. "How come I didn't hear about it?"

"Maybe you've been downtown drinking too much jasmine tea?"

Terry's heart sank to his boots. Jasmine was the new hostess, a Jap or a Chinese, at Mrs. Smedly's "boarding house." How in hell had his ma found out?

Ma continued before he could think of a reply. "Anyway, never mind about that. I didn't find out about them myself until day before yesterday."

Terry stared at her. "*You* didn't? How can you not find out about it? You take care of all the reservations."

"Megan did it."

"Did *what*?"

"Set up the whole thing. Oh, she told me about it, but I wasn't paying enough attention. She's been jabbering on the phone ever since her sister called last week. She's had her head together with Parley planning everything, and now all those Hollywood people are coming."

Terry sagged back into the chair. "*Who* is coming? How many? How long are they going to stay?"

Ma filled him in on the details. When she finished, all he could say was, "No shit!" Then, after a pause, he continued, "I don't see how you could let Megan do all—"

Ma slammed the rolltop of the desk shut, chopping off his protest. "I was busy taking care of your father."

The grim tone of Ma's voice made Terry feel as if he'd just come out of the chute on a bucking Brahma bull. How in hell was he going to get off without getting thrown or gored? Ma sounded so miserable; he'd never heard her like this before. But then, his pa had been out to the barn a lot lately.

Maybe he'd better just ask. "What's wrong, Ma?"

She sighed deeply. "I guess it's time I told you."

She was silent for a long time, looking into empty air. Finally he asked, "Told me what?"

"Close the door."

He did, shutting out the sound of Megan playing and singing for the guests. When he sat again, his ma said, "It was not an automobile accident that put your father in that wheelchair."

His pa had been wheeled home one night, around seven or eight years ago. Six months later they'd moved out West, ripping Terry away from his school chums and the home he'd known all his life. He thought he was over the resentment, but this new development brought it all roaring back.

"Oh. Well, are you going to tell me about it?"

Ma looked again at the door, gestured for him to come closer, and lowered her voice. "You know about your father's temper, right? Well, it got him in trouble with our, um, wholesalers. One of your father's retail customers called him a bad name, and he beat him to a pulp. Our friends didn't like that one little bit. You don't mess with customers, because, if you do, they go to another supplier."

Terry felt as if a little black snake of terror was poking him in the guts, trying to rip him open and get inside. "Ah, so, they . . . they did what?"

"He was found one night behind some packing cases on the Brooklyn waterfront. The police took him to the hospital. When he got out, he couldn't walk."

"But how did we happen to move here? Do you have any idea how miserable that made me?"

"I hope you don't think you're the only one who's miserable," she said acridly. "We tried to stick it out for a while, but with your father not able to work . . . uh, he heard about this ranch being for sale cheap, so then we sold everything to buy it. When his boss found out where we were going, he offered to stake us to a supply of flower pots."

Terry goggled at her. "Flower pots?"

"That's how the whiskey came into the country from Ireland. The crates were marked 'Ceramic Flower Pots.' A few did contain clay pots. Our people knew which ones they were. They'd take the inspector to see those, he'd sign off on those, and the rest would get to our wholesalers, and then to us.

"Anyway, our people called it 'opening new territory.' Said they'd give us another chance if we went West and stayed there."

"So, who in the hell are 'our people'?"

"You don't want to know, son. If you don't know, you're less likely to get hurt."

The idea of being hurt left Terry feeling weak. "Jesus, Ma. We don't have to deal with those people anymore, do we? We could make a living from the ranch. We're getting a good reputation back East as the best dude ranch in Wyoming."

"There's two things wrong with that. First is, we're not making a profit—yet. Second thing is, your father is in a lot of pain. The only thing that helps is a little of that good Irish whiskey he likes."

They sat in silence, measuring each other. "So," Terry said at last, "Megan has set up this whole thing with these Hollywood people?"

His ma nodded. "And we're going to have to do something about it."

"I'm not sure I understand." Terry inspected his fingernails. "Megan goes along with the business; she told me so herself. She thinks Prohibition is a waste of money." He looked up from his fingers. "Unless you think she'd do something . . . stupid?"

"I don't think anything right now. What I do know is she's running around out there like a mare in heat, bringing all sorts of strange stallions into town."

"But why would she do something like that?"

"You know how close she is to Sally Mann, right?" Terry

nodded. "So, what if she told Sally about it, and Sally called the Bureau of Prohibition and hinted they could send a Prohibition agent in with the movie crew?"

Sally was such a rabid prohibitionist, she just might do something sneaky like that. "Um. Yeah, well, so what do we do?"

"You did hear that she wants to go along on the pack trip?" Terry nodded. "Might be a good idea to let her go."

"Aw, Ma! You know I need her here."

"I suppose if you think she's more important than your own mother and father . . ." His ma sniffed and dabbed at her eyes. "We need you, too, you know. We're not getting any younger."

"All right, I'll think about it."

"You have to do more than just think about it. You have to pretend that you don't want her to go, tell her she can't go."

"Huh?"

His ma sighed impatiently. "Because if you do that, it will just make her want to go all the more."

"Oh. I hadn't thought of it that way." His ma was smart that way. He stood up to leave.

"And Terry?"

"Yes, Ma?"

"Best you don't go mentioning anything about lawmen to Megan."

"Yeah? Why?"

"Because that way, if she has anything to do with it and doesn't think we know, we can catch her out."

"Aw, Ma, Megan ain't like that."

"Just do as I say, son."

A burst of applause from the direction of the dining room made Terry remember Megan had been playing for the guests after breakfast.

His ma continued, "We're running low on vegetables. Tell

Megan to come in and get the shopping list."

Megan was just beginning the last verse of "Home on the Range" when she saw Terry passing through the living room. He stopped and, with exaggerated motions, indicated that she was to go to the office. She nodded and continued singing.

The guests always demanded the song, and she had played it so often, she was beginning to hate it. The guests always loved it, and this morning was no exception; they clapped and cheered.

"Okay, folks, that's it for right now. I need to get to work."

As the guests were rising and getting ready for the day's activities, Charity Palmerson said, "With a voice and talent like that, you could be in the cinema, Megan."

Megan felt a glow of pleasure work its way through her. She hoped she wasn't blushing. If she was ever going to be a professional, she couldn't blush on stage. "Why, thank you, Mrs. Palmerson."

"Oh, dear, call me Charity, please."

"Mom's right, Mrs. Foxworth." Bertie stood shyly beside his mother, his head hanging. "You sing real good."

"Bertie! She sings *well,* not good. And button up your coat. You'll make your bronchitis worse."

"Okay, she sings real *well* then."

Megan said, "Excuse me, um, Charity? I need to go talk to my mother-in-law."

The door was closed when she arrived. She knocked and heard Fiona say, "Just a moment." She waited patiently, waited some more, and finally knocked again.

"Yes, yes, coming." Fiona sounded annoyed and was scowling when at last she opened the door. Megan was still floating on a pink cloud of happiness. Darned if she was going to let Fiona yank it out from under her.

"Good morning, Mother Foxworth." She kept her tone light

and polite. "You wanted to see me?"

"Of course I wanted to see you. Why do you think I sent Terry to tell you? Anyway, come in and sit down." Megan lowered herself into the creaky leather embrace of the couch, folded her hands in her lap, and waited.

"Now that you've got that mob of Hollywood people coming, we're going to need more vegetables. I want you to go to Isaiah's. Here's a list."

Megan glanced at it. "You want *canned* vegetables?"

"Don't use that tone of voice with me, missy. Have you any idea how much work it saves us, to buy canned veggies? All that peeling and cutting and chopping we don't have to do? These new canned things are a godsend. Now get on with it."

Well, maybe they saved a lot of work, but they tasted like boiled cardboard compared to fresh. Some of these new-fangled inventions were not worth it, but Megan knew it was better to get on Fiona's good side.

"Oh! I'd be happy to." She hesitated, wondering if this would be a good time to bring it up. *Might as well try.* "You know, I've been thinking, Mother Foxworth. I'll bet the guests would love it if we put on a rodeo for them. Not a real rodeo, of course, but maybe they could do some barrel bending, maybe an egg-in-the-spoon race on horseback, that sort of thing. There's lots of fun things to do."

"A rodeo? What makes you think a little snip like you knows anything about what ladies and gentlemen would like? Do you have any idea how hard I've struggled to keep this ranch running? What with TT being locked in that wheelchair? Do you really think I have enough time for foolishness like rodeos for dudes and dudines who can barely stay on a horse in the first place?"

Megan roped all the emotions that wanted to leap out and hog-tied them. She'd let them loose and sort them out later.

She rose. "I'll go see Isaiah now, Mother Foxworth."

Megan drove mechanically, soothed by the familiar rattling rhythm of the big truck. To her right the sun blasted showers of golden light from the snowfields of the Tetons, and for a moment she and nature were one and the same thing. She felt as if a light inside her were guiding her and would help her give birth to all the music gestating within.

She was so wrapped up in her thoughts that when something went by in the opposite direction, throwing up a huge cloud of dust, she nearly lost control of the truck. A glance in the rearview mirror showed her Reverend Swanson's big black sedan dwindling to a flyspeck on the mountain scenery. She laughed quietly to herself. He would have been horrified if he'd been able to read her thoughts.

Now was a good time to pull out all those emotions she had hog-tied and let them loose. As her humiliation and anger broke their bonds, she realized to her surprise that she had already forgiven Mother Foxworth. *Oh, the hell with that Mother Foxworth nonsense.* She would call her Fiona from now on. Fiona was bitter and angry over the wound that had paralyzed her husband. A stupid automobile accident had shattered her dreams of a new future for themselves and their son. No wonder she was bitchy and bitter.

The truck rumbled over the timber bridge that crossed the creek, and Megan turned south toward town. As she did, a new thought intruded, dimming her glow of happiness: maybe TT and Terry were buying a lot more booze than they let on to and then maybe selling it?

On the paved road, the jarring rhythm of the truck smoothed out, and Megan concentrated on walking around the ranch in her mind, searching for possible hiding places for large quantities of whiskey. There sure was no room in the main cabin or in

the living room or kitchen, and all the guest cottages were occupied. The barn was filled with hay bales from the floor to the
rafters, from front to back and side to side. She was sure there
was no room in the bunkhouse either. Besides, if the hands had
found out about it, it would be gone the next morning.

No, the thought that her husband's family might be involved
in smuggling was unworthy of her. TT and Fiona owned some
of the best land in Jackson, a whole section, which made them
real rich. Why would they risk jail? Drinking it was one thing—
everyone did it—but selling it was something else. No, TT was
buying just enough for them and their guests.

Relief stampeded through her, leaving her feeling as if she'd
been released from jail. The only thing that still worried her was
that Terry was drinking a little bit too much every now and
then. She'd just have to talk to him about it and get him to cut
down. Then when he did, he'd understand how important her
music was to her, and they'd work things out.

To hell with canned vegetables. She was damned well going
to stop at Sally's. She'd buy some *real* veggies and peel, cut,
chop, and cook them for herself and Terry.

CHAPTER 6

Monday Afternoon, June 8

Sally Mann looked up from her hoe as the truck from the Rocking Lazy F Ranch squeaked to a stop in a cloud of dust. She expected to see Terry Foxworth get out and come wriggling toward her like the puppy he was, but it was Megan who stepped off the running board and walked toward her, waving.

Sally wiped her face with a red bandana and waved back. Ever since the death of her husband, her only source of support had been her truck garden. She worked twelve hours a day in the summer, planting, weeding, watering, and harvesting. The dude ranches all loved buying her vegetables, but making a living was interfering with her real mission in life: the Women's Christian Temperance Union.

After Herbie Mann drank himself to death, the WCTU had become Sally's new family. She threw herself into the fight against alcohol. The fight had kept her sane, but now it was driving her crazy. Booze was still getting into Jackson, and she was frustrated and melancholy over her lack of progress.

She'd never been able to have children, and Megan had become like a daughter to her. Now she swept her into her arms and hugged her tightly. "Ah, Megan, where have you been keeping yourself? It's been a coon's age since I've seen you. Let me look at you." She held Megan away and was surprised at the look of . . . was it guilt, or misery, or both?

"I know, Momma Sal. I'm sorry." Megan turned away and

brushed at her cheeks quickly. "Things have been hectic at the ranch."

Something more than a load of work was eating at her, Sally realized. After the scandal that had destroyed her father's career, Megan's plans for trade school had been cancelled, and the once-joyous child she'd known had become somber and altogether too quiet. For now, it was best to accept the fib.

"So tell me, what's making things hectic?"

Megan's face brightened. "We have a film crew from Hollywood coming! About fifteen people, I think. Luella's coming, and that director Steamer Daniels and his boss and, oh, a lot of other people."

"So you're going to need more vegetables than usual next week, right?" Megan nodded. "When are they arriving?"

"Next Tuesday. On the three-fifteen train."

"So soon? Oh, well, let's go have a look."

They moved together along the rows as Sally counted and calculated in her head, estimating when the next crop would be ready. "All right, if you can make do with a little less this week, there'll be enough next week."

As she uprooted carrots, beets, and onions and plucked tomatoes and green beans from their vines, Sally pondered whether to tell Megan about what she had learned. Perhaps she should, as it might knock some sense into her head.

"Here you go," Sally said, plopping a basket at Megan's feet.

Megan poked through the contents, estimating. "Fiona wants canned vegetables for the guests, but I want these for Terry and me." She carried the basket to the truck and loaded it into the back. "I suppose you'll be at the railroad station, with your WCTU ladies and the band."

"Of course we will."

The look on Megan's face told Sally she was embarrassed at the idea. Annoyance surged through her. The silly girl refused to take the threat of alcohol seriously. "Megan! We can't let an opportunity like this go by. The men who make movies are in a position to influence vast numbers of people. If we can just persuade them, they can send a powerful message of temperance to the world. Alcohol is evil, Megan, and that's all there is to it."

Megan climbed onto the running board of the truck. She seemed reluctant to speak but at last said, "I guess I just don't see it the same way you do, Momma Sal. All the men here work very hard. I can't blame Terry and the hands for having a little drink at the end of the day."

"If it was only 'a *little* drink,' Megan, but it's not. It's a national disgrace. It's destroying the moral fabric of our nation. It leads to prostitution, organized crime, and corruption among our politicians and police."

"That's only because it's illegal, Momma Sal. People always want what they can't have. It's Prohibition that's responsible for all that bad stuff that's happening."

Sally stared at Megan in shock and floundered around for something to say. At last she replied, "Look what liquor has done to poor old Buddy Brewster! He used to be an upstanding citizen of this community." She stopped, gasping for breath. "You come help me one of these days at the orphanage. You can see for yourself the results of that 'little drink' the men have. I want you to see the abandoned children, the wives who get beaten up because they try to stop their men from drinking."

Megan stepped down from the running board and threw her arms around Sally. "All right, Momma Sal, I owe you that much. I'll come around some day after the Hollywood people leave."

The soft answer calmed Sally, and she decided to tell her what she had done. "Thank you, dear." She glanced around to see if anyone might be looking. "I can tell you, because I trust you. I've been talking to people in Washington, and I'm finally going to get some help."

"Help? With what?"

"To tackle the problem of all the alcohol that's getting into Jackson. The Bureau of Internal Revenue is sending an undercover agent to look into the situation."

Megan sank down onto the running board with a gasp. "You've been talking on the phone? To the prohibition unit?"

"Yes. Why? What's wrong with that?"

"Oh, Momma Sal! I went to the movie last Saturday, with Gertie. You know, the switchboard operator."

A horrible feeling that she'd done something wrong crept up on Sally. "So . . . what . . . ?"

"Gertie listens in on people's conversations. She just loves to gossip, and, well, anyway, she whispered to me that someone is planning to kill us."

The ground shifted under Sally's boots. She collapsed onto the running board beside Megan. "Oh. I didn't know. About Gertie, I mean." Conflicting emotions shot through her like a twister ripping buildings apart. She couldn't sit here forever; she had to get away and think things out. One thing was clear, though: she had to protect this child.

"Megan dear, if Gertie loves to gossip that much, who's to say she's not . . . well, exaggerating to make it sound better?" She laughed, hoping it sounded light and dismissive. "Who on earth would want to kill you?"

Megan snuggled deeper into the copper bathtub. She'd returned from Sally's exhausted, only to discover that Terry had gone into town. She'd heated an extra large quantity of water on the woodstove and dumped it into the high-backed copper tub in their cottage bathroom. The legs of the tub were uneven, and it always tipped a little as she got in. Now she was finally beginning to relax. She poked at the long-handled bath brush, amused as it bobbed on the surface of the soapy water.

Sally's last words of this afternoon came back to her. *Who on earth would want to kill you?* Momma Sal was always so sensible. Megan knew from personal experience that Gertie loved to gossip—not only gossip, but exaggerate to boot. It made her life more exciting. But what if for once Gertie wasn't just trying to make herself look good? What if this time Gertie *hadn't* twisted what she had heard? Suppose a "Prohi" really was coming to town? Megan knew she had to find out where the booze was hidden. That way she'd know, in case.

Her chin was touching the water when a loud rapping yanked her out of her doze. "Miz Foxworth?"

At the sound of Junior's voice, Megan grabbed her bath towel and dragged it over the edges of the tub. The towel concealed her most important parts.

She fought to keep the panic out of her voice. "What is it?"

The door opened a crack. Junior was standing half turned away from her, looking at the floor. He shuffled his feet, darted his gaze at her, down to the floor, and then back to her.

"I was just thinking, you know, maybe you needed some more hot water. I could bring you some. I mean, if you'd like." He glanced up, and his gaze lingered on her longer this time.

"*No!* I mean, no, thank you. I have plenty. Good night, Junior."

He edged a bit farther into the room. His gaze wandered all around, coming back to settle on her, then to dart away again. His hands were inside his overalls; she could see them moving under the fabric.

"Well, how about I wash your back? I could get it real good and clean for you. You'd like that, wouldn't you?" He slid completely into the bathroom and closed the door behind him.

Megan pulled her towel into the water and covered herself with it. "Stop! Get the hell out, now!"

"Aw, now, Megan, no need to be that way. I've got a real nice surprise in here for you." He rubbed his crotch; she could see the bulge tightening the fabric.

"Get out or I'll scream."

A lupine grin smeared itself across his face. "Wouldn't do you no good. Ain't no one around, not way back here. You and Terry, you sure got yourselves a real private cabin."

Well now, she had a choice, didn't she? She could scream and try to run, but she had no doubt he'd catch her before she could get out the door. With every step he took toward her, his smirk deepened. She gathered herself for action.

He reached the edge of the tub. As he stared at her, she pulled the bath towel slowly away from her breasts. He leaned over, eyes widening, reaching for her, and she thrust the wet towel upward with all her strength.

The soggy, soapy mass thumped into his face and chest, blinding him. He staggered, grabbing for the tub. For a moment it remained in place. Then his feet slid from under him, and he went over backward, pulling the tub over with him. Megan and twenty gallons of hot, soapy water landed on top of him.

She rolled off him and stood up as he struggled to free himself from the clinging bath towel. She wielded the bath brush like the softball bat she'd used in school, fury and shame powering her swings. Despite her blows, he said nothing, only grunted as each blow landed. He crawled away on his knees, unable to free himself of the clinging towel and get to his feet on the soapy floor.

When at last he reached the door, he pulled himself upright on the door frame and glared at her for a while. When his smirk returned, she could see his gaze moving up and down her naked body.

"Bitch! You'll pay for this."

She slammed the door shut and dropped the latch in place before she gave way to the shakes.

The water in Pia's bathtub was getting cold. She opened her eyes with a sigh and turned on the hot water tap. Today was Thursday, which meant she had not heard from Uncle for three days. This probably meant Mr. Alan Segal had made a payment on his loan, which she prayed to God he had. She quickly ran through her ritual. She touched her right forefinger to each of the scars on her arm, starting at the top of the cross, and at each one said, "Mister Segal has made a payment; Tommaso and I are free."

Rearing Tommaso had taken every bit of strength and courage she possessed. As each year passed and he grew bigger and stronger, Uncle's demands had increased. She was to send Tommaso to him in Italy, to be brought up in the family tradition, which meant being cruel and domineering.

She had used all her wiles to keep Tommaso from him, but now he was nearly fifteen, the age Uncle had determined that Tommaso was "to become a man." How could she prevent it? She was running out of excuses to keep Tommaso near her. She thought again of the .25 Colt pistol in her purse. Maybe she could pretend to comply, take her son to Italy, and then find a way to kill Uncle?

She turned off the hot water and pulled the tray of manicure implements toward her. It rested on each side of the marble tub, with emery boards, cuticle scissors, nail buffers, and polish snuggled in a basket in the center section. She had finished nipping the last ragged cuticle from her fingers when there was a timid knock at the door.

"What is it, Tommaso?"

"Ah, a telegram has arrived for you."

The bath water suddenly seemed as cold as the arctic seas

she had read about. A person who fell overboard in those waters died within five minutes. She wondered if she had even that long to live. "Well, bring it in," she said impatiently.

"But Mama . . ."

"Just close your eyes, Tommaso. Quickly now."

Her son sidled into the room, one hand over his eyes, the other holding a yellow envelope at arm's length. She snatched it from him, and he hurried out, closing the door quietly behind him.

Pia closed her eyes and held the telegram in shaking hands for a long moment before she picked up her nail file and slit it open. The quarter-inch-wide paper strips from the Teletype machine, glued to yellow support paper, spelled out her worst fears.

CLIENT DEPARTING FRIDAY BY TRAIN FOR ROCKING LAZY F RANCH JACKSON WYOMING STOP. MAKE RANCH RESERVATIONS AND TRAVEL ARRANGEMENTS SAME TRAIN IMMEDIATELY STOP. IMPERATIVE YOU TAKE ALL STEPS TO PROTECT INVESTMENT STOP. UNCLE.

She couldn't help it. She knew Tommaso was probably hanging around outside her door and would hear her, but she broke down and wept anyway.

A timid rap at the door was followed by his voice, wavering: "Momma?"

"Go away, Tommaso, just go away!" *Damn Uncle to hell anyway.* She loathed him; she was bound to him by bands of iron. She was such a coward. After all, she had her .25 automatic; she could simply take a boat to Italy and kill him. Why couldn't she just do it? Because one of his brothers would take over and probably kill her. And then where would Tommaso be?

Her bath water had grown as cold as her soul. She dried, dressed, and went to the telephone.

The windows of the Cattleman's Cafe in Jackson Hole were heavily fogged, which was not surprising, given that the heat and moisture rising from the crowd inside was condensing on the rain-chilled panes. The good citizens were mostly quiet, spirits dampened by the gloomy weather. They slurped their coffee and ate steaks and fries drowned in ketchup.

Buddy Brewster was nursing a hangover, but there was nothing wrong with his hearing. He listened avidly as Gertie gossiped to a friend in the booth behind him.

"But I *heard* her," Gertie said in a stage whisper. Buddy could not see who she was talking to—probably some old biddy just as nosy as she was.

Her friend said something Buddy could not hear. Gertie's whisper turned indignant. "I promise you, she called the Prohibition Unit, and they said they were going to send a Prohi."

"Prohi?" her friend asked.

"That's what they call a Prohibition agent."

Several patrons rose and headed for the door, saying good morning to Gertie as they did. After that, Gertie's voice dropped, but Buddy had heard all he needed to know.

Sheriff Goodman was startled at the sound of a knock on the door of his private office. He looked up to see Buddy's nose pressed to the glass, fingers on one hand waving a little greeting. The only thing to do with Buddy was to ignore him, which proved impossible. The knocking only grew to the point where the sheriff feared the glass would shatter.

He shoved the door open, forcing Buddy to step back suddenly. He staggered a bit but remained upright. "What the hell do you want, Buddy? I'm busy, can't you see that?"

A foxy smile creased Buddy's face. "Sure, I kin see that, Sheriff. I wouldn't want to bother a busy man like you. Not even with really interesting news."

The sheriff snorted with laughter. "Now what kinda news could you have that would interest me?"

Buddy sniffed. "Maybe I might know something that would have to do with your . . ." His voice dropped to a hoarse whisper, and he looked around with care. "With your *business.*" He turned and walked away with injured dignity.

"Whoa, hold up there." The sheriff grabbed the back of Buddy's rain-soaked jacket. "Best you come in here where we can talk in private."

When Buddy sagged into a hard-back chair, the sheriff leaned in close and scowled. "Now just what in hell are you talking about? And don't try to pull any wool over my eyes, damn you."

Buddy leaned back and smiled a wide, shit-eating grin and said nothing.

The sheriff glared at him a moment, then seized his collar in an iron fist. Buddy's smile widened, and he yelled, "Help!" in a voice that could be heard in the next county.

The sheriff loosened his grip. "Damn you, stop that nonsense."

"Aw now, Sheriff, you wouldn't want to get the reputation for beating up on destitute old men like me, would you?"

The sheriff released his grip and sat back, fuming with frustration. "All right, damn it. Talk."

"Aw now, Sheriff, do you have any idea how thirsty a man can get?"

The sheriff scowled fiercely at Buddy, who only leaned back and contemplated his boots. At last the sheriff opened his desk drawer, rummaged in it, pulled out a half dollar, and slapped it on the desk.

"Aw now, Sheriff, this here news is worth a lot more than that." He counted on his fingers. "Maybe, I'd say, four times more."

The sheriff scowled at Buddy some more and at last put another dollar and a half down. "There, damn it: talk."

"Well, I just happened to hear . . ."

What Buddy just happened to have heard terrified the sheriff. He was damned if he was going to let Buddy know it, and he sat in stone-faced silence until Buddy stopped.

"Um. Well, thank you, Buddy. That's certainly worth thinking about." He considered a moment longer and pulled another dollar from his pocket. "And you don't need to think about it anymore, right?"

"Right." Buddy rose. "Thought you'd see it my way, Sheriff. You've just made ol' Buddy real happy."

He opened the door and turned back. "Know what?" The sheriff shook his head. "I'll bet they are going to send that Steamer, what's his name."

"That's crazy, Buddy. He's just an actor."

"Yeah, but he played the sheriff in that moom pitchure we seen a while back."

"So what?"

"So it's the perfect disguise, doncha see?"

"No, I don't."

"Well now, that's just it, won't no one believe he's a real law-man 'cause everyone knows he's just an actor, right?"

The sheriff needed in the worst possible way to be alone and ponder on this news. Best to humor Buddy and get him out the door. "I suppose that's possible, Buddy."

"Tha's what I thought." He sounded like a banty rooster crowing. "Ol' Buddy ain't so dumb after all."

CHAPTER 7

Wednesday Morning, June 10

Steamer was deeply, irrationally pleased with his recently acquired apartment. On the top floor of a new building on Franklin Avenue in Hollywood, it had tall windows and a high ceiling that filled it with light and air. Two bedrooms and two baths meant there'd be room for Allison—after they were married, of course—and their first child. For now she still had to sneak down the back stairs when she left. Gossip could ruin her career.

He stood looking out over the Hollywood Hills and all of Los Angeles. His new boots gleamed, his waist overalls were washed to just the right degree of softness, and his red-and-white shirt with pearl snaps fitted his body like its skin fits a snake. He was as ready as he was ever going to be to pop the question.

Down the hall the bathroom door opened and closed. Allison came to stand beside him and gaze out over the sun-splashed hills. He put his arm around her, felt her not so much resist as fail to soften and fit herself into his embrace. Perhaps she knew what he was going to ask. Perhaps she had seen the small, white box on the breakfast table.

"I'm famished, darling. Can we eat now?" she asked.

"In just a minute. Let me look at you." He turned her to him, nodded admiringly. In her latest incarnation, she was a knock-off of Louise Brooks, right down to the bobbed hairdo and string of pearls. She dyed her hair black now; she had been less successful as a blonde at hiding the grey.

"You'll do," he said as she lowered her gaze. "Come sit for a minute and have a Buck's Fizz."

Steamer had set the table with his best china and put a rose in a crystal vase at her place. He poured her glass half full of freshly squeezed orange juice and then filled it with champagne. She grabbed the bottle, avoiding looking at the small box on her plate.

"And just where did you get *French* champagne?" she burbled. "This is supposed to be Prohibition."

"Alan has a supplier."

"Oh, of course. Cheers." She clinked her glass on his and then drained half of it. "Ooh, that's good." She drained the other half. "Now, what about breakfast?"

He refilled her glass. "Allie, there's something I want to ask you." Her gaze struck the small, white box as if it were a rattlesnake, and she recoiled, taking another big swallow of the mimosa.

"Oh, Steamer, let's not be so serious. I had such an exhausting day yesterday. You have no idea. Francine was all thumbs when she was fitting my costume. And Eric, dear boy that he is, well, his makeup made me look like the bride of Frankenstein."

Steamer gently took the wine glass from her. He put the box in her hands. "Open it."

She did. She glanced at the ring inside and snapped the box closed. She leaned back and looked at him with an expression he had never seen before. "I don't think this is the time to talk of marriage, Steamer."

"Allie, I want you to marry me. No, listen to me." He took her hands in his, enclosing the box between them. "I love you, and I want you to be my wife. Look, I've opened my heart and soul to you. You know everything there is to know about me."

A tiny smile lurking at the corners of her mouth seemed to

say that she knew something more than everything. The idea alarmed him, and he pushed it from his mind. "We've been together for, what, two years? They've been wonderful years. There's no reason we shouldn't get married. We can continue our careers even though we're married. We don't have to have children right away."

"That's just it, you see."

Steamer frowned. "No, I don't see."

"Steamer, it's time for me to think about something other than a career as an actress." She smiled a hesitant and reluctant smile. "Look at me. I'm, well, middle-aged now. The mirror doesn't frighten me anymore, Steamer. I've had a good career, but it's time for something else."

"Something else?" He felt foolish echoing her words, but they had knocked any other response out of his mind.

"A family. Children. A white picket fence and a dog."

"But Allie, I thought we agreed. My career is just getting started. I need at least five more years to build a solid foundation under us before we do anything as drastic as have children."

The look on her face told him he'd used the wrong word, but he didn't have a chance to backpedal. "Steamer dear, I've tried to tell you for some time now." She leaned forward and placed her hand on his arm. "You're all involved in your *career*. It's an all-consuming passion with you and leaves very little of you left over for other people."

"How can you say that?" He felt his throat constricting. He knew he was speaking in a tight voice he hated but could not control. "I spend a lot of time with you, Allison. We've had a lot of fun together, haven't we?"

"Yes, but it's not that."

"What is it, then?"

She put the small, white box on the dining table in front of him and rose. "You're not playing with imaginary actors anymore, like you did when you were a kid."

"What does that mean?"

"It means that Daphne, and F-Stop, and me, and all the other people you work with, we're not cut-out paper dolls you can push around like stage props. You've got a lot of good ideas, Steamer, and you'll be a great director one of these days—if you can remember that you work with real, live human beings, not wooden statues."

She picked up her purse and moved toward the door. "I think . . . we should date other people. At least for a while."

Steamer felt a great, black fog creeping into his body and soul. "I guess that means you don't want to finish breakfast."

"No. And don't worry about driving me to the studio. I think it would be best if I took a taxi."

He stood in the open doorway listening to the clatter of her high heels on the back stairs. As the sound faded, he realized that at some level he'd known she would refuse. It would take several weeks, and an utterly and completely unexpected event, to make him understand why she had done so.

"Why so glum?"

Steamer looked up, startled out of his reverie. He'd driven to the studio, parked, and walked onto the set without conscious attention. Now Daphne was looking at him curiously. "Who, me?"

"Yes, you. You look like the dog just ate your script." Daphne giggled at her own joke. "Come in; sit down."

Steamer entered her dressing room, pulled the door shut behind him, and sank onto the couch. He stared at his boots for a moment before he replied. "I asked Allison to marry me."

"Ah. And she said no." He nodded. "I'm sorry, Steamer. I know how much you loved her."

"Yeah, well . . ." He sighed and sat up straight. "No use crying over spilt milk. How are you doing?"

They chatted about the weather and the other usual trivia, and he could see that she was, indeed, fine, which was to say, sober. "You've heard we're going to Jackson, to shoot on location, right?"

"Uh-huh. So what do you think about it?"

"I don't like the idea."

"Because?"

"It's too hard to control what I get on film. The lighting isn't reliable. If we start shooting in the sun and a cloud comes along, we have to wait until it goes away or the shots won't match. I like working in the studio with you."

"I do like the way you light me, Steamer. I mean, I know F-Stop does the lighting, but he always seems to listen to you."

"Yeah, well, then there's the thing of it. I can't move the camera, you know, make tracking shots or dolly shots. I mean, unless we lay dolly tracks and all that. I'll be stuck with the camera on a tripod."

A loud triple rap on the door was followed by a voice demanding, "Miss Divine? Are you all right?"

Daphne rose and opened the door just as Paul Marshal was raising his fist to knock again. "I'm fine, Paul. Come in."

When Paul saw Steamer, he quickly smothered the smirk that started to cross his face. "Good morning, Steamer. Actually, I was looking for you."

"Oh?"

"Yes, ah, Esse has been working all night. Here." Paul thrust a bundle of paper at Steamer. "This is the new stuff Alan wants to shoot in Jackson."

Steamer leafed through the script while Paul hung over him and enthusiastically jabbed his finger at the pages. "Look at that, isn't that great? And look at this scene. It's a real humdinger, isn't it?"

Steamer controlled his dismay as he paged through the new material. The script was loaded with shots of horses galloping and cowboys running, shooting six-guns and hitting each other with rock-hard fists. Then there were all the shots of Daphne reacting to all of this nonsense with shining eyes and gazing adoringly at so-and-so.

Paul said, "Great stuff, isn't it? It's really going to pump up the film, make it so much more accessible to the masses." *He sounds,* Steamer thought, *like an echo of Alan.*

He was saved from making a reply when Daphne jumped up and handed her copy back to Paul with a sweeping gesture. "That's all well and good, Paul, but I won't be needing this."

Paul looked at her as if he'd been pole-axed. "Why not?"

"Because I'm not going to Jackson, that's why."

Paul sputtered and mumbled for a moment. "Ah, does Alan know about this?"

"I've already told him," Daphne said.

Paul stood rattling the pages of the script, glaring from her to Steamer and back. "Ah, well, ah, remember the rushes at four this afternoon," he said and backed out the door.

Steamer and Daphne burst out laughing at the same time and laughed until their sides ached. At last Steamer was able to say, "Ah yes, you do know how to throw a monkey wrench into the machinery, don't you?"

Daphne smiled at him. "I'm just as bored with all those hicks in my hometown as you are, Steamer."

"Well, yeah, I guess I am—sort of. How long do you think it's going to be before you're struck by lightning?"

"I've told Alan I'm not going, and that's final. You can shoot all those gazing-adoringly shots here, can't you? After you get back?"

He'd probably have trouble matching the lighting, but he

could do it if necessary. He nodded, gave her a quick hug, and left.

He spent the rest of the morning shooting inserts and cut-aways. Jimmy could always edit them later to patch up mistakes and adjust the timing of the film.

As he worked, Steamer became ever more certain that film-ing on location would be a mistake. Daphne was too much of a wilting flower to work outdoors. When sober, she was capable of creating a luminous screen presence. Her acting would make or break the film, and all the galloping horses and flaming six-guns would not make the least damn bit of difference. He needed to film her in the studio under controlled lighting. Right now, though, he had to get to the screening room for the dailies.

The big movie screen splashed light and shadow on Steamer, Alan, and Daphne, who were sitting in the front row. In the third and fourth rows of the studio screening room sat several other members of the production team. They sat far behind Alan so they could comment—in soft whispers, not stage whispers—about the footage. If Alan should overhear, they would lose their jobs. The air was hazed with tobacco smoke from Alan's Havana cigar and from the Lucky Strikes, Camels, and Chesterfields of the others. Smoking was considered to be very glamorous these days.

The object of everyone's attention was the dailies, a positive print of the scenes filmed yesterday. The 35mm black-and-white negative film had been processed and printed at the lab, then stored in a temperature- and humidity-controlled vault. The negative was virtually priceless, as it represented hours and hours of expensive labor of a crew and cast of highly paid profes-sionals. These rushes revealed anything that had gone wrong and might need to be re-shot.

Six takes of a brief scene with Daphne were causing the most comment. Alan ordered them projected for a third time. On screen Daphne made a small, uncertain move to the left, then to the right and stopped. Her expression was mildly confused.

Steamer jabbed a finger at the screen. "Right there, see?" Alan shook his head slightly. "She did a little, sort of . . . well, a jig to the left, then to the right."

"So what?" Alan asked. "You know, the audience will just think she's happy, doing a little dance is all. It's good enough. Mark it, F-Stop."

F-Stop made a note on his pad. "A little dance, my ass," he whispered to Elizabeth, the art director sitting next to him. "She couldn't hit her marks. No way we could pull focus."

"Yeah, and she's getting fat, too," Elizabeth replied.

"Gin'll do that to you."

Daphne was not at all happy that Steamer had been—oh, so politely, of course—pointing out certain "mistakes" on her part. She leaned closer to Alan and held his arm in both hands. No one could see her doing this.

"It wasn't my fault, Mr. Segal." She called him "Mister" in public. "Steamer yelled at me just then, and it scared me." Movies with sound were a couple of years in the future, so directors could still call out directions to the talent during the shot.

Alan turned to Steamer. "You've gotta stop doing that, Steamer. When are you going to figure out that Daphne is sensitive? Treat her with respect, okay?" Steamer nodded agreement reluctantly. It would have to do.

The next scene was a two-shot with Douglas Cragmont, who played Daphne's husband. She was supposed to look at her child in a cradle and then up at Doug with an adoring expression. Her face conveyed something more like disdain. For the next two takes, Steamer had ordered F-Stop to reset the light in an attempt to soften her look.

"So, what's the difference?" Alan asks. "They look the same to me."

Steamer was flummoxed. Here he was, trying to make Alan see, but he was blind to nuances. "Well, you see, in takes three and four, I reset the lights. I wanted to show Daphne to her best advantage. We're shooting from her good side on these."

Daphne squeezed Alan's arm. "It's so hot under those lights. Have you ever sat under studio lights, Mr. Segal? They make you perspire so. And Steamer just wanted to keep on shooting and shooting."

"So look, Steamer," Alan said. "Try to get it in two takes from now on. Do I have to remind you that Daphne is the most valuable asset in my stable? If she gets sick because you're working her too hard, well . . ."

The remainder of the rushes went by without eliciting much comment. The people sitting in the back rows were busy with their own thoughts and plans.

Esse was scribbling notes for shots that could be made on location that would cut with the studio shots. Alan had thrown him a hard curve ball, upsetting the narrative flow of his script with this crazy idea of going on location.

Paul was juggling long, narrow strips of paper on his production board to create a shooting schedule that would minimize expenses. Each strip represented all the assets needed to get a particular shot "in the can" and ready to go to the lab. He moved them about, working to find the optimum arrangement.

In the projection booth, the last of the film ran through the arc-lamp projector. The tail end went flap-flap-flap against the machine, and the screen glared brilliantly white for a moment. The projectionist quickly doused the arc, and the screening room went dark.

★ ★ ★ ★ ★

As he left the screening room, so many thoughts stampeded through Steamer's head, they were kicking up a lot of dust. He was trying to blow the dust away to see his thoughts clearly when he felt someone plucking at his sleeve. Daphne was hurrying to keep up with his long-legged strides.

"Hey, cowboy, slow down. So, what did you think?"

There was no way he wanted to tell her the truth right now. The difference between her behavior this morning and now was marked: she was clinging to his arm, transmitting her unsteadiness to him. She'd been at the bottle between then and now.

"Not too bad," he lied. "Mostly I'm thinking about going to Jackson."

"You really don't want to go, do you?"

"Oh, come on, Luella. You know the life of a cowboy is greatly overrated. An old cowboy is a busted-up cowboy, what with always being thrown, kicked, and stepped on by pile drivers with four legs. Not to mention the dust, and you're always either too hot or too cold, and at the end of two months on the trail, you smell like a garbage can."

"I'm not Luella any more. I'm Daphne Divine, and I like civilization, thank you. But you're getting soft, Steamer." She said it in a bantering tone, but he sensed that she was serious. It gave him a twinge of anxiety.

"So, I'm getting soft, am I?"

She glanced up at him with a coy smile. "Oh, not really, but why not go up there and get out in the fresh air and sunshine, get back on a real horse, and sweep the cobwebs out of your head. You're getting too intense about your work."

He'd have to go, of course, if for no other reason than to keep an eye on Paul and Alan. No telling what they'd put in the can if he wasn't there to control their worst excesses. Alan was great at getting investors to back his projects, but his focus was first, last, and always on the bottom line. He was easily swayed by those around him.

"Okay, maybe that's a good idea."

"When are you leaving?"

"Friday."

"You're not going by automobile, are you?"

"No, by train. Alan has ordered his private car hooked on, so I guess he's taking Bettina with him." They had reached the studio floor. Steamer disengaged her arm from his. "I've got a few things to talk to F-Stop about. See you when we get back."

An hour later he was ready to leave. He felt like a piece of washing that had been put through the wringer too many times. As he passed Daphne's dressing room, he was startled to see her sitting outside, a glass in her hand.

"Hey, Steamer, guess what?"

He halted, hands in hip pockets, looking down at her. "I'm plumb out of brain power to guess with."

"I'm going to Jackson."

Steamer reared back, laughing. "I'll be damned. So what made you change your mind?"

"Since my dear sister, Megan, has gone to so much trouble to set it all up, I guess I kind of owe it to her."

"I see."

She had, he admitted to himself, come up with a pretty decent rationalization, given that she'd changed her mind only after he had told her that Bettina was going along. "What is your sister like?"

"She's a tweety bird."

Steamer laughed. "Now what in hell does that mean?"

"She sings sweet as a canary, but she's just a bird in a gilded cage. Heck, it isn't even gilded. Her husband made it for her out of baling wire. She's probably got so fat by now, she'll never get out of it."

"Oh."

"Is she going to be surprised to see me." Daphne rose, folded her canvas chair, put it inside her dressing room, and locked the door. "Help me find my chauffeur, will you?" She linked her arm in his, and they headed toward the parking lot.

"I'm going to take my wardrobe trunk. And of course I'll have to take Eric and Fayrene and Katrina with me." They were her hairdresser, makeup artist, and wardrobe mistress. "I told Alan he's just going to have to put a private car on for me, too. Say, I think there'd be room for you in there, too, a compartment to yourself, you know. What do you say?"

"I say, I'll think about it."

CHAPTER 8

Friday Afternoon, June 12

Steamer watched anxiously as the meter in the taxi clicked upward. He hadn't thought it would cost so much, but he sure as hell didn't want to leave his own car in the Central Station parking lot. It was a 1921 Stanley Steamer Model 735 B, and when he'd bought it, his friends promptly dubbed him Steamer. Three years later there was no undoing the nickname.

He'd slept badly for the past two nights. Allison's accusations had vexed him. Alan and Paul ignoring his ideas humiliated him. Two days of chewing over everything had done nothing but leave a bad taste in his mouth. The hell with them; he had more important things to think about.

His thoughts drifted back to what Daphne had said about her sister. A tweety bird, she'd called her, trapped in a cage of baling wire. He could imagine her now. She'd be dressed in a Mother Hubbard, the long sleeves pulled down to hide her washtub-reddened hands, the high neck buttoned tight to protect her virtue. Its loose folds would conceal a body like potato dumplings. As to her singing ability . . . Well, she'd plunk a few clumsy chords from an ancient guitar, and her voice would be reedy and thin like her sister's.

"Here you are, mister. That'll be two and a half bucks."

The cabby pulled Steamer's suitcases from the trunk and deposited them on the sidewalk. They were new, and he could scarcely afford them. Still, he wasn't going back to Jackson with his clothing in a canvas ice bag, as he had when he'd come to Los Angeles. He picked the suitcases up and moved toward the station. The facade glowed orange in the afternoon light. The bags were heavy, but he was going to be gone for nearly a month. Besides, the weather in Jackson was wildly changeable right now. He might need the warm clothing and rain gear he was bringing, and then again he might not.

Alan puffed on his Havana cigar. His gaze darted back and forth, even as he managed to keep up the semblance of a conversation with Paul and Steamer. He'd been worried that Pia Donatelli might appear, but the hour had passed with no sign of her. He'd obviously managed to reassure her last week. He allowed himself a small moment of pride at the way he'd handled her. He could relax, especially now that the last of the gear and supplies were going aboard the boxcar his production company had rented.

"So, Alan, is that a go?"

He pulled his attention back to Paul, who was looking at him questioningly; Steamer was frowning at Paul. He'd missed something. "Sorry, Paul. I was checking that last crate. What did you say?"

"I said, so that's the way we're going to handle the barroom brawl scene, right?"

Steamer thrust himself closer. "Damn it, Paul, I'm the director. Sure, that's a cheap way to shoot, but it's flat and boring. You see that, don't you, Alan?"

Paul and Steamer had been going at it ever since Steamer had arrived. Paul was jabbing at the scene strips on his production board, and Steamer was waving his shooting script in Alan's face. Problem was, they were both right.

Paul was a damned good production manager. He could think of more ways to suck the fat out of a script than anyone else.

Steamer was a great director, who created film magic out of a few black marks on a piece of paper. He needed them both. The film *was* running over budget; the rushes *were* something special. He needed a prize-winning film on a film-student's budget.

"Okay, knock it off for now. I'm tired of listening to both of you. Let's get aboard, where we can relax and have some lobster and bubbly. Our minds will work better that way."

Alan felt something slap into his leg and looked down. A boy of maybe twelve was twirling a rope as he pushed past Alan. The kid wore a miniature cowboy suit, one of the expensive kind from FAO Schwartz.

"Tommaso, apologize to the gentleman."

Alan wanted to shrink down inside his brown-and-yellow checked suit, to become a mouse and escape out one trouser leg. That way, the suit could remain there standing as his surrogate while he went away somewhere and vomited.

But Pia merely smiled a vague, impersonal smile, barely visible behind her black veil. She ushered the boy past him with a murmured apology. Two porters trailed in her wake, their baggage carts piled high with matching hatboxes, suitcases, and steamer trunks. She pointed imperiously: those in the sleeping car, those in the baggage car. When her orders had been obeyed, she distributed a tip that brought huge smiles to their faces.

He could see Bettina glance up from her conversation with Daphne and look at Pia with curiosity. His blood stopped flowing again. Pia seemed oblivious to him and everyone else, smiling at her son as he threw the loop of his rope at passers-by. He was beginning to hope again when Bettina's face registered recognition. She excused herself to Daphne and approached Pia.

"Excuse me," Bettina said. "Aren't you . . . I mean, I think you know my sons."

"I do, *signorina*?" Pia's smile was warm but puzzled. "I'm not sure how that would be possible."

"Oh, yes, they just sent us a picture from an Italian paper. They are on a tour of Italy. Dov and Gur Segal."

"Dov and Gur? Such unusual names . . . oh, yes! That was three months ago, at a major jumping event in Rome. Now I remember." Pia extended a black-gloved hand. "My name is Pia Donatelli. So. You are their mamma?"

Bettina beamed with pride. "Yes. I'm Bettina Segal." She turned, gestured to Alan to join her.

He found himself standing before them, smiling, shaking hands and making introductions without knowing how he had gotten from where he had been to where he was now. As soon as the introductions were over, Bettina and Pia ignored him. He quickly looked around for a polite excuse to leave.

Bettina said, "So, what is your son's name?"

"Tommaso. Of course, he wishes to be called Tommy, as he is now to become an American. I'm afraid he wants to be a cowboy, not a jumper."

"I'm so glad we're going to be traveling together," Bettina said. "Where are you going?"

"I am, how do you say, burned out? With jumping. I thought it might refresh me to learn something new about horsemanship. We are going to a lovely ranch in Wyoming. Perhaps you know of it? The Rocking Lazy F?"

"Oh! That's where *we're* going."

"So." Pia turned to Alan. "Mr. Segal, now I think I know who you are. You are a movie producer, yes? And are you going to this ranch for filming?"

He managed to nod and mumble answers to her stream of questions. He glanced around for help. Steamer was still arguing with Paul. "Hey, Steamer, come over here."

Introductions made, Alan said, "Steamer, Tommy wants to be a cowboy. Show him how to twirl that rope, why don't you.

Excuse me, ladies, but I need to go make sure all our equipment is loaded."

Pia could feel the anxiety rising in her like the pressure in the steam engine behind her. She was desperate to get aboard and get under way before Uncle found another excuse to punish her for delay. She thought she might have seen one of his men lurking behind a pillar, but she could not be sure. The departure was already ten minutes behind schedule; she could hear the conductor chastising Alan for the delay.

"Mother, look!"

She glanced down. Tommaso was swirling the loop of his rope around in a large circle a foot above the ground. Steamer watched with approval until Tommaso's concentration was interrupted by a loud blast on the steam whistle. The loop collapsed, but Steamer applauded loudly.

"Did I do this correctly, Mr. Steamer? Do you think I can be a cowboy someday?"

"You sure did." Steamer grinned. "And if you work hard, sure, you could be a cowboy."

He looked up at Pia, winked, and held out his hand. She responded automatically. His hand was warm and corded with muscle; she felt as if an electric current had penetrated her glove and touched the cold, empty place inside her. She covered her confusion by babbling her thanks for teaching her son.

"Sure enough. Nice kid you have." His gaze shifted behind her. "Hey, Daphne, you met *Signora* Donatelli yet?"

"Pleased to meetcha, Miss Donatelli." Daphne stuck her hand out like a man. "I hear you're going to the same ranch we are."

"Yes. Isn't that a coincidence? I am going to get away from the jumping for a few months, but I must be near horses. They are my life. And the fresh air will be good for Tommaso."

So this was the famous, glamorous Daphne Devine. She lived

up to her reputation, with a cascade of golden hair to her shoulders, flawless complexion, large bosom, and an hourglass figure. And, apparently this was what American men liked.

Pia was proud she had kept her slender figure after Tommaso's birth. Riding had done that for her, but Uncle had told her many times that she was plain, and that men did not like her. But she had seen the admiration in Steamer's gaze. He was a famous movie director; surely he was a good judge of beauty? The strange new feeling that had begun with his touch expanded inside her. What if she could be a famous movie star, like Daphne? She could hire bodyguards, and then Uncle wouldn't be able to touch her. The thought thrilled her.

"All aboard!" The conductor's shout was followed by a shrill blast from the train whistle, jarring her out of her thoughts. She realized Daphne had turned her attention to Steamer.

"Steamer? Which car are you traveling in?"

"Well, I guess I'm in one of the sleeping cars, Daph."

"Why don't you travel in my private car? There's an extra berth. That way we can talk about Wyoming and the film and all that."

"If you're sure you won't mind? I'd hate to disturb you."

"I won't mind. Besides, I'll have Fayrene to protect me in case you get fresh." Daphne smiled flirtatiously at him, but he ignored her expression.

"Okay."

Pia assumed that "getting fresh" meant making sexual advances, but Steamer seemed completely uninterested. She touched her cheek with her right hand. What a delightful thought! Should she question him about directing movies? Men were always flattered when you showed an interest in their work.

Silence and lack of movement awakened Pia. The train had stopped, and the rocking cadence of the rails that had lulled her into a deep sleep was missing. She retrieved her wristwatch from the miniature hammock over her berth; it was two A.M., which meant it was now Saturday.

She pushed aside the green, baize window curtain and peered out. They seemed to be at a station filled with people. Why would there be so many human beings there in the middle of the night in the middle of nowhere? Then she caught sight of Alan, Steamer, and Paul. Glancing at some of the other crew members, she realized something must be wrong.

She dressed quickly and went out. She fancied she could hear the stars crackling in the frigid desert air. She could make out storm clouds over the mountains in the distance, and a tumbleweed, driven by a strong north wind, bounced along the platform. A coyote yapped and howled. Well, she assumed it was a coyote; after all, this was the West, where they lived.

A dim, orange light shone through a window of a building a few meters down the track. She hurried toward it. Inside, a coal-burning cast-iron stove warmed the interior. The air seemed to quiver with suppressed anxiety, and no one looked up as she entered. People from the film crew mingled with the other passengers, who stood in knots of two and three, talking with quiet frustration.

Alan stood looking out the window with his hands clasped tightly behind his back. At a desk nearby, a man in a green eyeshade and sleeve garters sat near an apparatus she did not recognize. She moved closer to look at it, and it burst into a series of clicks so rapid, they sounded like the whirring of a cicada. It had to be a telegraph machine.

The sound might have been a shrieking siren from the effect it had. People stopped talking. Alan whirled around. "Well?" he demanded.

The telegraph operator shushed him and wrote rapidly on a pad as the machine spoke a language only he could understand.

When it went silent, he looked up. "Well, now, the boulders will be cleared off the track in about an hour, Mr. Segal."

"Thank God. Now look, I need you to send a telegram for me, to Jackson Hole. The people up there have got to know we're going to be delayed."

Alan's last word at last aroused Pia from the lethargy that had enveloped her. Delayed! Uncle would be furious. He'd ordered her to make sure the film was finished in the shortest possible time. He was not the type to accept any excuses—not even boulders on the track.

Despair threatened to swamp her. All she wanted was a small cottage somewhere and a good school for Tommaso. If that meant she had to live without horses the rest of her life, she'd make that sacrifice. Was there anything she could possibly do?

The passengers were beginning to return to the train and their warm berths. As she moved with them, she noticed Steamer studying her even as he pretended not to. His gaze darted her way each time she looked at him.

The open station door allowed the crowd to exit, but it also allowed blasts of frigid air to enter. It was not hard to begin shivering violently. She halted, managed to dredge up a sneeze and a cough, then slowly resumed her path. She sensed Steamer behind her, and a moment later felt his heavy coat settle over her shoulders.

"You're going to catch your death of cold if you keep running around dressed like that," he said.

She smiled up at him. "Oh, yes, it was silly of me to go out like this, wasn't it?" She slowed again, faked another sneeze, and this time his arm went around her. Men loved it when you confessed to some feminine frailty. It made them feel so strong.

They made their way back to the train, and the warmth of his embrace sent real shivers through her. As he helped her mount the steps, she pretended to catch her heel and fell backwards, forcing him to catch her. She twisted in his arms and smiled what she hoped was her most bewitching smile. "Oh, thank you, Steamer. I'm so clumsy tonight."

He merely nodded and walked her to her compartment. At the door she said, "I'd love to chat with you for a while, about movie-making. Tommaso is asleep. Won't you come in for a minute?"

"Ah, thanks, but no thanks." He yawned. "I'm sort of wrung dry, Pia. Had some bad news recently. So, see you in the morning, okay?" He kissed her forehead with a quick, fatherly kiss.

She nodded understandingly and slid the compartment door closed. Tommaso was indeed sound asleep in the upper berth. She sank into the lower berth and buried her head in the pillow so her sobs would not wake him.

CHAPTER 9

Saturday Morning, June 13

"And just what are you smirking about, missy?"

Fiona's caustic question, coming from close behind Megan, almost made her drop a dish. She lowered it into the wash water and turned. "Smirking?" She warmed her smile to a maximum. "I'm not sure I'd call it that, Fiona. I was just remembering a joke by Jack Benny I heard on the radio."

Fiona scowled and glared, lips compressed into a rigid line. Megan waited for an explosion; she assumed Fiona would have some reaction to not being called the required "Mother Foxworth." Yet it did not come, and Fiona stalked off in the direction of the ranch office.

Megan had heard a good joke, but it was the memory of Junior soaked with soapy hot water that brought the smile to her face. After he crawled out the door on Wednesday evening, she gave in and cried. For three days, she lived in fear of the retaliation he threatened, but today she was at last able to enjoy her triumph. The only times she had seen Junior, he was lurking in the distance.

She rinsed the last dish and stacked it on the wooden drying rack. As she dried her hands, her happy feelings drained away with the dirty dishwater. She'd seen all the signs in Junior and trusted him anyway. All right, she'd been naïve. Since knights in shining armor were in short supply right now, she'd have to take care of herself. Junior was still dangerous.

Lightning flashed outside the kitchen window. Megan automatically counted the seconds between the flash and the thunder. It was only three seconds now; the storm was getting closer. She hoped the rain would not be as heavy today as it had been yesterday. The guests were restless and unhappy at being confined to the ranch house.

Her mood brightened again as she thought of the people from Hollywood. They were supposed to arrive tomorrow; but Gertie's boy, Johnny, had just slogged through the rain from the telegraph office to deliver a cable. They'd been delayed because a section of track had been washed out in the storm or because there were boulders on it. She couldn't recall exactly when the train was arriving in Victor; it had been in the telegram, which she'd last seen in the office.

The door was open, and Fiona was absent. Megan went in and looked around. TT and Fiona had thrown out the ratty old furniture and brought in new office equipment. The old candlestick telephone had been replaced with a modern desk phone, heavy and solid as a granite boulder. A Remington Number One portable typewriter waited beneath a dust cover. Fiona would never learn to type; Megan was hesitant to use it. She was paid the same as a hand, fifty dollars a week, and the typewriter had cost the equivalent of three weeks' salary. She hated the idea that she might break it.

A brand-new Burroughs adding machine had never been used either. Megan rolled a sheet of paper into it, tapped in numbers and pulled the crank. She sighed. Why wouldn't Fiona let her do the accounts? If she used the Burroughs, she could do them in an hour.

The rain began with a roar. Megan pulled the paper from the adding machine, balled it up, and tossed it in the wastebasket. Now, where was that telegram? Fiona's desk was littered with papers, and the cable was nowhere in sight. She shuffled through bills from the feedlot and the farrier, advertisements for Absorbine liniment and Bag Balm and letters from dudes across the country. But she found no telegram.

The rain pounding on the shingle roof masked the sound of Fiona's entrance, but Megan sensed it. She turned just as Fiona was opening her mouth. "And just what do you think you're doing in here, missy?" Megan had been prepared to smile sweetly and defuse whatever Fiona might say, but the coldness of Fiona's voice scared her.

"Why, I . . . I . . . ah, I'm looking for that telegram."

"What telegram?"

Megan knew damned well Fiona knew damned well what she was talking about. "Why, Fiona, the one from the Hollywood people. Their arrival time is in the telegram. So we won't be late. When we go to meet them. We are going to meet them, aren't we?"

"Yes, of course. Seven fifteen."

"Thank you." Megan gestured to the adding machine and typewriter. "You know, you've got all this lovely new office equipment. If I could use it, I could do the bookkeeping for you in no time." Her next thought was sneaky and manipulative, but what the hell. "That way I'd have more time to take care of Terry's special needs."

Fiona's expression switched between suspicious and flattered several times. It settled somewhere in the middle as she said, "Well, I'll consider it. You know all I want, dear Megan, is for you to take care of your husband and your *family.*" She moved to the desk chair and lowered herself into it slowly. "I've so been looking forward to having grandchildren, Megan dear. You know Terry is our only child, so it's going to be up to you, my dear, to carry on the Foxworth family name. I'm depending on you, and I so hope you won't disappoint me . . . And close the door when you leave."

Megan managed to mumble some sort of appropriate response as she backed out of the office. She nearly bumped into TT, who had wheeled up silently behind her. They exchanged good mornings, and she held the door open for him. He wheeled through without another word.

"You're welcome," she said and resisted slamming the door.

She went outside, under the porch overhang, where she could be alone for a moment and think. She watched the rain slam down. Fiona always made her feel like a brood mare. And why was she always so damned suspicious of everything Megan did in the office?

The doubt grew slowly at first, coalescing from a dozen tiny incidents—"No need to look in there, dear. That's just old records, our private family records"—into a frightening suspicion that Fiona was hiding something in the bottom drawer of the file cabinet.

She was staring at the barn, feeling disloyal, when another suspicion joined the first: TT kept the whiskey out there. Could they be smuggling in more than they said they were, and were the records in that locked drawer?

The first thing to do would be to snoop in the barn to see how much booze was in there. It was raining too hard, and she'd get soaking wet if she went now; besides, it would arouse suspicion. Some time later, she decided, after the storm ended.

As soon as the door had shut behind him, TT said, "What was she doing in here?"

Fiona pushed a stack of papers together and joggled them into a neat bundle. "She was just being nosy. Looking for the telegram from the Hollywood people, she said."

TT glared at her. "Did you leave anything out, stuff she shouldn't see?"

"Do you think I'm a fool?"

"What's that stuff you're holding there?"

Fiona leaned closer. "It was on the bottom of the pile," she said in a forceful whisper. "I don't think she saw it."

TT grimaced. "Calm down, Fiona. We're in this together, and it's our necks. We can't be too careful."

Fiona went to the file cabinet. She took the key from the small brass pot behind a pile of junk on the top, unlocked the cabinet, yanked the middle drawer open, and slammed the papers into it. She re-locked the drawer and dropped back into the chair with a whimper. "Oh, God, TT, I want to go back to Brooklyn. I hate this hick town."

"Can't."

"Damn it, don't say that!"

"Can't help it. You know we can't go home."

Fiona put her head down on the desk and gave in to tears. TT wheeled closer, patted her on the shoulder. "There, there. We're just going to have to make the best of it, old girl."

Fiona sniffed and dried her eyes. "I got a letter from Susan yesterday. The opera season at the Met, she says, is spectacular. And there's a fantastic new artist. I forget his name. He's having a one-man show at the Gallery of Fine Art. Oh, God, I miss it so much. I want to shop at Saks and Lord and Taylor. I want an ice cream soda at Schrafft's. I want to eat steak again at Delmonico's."

"Ain't you heard? They went out of business two years ago." At this news, Fiona burst into renewed tears.

"Damn it, Fiona, don't do this. Get used to it here. If we go back, you know damn well they'll kill me. Then where would you be?"

She almost said, "At least I'd be in New York" but stopped herself in time. It was all TT's fault. If he hadn't lost his temper and beaten that customer, they wouldn't be in this mess. Their employers wouldn't have exiled them to this hellhole. Now she was stuck with TT forever; they had to get along.

"Yes, I know you're right. I just wish we could get out of this business." The look on TT's face finally sank in. She was suddenly scared out of her wits. "What?"

TT looked down, gripping his hands together so tightly, she could hear his knuckles cracking. "Our contact, um, met me in town the other day. Came up to me like a tourist asking for directions." He looked up, anger and despair written on his face. "They want us to move more stuff. As a matter of fact, they're sending a new shipment tomorrow night. A big one."

Fiona sat dumbfounded. "Where in hell are we going to stash it? There's no way we can hide any more in the barn. And the Hollywood people are arriving then."

"They'll be too tired to notice." TT banged his hands on the arms of the wheelchair. "Damn it. Let me think." He leaned back and closed his eyes; a few moments later they snapped open. "Got it!"

"All right, Mister Genius, how?"

TT ignored her sarcasm. "We'll build a platform we can hoist up to the rafters with a block and tackle. We can cover the stuff with a tarp in case one of the hands or a guest looks up there and gets nosy."

"So no one is going to notice a new platform and tarp?"

"Mmm. Hey, I know. All that old furniture we moved out of here is stashed in one of the stalls. We'll just say we need the stall and are building the platform to get the old stuff out of the way. We can put a few pieces around the edges to camouflage the shipment."

"Right." A skeptical note edged Fiona's voice. "So who's going to build it?"

"Terry."

Fiona snorted with laughter. "Terry's all thumbs."

"Junior Frampton has been hanging around sucking his thumb. He'd be happy to make a few extra bucks."

Fiona was uncomfortable with Junior being in on the secret, but she could always control him. Money had a funny effect on him: it glued his mouth shut. "Okay, get to work."

"Right. I'll go find Terry. We've got to get moving on this if it's going to be ready by tomorrow night." TT wheeled around and out the door.

As the squeak of the chair's wheels faded, Fiona laid her head on the desk with a whimper. Prohibition was stupid. It was sure to fail, and the sooner the better. People always wanted what they couldn't have, and the more they couldn't have it, the more they wanted it.

How in hell had they gotten into this mess? That was a stupid question; she knew how it had happened. First it was a few bottles for themselves. Then it was just a few bottles for their close friends. But then it was a few bottles for their not-so-close friends, and then they were in the business. Now they had to supply their guests. Fiona felt sure she could trust them to be discreet. It was another thing to expand their customer base. Could they do it without getting in trouble with the law? Bitter regret flooded over her—now they had a wolverine by the tail.

She sat up with her heart hammering. Megan! What was that little snip *really* doing in here? An unpleasant suspicion formed at the back of her thoughts. Megan was always saying Sally Mann was like a second mother to her. Sally was also a rabid prohibitionist. In this case, did one plus one equal much more than it normally did? What if Megan was being more than just nosy? What if she was spying?

The thought twisted Fiona's mind into an uncomfortable shape. Megan was a cute, harmless, fluffy little thing—or was she? Terry seemed to dote on her. She was being a fairly good wife to him, and he seemed happy with her.

She looked up at the sound of a knock. Terry was lounging against the door frame, a hand-rolled cigarette in the corner of his mouth. "Pa just told me about some damn platform he wants me to build." He squinted against the smoke rising past his eyes. "Gave me some story about we need them stalls. What's going on?"

Damn TT. He'd left it to her—again—to do the dirty work. "Come in, son, and shut the door. And take that cigarette out of your face and sit down."

Terry made a sour face at her, but he put his smoke out in the ashtray and flopped into a chair. "So?"

Fiona sighed. "You're right. We don't really need to move the stuff out of that stall. But we *do* need the platform."

"What in hell for? It's going to be a lot of work."

Fiona opened the door, peered out in both directions, then shut and locked it. "Our people back east have decided we can handle more business here."

As she explained, Terry sat with his left leg crossed over his right knee, all the while jiggling his left foot. When she finished, he looked as if he were feeling sick. "So," she said, "now do you understand?"

"Yeah. We're getting another shipment of flowerpots."

Fiona's smile was grim and brief. "You got it."

Terry heaved himself upright. "I'll go get to work on the platform."

"Get Junior to help you. I'm sure he'd like to pick up a few extra dollars."

"Okay."

"Wait! Before you go, there's something else."

Terry slopped back into the chair. "What?"

"Ah, well, just a while back I caught Megan in here. I think she's been snooping into the family business. I think she may have been in the middle drawer."

Terry glared at her. "Aw now, Ma, that don't sound like Megan. She's always respected your privacy."

Fiona simply looked him in the eye until the light dawned. He looked down, scuffed the floor with his boot, then looked up. "Okay, yeah, I suppose she could find out something she shouldn't. But, Ma, Megan's against Prohibition—says she thinks it's stupid. She wouldn't tell on us."

Fiona sighed. Was her son really that naïve? "You're forgetting something."

"Yeah? What?"

"Megan has been like a daughter to Sally Mann much longer than she's been a member of our family. You just think about that for a while."

The expression on his face changed slowly from smug to worried. He stared into the distance for a moment, then nodded several times slowly. "Oh, yeah. Maybe you're right."

"That's not all." Fiona waggled her finger at him. "There's a rumor been going 'round town. Seems like Sally's called the Prohibition Unit, got them to send someone undercover."

He stared into space some more. "Yes, and?"

"And you just told me that it was Megan who arranged for those Hollywood people to come."

"So maybe . . . ?"

"So maybe one of those guys from Hollywood might be the agent in disguise?"

"That's a crazy idea!"

"Is it?"

Terry sat rock still, his gaze fastened on Fiona's face.

She said: "Sure would help keep her nose out of the family business if she had a baby to take care of. Are you sure you're doing your job as a man?" The stricken look on Terry's face warned her that she might have pushed too hard.

"Damn it, Ma! She lets me do it any time I want. What the

hell else can I do? Maybe she's got something wrong with her female plumbing, you know?"

Fiona nodded slowly. "That might be. Now go on out there and get that platform built. You haven't got much time. They're arriving day after tomorrow."

CHAPTER 10

Sunday Morning, June 14

Steamer sat alone on the observation platform at the rear of Alan's private car. The others were inside slurping down coffee and rolls. He'd come out for fresh air and to get a moment away from the wrangling. He watched the tracks recede ruler straight and then dwindle to a point at infinity; the glare of sunlight on the corrugated iron roofs winked out as it disappeared behind a hill. His nostrils stung from the acrid coal smoke blowing back from the engine.

Alan had been in a foul mood since the delay yesterday. Steamer wondered why. They were going to be a day late; was that such a big deal? The only thing that had calmed him last night was when he stomped into the station office and demanded to send a telegram to the ranch.

"Steamer!" Steamer looked around. "Come back in," Alan shouted. "This is important!"

Inside, the clickety-clack of iron wheels on iron rails diminished. He sank back into his chair as Sam, the steward, approached. "More coffee, Mr. Daniels?" Sam's face was as black as the coffee he poured; his smile was as wide as the horizon. He put a fresh Danish on the plate beside Steamer and disappeared into the small galley.

"Now then, Steamer. Let's get back to scene thirty-seven," Alan commanded.

Steamer nodded and listened with half his attention as Alan

talked, poking at the script with one finger. It gave him a chance to study the others. Daphne sat with her legs curled beneath her, reading. Bettina knitted. Pia, a perky smile on her face, watched and listened intently. Something about the woman intrigued Steamer. She had inserted herself into their company shortly after departure, and now she had somehow become one of them.

"So, what do you think?" Alan looked at him expectantly. Paul tapped his fingers quietly on his production board with a faint smirk on his face—which told Steamer that nothing he had said previously had changed anything.

"Same thing I've always thought. Look, Daphne is going to . . ." What he'd been about to say was, "save this production from your ham-fisted bungling." Given that he still wanted his job, he instead continued, "Daphne is going to make this thing an even bigger success than—Well . . . she's going to light up the screen." *She'll light up the screen,* he thought, *if I can just keep the camera moving to cover up her mistakes and keep lighting her to cover up the fact that the booze is getting to her.*

"That's why," he said hurriedly as Alan opened his mouth, "I want to light her properly. And I've already worked out a scheme of moving camera shots that will make her look . . ."

"Damn it, Steamer!" Alan swiveled his chair around to face him directly. "How many damn times do I have to tell you? Your artsy-fartsy camera moves are going to take too long. Besides, I just got a weather report at the last station. It's been raining heavily up there. That's going to delay us."

"Excuse me, please?"

The sound of Pia's voice surprised Steamer. Her smile, bright as a 10K Klieg light, shone on Alan. He melted under it. "Yes, Mrs. Donatelli, what is it?"

"This is so fascinating, all this movie talk. Do you mind too much if I ask questions?"

"Not at all. Ask away."

"Now this matter of the time it takes for shooting. It seems to me that Mr. Daniels's ideas are so interesting." Her smile turned on Steamer briefly. "Is it so much more expensive to film them his way?"

Paul harrumphed himself into the conversation. "You see, Mrs. Donatelli, to get the shot like Steamer wants it, we have to put the camera on a moving platform. We call it a 'dolly.' Then, when we shoot outdoors, we have to lay down a sort of track for it to roll on, because the ground is too uneven. All of which takes a lot more time."

"And," Alan added, "as I'm sure you know, time is money."

A small frown appeared on her face but quickly vanished. Steamer wondered if it was because of Alan's patronizing tone—or was there something else behind it?

"Yes, of course." Pia turned to Steamer. "But there must be another way to do this, yes?"

"Sure." Steamer kept the annoyance he felt out of his voice. "We put the camera on a tripod, we turn the crank, and we get the shot. It's been done that way since the Lumiere Brothers scared people to death."

"Oh!" She put her hand to her mouth. "How was this?"

Steamer laughed. "They put a camera on a tripod and filmed a train coming into a station almost head on. People thought it was so real, they were sure it was coming through the screen. They screamed and ran out of the theater."

She frowned briefly again, and again her smile quickly returned. "Ah. I understand now. Thank you for explaining this to me."

Alan said, "So, that's settled."

Steamer realized his surprise was showing. What the hell had happened? It was as if some secret signal had passed between them, and he'd been out-voted. Was it because he'd used that stupid example of the Lumieres?

The conversation moved on. He was too tired to argue any longer. In some way he did not understand, Pia's presence had shifted the balance.

His thoughts drifted back to an earlier time, a happier time . . . He was sitting on the floor of his parents' log cabin. He could hear his mother swishing dirty clothes in soapy water and rubbing them on the washboard. Light from the fire illuminated the stage he had built out of an old soapbox and the cutout characters he maneuvered on it. He'd been working on this play for days now, and the hero was just about to rescue the heroine . . .

Pia saw that Steamer had fallen asleep. Her emotions were bouncing around like the tumbleweed she'd just seen blowing alongside the track. He seemed so genuine and sincere, always with a warm smile on his tanned face. Tommaso followed him around like a puppy. It didn't hurt that he was so handsome. He reminded her of a stallion, and she wondered what it would be like with him. Panic touched her. She tried to force her emotions away from that subject, but her mind refused to obey and circled back. Would he be cruel afterward?

Stop it! Thinking that way was useless; he was the enemy. Uncle had made it very clear: see that the film is finished in the shortest possible time at the lowest possible expense. It made no difference that Steamer's ideas about filming were so interesting and new; they were *expensive*. There had to be some way to keep him under control, but how?

"Mr. Segal?"

Alan looked up from the script he and Paul were discussing. "Yes, Mrs. Donatelli?"

She smiled and leaned toward him. "Please, you must call me Pia, yes?"

A hesitant smile spread across his face. "Yes, and you must call me Alan, of course."

Bettina glanced up from her knitting, lips pressed tightly together and with a speculative look in her eyes. She gazed steadily at Pia for a moment, then back down at her knitting.

Pia ignored the warning. "Yes, of course, Alan. I simply wanted to say that your shooting plan sounds exciting. I had no idea movie-making could be so thrilling. You are a lucky man to be able to work in this marvelous new industry."

Alan beamed with pleasure. "Thank you, Pia."

"Mother?" She turned. Tommaso stood at the entrance to the private car, twirling his rope.

"Tommaso, darling! Come to Mother." The boy was obviously bored and restless, but she could not take the time just now to play with him. He sat on the floor beside her chair, flopping his rope back and forth. She ruffled his hair as she continued talking to Alan. "What a coincidence that we're going to the same ranch. I do hope you won't mind if Tommaso and I watch while you work?"

Alan beamed at her. "We wouldn't mind in the least, except that we are packing back into the wilderness to do most of our filming."

Mild panic tapped at Pia's heart. She wouldn't be able to keep track of them while they were away from the ranch. "Oh! I see. Well, I had been thinking of asking you . . ." She paused and looked down as if embarrassed. She didn't want him to think she had planned what she was about to say. She fiddled with the pages of her book.

"What is it, Pia? I can't say yes or no unless you ask me."

She looked up, hoping she was blushing. "I thought I might offer to be a consultant on the film. I am a champion jumper, you know, and . . ."

"Yes," Alan interrupted. "I'm quite familiar with your career,

Pia. You are famous. The problem is, well, we can't afford to pay you."

Tommaso rose and left with a disgruntled glance at her. She'd have to pay attention to him shortly. "I would not ask for payment, Alan. The truth is, Tommaso suffers from bronchitis. Our doctor has advised me that he must get much fresh air and exercise. And he would be so excited to see the real American West."

"Ah, well." Alan glanced up. Pia followed his gaze and saw Bettina frowning with tightly pursed lips. "I'll have to think about it, Pia. This isn't going to be a picnic in the park. We will be camping out, sleeping on the ground, that sort of thing."

"That sounds like such a wonderful adventure! I would not want us to be a burden on you. I would pay our share of the expenses, of course."

Alan squirmed slightly in his armchair. "Ah, well, let me think about it and ask the others. We are a very tight-knit crew, and they would have to accept you as well."

"All right, I understand." She rose, turned away, and turned back with a smile. "I thought perhaps I could do a jumping scene, so as to rescue someone from peril, you know, to add to the excitement of the film."

She could see Alan was sorely tempted, but he glanced at his wife and muttered, "Well, maybe; I'll have to think about it."

It was time to disarm Bettina. Pia turned to her. "I do hope I will have a chance to talk with you, Bettina. About how you raised your sons. They are such gentlemen, just as I want my Tommaso to be." She smiled at Bettina and saw her soften ever so slightly.

There was a small, strangled snort behind her. She turned to see Daphne struggle to her feet, stagger, and clutch the chair to keep from toppling. Alan leaped from his chair and helped her to stand.

"I'm so sorry Alan," she said with a giggle. "Gotta go to the, um, to take a little nap."

Pia rose and took Daphne by her other arm, and together she and Alan got her into the bedroom car. Alan waved off her offers of further help and lowered Daphne onto her berth. Pia decided to use this opportunity to use the lady's lounge herself.

As she was exiting five minutes later, she hear Alan's voice rise in anger. She pulled back out of sight to listen.

"Where in hell did she get it, Fayrene? I thought I told you to hide it from her."

Fayrene was Daphne's makeup artist and personal maid, and she wasn't taking any guff from Alan. "Mr. Segal, there's only so damned many places to hide stuff on this train. I don't know where in hell it came from, or how she got into it this morning. I heard her moving around last night, but she said she was just going to the potty."

"Well, get rid of it. If she gets into it again, you're fired."

Pia waited until she heard the door between the cars open and close, then stepped into the corridor. She pretended to be looking at her hairdo in her hand mirror. Fayrene ignored her as she went past, and Pia angled the mirror so she could watch. Fayrene ducked into Daphne's compartment and emerged shortly with two bottles half full of a clear liquid. She looked, left then right, obviously searching for a hiding place, then disappeared around a bend in the corridor. Pia followed after her, but by the time she caught up with her, Fayrene was moving down the corridor empty handed. Where had she hidden the bottles so quickly?

Steamer was annoyed. His heroine was not supposed to scream now.

He woke with a jolt; the scream had been real. He jumped up and shook his head to clear the fog. Alan, Bettina, and Paul were sitting as if paralyzed.

The door at the end of the private car burst open. Pia ran in, her dress torn and dirty. "Help me! Tommaso, he is trapped."

Steamer dashed to the door and banged it open. He was assaulted outside the peace and quiet of the luxurious car by the loud clatter of the wheels, acrid smoke, and the jolting, swaying movement of the train. Tommaso was hanging upside down between the cars. From what he could see of his face, the kid was terrified. He was clinging to the coupling with tight, white fists.

Pia came up behind him, peered over the railing. "I'll pull the emergency cord!" she shouted.

Steamer grabbed her arm. "Don't! The sudden stop could shake him loose. I'll get him."

Tommaso slipped closer to the tracks and yelled with terror. The train was moving at least fifty miles an hour; if he fell, his brains would be splattered over the rough wooden ties. Steamer started to climb down between the cars but stopped when he saw Tommaso's rope hanging within reach. He seized it, quickly opened the loop, and aimed to drop it over Tommaso's right leg. He was thrashing around, and it took two tries before Steamer was able to pull the rope tight around his ankle. He pulled—but Tommaso remained where he was.

Steamer hitched the rope to the railing. Tommaso now could fall no farther. Steamer lowered himself cautiously to where the boy hung. His eyes were screwed tightly shut, the strap of his overalls hung up on a brake-line coupling. No wonder Steamer hadn't been able to pull him up by his leg.

Steamer maneuvered himself so he could reach the strap on Tommaso's overalls and wriggled himself into a position where he could reach the Barlow knife in his right front pocket. He opened the blade.

Somewhere in the confusion above him a woman's scream

was choked off. A quick look revealed Alan, Bettina, and Paul staring down at them. Pia stared at him with a horrified expression on her face and her hand over her mouth.

"I'm going to cut Tommy loose!" he yelled. "Take up tension on the rope and make sure he doesn't fall any more when I cut his overalls."

Paul nodded, and he and Alan grabbed the rope. Steamer seized the strap with one hand. Tommaso opened his eyes, saw the knife blade, and screwed them tightly shut. "I have to cut the strap, Tommy," he said in what he hoped was a soothing voice. "We'll have you out of here in a minute. Just relax."

The roadbed was particularly rough here; the train jolted and swayed. A sudden lurch twisted Tommaso away, tearing the strap from Steamer's grip. He realized he would have to use both hands to cut it.

He released his hold on the train—and instantly slid closer to the track. He grabbed the railing again; he was going to have to change his position so he could grip with his legs. The acrid smoke blowing back from the engine and the grit swirling up from the track stung his eyes and blurred his vision. The stark contrast of the late afternoon light made it even harder for him to see. He maneuvered his right leg until he felt it go over the edge of the platform, and he was grateful when he felt someone grab it firmly. After that, it was a moment's work to cut the strap and yell, "Pull!" When Tommaso was safe, hands reached down and pulled him onto the platform.

CHAPTER 11

Sunday Afternoon, June 14

Back in Alan's private car, Pia found herself shaking and sobbing and clutching Tommaso tightly. He was the only thing of value she had in the world, and the thought of seeing his battered body under the train had driven her mad with anxiety. Now that the crisis was over, she was burning with shame that she had, even for a moment, suspected that Steamer had intended to kill Tommaso with his knife. That was the sort of thing Uncle would have done out of annoyance with what he would have seen as Tommaso's foolishness.

After a while the storm blew over, and anger took its place. Pia thrust Tommaso away from her and glared down at him. "Tommaso, how could you be so foolish? You are a very bad boy, and I'm going to have to punish you."

A strong, warm hand gripped her arm. Steamer was looking at her with a faint smile. "You know, Pia," he said, "I expect Tommy has learned his lesson, haven't you, Tommy?"

Tommaso nodded vigorously. "Oh, Mama, I'll never do that again. I promise."

"See there? I reckon punishment won't help, Pia." Steamer patted Tommaso on the back. "But a hot bath and clean clothes might do a lot to restore a guy's confidence in himself."

"Oh, yes, thank you. I don't know how I can ever thank you enough. Tommaso means the world to me and . . ."

The look on Steamer's face told her she was babbling to

cover her confusion. *Was there really a world without pain and punishment?* The question twisted through her in a dozen variations as she got her son bathed and dressed. The warmth of Steamer's hand seemed to linger on her arm, making her feel light-headed.

Reality returned in a shower as cold as the rain now slashing down outside. No, Uncle would hound her to the ends of the earth. He'd kill Steamer, too, if he thought she was involved with him. He'd take her son away from her. The last cigarette burn, the one at the bottom of the cross, itched. She wanted to scratch it furiously, but then it might become infected. Uncle was the person who really loved her; he had taught her that suffering is necessary. It was he who made her a champion.

She and Tommaso returned to the private railcar in time for dinner: raw oysters, consommé madrilène, venison with oven-roasted potatoes and steamed vegetables, a delicious French claret, chocolate ice cream for Tommaso, and peach melba for the adults. She could, she decided, become accustomed to this mode of travel.

After Sam cleared the table, Pia returned to her comfortable armchair. Steamer was playing cowboy with Tommaso. Her gaze drifted to the view passing outside. The sun was going down behind jagged mountains, but she could still see telegraph poles whipping by with monotonous regularity. The sight soon mesmerized her, and she slipped into a comforting fantasy: she, Tommaso, and Steamer living on a small ranch, just the three of them, and no one within a thousand miles to threaten her.

A brilliant flash of lightning yanked her back to reality. The accompanying thunder sounded like the doors to hell slamming open. Another flash revealed monstrous dark clouds massing around the train. She shivered. She still had to ensure that the production was finished in the shortest possible time, which meant she still had to stop Steamer from wasting time and film with fancy camera moves and special lighting. All he seemed to use them for was to make Daphne's zaftig figure and blonde curls look good on screen.

Should she eliminate Steamer? The thought was obscene. He had, after all, saved Tommaso's life. Besides, he was essential to the success of the film. No, she'd have to find some other way to speed up the production. Maybe she could push Paul to cut back on the shooting schedule. She could work on him, even though he was physically repulsive to her, with those rolls of fat bulging out here and there.

"Mama? I'm tired." Tommaso stood before her, yawning prodigiously. Pia shook herself and looked around. The lounge of the private car was almost empty; people had slipped off to their own compartments while she was scheming.

"All right, young man. To bed with you."

Alan and Bettina barely looked up from their books when she said good night.

Her plan wasn't a very good one, but it was the only one she'd been able to come up with: keep Daphne sober. To do that, she'd first have to cozy up to her and pretend to be her pal. If she pretended to share her weakness for alcohol, Daphne would tell her where she had hidden her bottles.

She stood on tiptoe and peered into the upper birth. Tommaso was now sleeping soundly. Pia shook her silver flask gently. Her precious supply of calvados had diminished over the past few years, but there was at least half of it left. She had no idea how much it would take to get Daphne drunk, and, once the brandy was gone, she had no idea where to buy even bathtub gin. She slipped the flask into one pocket of her bathrobe and her nickel-plated .25 Colt into the other.

She walked softly along the corridor, then laughed at herself. Who could hear her footsteps over the rattle of the train? Outside she saw the gleam of a campfire. It was so far away, it almost seemed to be one of the stars peeking from between the clouds. Was it cowboys or Indians? She laughed at herself again. She knew so little about this strange country, but perhaps someday soon she'd be sitting beside a campfire, surrounded by cowboys.

Her knock was answered by a rustle of frantic movement inside, then Daphne's quavering voice asking, "Who is it?"

"It is I. Pia."

The compartment doors slid open a crack. Daphne peered out, blinking owlishly. "Hi, Pia."

Pia looked at her feet. "Oh. I'm sorry to disturb you. It's just . . . I'm so, well, a little scared. I thought perhaps we could . . ." She allowed her voice to trail off with a little sigh.

"Oh, Pia, of course! Come in." When they were seated on opposite ends of the berth, legs tucked under them, Daphne said, "All this is so new for you, isn't it? I guess I'd be a little scared if I was traveling all alone in Italy."

They chatted about the train ride for a while, until Pia saw Daphne was getting bored. If she were going to make a move, she'd better do it soon.

"I was wondering . . ." She hesitated and tried to look guilty. "I happen to have, uh, some brandy." She pulled the silver flask partway from her pocket. "Well, anyway, I was wondering if you'd join me in a little toast to the success of the movie?"

"Oh, gosh, thanks, Pia." Daphne's face relaxed into a big smile. "I knew I could trust you, and thanks for the offer, but I prefer"—she pulled a bottle from behind her pillow—"martinis."

Pia put her hand to her mouth. "Oh, my goodness. I do hope that is high-quality gin. Don't people die from drinking bathtub gin?"

Daphne's smiled vanished, then reappeared almost instantly. "Of course it is." A quaver in her voice betrayed at least a smidgen of doubt. "My, um, supplier handles only the best stuff." She sniffed. "Not like Alan's."

"How clever of you." Pia leaned closer, lowering her voice to the let's-share-a-secret level. "But aren't you afraid of being caught? Where do you hide it?"

Daphne, suddenly frightened, drew back and stared suspiciously at Pia. "You mustn't tell Alan! He thinks I'm naughty when I drink, but he just doesn't understand. You won't tell, will you?"

Pia patted her on the hand. "Of course not, Daphne! It must be so tiring, working all day under those lights and having to say the same lines over and over. I do understand."

Daphne sank back against her pillow. Her eyelids were drooping; her head was wobbling. "Oh, thank you." She giggled. "Fayrene thinks she's so clever. I told her once I was terrified of electricity, so of course I hide it in that electrical compartment thingy."

They talked a moment longer until Daphne's eyes closed permanently, and she began to snore. Pia rose and was sliding the compartment door open when she heard the door at the end of the car open and shut. She pulled back inside, pulled the door shut, and held her breath.

A gentle knock was followed by Alan's voice. "Daph? You awake?"

Pia scrambled under the lower berth and scrunched up as far away as she could. A louder knock was soon followed by the door sliding open. Alan's bedroom slippers appeared in her line of vision.

"Daph?" The berth above her shook; Alan was obviously trying to wake his slumbering mistress. When this failed, he cursed and ripped open the door between the compartments. Fayrene and Katrina, her wardrobe mistress, shared the adjacent cabin. Alan's snarl woke them both; he ordered Fayrene to come and look at Daphne.

"I swear to God, Alan, I hid the stuff."

"Goddamn it, where? Under her pillow?"

Pia smothered a laugh as Fayrene continued, "I hid it—hey, maybe that woman Pia saw me hide it. She was right around there at the same time. She'll tell you I'm telling the truth."

"I don't give a damn what she says. If I find Daph drunk one more time, you're fired."

Pia waited until she was sure Alan had truly left, then crawled from beneath the berth, covered with dust and dirt. Back in her own compartment, she gave in to the fear she had suppressed while hiding. Alan had a tough reputation. There were always rumors about how his competition had died "accidentally" or been crippled for life. But rumors, in her experience, almost always had some basis in fact.

If Alan discovered she had been in Daphne's compartment and had actually shared liquor with her—well, maybe he would arrange an "accident" while she was on the trail with them. What would happen to Tommaso then? She thrashed back and forth in her berth, the rhythmic click-clack of the wheels no longer a soothing sound. *Now what?*

Then she knew what she would do. In the morning she'd take the remaining bottle of martinis from its hiding place and take it to Alan secretly. She'd tell him she was well aware of Daphne's reputation as a lush, and that she'd gone to Daphne's compartment to help him by keeping her sober. She'd explain that she'd found her drunk, but that his knock had frightened her and she'd hidden under the berth.

She smiled with satisfaction. That was just the sort of unbelievable detail that would convince him she was telling the truth. She'd end by warning him to keep better control of Daphne—unless he wanted more trouble than he was already in.

She was sliding into that delicious state between dreaming

and waking when a thought ambushed her: what if Daphne woke up thirsty in the middle of the night? The first thing she'd do would be to head for the electrical "thingy" and retrieve her bottle.

Pia rose again, put on her bathrobe and slippers, and walked warily down the corridor. Soon she spotted a small metal door labeled "DANGER—ELECTRICAL EQUIPMENT—KEEP OUT." She peered inside. All those wires looked dangerous, but she probably would not be electrocuted if she did not touch any of them. The bottle of pre-mixed martini cocktails rested at the bottom, clinking against the wires with the rocking of the train. She reached in slowly and with great care; moments later the bottle was stashed out of sight beneath her robe.

She realized she couldn't hide it anywhere in this car. Drunks were clever little monkeys when it came to protecting their supply, and Daphne would have cataloged every possible hiding place in the car. She'd just have to hide it somewhere else.

She decided on the coach-class cars at the head of the train. They were full of ordinary people, poor people, people in worn and patched clothing, men unshaven and women with frowsy hair. It was the sort of place Daphne would never go. Pia started forward; she'd pretend she was a little drunk if anyone asked questions.

The third car ahead smelled of unwashed humanity, dirty nappies, and sour beer. The light was so dim, she could barely see to find her way to the other end of the car, where she now knew the electrical panel would be. She was halfway through the car when the train lurched, throwing her toward a figure hidden behind a newspaper.

The next five seconds were to be the most terrifying in Pia's life.

In the first second, she put out her hand to steady herself and swayed against the newspaper, pushing it into the feeble light of the car. She could clearly see the print; it was in Italian.

In the next second, the man behind the paper looked directly at her, annoyance reflected in his twisted mouth. Then his expression changed like the lightning flashing outside: recognition, guilty surprise, angst, fear, and uncertainty lighted his face in rapid succession.

In the third second, terror clutched Pia's innards.

In the fourth second, she decided to live, to bluff it out and to let Uncle's agent know she was through being intimidated. She dropped the bottle of martinis and then her .25 pistol. They landed on the wooden floor of the coach with a loud double clunk.

What followed thereafter was worthy of the *commedia dell'arte all'improviso*. Pia and the hit man might well have been playing two of the stock roles in that ancient Italian theatrical art. She, the devastated wife, hiding liquor from a drunken, abusive husband, flung herself (metaphorically) on his honor to keep her secret and help hide the bottle. He played the gallant military officer (full of false bravado) who would defend her to death against such a brute. They exchanged apologies, brief explanations, expressions of concern, polite inquiries as to the purpose of their voyage and their destinations, best wishes for a successful outcome, and polite good-byes.

Throughout her performance, Pia stood erect and looked the man directly in the eye. She fondled the nickel-plated pistol she had slowly and subtly replaced in her pocket. But it wasn't until the curtain fell, and Pia was backstage alone in her compartment, that the play expanded into sobs. Tommaso woke, climbed into the berth with her, hugged her tightly, and cried himself to sleep.

CHAPTER 12

Monday Morning, June 15

Megan was almost sorry she had pushed to be included in the welcoming party. It meant that they had had to leave at five. The ride over the Teton Pass to Victor, Idaho, had been, as always, rough and interminable. Now Terry and Fiona waited outside on the platform. She had yawned and excused herself to use the ladies' room and then decided to wait inside. Her little excursion in the middle of the night had left her feeling droopy this morning.

She had been sure the rain would never end, but it had, sometime after midnight. She had taken the opportunity to sneak out of bed and go to the barn to reconnoiter. Two of the horse stalls were now empty of the old furniture that had cluttered them. More horses were coming, Terry had said, which made sense inasmuch as they were facing an influx of unexpected guests. There was nothing suspicious about that.

Fiona's bossy attitude was driving her crazy, but her victory over Junior had more than compensated for that. She'd seen him lurking around their cottage, but he hadn't tried to assault her again.

Well, damn it, all she wanted was to be accepted as a full contributor to the family and the welfare of the ranch, and all she asked in return was a chance to go to the movies every once in a while. Mild guilt, at being suspicious of her own family, crept over her. They deserved better from her. So what if they were bringing in a little liquor now and then for the guests? Prohibition was stupid.

There *was* that rumor going around, that the Prohibition Unit was sending an undercover agent to spy on them. He was supposed to be one of the Hollywood people, so if someone really was coming, it was a good thing that she hadn't found anything.

She put all her worries out of her mind as a commotion outside drew her to the window. Sally Mann, her WCTU ladies, and her band were arriving. They gathered on the platform and began to practice their music. Megan wanted to stick her fingers in her ears, but if she did, Sally might turn at exactly the wrong moment, look at her, and be hurt by her disloyalty.

It wasn't that the music of the WCTU band was too loud. It wasn't—as long as Megan stayed inside the station. It was just that the trumpet player sounded as if he'd been sucking on green persimmons since birth. It didn't help either that the fat man playing the tuba was doing so with all the enthusiasm of a man standing on the gallows.

Train number forty-seven departed from Ashton at five thirty in the morning and was supposed to arrive at seven. She glanced at the big Regulator clock on the wall. It read seven fifteen, which meant that, since she could now hear the whistle, it would be as on time as it ever was.

The WCTU contingent surged forward, waving placards that proclaimed, in heavy red letters: *LIQUOR IS EVIL* and *GOD ABHORS ALCOHOL*. The volume of their hymn increased to counteract the screech of brakes and hiss of steam. The door to one of the cars opened, and the conductor stomped on the lever that lowered the boarding steps. Megan put her fingers in her ears mentally and left the shelter of the station waiting room.

She waited patiently as people she did not know exited the cars. A man in a ridiculous checked suit stepped down, puffing on a huge cigar. That had to be Alan Segal, the producer. The woman behind him could only be his wife, Bettina. Megan saw her speak sharply to him; he checked, as if his wife had jerked an invisible leash. A fat man waddled down next; Megan felt sorry for the horse that would have to carry him. The thumping loud music and vigorous exhortations from the WCTU halted the Hollywood contingent in their tracks. It was as if a stampede had charged toward them.

At last Luella appeared. She descended to the platform and stopped to smile and wave. Her gaze darted around the crowd until it touched on Megan, and as they made eye contact, she burst into a huge smile and waved.

Megan was waving back when a man appeared behind Luella and stepped down to stand close behind her. She recognized Steamer Daniels, even as he turned to see who Luella was waving at. Then he was gazing directly into her eyes, his mouth half open in delight. The music and tumult of the crowd faded away, and she stared back, as light-headed as if she'd just had a whiff of laughing gas at the dentist's office. He was even more virile in person than in his pictures. She was aware of what she was doing but could do nothing but stare, hand to throat, scarcely breathing.

Then suddenly Luella was in front of her, and she was hugging her. They shed a few happy tears and laughed, and Megan hugged her back.

Luella was carrying a large, fancy box under one arm. "It's for you," she said and handed the box to Megan.

"What *is* it?"

"Don't open it here. It's a dress. The latest thing in Hollywood fashion. You'll look smashing in it."

Terry had waited anxiously, looking up the track to see if the choo-choo was coming. He'd loved trains ever since he and Ma and Pa had travelled from Brooklyn to Wyoming. It was a real pretty morning. The sky was spotted with puffy, white clouds. Last night Megan had let him do it twice. Things were finally going the right way with her.

A big bunch of Mrs. Mann's WCTU ladies had crowded onto the platform along with the band, which started playing loudly. Terry could hear the train arriving, and the women started waving their stupid cards and singing their hymn. It was going to be hard for him to get the guests and all their baggage through the crowd and loaded into vehicles. *Shit.*

Someone nudged into him from behind, and he turned to see Buddy shoving in between himself and Ma. "Hey, Buddy, don't push like that," he snapped.

"Aw, now, Terry, 'm sorry. You know how it is sometimes. Man loses his balance once in a while. Howdy, Fiona, how're things with you this morning? Ever'thing all right with TT? How come he ain't here?"

His ma looked down her nose at Buddy. "I'm fine, Buddy, just fine. TT is taking care of things at the ranch. What are you doing here so bright and early in the morning?"

Her sarcasm whizzed past him. "Why, same thing you are, Fiona. Came to see all them Hollywood people. 'Specially that Steamer Daniels guy."

Ma frowned. "Why especially Mr. Daniels?"

"Why, doncha know, Fiona?"

"Why, no, Buddy, I don't know, or I wouldn't have asked you."

Buddy leaned in closer. "Why, he's a lawman. In disguise."

The look on Ma's face worried Terry. "That's ridiculous, Buddy. He's just an actor. And now he's a director."

"Yeah, but he played that lawman in that film, remember?"

"So what?"

"Tha's it, doncha see? Everyone thinks he's just an actor, see, and no one won't suspect him of being a real lawman."

"I find that hard to believe."

A wounded look crossed Buddy's face. "You don't believe ol' Buddy, you jus' ask Sheriff Goodman."

"Sheriff Goodman knows this Mr. Daniels is a lawman?"

"You betcha. When I told him my idea, he said . . . what he said was, 'I suppose that's possible, Buddy.' "

"Just 'possible,' not definite?"

"Aw now, Fiona, you don't think the sheriff is going to admit it right out in the open like that, do you? That'd jus' blow his cover."

His ma sniffed. "Well, thank you for the information, Buddy."

Buddy smiled triumphantly. "Ol' Buddy ain't so dumb after all," he crowed.

Terry glanced at his wife. "You hear that, Megan?"

"Hear what?" She turned, and her gaze focused on him. "Oh, you mean what Buddy said? Yes, I heard."

Ma was glaring at him. "Have you heard anything about this before, Terry?"

Terry studied his ma's face. She looked real worried. "Nothing, Ma."

"Best you find some time to talk to the sheriff, all right?"

"Okay."

"Oh, look." Ma pointed toward the train. "That must be him, behind Luella."

The man behind Luella had a funny expression on his face, like a calf bawling after its mother. Terry turned to see what he was looking at.

He was looking at Megan. She was holding her hand to her throat.

Steamer had slept poorly, tormented by memories of Allison's accusations. Alan's private car, the crew's sleeping car, their baggage van, and one second-class car full of ordinary passengers had been switched to a local train in Ashton, at five ten in the morning. This did nothing to improve his mood. Now that the train was slowing for its final stop at Victor, all he wanted to do was get the shoot over and done with and get back to Hollywood—and perhaps rescue his relationship with Allison.

Alan, Bettina, Paul, and Daphne were all waiting in line ahead of him to detrain. The door opened, and a blast of martial music rammed into the car. Steamer peered out a window. A four-man band and a gaggle of women waving signs reading "Abstain from Alcohol" greeted his gaze. *Great, just great.*

He stepped down beside Daphne. She was waving at someone, and that someone was waving back. He felt his heart lurch.

The woman embracing Daphne could only be her sister. Some tweety bird. Hell, she looked more like a falcon. Her hair was a deep, rich auburn; sure, a good hair stylist could work wonders with it, but anyway . . . Yes, her hands were red, but there was no Mother Hubbard dress to conceal a figure with all the curves in the right places.

He realized with a shock that her grey eyes were locked on him, her mouth open and her hand to her throat. His delight smashed into a thousand pieces as he remembered she was married. He broke eye contact and managed to stumble off the train without falling.

Megan remembered to breathe, glad Steamer had looked away first. She would have stared at him all day if he hadn't. The music and the voices of Sally's ladies rose again to their normal level. She had to move. She had to do something other than stand like a statue. She was desperately curious about Steamer now that he was no longer an image on paper. A thousand questions whirled through her, and her impulse was to go to him—until she noticed Terry and Fiona looking at her.

Had they seen her staring at Steamer? The look on Fiona's face told her that she, at least, had seen and understood. The pain of coming back to reality was almost too much to bear. *Get a grip on yourself, Megan. Do you want to destroy everything just for a romantic whim?* She directed her footsteps toward Mr. Segal. She had, after all, arranged everything, and he'd expect her to be the liaison between his crew and the ranch. If she threw herself into work, maybe she'd be able to forget what she had seen in Steamer's eyes.

Terry was pretty damned sure Steamer Daniels had been looking directly at Megan, but somebody had walked in front of him, and he didn't see if she was looking back. By the time the guy moved, she was walking toward the guy in the funny suit with the big cigar. What the hell was Daniels doing making goo-goo eyes at her?

He got real uncomfortable suddenly. Everyone knew Buddy was a sot, so why would the sheriff believe anything he said? Could Buddy maybe know something after all?

"Ma?"

"What?"

"Did you see that guy looking at Megan?"

"Oh, I saw her looking at someone. Was it that Mr. Daniels she was watching?"

"I reckon so."

"I wouldn't worry about it, son. I've seen Megan mooning over his picture in the movie magazines."

"What does that mean?"

"Oh, nothing, dear. You know she's always infatuated with movie people. I'm sure she'll get over it. My, he's so virile. And handsome, too."

Terry wasn't sure what virile meant. Maybe he'd better look it up in that word book. But the guy was a good-looker, for sure. That uncomfortable feeling came back. Was Megan maybe . . . ? No, that was silly. She'd never met Mr. Daniels, so how could she be in love with him? Besides, she was letting Terry do it as much as he wanted, and she was being a real good obedient wife.

"Ma?"

"Now what?"

"Do you believe what Buddy said? Maybe that guy Daniels *is* a lawman."

Ma pursed her lips and looked thoughtful. "Well, now, Buddy is a worse gossip than Gertie . . . but it wouldn't hurt to check around a little. Tell you what: you drop in on the sheriff, and maybe I'll run over to Sally's and sniff around."

Terry nodded. "Good idea, Ma."

Ma's gaze shifted to something behind him. "Now who in hell is that exotic creature?"

Terry swiveled around to look. That exotic creature was a real good-looker with black hair and a nice figure. She looked foreign somehow. Since she was following Megan toward the ranch touring car, she had to be an actress.

Pia had stepped down into the crowd on the platform. She'd expected to be greeted by someone but found herself ignored. All the people who seemed to work for the ranch were obviously enthralled by the Hollywood crowd, swarming around them like bees around ripe flowers. Tommaso was deeply engaged in twirling his rope.

"Tommaso, go find a porter to fetch our baggage. Quickly now."

He coiled his rope. "Please, Mama, you must call me

'Tommy' now. We are Americans now, and it will be more appropriate."

This was the third time he'd asked, and she was exasperated. "Oh very well, all right, now go find a porter."

Tommaso trotted off, and she glanced around at the scene. The air was crisp and cool, and the sun felt good on her skin. She was beginning to relax and enjoy herself when she saw Uncle's man climbing down from the second-class car. He smiled and nodded to her. She turned away in panic to see a hard-faced man trotting toward her on bowlegs. He wore a shiny badge on his shirt, just like those she'd seen in the movies. How quaint; she really was in the Wild West now.

"Mornin,' ma'am." He raised his hat, then settled it back on his head. "My name is Joe, Joe Goodman. I'm the sheriff for this county. And who might you be?"

Even without the badge, she would have known he was some sort of law enforcement officer. He exuded that sense of arrogant power all policemen did. She raised her veil and gazed at him. "How do you do, Sheriff? My name is Pia, Pia Donatelli. This is my son, Tommaso . . . I mean, Tommy. He insists we are American now, and I must call him an American name."

"You going out to the Rocking Lazy F ranch?"

"Why, yes. Yes, I am! Could you possibly find someone to help us with our baggage?" She gestured at the pile of valises, hatboxes, and steamer trunks the train porter was piling up behind her.

The sheriff's eyes widened as he took in the size of the pile. He glanced around. "Looks like Bill is helping all those Hollywood people. I'll be happy to get your gear to the . . . say, are you one of them?"

She laughed her little tinkling laugh designed to delight men. "Well, yes, I am." She was sure that by the time he might catch her in the lie, she would have convinced Alan or Steamer to hire her. "Could you really help me?"

"You bet. I just knew you were an actress." He eyed her baggage. "You wouldn't have any liquor stashed in them bags, would you?"

She shook her head demurely. "Good heavens, no!"

"That's good. Sounds like you're Italian, right?" She nodded. "Some visitors here don't seem to realize we have Prohibition in this country. It's my job to enforce the law in Jackson County." He nodded, a self-satisfied smile on his face. "I do a damn good job of it, too."

"I'm sure you do, Sheriff."

A few minutes later her bags had been piled next to the touring car. The sheriff tipped his hat again and held out his hand. "Sure glad to meet you, Miss Pia." He hesitated a minute. "Would you, ah, mind if I called on you out at the ranch? Maybe I could take you riding or something?"

Feeling it was best to discourage him right away, she replied, "Thank you for the offer, Sheriff. I'd like to, but my schedule?" She shrugged. "You know, we're going to be working day and night."

"If anything should change, you could just ring me at the office. Fiona knows the number."

"Fiona?"

"Oh, right. You ain't met her yet. She and her husband, TT, run the ranch."

"TT? That is his name? How unusual."

"Stands for Terrible Terry. He's Irish. It's said he had a terrible temper when he was younger. Got him in trouble, too."

"I see. Well, thank you."

The sheriff tipped his hat again and left. Now that she didn't have to keep her guard up, she could relax a bit and look around. She sighed. It was so bucolic and peaceful here, she could almost imagine a world without Uncle. She bit her lip to keep from crying. Uncle would never leave her alone until she finished the job. How would she keep an eye on the production if they went off into the wilderness? She had to stop them from doing that somehow.

The Hollywood people were moving purposefully back and forth, loading a mass of equipment into a truck. Alan was directing the affair, waving and pointing with his cigar and shouting orders. Daphne was surrounded by people from the town. They were gazing at her worshipfully as they pestered her with questions. *Local girl makes good,* Pia thought with amusement.

Where was Steamer? she wondered. Then she spotted him talking to one of the women from the ranch. Pia was looking away when something about their behavior struck her as odd. She turned back to study them. They were . . . they were avoiding each other while being oh, so polite. But . . . they were attracted to each other at the same time. No, not just attracted: deeply and hopelessly in love.

Angry jealousy threatened to overwhelm Pia. Steamer had turned her down, and she was at least as attractive as that woman, if not more so. What did he see in her? She was pretty enough, but she was a Percheron, not an Arabian; she was a sturdy workhorse, not a purebred.

Pia walked over to them. "Hi, Steamer." She ignored the woman. "Is everything going all right?"

Her greeting snapped the spell holding them enthralled. Reluctantly, Steamer dragged his attention away from the woman. "Uh, yes, Mrs. Donatelli. This is Mrs. Foxworth, um, Megan Foxworth. Megan, Pia Donatelli."

Ah, Pia realized the problem. She was married and most uncomfortable now that she'd been caught wearing her heart on her sleeve. Something was very wrong here.

"So glad to meet you, Mrs. Foxworth." Pia laid a slight emphasis on the "Mrs." "You are, what is the word you use, a 'hand' on the ranch?"

The Foxworth woman frowned briefly but then smiled. "We usually reserve the word 'hand' for the men. Although I suppose I'm a 'hand' in a way, as well. My husband's parents own the ranch. Terry and I help them manage it."

Steamer said, "Megan made all the arrangements for us to come up to the Rocking Lazy F and shoot here. As well as all the arrangements to pack into the backcountry and shoot there."

"How clever of you, Mrs. Foxworth." She laid a hand on Steamer's arm. "Speaking of all that, Steamer, I'm sure that by now you've come up with a way to include me in the film, yes?" She turned quickly to the Foxworth woman. "You see, in Italy I am a champion jumper. Steamer and—oh, yes, of course—Mr. Segal, have considered putting me in the film. To do a jumping scene, in which I rescue someone."

She quickly explained about Tommaso needing fresh air, how she had agreed to pay for their share of expenses, and how she was so happy to have found something to keep her occupied. She went on to share that this was her first trip to the West. When she finished, she saw that Megan and Steamer both looked mildly confused, which was good. She could tell Alan that Steamer had agreed to it, and Steamer wouldn't remember, as he was so besotted with Mrs. Foxworth.

CHAPTER 13

Tuesday Morning, June 16

A sound she could not at first identify awakened Pia. She sat up and gazed about, disoriented and groggy, until the odd-looking walls resolved themselves into pine logs. After another moment the noise revealed itself to be rain thrumming on the roof. Oh, yes, she remembered now. There'd been the long train ride and the cold, uncomfortable car ride over the Teton Pass. She was in the log cabin at the Rocking Lazy F ranch. Where was Tommaso?

He was not in his bed, and she panicked for a moment before she remembered she'd told him he could get up whenever he wanted to, as long as he stayed where she could find him. A faint odor of frying bacon told her where he would be. She rose, washed, and dressed. The ranch provided umbrellas for their guests, which was a good thing. The rain was coming down in buckets.

The dining room in the main cabin was nearly full. Tommaso was eating with several other boys and girls. When she kissed him, he barely looked up to say good morning. He was listening wide-eyed to some tale the other boys were telling as he stuffed his mouth with pancakes.

"Good morning, Mrs. Donatelli." Megan Foxworth appeared from the kitchen carrying a tray covered with platters of bacon, sausage, pancakes, and something white and mushy. Oh yes, probably this was hominy grits.

"Oh, please, we must not be so formal, yes? You must call me Pia."

"Well, sure. And you call me Megan, okay? Have a seat, and I'll bring you some coffee."

As she passed, Pia could see that Megan carried the tray as if it were heaped with pillows. Pia could see Steamer was trying hard to avoid looking at her and doing a poor job of it. Jealousy roiled through her. How could he be in love with this country bumpkin?

Dangerous thinking, Pia. Never underestimate your enemy. Megan was really quite pretty, with a mass of long, auburn hair that caressed her face and shoulders with her every step. On further examination, she did not look like a draft horse; rather, she was one of those fast, nimble horses cowboys rode when they were roping cows. So Megan was not a thoroughbred like herself, but probably just what Steamer would want. Now, how could she get him to change his mount of choice?

Steamer was not the only person covertly watching Megan. The owner's wife, Fiona, was moving about and chatting with her guests, but her gaze stabbed back and forth from Steamer to Megan, Megan to Steamer, evaluating and judging every tiny involuntary movement and every last flicker of emotion. Ah, yes; Megan was married to her son. Fiona was a lioness guarding her cub.

A place at the table next to Steamer beckoned to her. She pulled the chair away and, as she lowered herself to the seat, swayed slightly so that she brushed against him. "Oh, I'm sorry. Good morning, Steamer."

He turned to her as if coming out of a mesmerist's trance. "Pia. Hi. How are you? Did you sleep all right? How is Tommy?"

"I had a wonderful sleep, thank you. And, as you can see, Tommaso is completely ignoring me."

Steamer laughed. "I'd guess he slept well, too. He came charging in here like a hungry wolf this morning."

"Oh, I am so glad to hear that." She placed her hand gently on his forearm and gazed up at him. "I am not sure I will ever be able to thank you enough for saving my son. He is all I have, and . . ." She looked down and sniffed. "Anyway, thank you."

Megan leaned in between them and banged a mug of coffee down in front of her. "What would you like for breakfast, Mrs. Donatelli?"

"I think just some toast, please. And please, do call me Pia, yes?"

Steamer said, "If you're going to be riding and spending the day outdoors, you'll burn a lot of energy, and you'll be hungry before lunch if you don't eat more at breakfast."

"I'm so accustomed to a continental breakfast, but perhaps you are right. I'll eat more tomorrow." Her toast arrived; she buttered it and spread it with honey. "Do you think you might be able to take some time to go riding with Tommaso and me? It would make him so happy if you could."

His smile faded. "Ah, well, maybe, but I'm going to be pretty busy." He paused, frowned. "And you are, too, aren't you? I mean, I hear you are going along on the trip."

"Yes, I've arranged it with Alan." She hadn't, not really, but maybe he wouldn't think to ask Alan about it. "We'll have a chance to ride together then, won't we?"

"Ah, yes. I've got to go now." He gestured to where Alan and Paul were rising from the table. "We're going to unpack and check all the equipment. Not much else we can do in this weather."

Pia watched him walk off as she buttered and honeyed another piece of toast. As she bit into it, she realized Steamer was right about eating more. A warm feeling rose in her. He really was concerned about her health, which was something

Uncle never was. Steamer would protect her from Uncle—if only she could turn his head in her direction.

"Mom?"

She realized Tommaso was standing beside her. "Mom? Why are you suddenly calling me Mom?"

He scuffed his feet on the floor. "That's what all the other kids in America call their mothers," he said.

She laughed. "All right. You're right. We are Americans now."

"Can I go out and play in the barn? With the other kids?"

"Yes, you *may* play with them. And if you need me, I'll be in our cabin. I have to unpack all our clothes." Tommaso ran off.

Pia was about to rise when she noticed Fiona moving in her direction. She handed her the yellow envelope. "Telegram for you, Mrs. Donatelli. Came earlier this morning."

Pia sank down into her chair and ran her finger under the flap. It opened easily. It was, as she suspected, from Uncle. Her heart curled up and turned brown around the edges as she read the familiar code. She was to make every effort to ensure the production was completed as soon as possible at the least cost. But that wasn't what pained her. It was the final sentence: "Do not allow yourself to be distracted by a man, Pia darling. Your loyalty must always be to me and to our cause."

She held the telegram in her lap under the table and methodically tore it into tiny pieces and pushed them into her pocket. She finished her toast and coffee and left the table. As she passed the kitchen, she glanced in. Megan was up to her elbows in soapy water, scrubbing dirty pots and pans. Steamer was drying them. They were deep in conversation and did not see her. The warm feeling she had felt for him evaporated as jealousy seethed through her. She wanted to kill him. That way, if she couldn't have him, neither could Megan.

The next instant shame overwhelmed her. How could she be so callous? He'd saved Tommaso's life, hadn't he? What about killing Megan? With her out of the way, she would have a chance to prove to Steamer that she was the right woman for him. But no, she couldn't do that either. She was not a murderer.

She went out and stamped through the puddles, splattering water on her riding pants. She had to get free of Uncle—but she'd never be free of him until he was dead. She stopped, heedless of the rain soaking her clothing. She'd have to kill him if she was ever going to be free.

She started walking again, fantasizing about how she would do it. She could leave Tommaso here. Bettina and Megan would take good care of him while she went to Italy. She knew exactly where and when she would find Uncle sleeping. She would creep in and kill him with her .25 Colt. Would one shot kill him? She suddenly realized she had no idea how powerful the little pocket gun was. How could she test it? Ah, yes, she would ride out by herself one day and find one of the ranch animals to test it on.

Two hours later she had unpacked all their clothing and put it away in drawers or on hangers. She sat down to rest a while and realized she was hungry. Lunch would not be served for another hour, and she appreciated the wisdom of Steamer's advice.

When Steamer had appeared in the kitchen and offered to dry the dishes, Megan was, for once, grateful for the huge pile of dirty pots and pans. She could slosh them noisily in the soapy water and bang them in the draining rack to conceal her agitation. Last night's dreams had been disturbing, but pleasantly so, and she had awakened feeling wetness between her legs. Thank God Terry had risen early—that way she'd had time to rid herself of this strange new sensation.

Except it hadn't worked out that way. Steamer had showed up and insisted on drying. He'd kept up a constant stream of innocuous questions and comments, but she was beginning to relax a bit and keep up her end of the conversation. Yes, she could do it now; ignore him, forget him, and keep her commitment to her husband and her family.

But then, what if Steamer was the undercover agent who was supposed to be coming? She nearly dropped the big ceramic platter she was scrubbing. Why not just tell him the rumor and see what kind of reaction he had? If he looked guilty, it would be easier to keep away from him.

"You most likely haven't been in town long enough to hear the rumor that's going around," she said.

He took the platter from her. "What rumor is that?"

She leaned closer, lowering her voice. "There's supposed to be a lawman coming, an undercover agent or something from wherever it is they work. To spy on people here, find out if there's any illegal liquor getting into town."

"Well, is there?"

The pan she was washing slipped back into the water with a splash. She ducked her head, hoping she didn't look guilty. "Prohibition is stupid," she said, more forcefully than she'd intended.

"You didn't answer my question," he said. "About liquor getting into town."

Panic rose in her, and she struggled to remain calm. A half truth would be better than a lie. "Well, yes. Just a little bit though." He'd find out eventually anyway. "TT says we have to have a few bottles, for the guests who want it."

"I agree with you. Prohibition is stupid." He frowned at her. "I haven't got any idea if the Bureau of Internal Revenue uses undercover agents in its Prohibition Unit. But Prohibition *is* the law. You might want to be careful what you do."

Her confusion returned more strongly than before. He was warning her personally, wasn't he? A quick glance at his face told her: yes, he was. She could only assume his warning came because he really *was* an undercover agent. But why would he warn her personally? She knew why, and the admission that she did know nearly made her faint. He was in love with her.

She somehow managed to finish washing up without making a fool of herself. She was searching desperately for an excuse to get away so she could go off and lick her wounds when Fiona yanked the kitchen door open. It was the first time she'd ever been happy to see her.

"Hi, Fiona. You startled me."

Fiona's lips twitched. "Good, you're finished with the dishes." Her gaze shifted to Steamer. "I thought you were supposed to be helping get your camera stuff ready, Mr. Daniels. Megan has a chore to do."

"Now don't you worry about that, Mrs. Foxworth. We've got plenty of time, what with all this rain. It's been nice chatting with you, Megan." He hung the wet dishtowel on the hook, nodded to Fiona, and left.

"What kind of man dries the dishes?" Fiona muttered. "Now, missy, Mrs. Segal wants a bath. Get on over to their cabin and help her."

Megan was just past the entrance to the ranch office when she sensed movement behind her. She turned to look and was rewarded with a glimpse of Junior as he shut the door behind him. Now what in hell was he doing visiting Fiona? She had told him never to come near her again, but that didn't mean Fiona couldn't hire him occasionally for odd jobs. She continued on her way toward the Segals' cabin.

The pounding rain outside was a perfect match to her mood. Her heart was drowning in a hard, cold rain of disappointment. The arrival of the people from Hollywood had changed nothing. Besides, Fiona knew exactly what was going on between herself and Steamer. She was doomed to live out the rest of her life on the ranch. *So stop whining, Megan. You made your bed, now lie in it.* She'd said that to herself before, hadn't she? Yes, she had.

She knocked on the guest cabin door. A cheerful voice called, "Enter."

Bettina Segal was an imposing woman, even in a nightgown and bathrobe. Tall and solid, she looked as if she would never take any guff from anyone, but her eyes were smiling.

"Good morning, my dear." Bettina drew quite close and peered at her. Megan realized she probably needed eyeglasses but was too vain to wear them. "You are TT and Fiona's daughter-in-law, aren't you?" Megan nodded. "I'm so glad to meet you. Are you going to help me with a bath?"

"Yes, ma'am. I'm going to—"

"Oh please! Not ma'am. Name is Bettina."

With that, some of Megan's disappointment went away for a while. Bettina was warm-hearted, charming, and funny. Megan had expected a snooty high-society dame, and Bettina was the opposite. Nothing fazed her: the high-back copper bathtub was just like the one she had used as a girl, and the cabin was charming and quite comfortable. They quickly fell into an easy exchange of personal stories.

"So then," Bettina said as she was drying herself, "what do you see in your future? Will you be running the ranch someday?"

"Ah, no. I mean, I don't think so."

"That's not what you want?"

Megan hesitated. Should she trust this stranger with her dreams? If she didn't tell someone soon, she would die of misery. She didn't have to say anything about the family business or her marriage. She settled on saying, "I just envy you so. I think it must be the most wonderful thing in the world to make movies."

"I don't know much about that, my dear. I am just a housewife. I've raised two sons, although they're out of the house now. But I do know Alan, and Steamer and Paul, and your sister all love the business."

"It's just magic, seeing all those wonderful stories like that. I wish I could do something like that."

Bettina nodded thoughtfully and studied her for a moment. "You are really quite good-looking. Not beautiful—no, don't be disappointed—you're better than beautiful. You have a strong, interesting face. The camera would love it. With a good hairstyle and makeup . . . do you have any talent?"

Megan was taken aback by this frank appraisal and the direct question. "I sing a little."

"Just a little?" Bettina laughed. "My guess is you sing more than a little. I'll tell Alan. You can sing for him. He's a good judge of voices."

Megan floated back to her own cabin on a pink cloud.

Fiona had heard the office door click shut and looked up to see Junior glaring at her.

"Damn, you scared me, Junior. What the hell are you doing, sneaking in like that?"

He dropped into the chair with a thud. "Megan."

"Megan *what*?"

"She seen me coming in." He leaned over and ejected a stream of tobacco juice into the cuspidor.

"So?"

He glared at her a moment longer, then said, "You wanted to see me?"

Fiona leaned back in her swivel chair. "Lock the door."

She felt as if every part of her body was wrapped in barbed wire, and a giant pair of fencing pliers was twisting it tighter ever minute. The new shipment of Irish whiskey was safely stored in the new elevating platform—but how in hell were they going to get rid of it all? If they didn't sell it soon, their eastern connections wouldn't put TT in a wheelchair; they'd put him in a pine box. And maybe they would do the same to Terry. The thought made her feel faint.

She'd had a funny feeling this morning when the telegram arrived for Pia Donatelli, so she'd steamed it open—and nearly had a heart attack. It was in code! Who in the hell was this Italian bitch, and who did she work for? Could it be their Eastern connection or the government?

And Megan, that sneaky little minx, had been seeing a lot more of Sally Mann than usual, and Sally was more than a little crazy on the subject of Prohibition. Megan made a lot of noise about how she thought Prohibition was stupid, but that could be a cover for her real motives. She and Sally were most likely in cahoots and had arranged for the law to come to town.

Fiona had been in the dining room, talking to Pia and Tommy, which had given Megan and Steamer the perfect opportunity to talk privately. What kind of man dried the dishes, for chrissake? He had to have been passing the latest information to her.

And if all that wasn't bad enough, she had finally decided that Buddy's news was probably true. It made a lot of sense. "He's just an actor," is what everyone would say. Sheriff Goodman was out of town for two days. She could not wait that long to confirm what Buddy had said.

She leaned forward, folding her hands on the top of the desk. "I hear you've been hankering for one of those new Ford pickup trucks."

Junior sat up straighter. "Sure is funny how rumors get around this town."

She nodded. "Yeah. Anyway, there might be a way to earn one. Something you might do for us."

"So tell me."

Fiona ticked off the points on her fingers as she gave him a brief summary of her worries. She finished and settled back in her chair again.

"Sounds like you got your tail real deep in a crack, Fiona. Why don't you get Terry to give you a hand with this?" Fiona merely stared at him until he smirked and nodded. "Yeah, right," he said. "So, what're you suggesting?"

"How about an accident?" A look of smug pleasure rolled over his face. She hated that look and realized she'd just gotten herself in deeper shit than before. She was going to have to do something about Junior when this was all over.

"Well now, let's put our cards on the table, Fiona. We're talking about *Megan* having an accident, right?"

"Keep your voice down!" She nodded. "Don't kill her. Just make her not pretty anymore, so she can't act in the movies."

"How?"

"Use your imagination, Junior! Fake a fall in the kitchen, cut her with a knife, dump hot water on her face. Anything to uglify her. And that Italian bitch. Five hundred in cash for her. Same thing."

"You've got a deal." Junior's grin threatened to split his face into top and bottom halves. "How 'bout a down payment?"

Fiona opened the middle drawer of the file cabinet and handed him a hundred dollars.

As he rode home from the ranch, Junior's thoughts were hog-tied to one subject: if he was to cause Megan to have an accident, he had to persuade his pa to hire him on as a trail hand for the film crew. That would be one real tough proposition, seeing as how he'd told his pa that he could take his damned religion and shove it where the sun don't shine. Pa was such a damned hypocrite, always lecturing him about being godly and all that, and then doing everything un-godly behind his back. Well, if he pretended long enough and hard enough that he'd seen the light, Pa would forgive him.

The hot bath water was beginning to cool, but Megan was reluctant to rouse herself. She had been rehearsing the songs she was going to sing for Alan and was in the middle of her newest idea when a loud knock snapped her out of her reverie.

"Terry?"

The door swept open. "You got another husband you've been hiding from me?" He grinned at her as he pulled off his blue, silk shirt, then jammed his heels in the bootjack and levered his lizard-skin boots off his feet. He was pulling off his waist overalls when he suddenly looked up. She shrank down in the tub; that look in his eyes meant only one thing.

He leaned over the foot of the tub, and his gaze swept up and down her body. "Now you're lookin' real inviting in there. Come on out and let's do it. Or maybe I'll get in, all right?"

He was in a good mood, but memories of Junior's assault of the day before made Megan cringe inside. She whimpered, only a little one, but he stopped.

"Something wrong?"

"We've been doing it a lot lately. We did it twice last night. I'm kinda sore down there, Terry. Could we wait a night or two?"

"Okay," he said and backed off. "So how about you get out and get me some hot water so I can take a bath?"

She was surprised at his quick retreat. What was going on? She climbed out of the high-back copper tub, dried, pulled on her bathrobe, and put the kettle on the stove to heat.

"You took one last night," she said, keeping a smile in her voice. "You going out or something?"

"Going to town."

"Before supper?"

"Yeah. Mrs. Segal, she told Ma, and Ma told me. Seems like her husband . . . what's his name? Oh yeah, Alan. He's offered to throw a big party tomorrow night, wants music and everything."

"Really?"

"Yes, indeed. So Ma wants me to get on into town and talk to Glen May, you know, about his orchestra playing at the party. And go to Isaiah's and order more food. And let folks in town know about it. Alan has invited anyone who wants to come."

The kettle was boiling. Megan poured the hot water into the tub, then pumped up a bucket full of cold and added it. Terry climbed in. "Scrub my back, okay?" He looked up at her. "Ma said something about Bettina said something about you singing for Mr. Segal. That right?"

She nodded, not trusting herself to speak.

"You know I don't hold with you doing that, Megan." He climbed out, and she handed him a towel. "You're getting ideas that just don't mix with marriage. It's all right if you amuse yourself with plunking on that autoharp, but you're my wife now. I need you here. Ma and Pa ain't going to be around much longer, and I'm going to need you to help me run the place." He finished dressing in clean clothing. "And it would sure help if we had a passel of kids to help out too."

"All right, Terry. I . . . I'll . . . keep trying. You have a good time in town."

"Don't wait up for me. I might be late."

When he was gone, she went to her closet. She'd hidden the box Luella had given her at the railroad station on the top shelf, behind a pile of clothing. This was the first chance she'd had to open it, and she was dying to see what was in it. She reached it down and put it on her bed.

She blew out the lantern; she didn't want Fiona to think she was still awake and come snooping. She lifted the garments from the box and carried them to the window, where moonlight shone brightly into the room. The top was of soft, white cotton in an off-the-shoulder design with short ruffled sleeves. The skirt looked like a Mexican serape in vibrant colors with lace trim around the bottom.

She gasped with pleasure and held them in front of her. A small reflection of herself in one windowpane confirmed that they fit her perfectly. Music rose inside her, the tune and lyrics from "South of the Border." Her feet followed her heart, and soon she was whirling about, her bare feet tapping the rhythm on the floor as she sang the words. The skirt flared upward and the windowpane reflected her bare legs moving in four-four time.

CHAPTER 14

Wednesday Evening, June 17

From her cabin, Megan could hear the sounds of the party in full swing in the main lodge. No one seemed to have seen her sneak out. She pulled the kerosene lantern closer and checked her makeup. Not too much, but just enough to help her look better in the artificial light of the lodge. TT and Fiona had installed electric lights there a year ago. Megan hated the harshness of the incandescent bulbs, but they would assure that her performance would be seen.

She rose and pulled on the skirt Luella had given her and then the blouse, tugging and tucking until they fit properly. She blew out the lantern, picked up her autoharp, opened the door, and started walking toward the main lodge. The sky had finally cleared, and bright moonlight bathed the yard and barn. Movement at the edge of her vision made her draw back so she was completely in the shadows.

It was Terry. He was tiptoeing, which was ridiculous behavior given the noise of the party. Every so often he'd stop to scan the yard. *What in heck is he doing sneaking through the night like that?* Megan watched as he vanished into the stygian interior of the barn. She laid her autoharp carefully on the bench outside the kitchen and darted through the yard to the side entrance of the barn.

Once inside she heard a strange sound, like the squeaking of mice. She moved toward the sound, sticking to the shadows and walking as carefully as if she had been walking on eggs. Terry was . . . *What on earth is he doing?* Something descended into sight, and she realized the mouse noise was the squeaking of a block and tackle; he was lowering something from the rafters.

She held herself rigidly still, breathing in a slow, shallow rhythm. The platform touched down, and Terry threw back a tarpaulin covering, revealing dozens of boxes of Irish whiskey. The shock of what she was seeing nearly made Megan cry out. A huge quantity of whiskey was concealed under that tarp, a quantity that could mean only one thing: her family was smuggling commercial quantities of illegal liquor onto the Rocking Lazy F. They had lied to her; they'd almost certainly been lying to her for months now. The implications made her dizzy, and her legs felt weak.

Terry hoisted the platform back into place and left with several bottles. She waited a few minutes, then crossed back to the main cabin, keeping to the shadows. She collapsed on the bench beside her beloved autoharp. Her mind darted over her options like a hummingbird darting from flower to flower. Should she remain loyal to her family and keep her mouth shut? Or should she tell Steamer? But if she told him, she might lose him. Oh, what the hell nonsense was she thinking; he was the *enemy.* He'd arrest her and throw her in jail for years. And even if that didn't happen, their suppliers would be angry, dangerously angry. So Gertie had been right after all: her life was in danger.

Inside, the band struck up "Beer Barrel Polka," and she heard Glen announcing that it was now time for "The Jackson Hole Stomp." She was going to sing when it was finished and when everyone would be tired and pay attention. She'd think more about what she'd seen later. She rose and went inside, failing to notice Fiona standing motionless in the shadows by the kitchen door.

"The Jackson Hole Stomp" was in full swing when Megan slipped into the main cabin through the side door. The solid oak floor vibrated under the influence of hundreds of stomping boots as dudes and dudines joined the hands of town folks in the fun. They swirled around in the steps of a classic polka as interpreted through the sensibilities of the American West. She stood on the sidelines clutching her autoharp to her chest, which made it easier for her to conceal the fear slowly eating her alive. The longer she thought about the implications of what she had seen in the barn, the more helpless panic grew in her. At last one thing became clear: her only hope lay in standing foursquare and firm with her family. Her dreams of a singing career were just empty, foolish dreams. Terry was going to be angry with her for disobeying him, but she would make it up to him later. Because one time, just this one time, she was going to perform in public.

The dance ended with a final deafening stomp as one hundred boots slammed on the floor as one. As the cheering and clapping died down, Glen raised his arms for quiet. "Now that was one of the best 'Jackson Hole Stomps' I've ever heard. You all did a great job, and I'm sure you all could use a little rest. So—I've got a special treat for you tonight. Our own lovely Megan Foxworth has a voice so, well, so . . . I'm not even going to try to describe her voice. I'm just going to let her show you. Megan?"

She was amazed at the calm sense of purpose that overcame her and pushed her fear and panic into the background of her thoughts. This sensation, so new and strange, she'd examine later. Her friends from town were turning to whisper to each other and watching her with amused curiosity. She continued with her head high.

Steamer stood at the forefront of the people from Hollywood. Alan and Bettina, Paul Marshal, Mrs. Donatelli, and all the technicians were gossiping under their breath as she reached the front and turned to face them. She instantly noticed Terry, Fiona, and TT watching her with dour expressions. The hell with them for now; she'd deal with them later.

"Thank you, Glen." She took a deep breath. "I want to dedicate this song to my wonderful husband, Terry, and to my in-laws, Fiona and TT Foxworth." She wanted to add more, but realized she had better sing before she lost her nerve.

She struck the opening chords and allowed herself to become one with the music. The words of "Red River Valley" poured from her heart and soared out over the crowd. Soon she was swaying to the music, then dancing, with her new skirt swirling between her legs, the blouse caressing her breasts.

The final chord died away, and she came back into herself. Was something wrong? They were so silent—and then she saw that some of her friends were dabbing at their eyes and sniffing. Steamer and Alan were staring open-mouthed at her. Terry, Fiona, and TT looked baffled and angry. The silence ended with a roar of applause and cheering that left her stunned.

Then Steamer, Alan, and Bettina were pushing through the crowd, followed by her family, and they were all congratulating her and exclaiming in surprise, and it was never going to stop.

Alan finally said, "My God, Megan! That was an incredible performance. Look, I want you to do a screen test. Hell, I want you to come along on the trip. We'll find some way to get you into the story line. We can't record your singing yet, but that's coming soon. In the meantime we can send you around the country when the film premieres, and you can sing accompaniment. And we'll use the new electric recording technology and make some records and get you on the air in every radio station in the country."

"I'm sorry, but I can't do that, Mr. Segal." She wasn't sure how she'd gotten the words out, but there. It was done. The haunted expression on Steamer's face would remain with her the rest of her life.

"What do you mean, you can't do that?" Alan looked as if she had slapped him.

"My place is here with my family, Mr. Segal. Terry needs me. We have a business to run. Dude ranching is a good business, and, well, it's what we do best."

Terry gave her a big hug. "About time you came to your senses, Megan." He turned to Alan. "Real nice of you to offer, Mr. Segal, but Megan is just a hometown girl. Her place is here with us, on the Rocking Lazy F."

The band started playing again. Megan drifted slowly through the crowd, chatting with her friends. The dancing had started up once more, and she was able to slip out and go to her own cabin for the privacy she needed to sort out her conflicting emotions.

Terry was tempted to knock back the shot of whiskey but sipped it slowly instead. It was really good stuff, and he wanted to enjoy it. By God, Megan had finally gotten some sense in her head. She knew which side her bread was buttered on, and he'd been the one to convince her. He was real glad he'd put his foot down. Or had he? He'd seen her looking at that Steamer guy, and him looking back at her, and that had made him real jealous.

No, now that he thought about it some more, he was wrong. She had just been nervous about performing in front of all those professionals from Hollywood. After all, Mr. Segal had offered her a film test, and she'd turned him down flat. That had to mean she'd come to her senses. He knocked back the rest of the whiskey. He'd go tell Ma and Pa. They were probably as happy as he was.

A light was on in the office, but when he tried the door, it was locked. He rattled the knob and saw a shadow moving on the rippled glass. The door opened, and his pa gestured for him to come in.

"Well now, isn't that something?" Ma said. "Turns out Megan has a good voice after all."

Terry grinned with pleasure. "Yeah, how about that? Sure surprised me."

"And then that Mr. Segal offered her a screen test," Pa added. "And he wants her to go on the trail ride with them."

"Yeah, but she turned him down. Ain't that wonderful?" Terry looked expectantly from one to the other. "Looks like I've finally knocked some sense into her head."

"Don't say 'ain't,' " Ma snapped. "You learned better English than that, son. Now, let's take a good look at what's really going on here."

Terry's pleasure slowly congealed into a rancid lump. "What's really going on here? You mean, Megan's doing something wrong?"

TT leaned forward in his wheelchair. "Listen, son, your mother caught her snooping in the barn."

"She wouldn't do anything like that . . . I don't think. Would she?"

Ma said, "It was when you went out to get another bottle or two. She was sitting on the back porch plunking on that damn autoharp, when you went out to the barn."

"How do you know that?"

"I was standing back in the shadows. She didn't see me. I watched her get up and follow you to the barn. Went sneaking in the side entrance. She didn't leave until after you'd gone. Did you lower that platform?"

"Well, yeah. But still, I just don't see her being a tattletale. You know, how many times has she said Prohibition is stupid?"

Ma nodded. "Right. But you do remember what Buddy said

150

yesterday? That Steamer Daniels is an undercover agent? Said the sheriff backed him up on that?" Terry nodded. "So did you ever think she might be saying she wouldn't go on the trip just to throw us off the track? Those Hollywood people are going to be around here for, what? Maybe three days, until this storm blows over. Plenty of time for her to slip him information, sneak him out to the barn some night when we're all asleep, show him the evidence."

Ma sniffed, holding back tears. "Then what do you think will happen to your father and me? If we aren't thrown in jail by the government, our suppliers won't like it, not one bit. Do you want me to wind up in a wheelchair, like your father?"

"Or dead?" TT added in an ominous voice.

Terry swallowed hard. "I guess I just didn't think of all that."

Ma laid her hand on his arm. "Your father and I aren't getting any younger, Terry." She wiped her eyes on the back of her hand. "We aren't going to be around that much longer. We need you more than she does. Besides, she isn't one of us."

"Well . . . so what do you want me to do?"

"Tell her she has to go on the trip with them," TT said. "Tell her we've got some financial problems, and it would really help for her to earn that money Mr. Segal said he'd pay her."

Terry nodded. "Sure, I could do that." He paused, frowning doubtfully. "But what good would that do?"

His parents looked at each other for a long, silent moment. Then Ma said, "It will get her out of town for a while and give us time to come up with an answer."

"Oh." Terry was crushed that he hadn't thought about all those things. "Well, okay, I guess."

"Don't worry about it, Son. We'll figure it out somehow." Ma sniffed hard and wiped her eyes again. "Thank you. You're a good son. You have no idea how much we appreciate this."

"So, what do I tell her? I mean, about our money problems?"

Ma ticked off on her fingers half a dozen problems. They were not true, she assured him, but they sure sounded realistic.

When she left the party, Megan had gone to the cabin she and Terry lived in. Brilliant moonlight poured through the windows; there was no need to light a lamp. She stumbled to her favorite chair and wept savagely. All the evidence had been there in front of her all along, and she had deliberately ignored it. She had been a deluded dreamer, and now she was trapped. The worst part of it was that she'd made the trap herself.

The storm of tears abated, and she sat quietly, searching for any possible way out. Steamer loved her, she was sure of that. What if she ran away with him? *He's not going to ask you to run away with him, Megan.* Besides, there'd be the pain of divorce, the certain scandal that would follow, the uncertainty . . . no, it was unthinkable. She'd just have to make the best of it.

The sound of the door opening snatched her from her misery.

"Megan? What in hell are you doing sitting in the dark?" She heard Terry's footsteps on the wooden floor, like the scritch of a wooden match. The light of an oil lamp came closer, and he was gazing down at her. "You all right?"

She smiled. "Yes, of course I am. The moonlight was so bright. I was just enjoying it. Is the party over?"

"It's breaking up. Ah, look, I've got something to ask you."

"So, ask."

"Well, Ma and Pa and me, we've been talking, and, well, I hate to tell you this, but we're having a bit of trouble. About money."

No wonder Fiona didn't want me doing the books. She didn't want me to find out. "I'm sorry to hear that. But what can I do?"

"We'd like you to go ahead and go on the trail with the Hollywood people."

Megan was certain the joy that exploded in her heart would

burst out on her face and betray her. She gripped the arms of the chair tightly. "Go . . . on the trip?"

"Well, sure. I mean, Mr. Segal offered to pay you, didn't he?" She nodded. "That sure would help us out."

Thoughts tumbled through her head like boulders falling down a mountain. Was there something else going on behind this sudden change of plans? "I didn't have any idea we were in financial trouble, Terry. Can you tell me more about it?"

"It's like this." He talked for several minutes. She was reluctant to believe him at first, but as he added details about how things had gone amiss, she came to believe he was telling the truth. They really did need the money she could earn.

"Okay, I'll talk to Alan tomorrow and tell him I've changed my mind. *If* he still wants me to go along."

Junior ambled past the door to number twenty-seven on Second Street, pretending he was not the least bit interested in going there. At the end of the block he stopped and looked back; no one was around. He returned quickly, knocked, and slid through the door when Madame Caitlin opened it. She was always "Madame Caitlin," never just Caitlin. Such familiarity would get you ejected before you could say Jack Robinson.

"Well, well, if it isn't Mr. Parley Frampton Junior. How are you, lad?" Her Irish accent was so thick you could spread it with a butter knife. "And why are we not at the Clubhouse drinking tonight?"

Junior removed his sheepskin jacket. "Nothing going on there."

Madame Caitlin peered at him with one eye closed. "Why not?"

"Glen's band is over at the Rocking Lazy F. That producer guy from Hollywood is throwing a big party." He grinned. "Hell of a good party. Made me hanker for some lovin'."

"So, sit down, make yourself to home." She poured him a shot of whiskey, compliments of the house, as always. "And what would you be fancying tonight?"

Junior grinned. "Jasmine."

"Jasmine? Oh my, are we feeling flush tonight." Jasmine was her newest girl, still young and fresh—and expensive. "What did you do, win at poker?"

"Never mind. I can pay."

"She's still with another client. You'll have to sit and wait. And that will be fifty dollars. Have another shot."

Junior sank down into the cushy armchair and closed his eyes. He fondled the one hundred dollars Fiona had given him. He was sure going to have a lot of fun when he had that new Ford pickup truck. Maybe he could even take Jasmine out for a ride. She'd like that.

He started to think about what he was going to have to do to earn that truck. His happiness eroded a bit, revealing the hard substrata of reality. Fiona hadn't said, but Junior knew that by "accident," she meant something that made Megan dead. Now that he was thinking about it, he was beginning to regret agreeing to her plan. If he killed her, he'd never be able to bring her into the Kingdom of Heaven.

It was just a week ago today that Megan had thrown him out of her bathroom. He'd prayed on that all week and finally realized that she was just plain ignorant; she had no idea how deeply she had sinned. She had rejected his saving grace and forfeited her chance to enter heaven. All right, so he wouldn't kill her—at least not until he'd given her a chance to repent and accept his blessing.

He heard the back door open and close. Madame asked her clients to leave by the back door. That way there'd be no embarrassment of running into someone they knew.

Moments later she came in, took his fifty dollars, and led him to Jasmine's room. He could hear her crying softly as he opened the door, but the moment he entered a big smile crossed her face.

He'd had his fun with her and was buttoning his jacket when he saw that the man ahead of him had left his gloves behind. He picked them up—and nearly peed in his pants from surprised terror. Made of buckskin with fancy beadwork decoration on the back, they'd been made for his pa by a local squaw.

As he realized the value of what he held, his fright gave way to a slowly building sense of triumph. He had no idea how he was going to use them, but now he had Pa by the short hairs. A time would come when he could return them. He could not wait until he saw the expression on Pa's face when he told him where he'd found them. He tucked them inside his sheepskin coat.

"Hey, Junior!" Jasmine said. "Those ain't your gloves."

"I know. They belong to my pa. I'll take them back to him."

CHAPTER 15

Thursday Morning, June 18

Despite the rain pounding down outside, Fiona was sure she could see a brighter day coming. Terry had told her, before he went off to work, that Megan had agreed to go along on the filming trip. Their phony financial problems had convinced her. She was to ask Alan this morning if she could change her mind and have a job on the film.

The party last night, besides being a big hit with the guests, had proven to Fiona that her intuition was right. Steamer Daniels had gotten drunk—or so he'd have her believe. His act wasn't quite convincing, however, and she was sure he was faking it. Undercover agents for the Prohibition Unit would sure as hell not drink, so he'd been drinking to prove he was anything but.

She laughed to herself as she served breakfast. Did he and Megan think they were really fooling anyone? Each had tried quite desperately to pretend they had not the least interest in the other, but it was as plain as the nose on your face they were nuts about each other. Hell, they might even have met secretly and fallen in love at Sally Mann's farm when they were planning whatever it was they were planning.

Alan and Steamer had been going at it ever since they'd sat down to eat. Fiona had no idea why they were arguing so fiercely, but Mrs. Donatelli was listening in with a rapt expression.

Steamer flagged Fiona down as she laid another platter of bacon in front of them. "Mrs. Foxworth, tell him."

"Tell him what?"

"That all the gorgeous scenery is right here in the valley. Tell him there's no need to go off into the wilds just to shoot great scenery. It will save us a *lot* of money. We can go out in automobiles and shoot."

Alan said, "Yeah, I know, Steamer. That's not a bad idea. This damn rain has sure screwed us up."

Stark fear struck Fiona. Steamer obviously wanted to stay in town where he could snoop around. Time was running out; she had to do something to keep herself and TT out of jail. The Hollywood people just had to go out into the backcountry and give them time to hide the new shipment. She poured herself a cup of coffee and sat down. "Well, now, Mr. Daniels has a good point, but—"

"There, you see, Alan?" Steamer said.

"Now hold up a minute, Mr. Daniels, I said *but*."

He gave her a sour look. "But what?"

"This valley has become very popular with easterners." She turned her focus on Mr. Segal. "You probably don't know it, but the dude ranching business has grown into a big money-maker, and hundreds of people come through here every year, meaning thousands have already seen all the scenery here in the valley."

Steamer started to interrupt, but she held up her hand. "Besides, Megan has gone to all sorts of trouble to set up the trip for you, made all the arrangements with Parley, reserved the horses, and that sort of thing." She glanced at Steamer. "She'd be brokenhearted if you cancelled all your plans."

Alan let out a loud crow of laughter. "There, you see, Steamer? Now just be a good boy and get ready to get the hell out of here as soon as this damn rain breaks."

Fiona turned to Steamer. "And, speaking of being broken-hearted, you all are going to be broken-stomached if you don't have enough to eat in the backcountry. Can't just pop into town from out there and grab more groceries, you know. It'll be at least a two-day ride back in."

"What's that got to do with me?" Steamer asked.

"You could go to Isaiah's with Megan, help her with the shopping."

That had been a sudden inspiration, to throw them together and give them enough grain to founder themselves. The look on Steamer's face told her it was going to work. "Besides, if she's going to go along, you might . . ."

"Going along? But she . . . I mean . . ."

"Didn't you know? She changed her mind last night after the party, told Mr. Segal this morning that she'd really like to go along."

"Oh."

"So what I was going to say was, if she's supposed to have a screen test, you're going to shoot it, aren't you?" Steamer nodded. "So, you go along to help her with the groceries, and you can give her some tips on how to look good for the test." Steamer nodded. She could see he was fighting to control his expression.

Steamer was just as glad the road was wet and sloppy. The sound of water splashing into the woods on each side combined with the rough ride made it impossible to talk. Megan was driving with relaxed concentration and handled the heavy vehicle with a skill that he admired.

Damn Alan anyway. Larking off into the backcountry was a stupid idea. They could damned well get to gorgeous scenery by road, which would save them all kinds of money. And then he'd gone and invited Megan to come along *and* have a screen test.

How in hell was he going to be able to ignore her?

And what in hell was going on with her husband and his parents? There'd been a lot of furtive comings and goings last night, and a suspicious amount of Irish whiskey appearing out of thin air. He risked a glance at her. She was staring straight ahead, her jaw set. That made it easier for him to ignore the pain in his heart.

Steamer's glance had nearly made her miss the shift into high gear. She felt as if she were being torn apart by fear, suspicion, anger, and heartbreak.

So maybe she wasn't going to be killed, but she'd be arrested and thrown in jail. Her husband and in-laws were almost certainly smuggling huge quantities of whiskey into the ranch. And they were lying to her about it. Had they not told her the whole truth about their financial situation? Were they in debt to their suppliers? If so, perhaps they were going to be killed after all. So where did loyalty to family end and self-preservation begin?

She turned onto the main highway and mashed down on the accelerator. She'd keep her mouth shut and play the game for now, and, above all, steer clear of Steamer. His arrival had shown her that her marriage was a sham. If she didn't keep away from him, she was liable to throw herself into his arms and say to hell with the consequences. *That* would be a disaster.

Megan braked the truck to a clattering halt in front of Isaiah's General Store. Megan saw Buddy sitting in the battered old armchair that was his home away from home. The noise of the truck stirred him from his alcoholic fog. He looked up, and his face brightened as his gaze landed on Steamer.

As they entered the store, Megan sensed Buddy following them. His behavior was a bit odd, but she dismissed him from her mind. Her shopping list was long and her time short; the expedition was to start tomorrow, and all the food and gear had to be loaded and ready by the morning.

"Mornin', Megan." Isaiah greeted her with his usual lopsided grin that revealed his chewing tobacco–stained teeth. "Who's your friend?" He sounded like a giant bullfrog desperate for a mate.

"This is Mr. Daniels, Steamer Daniels. He's the movie director, from Hollywood. You must have heard they were coming."

A look crossed Isaiah's face that told her he had indeed heard the rumors. To cover it, he dove behind his counter, rummaged around a moment, then handed her the latest issue of *Photoplay*. Isaiah had just started displaying a few of the most popular magazines: *Colliers, Saturday Evening Post,* and *Time*. He also brought in copies of several movie magazines, which he set aside for her.

She felt her face go red with embarrassment. Steamer stood right beside her. He'd probably think she was some sort of dizzy teenager for reading those magazines. He merely smiled at her and looked around at the store. She handed Isaiah twenty cents. "Thanks, Isaiah." She thrust the periodical quickly into her shopping bag. "Got a big list of stuff we need. Tomorrow we're packing the film crew out to the backcountry for a week." She glanced at Steamer. "They want to shoot scenery no one has filmed before."

Steamer turned from his scan of the store. "What you haven't heard, Isaiah, is that Megan is going to be part of that scenery." Isaiah gave him a quizzical look. "We're going to shoot a screen test of her."

"No sugar! Hey, Megan, that's great. That's real nice of you, Mr. Daniels. Megan sure deserves a break."

Megan had a sudden suspicion someone was staring at her and looked in the flyspecked mirror behind the counter. Buddy was studying Steamer with an intent look. What on earth was going on with him?

She pulled her shopping list from the bag. "All right, let's get started. We need fifty pounds of potatoes, Isaiah. I hope you've got enough?"

"I reckon. I'll get Frank to help."

Frank was Isaiah's half-wit helper. Many of the townspeople ragged on him, calling him "Droopy Drawers" for his perpetually sagging pants. He may have been simple-minded, but that was no excuse to treat him badly, Megan thought.

When Frank saw who he was to help, he beamed at her. She wondered if she was the only person who treated him with dignity. "Morning, Frank. This is my friend, Mr. Daniels. Now, we need twenty-five pounds of onions. And the same of apples."

"Right away, Miss Megan. I was just sweeping up. We caught a couple of—"

"Frank!" Isaiah snapped. "That's enough."

"Yessir." Frank trotted off toward the back.

Megan began moving through the store, selecting items and adding them to her shopping bag. Steamer tagged along, keeping up an easy flow of conversation.

"That bag looks like it's getting heavy," he said. "Why don't I take it out to the truck? You've got some more bags out there, right?"

She surrendered the bag to him. "Thanks. And, yes, do bring in some more gunny sacks."

Buddy peered around the end of the shelves she was walking along. He was beginning to annoy her. "Buddy, shoo. You're being a pest."

He sidled up to her and whispered, "Aw now, Megan, I was just wanting to see how a secret agent operates."

"Secret agent?" Her heart started thumping as her thoughts went back to the day the Hollywood people had arrived. She'd forgotten those rumors. Or, rather, she had put them out of her mind deliberately. She hadn't wanted to think ill of them. "That's ridiculous, Buddy. He's just a director and an actor."

He slid even closer. Megan was sure she could smell preserved meat with his breath. "Tha's just it, Megan." He told her his theory about the perfect disguise. "Wha's more, Sheriff Goodman confirmed it. You can ask him if'n you don't believe me."

"Shh! Here he comes. Now get out of here."

Questions and protests stampeded through her mind. She had to do something to maintain her calm, especially now that Steamer was once again close by her side, still chatting as if nothing was wrong. She handed Steamer the list. "Here, you read the list to me. It will save time."

She scuffed through the sawdust on the floor. Isaiah scattered it throughout the store. Sawdust helped pick up the dirt and bits of foodstuffs when Frank swept the floor. "Let's see now . . . we need twenty-five pounds of bacon and forty T-bone steaks."

She continued around the store, adding two dozen number-ten cans of food: carrots, peas, succotash, beets, peaches, and pears. She hated the taste of canned food compared to fresh, but it saved hours of work in the kitchen.

She stepped up to the meat counter—and stepped on something soft and squishy. It was a dead rat. So that was what Frank had caught. She stepped back in disgust—and into Steamer. His arms went around her.

Years later, memories of that moment would return, bright and clear and poignant. But in this year, this day, this moment, Megan was merely confused. The only thing she knew was that she loved him—and that he was a dirty, lying rat. He was cold-heartedly playing with her, too, using her to gain information; when he had enough, he'd arrest her and all her family.

He steadied her on her feet, and she extracted herself from his embrace with a small, embarrassed smile. Now what the hell was she supposed to do? At the party last night, Steamer had seemed to be rather drunk. He'd been pretending, of course, and stayed sober so he could watch what was going on. How much had he seen? What did he know already?

She wiped the back of her hand across her forehead. "Sorry. That was some party last night."

He grinned sheepishly at her. "Uh, yeah. I don't usually drink that much. Come to think of it, I don't really like booze that much."

Steamer trotted back and forth from store to truck, his arms laden with food. Megan's scent seemed to cling to him. Whatever perfume she wore, it was light and mildly spicy and did not overwhelm her natural clean smell.

Her response to stepping on the dead rat had left him more convinced than ever that she was the woman he wanted. Her lack of squeamishness told him she'd be able to handle the tough parts of life. The feel of her firm, slender figure threatened to crack the shell of armor he was trying to build around his heart.

He'd heard her singing "Beneath Still Waters" for the guests after breakfast, and her voice had made his heart ache. And last night she'd turned down Alan's offer with a guilty look. She'd somehow knuckled under to her husband and his parents— Steamer was sure of that. Something was lurking beneath the surface of their lives, like a cougar creeping up on its prey.

He was about to step into a nest of vipers, and for his own sanity, he had to find some way to stop this. Ah, he'd tell her about Allison. Of course, he'd have to bend the truth a little, but it would work.

★ ★ ★ ★ ★

Megan focused on the road, ignoring Steamer, who sat grimly silent beside her. Buying and loading all that food had taken longer than she'd planned, and now the sun was dropping behind the Tetons, bloodying the peaks with dying light. She pressed harder on the accelerator. She wanted to get home before dark.

A mile later, the right rear tire blew out with a loud pop, and the truck sagged and dragged to a stop. Steamer's eyes snapped open. They looked at each other and burst into laughter.

"Well," Steamer said, "we can't sit here until morning. Let's get it changed."

They worked together to jack up the truck and loosen the lug nuts. He handed them to her to hold while he removed the wheel and brought the spare into place.

The weight of the big lug nuts in her hand gave her an opportunity to break the silence. She dropped one, exclaimed, "Oh, damn," and bent to pick it up. Steamer looked up from his task.

In a tone as casual as she could manage, she asked, "You know a lot about me, Steamer, but I don't know much about you."

He cranked down a nut with the wrench. "So, what would you like to know?"

"Well, you must have a girlfriend, right?"

"Yes, her name is Allison. I asked her to marry me just before I left."

He tightened the last nut, ignoring her. She controlled her impatience and kept her tone light and social. "And? Did she accept?"

"Uh, well, no. She said no."

"Oh."

★ ★ ★ ★ ★

A half hour later they drove under the sign at the entrance to the Rocking Lazy F ranch. A few yards along, Megan saw movement outside Pia and Tommy's cabin and slowed to watch. Someone was getting into a truck; she recognized Parley as he got in, slammed the door, and drove off. For a brief moment, his headlights shone on Pia, who shielded her face and ran into her cabin.

"Mom! What's the matter?"

Pia nearly jumped out of her skin. Tommaso was supposed to be asleep, but she'd stumbled over the threshold and slammed the cabin door hard against the wall. No wonder he'd awakened.

"Nothing. Go back to sleep."

"But, Mom—"

"Tommaso! Please, just go back to sleep. Leave me alone." She regretted immediately speaking so harshly to him, but she needed time alone.

He reluctantly slid back under the covers. "G'night, Mom."

"Sleep well, darling."

"Nothing" was the price she'd had to pay to ensure she was included in the party going into the backcountry. She crossed the cabin and went into the bathroom. The kerosene lantern was not very bright, and she pulled it closer so she could examine herself in the mirror.

Parley had been rough on her. Her mouth and cheeks ached from the impact of his heavy beard; her tongue felt as if it had been pulled out by the roots. She desperately wanted a hot bath to wash away the foul scent of him, but there was no one around to heat water for her. She pumped the tub full of cold water anyway and shivered her way into it. After a while the pain in her vagina eased, and she washed, dried herself, and crept into her own bed.

Stupid barbarian cowboy. They'd been discussing plans for the forthcoming trip when she mentioned that she would ride her jumping saddle.

"Like hell you will," he'd said in a cold voice.

"Please? I do not understand. Why not?"

"Too dangerous."

She'd laughed and smiled at him. "Still I do not understand. Why is it more dangerous than one of those monstrous things you put on a horse?"

He'd glared at her, lips compressed. "Too damn easy for you to fall off. Nothing to hang on to."

"Hang on? Do you mean I am supposed to hold on to the saddle?" She'd heard the note of incredulity in her own voice.

"Maybe you ain't got a clear picture what it's like back there. The trails are rough, real steep up and down. Narrow, too. You'll look down one side of your horse, you'll look straight down a thousand feet."

A peal of laugher had burst from her. "So what? Did you not know I am a champion jumper? Hold on to the saddle? How would I control my horse over a jump if I did that?"

The laughter was a mistake. His face had hardened. "I'm the trail boss, and what I say goes. You ride a stock saddle, or you ride a chair here in the lodge."

She'd dropped her protests after that, until he'd gotten out of his chair to go home. She'd trailed him out the door and put both hands on his arm. "Perhaps we could discuss this further, in, ah, in private?"

No man treated her that way and got away with it. He'd have to die, of course, but how? That was the problem.

That he was strong and powerful, he'd demonstrated beyond doubt. That he was cunning and determined, she now knew. As the trail boss, his word would be law. If he died during the trip, who would lead them? She certainly would be a babe lost in the woods, and she suspected all the rest of the Hollywood people would be as well.

She'd offered herself to him voluntarily, and there'd been no need for him to treat her like dirt. She'd somehow find a time to kill him—and then whimpered as she remembered her doubts about the killing power of her Colt .25. It was time to end her doubts.

She dressed in dark clothes and crept out into the night. On her ride this morning she'd seen several calves in the pasture. It was a long walk from her cabin, but the distance would make it unlikely that the shot would be heard.

When she finally got back into bed, she was severely disappointed. The calf had not dropped dead but only bucked, bawled, and run away. Her pistol was not as powerful as she'd hoped.

Junior had been slouching in the second-best armchair at home, consumed with rage. Jasmine was *his* woman, and the sight of his pa's gloves in her bedroom had nearly destroyed him—until he'd figured he could use them against him somehow. But he'd still found no way to use his new weapon, no matter how he twisted and turned things around.

But now maybe he wouldn't have to. Pa had shoved the door open with a big grin and a howdy. He came back into the parlor with a mug of coffee and dropped into the best armchair. "So, son, what brings you here? You out of clean clothes? Money?"

Junior swallowed the poisoned words he wanted to spit out. Pa had just given him the perfect excuse. "Um, well, I *could* use a little extra cash these days."

His father's smile turned into a sneer. "And just how did you plan to earn a *little* extra cash?"

Junior hesitated. If he'd misjudged his father's mood, this could turn into a disaster. He was going to have to kiss his ass anyway, but maybe it wouldn't be so bad. "Well, I thought maybe you could use an extra hand. On the trail. With all those Hollywood dudes, I mean." He held his breath, waiting for the explosion.

"Do you expect me to take a backsliding heathen like you along?" His father's voice rattled the windowpanes. "A punk kid who mocks God, who ain't been in church in months, who doesn't honor his father and mother?"

"Pa, please listen. I've seen the light; I really have. You're right, about God and all, and I want to come back into the fold. To learn more about the love of God." He hesitated briefly; was he overplaying his hand? "From you."

"Oh, yeah?" Pa glared at him for a long time, then his expression softened. "You don't expect me to believe that, do you?"

Junior kept an earnest, pleading look plastered on his face. "I do for true, Pa. I know I've been wrong, and all I ask is a chance to prove it to you. That's why I'm here."

"All right. We'll pray on it. God will look into your soul and judge you."

They knelt side by side before the large gold cross in the family chapel. An hour of fervent prayer later, and Junior was sure his knees would crack when he stood, but Pa had agreed to take him along.

CHAPTER 16

Friday Morning, June 19

Megan stretched her arms along the top rail of the fence and closed her eyes. The morning sun poured down out of a cloudless sky. It warmed her body but did nothing to drive away the vexation and humiliation she'd felt after she and Steamer left Isaiah's yesterday afternoon. Now that she knew he was a Prohi agent in disguise, it was clear as the sky above that his "love" for her was a despicable act designed to get evidence against her family. How could she have been so blind?

If Steamer got the evidence he wanted and the Prohibition Unit arrested them, it would mean the end of all her hopes and dreams. It would mean jail for all of them. No matter how she felt about Terry, his witch of a mother, and poor old crippled TT, she had to protect them. *But how?* she wondered.

If only she were rich, she could hire lawyers to protect them. The movie projector in her head started up, throwing images of the future on the wall of her imagination. There she was, up on the silver screen, bigger than life, in one of her favorite roles: a world-famous singer. Her singing and playing would give women strength and courage and make strong men weep, and she would earn a lot of money.

Stop daydreaming and face reality, Megan. She had about one chance in a million of that ever happening. But what if Steamer was *not* a secret agent? What if he really was just a movie director? She felt a spark of hope; maybe she could ask Sally Mann.

But it was too late for that, as they were leaving shortly.

She opened her eyes. Parley was directing the loading of a large truck as a dozen people moved purposefully about, loading boxes, bags, and strange-looking apparatuses. Alan had decided the weather was going to cooperate and ordered them to get loaded and get on the trail. Steamer stood near the truck with a pad of paper in his hands. *Probably a checklist,* she decided.

Two men appeared, struggling under the weight of a large steamer trunk they dropped on the ground with a bang. *Daphne Divine* and *Segal Studios* were stenciled on the trunk's side. It had to be her wardrobe trunk. She could see Parley glowering with anger at the whole process: he'd had no idea—neither had Megan, for that matter—about the amount of gear the film crew would bring. He'd had to rent an extra truck and more pack mules.

And just where was Luella? She looked around but did not see her. She was sure to be sleeping late, as she always did. Megan would go fetch her shortly, but for now she just wanted a few more moments with her fantasy. She closed her eyes again. She had to figure out some way of worming Steamer's secret out of him.

A faint tingling sensation crossed her eyelids, as if the tip of an angel's wing had brushed them. It had to be the sunlight, didn't it, or her imagination? But the sensation grew stronger. She cracked her eyelids open. Steamer was watching her. Not just watching her, but . . . *sketching* her?

She pushed away from the fence and strolled over to where he stood looking down at the paper in his hand. "May I see it?"

He'd obviously not heard her approach. He looked up with surprise, then back down at the sketch pad. "It's not finished yet."

"Why are you invading my privacy?"

He ducked his head. "Well, I suppose you could look at it that way." He slapped the pad shut and turned away. "My apologies."

Annoyance prickled through her. "I still want to see it."

He hesitated, turned back, and handed the pad to her. He'd sketched her leaning against the fence rail, arms outstretched along the top. Her posture had tightened her shirt across her breasts, and he'd made her look glamorous, exciting, and sexy. A new and different movie scene flashed on: Steamer directing her in the role of a sultry temptress. She would have run that scene all the rest of the day and night—except that she could see Tommy galloping her way, with his mother trailing behind him.

She handed the pad back to Steamer, controlling her rampaging emotions. "Thanks. You've made me look like a floozy." Which was not true; she was flattered and flustered by the sketch, but she was damned if she was going to let him know that. If she was nasty to him, maybe she could push him into showing his hand.

Steamer merely waggled his head slowly from side to side. He was saved from having to reply by the arrival of Tommy and his mother.

"Good morning, Mrs. Foxy," Tommy said.

"Tommaso!" Pia grabbed him. Megan thought she was going to hit him, but she pulled him closer instead. "You must call Mrs. Foxworth by her proper name."

Tommy squirmed in his mother's grip. "That's what Steamer calls her," he said with a defiant note.

Megan blushed, then giggled helplessly as she saw Steamer gazing off into the distance with an innocent look. "It's all right, Mrs. Donatelli; I don't mind. He can call me that if he wants." She turned to Tommy. "Just don't call me late to dinner, okay?"

He looked at her, mouth half open, frowning with puzzlement, then burst into laughter. "Oh, I get it! That's an American joke, isn't it?"

Megan nodded. She could see Parley moving toward them; his men were closing the doors of the rented truck. "Right. Now then, are you all ready for the big adventure?" she asked as Parley loomed ever larger.

"You betcha, Mrs. Foxy. Hi, Mr. Frampton."

Parley barely glanced at Tommy and deliberately ignored Steamer. "We finally got all that damn gear loaded, Megan. We're going to the trailhead, start packing this crap on the mules, then head on out to the first campsite. There's another truck coming in a few minutes to haul all them film people out. And you, of course."

He turned to Pia. "Morning, ma'am. There's room in the truck if you'd like to ride out with me?"

Megan saw Pia stiffen and draw back slightly. Her voice trembled a bit as she said, "Thank you, but I'd rather ride out with the film crew."

"Suit yourself." He spun on his heels and marched off toward the truck.

Megan saw Pia relax and realized she was terrified of Parley. Now that she was paying attention, Megan saw that Pia had tried to cover a bruise on her cheek with heavy makeup.

Come to think of it, there'd been rumors and gossip about the Framptons when they had arrived in town two years ago. They'd had to leave Ashton, up north, for some reason never made clear. Megan normally hated rumors, but Doc Byrne had mentioned that Mrs. Frampton was recovering from a broken arm.

Her speculations were interrupted when she saw Pia move closer to Steamer and put one hand on his arm. When he glanced down at her, she smiled a big, sunny smile.

"Steamer, would you come look at Tommaso's saddle, please?

I want to make sure it is suitable for him."

"Of course, Pia."

"Come along, Tommaso. I'm sure Mrs. Foxy has work to do."

Megan clamped her mouth shut. Steamer was a lying rat and a threat to her family. Besides, she didn't love him. So why was she feeling jealous?

A grinding noise interrupted her speculations. A two-ton truck of indefinite vintage squealed to a stop with a clatter of its faded red stakes. The sides could be left in place to contain a load of calves or removed to allow the flatbed to be loaded with bales of hay.

Junior Frampton jumped down from the cab. When he saw her, his manner changed abruptly from arrogant to self-conscious. He tipped his hat to her. "Morning, Mrs. Foxworth."

After she had chased him from her bathroom covered in soapy water, he'd not come near her for days. Now here he was, too close for comfort, acting like an eager puppy. Her heart retreated into a dark corner, growling a warning. He had, somehow, changed, but she was sure he was still dangerous.

"Good Morning, Junior. Nice weather."

He inched closer. "Uh, ma'am, if you don't mind, could I talk with you for just a minute?"

"What is it?"

He came closer and lowered his voice. "I just wanted to apologize for, uh, well, what happened Thursday night. I'm real sorry it happened, and I pray you can find it in your heart to forgive me."

Her heart growled a louder warning. People don't flip one hundred-eighty degrees in two days. She nodded, a tiny inclination of her head. "All right. Just don't let it happen again, or I'll tell your father."

"Oh, no, ma'am. I promise."

"All right." She frowned at him. "Come to think of it, why are you here? Last time you said anything about your father, you told me he was furious with you. I thought you and he were on the outs."

"Oh! What happened was, Pa and me, we sort of patched up our differences, so he asked me to come along and help. 'Sides, Terry asked me to sorta keep an eye on you."

An alarm sounded in her mind, as faint and distant as the whirring of a rattlesnake hidden deep in the brush. "Keep an eye on me? What on earth does that mean?"

"Well, you know, just to make sure you're safe and all."

"Oh. I see. How sweet of him." She frowned. "But your father . . . he's not angry with you now?"

"Not anymore." He leaned forward eagerly "I had a revelation right, uh, after I left your bathroom. Anyway, God told me it was my duty to ride beside Pa on this trip. I see now that Pa was right, God *is* up there, and I'm going to be down on my knees every night praying to Him to forgive me. And I'm askin' Pa to pray right alongside me."

He pulled something from the front pocket of his overalls. "TT loaned me his Colt .45." She recognized the pearl-handled revolver. It was TT's pride and joy, a commemorative model with gold engraving on the barrel.

"What for?"

"Protection."

"From what?"

"Uh, well, cougars and other things."

Which was foolish, she thought. Cougars were probably more afraid of men than men were of them. Especially with such a large crowd, the nearest cougar would be miles away. But she said, "Oh. That's sweet of TT. Now I think we'd better get these dudes aboard, don't you?"

"Yes, ma'am. I'll go herd them over."

174

Had Junior really reconciled with his father? Parley had been livid for years about his son's backsliding and his refusal to accept the god his father revered. Junior reminded her of a puppy that had alternately been kicked, then petted, and didn't know if it should bite or lick.

Her sense of alarm receded, leaving her wondering why she'd been worried. It was sweet of Terry to be concerned, but Junior was, after all, a paid hand. He'd do as she told him, and of course she could take care of herself.

She saw Junior open the rear entrance to the truck and put the loading ramp in place. The Hollywood crew began gathering their saddlebags and moving toward the truck. Everything was going to be all right.

Except maybe the weather; a cloud shadow had fallen on the truck. She looked up. Dark clouds had begun to munch on the blue of the sky, swallowing the light. She checked to be sure her saddle slicker was tied tightly across her saddlebags, then moved them closer to the truck.

Junior now strode down the loading ramp and stood, hands on hips, surveying the gathering film crew. "Mornin', everyone. You all ready for the big day?" A cheer answered him. "Well then, let's get loaded up." He stepped aside, bowed, and made a sweeping gesture at the narrow ramp.

"Ooh, wait a minute."

Megan watched in disbelief as Luella sashayed through the crowd. Now where in hell had she been hiding herself? *In bed*, Megan guessed, from the looks of it.

Several gobs of fresh horse plop had fallen from the truck; she was eyeing these morsels with comic distaste. "Do you mean," she cooed, "that you use this truck to carry both cows *and* humans, Mr. Frampton?"

"Only truck we have, ma'am."

Luella gazed at him wide-eyed. "You mean we have to ride in

there with all that cow poop?"

Megan bit back a cry of warning as Junior moved closer to her sister. In a voice that could magnetize water, he said, "Well now, ma'am, why don't you just call me Junior?" His gaze measured her from top to bottom, bottom to top, and then stopped one-third of the way down. "You folks brought so much gear, we had to borrow another truck. And just who might you be?"

"Daphne Divine."

This time Megan had to bite back a shriek of laughter. If the camera had been rolling, Junior's expression would have won a prize. He looked as if he'd stepped off his horse in the middle of a stampede.

Megan had to give him credit. He remounted quickly and with little apparent damage. "Well, now, Miz Divine, there's a tarp on the floor, to protect you and your gear." He paused, as if for her approval. She continued to smile at him. "Tell you what, though. You can ride in the cab with me, okay?"

She nodded, and he escorted her to the high step to the cab. There she wriggled awkwardly for a moment in her tight riding skirt, then beamed a helpless look at him over her shoulder. He boosted her into the cab with both hands on her bottom.

The watching cast and crew burst into applause, then began climbing the ramp. It was a good thing Parley had already departed for the trailhead. If he'd seen his son's actions just now, the resulting explosion would have been heard for miles. Megan reached down to pick up her saddlebags.

"Now then, Megan, whyn't you let me help you with them bags?" Junior's tone of voice had been deferential, but she wondered if mice, waiting for the rattlesnake to strike, felt the same way she did. The urge to bolt and run like hell in the opposite direction nearly overwhelmed her.

No, she'd be damned if she was going to let their hired hand intimidate her. She clutched the bags closer to her. "Ah, no thank you, Junior. You know I always handle my gear myself."

He reached again for the bags. "Aw now, I just want to make it up to you."

She pulled back and lowered her bags to the ground at her feet. "Are you going to continue to work for us, Junior? Or will you be working for your father from now on?"

An ugly expression came and went in an instant, frightening her. He reached again for the bags. "No need to be unpleasant, Megan. I done apologized to you."

A voice behind her said, "The lady said she wanted to handle them herself."

Junior's gaze shifted over her shoulder. "Well now, if it isn't Mr. Steamer Daniels." He said "Steamer" the way little boys say "nyah nyah." "That's a mighty unusual name."

She waited for an angry response from Steamer, but he only shrugged. "Yep. Bought myself a Stanley Steamer automobile a while back. So being as my real name is Stanley, my friends started calling me Steamer. Sort of stuck." He looked Junior up and down. "And what were you named after, Junior?"

Junior's mouth twitched as he studied Steamer's clothing. He was dressed like a movie cowboy: white ten-gallon hat, red bandana at the neck of his sky-blue, silk shirt. His waist overalls were spotless and pressed, cinched in place by a stamped leather belt with a large silver buckle.

"Me and the boys," Junior whispered, "have ways of dealing with smart-ass *dudes.*"

"Now here I thought real cowboys always took care of their own problems, without help."

Megan was sure Junior would explode, but he fired a poisonous look at Steamer and reached for her bags. Steamer bent down at the same time. Megan thought they were going to have a tug of war, but Junior was suddenly pivoting back and forth, and the bags landed on his boots with a thump.

What had Steamer done to throw Junior off balance? It sure looked like he'd used some sort of oriental fighting art he'd learned for a movie.

Junior jerked his scuffed, dirty boots from beneath the bags, tensed to swing a punch, then glanced covertly at the crew, who were watching in silent curiosity. A vicious smile broke across his face. "Well now, I reckon you owe me a boot shine, Mr. Daniels. I'll be around to collect when we get to camp tonight."

"I guess you'd like a spit shine, right?"

Junior's face darkened, and Steamer saw him tense to swing again. A piping voice interrupted him. "Would you like some help with that, Mrs. Foxy?" Tommy was clumping toward them in his new cowboy boots. "Hi, Steamer. Hi, Mr. Frampton." He pivoted on his heels, toes raised off the ground. "Mr. Frampton, Mom says I can't ride a wild mule, like Steamer said I could. Why not?"

Megan could see this was all news to Junior, an impression confirmed by Steamer's innocent look.

Junior said, "Ah, well, no, that just won't work. You're not strong enough."

"Aw, please? Steamer said I could."

Junior gave Tommy a clumsy pat on the head. "I doubt if Mr. Daniels here would know the difference between a mule and a Percheron. Takes experience to ride a mule. Doesn't matter how strong you are."

Tommy looked at Steamer, and his face crumpled with disappointment. "It doesn't?"

"Nope." Junior turned away with a smirk.

"But Steamer said—"

"Steamer don't know jack shit about livestock, and you're stupid if you listen to a drugstore cowboy like him." Junior moved away toward the cab of the truck.

Tommy swiveled violently on the heels of his boots, fighting tears. Megan turned away. If she could only have a son, a son as adorable as Tommy, things would be all right at home.

Steamer squatted on his heels, bringing his eyes to Tommy's level. "Let me feel those muscles." Tommy sniffed and halfheartedly bulged his biceps. "No, come on. Make a real muscle."

Tommy strained mightily as Steamer felt both biceps and then his forearms. "If Junior had felt those muscles, he wouldn't have said that." Steamer rose to his feet.

Megan sensed someone at her side and turned. Pia had come up quietly to join them. She gazed at Steamer with open admiration.

"Are you sure?" Tommy's face glowed as Steamer nodded solemn reassurance. "I guess he don't know me real well, not like you do, Steamer."

"Well, if it was up to me, I'd let you ride a mule." Steamer paused, gazed thoughtfully at Tommy, and shook his head. "Except that—Oh, never mind." He turned as if to walk away.

"Never mind *what*?"

"Ah, well, no. I don't think they'd have any of them here. Say, Pia, why don't—"

"Any of what?" Tommy's voice ratcheted up another notch.

"Well, um, those Grand Canyon Jumping Mules."

"Jumping Mules? You mean like Mom's jumping horses?"

Steamer rubbed his face and gazed at Tommy as if gauging what he should reveal. "No, not exactly. See, one day a couple of years ago, one of the mules they use to ferry dudes down to the bottom . . . well, it just jumped off the trail."

"All . . . all the way down?"

"Uh, yeah. 'Course, the dude riding it went all the way down, too."

"That's horrible!"

"Yes, but it turns out, only one mule had this defect . . . but then some of her children also jumped, and . . . well, you see the problem."

"Did she have many children?"

"Unfortunately, yes. She did."

Steamer could see Pia's gaze alternating between him and Tommy, her expression a mixture of disbelief and curiosity. "But Steamer, there must be a way to tell which ones inherited her defect?"

"Yeah, how about that, Steamer?" Tommy said.

"After a while, someone remembered that old Nellie had one blue eye and one brown eye, and so did all the ones who jumped later. So they're pretty sure that's how you tell, and so no one puts dudes on any mules with the same problem."

"Hot damn! Come on, Mom, let's get going. You too, Mrs. Foxy." He seized his mother's hand and led her up the ramp.

CHAPTER 17

Friday Morning, June 19

Pia was more or less satisfied. She'd had a quiet conversation with Alan after breakfast that would, to an outside observer, have appeared warm and friendly. The content of that conversation was, however, far from friendly. Her warning had resulted in a promise from him to rein Steamer in, to control his profligate shooting method, and to finish the production pronto (as they said out here).

The truck was tightly packed with humanity, so there was not much room to jostle about as it passed through the ranch gate and onto the highway. Which meant she was frequently pressed against Steamer and had an excuse to steady herself with a hand on his arm, a smile, and a murmured excuse for her clumsiness. This in turn gave her an excuse to open a conversation with him.

"I'm so curious about this screen test you've promised Mrs. Foxworth, Steamer. It sounds, well, so difficult. But then, I hate tests!"

He smiled down at her, and her heart fluttered. "I doubt it will be difficult for her, Pia. She's really quite beautiful and extraordinarily talented. Too bad we can't capture her singing right on the film, but then I hear they're working on that. The movies will talk, soon. Sing, too."

"How fascinating. But tell me, will it take a long time? To do it, I mean?"

"Depends. She deserves the best possible chance to do well, so I want to shoot several setups with her. And be sure that her costume and makeup are right." He glanced up at the sky, now a dark grey. "The weather has to cooperate, of course—but then, that applies to the whole shoot. If it rains, well . . ."

"Oh, I'm sure the weather will change. So, how long would all that take?"

"Two or three hours, perhaps half a day."

"I see." She felt like snarling at this bad news but forced a smile. "Thank you. This movie-making is so fascinating."

She was angry, and she knew the emotion came from fear. Uncle had given her orders to see that the production was finished in the shortest time possible with no more extravagant measures. "Get the film in the can now," was how he'd put it. The weather was turning nasty, and, on top of that, Alan had obviously not said anything to Steamer yet. She didn't want to think about what Uncle would do to her, or to Tommaso, if she failed.

Her uneasiness deepened as she tried to think of ways to speed things up. She'd discarded several ideas when the solution came to her. Of course! Kill Megan! Or maybe not kill her, but just disfigure her. Pia could spill hot food on her face; she'd find something that would work.

Beside her, Steamer made a little groan. She glanced up at him. He looked worried. "Is everything all right?"

"Huh? Oh sure, just thinking," he replied without looking at her.

Steamer was worried, but not about the weather or production problems. After tussling with Junior over Megan's saddlebags, he'd realized that Junior was made of granite, oak, and rawhide lashed together with baling wire—and that *he* had become soft. He'd spent too many years in the easy life in Hollywood with no outdoor work and not much exercise. Junior would whip his ass in any fight, and a fight seemed inevitable.

But why in hell was Junior so hostile toward him? Okay, he was a stranger who'd just landed in a tightly knit community. His appearance would have caused less disruption if he'd been an Eskimo or a Chink or a Jap. Not that there was anything wrong with the Japanese. His jiu-jitsu instructor had been a charming, witty, and intelligent man.

Back to thinking about Junior, Steamer knew that Junior was their hired hand. He'd be loyal to his paycheck and feel he had to protect the boss's wife from preying outsiders. It made sense. So how did Steamer avoid a fight? Stay the hell away from Megan, far away, no matter what his heart wanted.

He felt a gentle, warm hand on his arm. He looked down, and his good intentions evaporated like mist in the morning sun.

As the truck rolled farther and farther from the ranch, Megan felt the ice inside her break up and release an avalanche of humiliation, frustration, and annoyance. When the worst of it had passed, she cursed silently. *Damn Junior, damn Fiona, damn Terry.* Husband, home, and in-laws were all anchored inside her like porcupine quills. Even if she had the right to pull them out—which she did not, did she?—there was the pain—oh, the pain.

She glanced aside at Steamer. He was deep in conversation with Pia, who was smiling and touching him to emphasize whatever it was she was saying. *Damn Steamer, too.* He was swallowing all her sugarcoated flattery and smacking his lips.

Megan inhaled deeply as the truck rolled through the great basin that formed the "hole" that was Jackson Hole. She wanted to sort out the smells of pine, horses, dust, and good clean air. She had smelled nothing but dirty dishes and cow-shit–stained overalls for months. As the town receded, the white-nippled peaks of the Grand Tetons rose before them; the Snake River glittered like a scar across the rib cage of the range. Brilliant sunlight and deep shadows fell across the landscape, and steam rose from the rain-soaked earth where the sun touched it. Thank heaven the rain had stopped.

Then her humiliation and annoyance struck her again. How was she supposed to unravel this gigantic knot of a problem? She had to find out what Steamer was up to. Was he really a secret agent, sent to find evidence and arrest them all? It wouldn't do any harm if she were friendly to him, would it? If she behaved like an old sourpuss, she'd never get anything out of him. One catches more flies with honey than with vinegar. All she had to do was remember he was the enemy, and she'd be all right.

She looked up at Steamer. He'd finished talking to Pia and was gazing off into the distance with a worried expression. She laid her hand on his arm. "Steamer, tell me something about this screen test you're talking about. I'm kind of worried about it."

The warmth of his smile nearly undid her resolve, but she kept a cool, professional distance. She'd read about screen tests in movie magazines and dreamed of one day having one. Now that it was an imminent reality and no longer a dream, she was truly nervous. But by the time Steamer finished his patient coaching, she was confident she could pull it off.

Doodah, Shorty, and Curly watched from the fence as the truck bumped to a halt in a large clearing. Several dozen horses and mules milled about in the corral behind them, hooves squelching in the mud. Off to one side, a large canvas fly covered the kitchen. A wooden shed for gear stood behind the corral, and, tucked discreetly in the woods a dozen yards away, were two privies.

Doodah Cummings wore a pair of bib-and-brace coveralls two sizes too big for him, heavy work shoes, a red bandana, and nothing else. He watched as Junior jumped down and raced around to open the door on the passenger side. He muttered, "Oh, no," as a curvaceous blonde wriggled to the ground.

Shorty straightened his six-foot, seven-inch frame and asked, "Now what's that supposed to mean?"

"Oh, yeah, you ain't been riding with us long enough to know what's going on." Doodah dropped his voice to the back-fence gossip level. "Junior, he'll screw anything he can get into his bedroll. He wants all the heifers to himself."

"So?"

"So his pa is always talking religion at him, about how he ain't supposed to do it unless he's married."

"So why don't he just leave Junior behind if he's so worried about the dudines?" Shorty asked.

"He generally does." Curly Martin pulled off a disreputable hat, revealing a head of bare skin that he scratched vigorously. "I don't get it. Parley, he's never wanted his boy along on these trips before. They been fighting like two cats in a gunnysack for years. Anyway, you can't have no more than one bull in a pasture."

"Do you reckon he's ever going to get around to letting them dudes out?" Shorty asked. "Should I go help?"

Doodah spat a stream of tobacco juice. "Looks like he's getting to it now."

Junior put the loading ramp in place, and the dudes began straggling down, carrying their luggage. There was an interruption in the flow of people, and a boy appeared at the head of the ramp.

"Hey, Mom! Watch!" he yelled and went down on all fours

and crawled down the ramp, mooing loudly. Another man went down behind him, mooing even louder, and they collapsed in a heap at the bottom. The dudes applauded.

Shorty said, "Well, them two is going to be fun to have around."

"Hey, Doodah." Curly shoved his hat back on his head. "Do you reckon the kid is his son?"

Doodah said nothing but whistled "doodah, doodah" instead.

Curly looked at him with a frown. "Ain't never heard you say that before. What's wrong?"

"Nothing. I know that guy," he said in a hoarse whisper. He put his finger to his lips, jumped down, then slid along the fence, keeping his face turned away from the dudes. "Don't say nothing."

"Now what in thunder is he up to?" Shorty asked.

Curly watched Doodah sneak away. "Damned if I know."

Steamer looked up from his sketch pad as he heard his name.

"Come on over here," Alan called. "We need to talk."

Steamer closed the pad, slid it into his shoulder bag, and ambled over to where Alan was conferring with Esse and Paul. They were leaning against the front of the truck. Someone was still in back, moving around and jiggling the truck. Pia stood slightly behind Alan, listening. He could see Alan was in a foul mood.

"What's up?"

"Parley just told me we'd better stay put tonight. The weather."

"Seems like a good idea," Steamer said. "We could—"

"Wait one damn minute!" Alan was red faced. "I'm not finished. He said it was up to me, and I say we're moving out. We're talking about how we can adjust the production schedule."

Steamer looked around. The film crew was gathering and

stacking the production gear in one place; Parley's hands were doing the same with the food and camping equipment.

"Alan, hang on one minute. Look at that sky."

Everyone looked up. Blue sky still showed above them, but dark clouds were closing in like a noose tightening. Alan glowered at them.

"Make sense, Alan," Steamer continued. "We can't shoot in the rain. If the cameras get wet . . . and what about Daphne's costumes? If we shoot now, it will cause a delay ten times as long as if we wait for the sun."

Alan jammed his hands in his coat pockets and scowled fiercely.

"Look, I'll tell you what we can do," Steamer said in a reasonable tone. "I'll just take a camera and one reflector, and we'll just go over there and shoot the screen test of Megan."

Alan glared at him. "All right, all right."

Steamer saw Pia give Alan a slight nudge. He would have missed it if someone moving in the background hadn't pulled his attention in her direction. What was that all about?

"Okay, but no more than one reel," Alan said. "And that better be the end of this screen test shit. I'd hate to lose a good director who can't control shooting costs."

"Okay, okay." Steamer looked around for Megan. She was nowhere to be seen. He strode off in search of F-Stop. Megan would turn up eventually.

Sheriff Goodman had called it quits for the day and was inserting the key into the door when he felt someone tap him on the arm. He turned, startled. The man behind him was, beyond any doubt, an easterner. He wore a snappy double-breasted, three-button suit in a light-grey wool with peaked lapels on the coat and cuffed trousers. The suit was tailored to perfection and must have set him back a good twenty-five dollars.

The sheriff wanted to get home to his dinner, and this interruption did not sit well with him. "Something I can do for you, mister? It's after hours."

The stranger reached into the breast pocket of his coat and pulled out a leather case. The sheriff caught a brief glimpse of a brass badge before the man flipped it closed. "Ray Drago. From the Prohibition Unit. Can we go inside?"

The sheriff nodded weakly and fumbled with the key for a long moment, giving himself time to calm down. What in hell was a federal agent doing here, and how could he get rid of him without raising his suspicions?

They entered the office, but the sheriff remained standing. "Can we make this quick? Like I said, it's after hours, and my wife is expecting me home for supper."

"Yes, of course." Agent Drago smiled a polite but cold smile. He extracted a piece of paper from his pocket and handed it to him. "Have you seen this woman?"

"Why do you want to know?"

Drago's jaw twitched, and he took a deep breath. "I'm here to enforce the provisions of the Volstead Act of 1919, which, as I'm sure you know, prohibits the manufacture and sale of alcoholic beverages in this country. She is a person of interest in a case I'm investigating. Of course, if you think someone is covering up for her . . ."

The sheriff swallowed hard. "I see. Well, she came into town on Monday. She's with those folks from Hollywood."

Drago looked at him without blinking. "And do you know where she might be at this moment?"

"I do. She went out to the backcountry with them. They'll be camping at Leidy Lake."

"How do I get there?"

"First off, you'll have to drive out to Kelly, about thirty miles from here. Then you'll have to rent a horse at Jason's livery and ride about five or six hours." He gestured out the window. "In the rain."

Drago seemed to sag slightly. "I see." He held out his hand. "Thanks for the information. I wasn't expecting this, and I'm going to have to contact my superiors for instructions. Where is the telegraph office?"

The sheriff gave him directions, showed him out the door, and once again locked it. As he walked home, he thought back to how Agent Drago had flipped his badge in and out so fast. He wished he'd gotten a better look at it—but he wasn't about to ask him. The less he had to do with the Revenue Department, the better.

CHAPTER 18

Saturday Morning, June 20

Steamer awoke before sunrise, dressed, and went to use the latrine. It was quite luxurious for such a facility in the wilderness: a folding box, with an open bottom and a toilet-seat shaped hole in the top, was placed atop a three-foot-deep hole. A roll of toilet paper adorned a forked stick jabbed into the ground close at hand. A blue tarpaulin around the men's facility provided privacy; a red tarp shielded the women's.

He walked back to the main campsite just as the sun sent a ruddy shaft of light into the open cook tent. It filtered through smoke from the fire before continuing on to illuminate the two women sitting inside. Betty, a weatherworn blonde, was thrashing chords from a guitar. Although she never quite got them right, neither did she make the same mistake twice. Joellen, equally weatherworn, was draped across a pile of firewood like a dozing cat. Her dark hair glowed in the sunlight, and one finger attempted to keep time with the music.

As his shadow fell across Joellen, she opened her eyes. "Hey, Betty," she called, "we got a customer."

Betty put her guitar away and turned to him. "You hungry, Mr. Daniels?"

"My name is Steamer, and, yes, I could eat a horse."

The corners of her mouth turned up. "You must want to walk home."

Steamer laughed. "I'll settle for eggs and bacon. And coffee."

190

He peered into a pot sitting at the back of the cooking grill. "I don't suppose that would be grits, would it?"

"It would," Betty said. She banged a spoonful onto his plate. "Eggs coming up." She tipped the big blue-enameled coffeepot over his tin cup, then flipped two fried eggs onto his plate beside the grits.

Joellen held a pitcher of batter over the griddle, ready to pour. "Hotcakes, Steamer?" Her smile was wide and inviting.

"Not now, thanks." The rest of the film crew was lining up behind him, and he moved aside. "Maybe when I finish this." He sat on a packing case to eat and watched as his friends and co-workers were served breakfast.

Movement outside the cook tent caught his attention. He saw F-Stop plant the camera in place facing the chow line, with Alan behind him issuing orders. A waste of film, he thought; none of this footage would cut into the story line.

He was mopping up the last of his grits when he saw Tommy approach the two cooks. Paul Marshal hovered close behind him. Tommy had obviously never seen food cooked over an open fire and was bursting with enthusiastic curiosity. Paul waited, shifting from one foot to the other. His rolls of fat jiggled up and down, and he drummed a nervous tattoo on his plate with his fork.

Then, just as Betty lifted a spatula of fried eggs toward Tommy's plate, Paul thrust his plate above Tommy's, and the eggs plopped onto it.

"Hey, those were my eggs!" Tommy squawked.

Paul smirked at him. "Next time don't ask so many questions, kid."

"Hey, you!"

Paul stopped and turned. Joellen rose and waggled a two-tined pot fork at him. "You pull a stunt like that again, mister, and I guarantee you'll be the last person to eat at every meal.

Now apologize to the kid, or I'll shove this thing where it will do you some good."

Paul stared at her in surprise, muttered something that might have been an apology, then waddled outside. Steamer saw Pia glaring angrily at him as she hugged Tommy; Betty and Joellen fussed over him and added a large stack of hotcakes to his plate.

Pia said, "Come sit outside and eat, Tommaso."

He gave her a withering, disgusted-little-kid look. "My name is Tommy now, Mom. And I want to sit beside Steamer."

Pia sighed. She didn't blame Tommaso. She wanted to sit beside Steamer, too, but settled for sitting beside her son. "What are they doing, Steamer?" she asked, pointing to Alan and F-Stop.

"Wasting film." The look on her face surprised him: disapproval and even anger. *What was that all about?* he wondered.

"Tommaso, please get me more coffee." When he rose with her cup, she slid closer to Steamer, making a whisper of contact with him. "Please explain."

"None of the stuff they're shooting now will cut with the studio stuff."

"Cut?"

"That means it can't be edited into the story line as we've already filmed it. That is, there's no way Snips will be able to fit this footage into the story. Unless."

"Go on."

"Unless the story is re-written."

"And that would take more time."

"Yes. The scenes we shoot have to fit into a logical flow to keep the audience from becoming confused."

"I see." She smiled a small, worried smile. "Thank you for telling me. This filmmaking is such a fascinating business, isn't it?"

"Yes." He rose. "You'll have to excuse me now. This is a good time to shoot the screen test of Megan."

Pia had felt something very close to terror at hearing Steamer say Alan was wasting film. If Alan was filming material not in the script, it probably meant he intended to use it. That would mean the script would have to be rewritten, which meant further delay. The cigarette-burn cross on her left arm throbbed with pain. Utter despair, never far away, crept closer. The only thing she had ever wanted was to be a normal wife and mother, but Uncle had denied her that.

Memories of Ramon burst from the locked cabinet in her mind. They had met on the jumping circuit, fallen in love, and run away. Uncle had found them, and now Ramon was dead. All she had left of their love was Tommaso.

For a moment she considered trying to disappear into the wilderness here to make a life for herself and her son far away from Uncle. She quickly gave up on the idea. She had no idea how to survive here, and she would always be an alien in this strange world.

Alan had listened to her, stone-faced, then insisted his ideas would work. He'd argued that he had the right to film what he damned well pleased if it made for a better movie. If she wanted it completed on schedule, she'd damned well better back off and leave him alone. And yes, he'd have the script rewritten if necessary.

She'd listened with growing fear, then told him to stop wasting film and time, or else she would cable Italy and give the order for his sons to be taken as hostages. That produced a few cracks in the marble slab of his face, and he agreed to move the production along faster.

As she'd walked away, she'd considered recommending to Uncle that Alan's sons be kidnapped in any event. That would convince Uncle that she was being serious about protecting his investment.

Between then and now, however, something happened to throw her into a new dilemma. She'd perched herself on a fallen tree to watch Steamer film the screen test of Megan. The preparations had taken over an hour. Fayrene fussed over Megan, trying first one shade of pancake makeup and then another as Steamer scrutinized the results. Katrina draped one outfit after another on her until Steamer was finally satisfied.

He devised a simple scenario for the screen test. Megan was to walk into the scene, showing great sorrow; she was then to sit, play her autoharp, and sing a lament for love lost. By the time F-Stop was ready to crank the camera, Pia was desperately impatient and worried sick about the delay.

The result left her stunned. This simple country girl, this unsophisticated American frontier woman, had star quality. Pia at first mistrusted her own evaluation, but it had been confirmed by the applause of Steamer, Fayrene, and Katrina, as well as by the handful of people who had straggled over to watch.

And then, as if that were not enough, her voice proved to be liquid gold. When the movies talked—and that would not be long now—the combination of her looks and her voice would be, as the Americans put it, dynamite.

On the other hand . . . oh, God, on the other hand, Pia felt like pulling out her .25 pistol and shooting Megan then and there. One would have had to be blind and deaf not to see that Megan and Steamer were hopelessly in love, which meant she had little chance of snaring him for herself. Plus, killing Megan to speed up the production process would be killing the goose that laid the golden egg.

Hope and excitement rose in equal measure in Pia as she realized she could take credit with Uncle for discovering Megan. She was certain to be a major star, a valuable property to the studio and a big moneymaker. Uncle would like that and would perhaps forgive any delays.

She looked up as a shadow fell across her. Parley stood over her, an angry smirk on his face. He held a yellow envelope in his hand, which he thrust out to her. "You must be pretty damn important to rate a special-delivery telegram."

"I'm sorry? I don't understand."

"Messenger just rode in from town with this." He flapped the envelope in her face.

Dread crept up on her as she opened it. Uncle's message warned her that he had not heard from her for five days, and that he was impatient for news of the film. It closed by telling her that if she got involved with another man, Uncle would see to it that Tommaso died.

Megan could finally examine the turbulent emotions she'd pushed beneath the surface because of the hectic events of the day. Alan had decided to move on down the trail to reach what he called "real wilderness." Now the late afternoon sun was vaporizing raindrops on the pine needles and wafting their pungent scent into the air along the trail. Nevada was moving at an easy walk, his nose almost touching the tail of the horse ahead. Megan had no need to guide him.

Her screen test had left her floating ten feet above the ground. The sudden and unexpected applause at first stunned her and then filled her with hope. Was it possible she might, at long last, be able to fulfill her secret dream? Steamer had assured her that her voice, her face, and her figure all but guaranteed her success in Hollywood. He was the most wonderful man she had ever met, and he obviously was in love with her. In the next instant she was ten feet underground. Yes, Steamer was charming, but he was the enemy. He was charming and kind and pretending to be in love with her because he wanted information from her, and then he'd arrest her for complicity in bootlegging. It made no difference whatsoever that she was in love with him. She'd cry later tonight, alone in her tent.

Nevada jolted to a halt beneath her. The trail had grown wider and flatter, and she could see a small meadow through the trees ahead. She could hear the riders behind her coming to a stop, like an accordion collapsing.

Paul Marshal came riding back along the trail. "What's up, Paul?" she asked as he rode past her.

"Steamer wants to shoot a scene with Daphne up ahead. Good location, great light. Have you seen her?"

Megan realized with a start that she had not seen her sister for some time now. She turned in her saddle and looked back. Daphne and Junior were just appearing around a bend in the trail a hundred yards back. She could see Junior reining his horse in and holding her reins as well, to slow them down. He said something and was rewarded with a shriek of laughter from Daphne.

"Hey! Daphne!" Paul bellowed. Daphne looked up. "Get on up here," Paul said in a voice only slightly quieter. "Steamer wants to shoot scene forty-seven up ahead. And hurry up. The light is going."

Junior urged their horses to a trot. Megan could see Daphne clinging tightly to the saddle horn. They rode forward and halted on the trail beside her.

"You go on ahead now, Daph," Junior said. "And remember, we got a date tomorrow night. Up at our hunting cabin." Daphne nodded and reluctantly kicked her horse into a trot.

Junior stared at Megan. His smug, self-satisfied grin threatened to eat his ears.

"And just what the hell does a date tomorrow night mean?" Megan hated herself the moment the words were out of her mouth. He'd baited the trap; she'd swallowed not only the bait, but the trap as well.

"Well now, Mrs. Foxworth, I don't know as that's any business of yours. Your sister is a grown-up, adult lady, right? And what she does is her own business, right?"

No, not right. She *was* her sister's keeper. "Daphne is still a child in many ways, *Mr.* Frampton. She has, well, a weakness. I'd hate to think you'd be taking advantage of her."

Junior waved his hand in front of his nose. "Yeah, you can smell her weakness a mile away. But don't you worry none, Mrs. Foxworth. I'll take *real* good care of her. We've got a nice bathtub up there." He leaned both forearms on the pommel of his saddle and smirked at her. "Best you mind your own business. *And* keep away from Mr. Daniels. You sure wouldn't want to do anything to hurt your in-laws." He gathered his reins and moved off. "Especially as Fiona has been so good to you, taking you in and all that," he said over his shoulder.

Megan hung her head and pulled her hat low to hide the shame burning on her face. How had Junior found out? After her father had been convicted and jailed for embezzlement at the bank, her mother had been desperate. They had no money, and the charity and forgiveness of neighbors went only so far.

So when the new folks from the east showed up, her mother went to work grooming them. Terry Foxworth had proposed within six months. Megan felt as if she'd been sold to the highest bidder.

CHAPTER 19

Saturday Afternoon, June 20

Alan knocked back the remainder of his whiskey. The weather had been dry and warm, and F-Stop had knocked off scene forty-seven and another besides. Things were going well.

He looked around. They'd ridden only four miles, but the meadow in which they were camped was perfect for filming. They'd be able to set up and shoot a dozen of the outdoor scenes here. Parley and Megan had set up the tents under the trees, far enough apart to ensure everyone privacy. A couple of his hands had dragged some big logs into camp and set them up in a square around the fire. Now a ruddy sunset decorated the sky to the west.

Paul plopped down on the log beside him. He started juggling strips on his production board and jabbering about the shooting plan for tomorrow. Paul had everything under control; tomorrow was going to be another good day.

Alan let his attention drift. Everyone—cast, crew, and Parley's hands—was in a jolly mood. They were seated around the blazing fire. Dinner was over, the stars crackled like cold fire overhead, and Betty's guitar filled the night air with rowdy songs. The voices of those singing along sounded wonderful, but then TT's good Irish whiskey might have had something to do with that. He'd had a bit more than usual himself, he realized; it was time to stop. The hell with it. He was having too good a time. He reached for the bottle at his feet—and stopped when he saw Pia.

She was glaring furiously at him. *Fuck her.* He tipped the bottle over his glass, then lifted it in a salute. *Yeah, fuck her.* She'd threatened to cable her mysterious "patron" and order his sons kidnapped. At first he'd been weak with fear. Not for himself, but for his boys. He soon realized hers was an empty threat. She didn't know the trails, and even if she tried to ride out, he could ride after her and stop her.

He could kill her if necessary. He recoiled at the thought. "Thou shalt not kill," the Bible said. No, that was unthinkable. If she had an accident, though . . .

"Alan?"

Bettina was looking at him. "Yeah?"

"Honey, you're drinking a lot."

"Yeah, maybe I am."

"When you do that, it means something is wrong. What's going on?"

"Nothing."

"When you say 'nothing,' I get suspicious."

"No, really. I just remembered I need to tell Steamer something tomorrow."

Tuning her autoharp gave Megan a chance to watch people unobserved. They assumed her attention was so focused that she couldn't pay attention to them. But she could—and did.

She'd seen Pia glowering at Alan and seen him toast her with a sardonic grin. She'd seen Junior smirking at her throughout dinner as he fondled Luella. He'd been daring her to do something about it ever since he'd warned her on the trail this afternoon: *You sure wouldn't want to do anything to hurt your in-laws—especially 'cause Fiona has been so good to you, taking you in and all that.*

Sure, she'd been taken in, in more ways than one. Fiona had

sensed Megan's desperation within minutes of their first meeting. Fiona had twisted and prodded and pried at her until she'd said "I do." Now Megan had a husband and a new wringer washing machine, but she was still a household slave. She had to get out of Fiona's trap—but how?

The price of betraying her family would be jail. She'd be tarred by the same brush as her in-laws and sentenced for violating the laws of Prohibition. No jury would ever believe she didn't know about the barn full of illegal whiskey. Even if she pretended to be innocent, Fiona would drag her down into the mud with her.

The price of being loyal to her family would be a lifetime of slavery to the mob—and maybe even death. Gertie might gossip, but she didn't lie. Someone was coming to kill them all.

She sighed and made up her mind. Being in jail would be far better than being dead. She'd confess everything to Steamer and agree to testify. Maybe she'd get a lighter jail sentence that way.

She rose. The chatter around the fire quickly died away as she struck the first notes on her autoharp.

The last notes of "Good Night, Irene" soared into the cold, crisp air. A silence that seemed to last forever left Megan feeling as if she were in suspended animation. She could see surprised looks on the faces around the campfire, and she waited for them to light up and for hands to move and bang together.

When the applause came, it came like a roaring wind, like a spring runoff tumbling down a bouldered river. She bowed, nodded, mumbled thank-you, and made her way back to her seat on the log beside Steamer without tripping over her own feet.

She began, with slow and deliberate movements, to put her autoharp away in its case. Beside her Steamer said, "You look like you've been smacked upside the head with a two-by-four. You all right?"

She closed the case, latched it, and turned to him. "Am I really that good?"

He gave her an exasperated look. "Shit, Megan, didn't you hear that applause? That's a tough audience out there, your friends and neighbors. 'Aw looky, ain't she cute? Thinks she can sing and don't know she's got a voice like an axe on a grindstone.' If they *really* didn't like your voice, all you'd have gotten would have been a quiet little pitter-patter, just to be polite."

"But I . . ."

"No buts! No false modesty, please. Inside, you know damned well you're that good."

Oh God, you don't understand! I do *know—and that's the problem. I now have the power to change my life—and it terrifies me.* "Yeah," she said and looked away, staring into the light of the campfire. "I know. Mom swore she could hear me singing in the womb. And now I've got all these songs locked up inside me, and they're going to rot and die if . . ."

"If what?"

"Oh, never mind." When his smile changed, she realized she'd spoken harshly. "We'll figure it . . . *I'll* work it out," she finished, touching him lightly on the arm.

"Well, I'm damned sure your screen test is going to get you an offer from Alan," he said. "Then you'll have to come to Hollywood."

"Well, when I do, I'll look you up. So tell me, what's it *really* like down there?"

Steamer was sure Megan had opened up to him. Then when she said "never mind," he felt like a starving man who is allowed a glimpse of a banquet before the door is slammed in his face.

"Ah, well, it's like no place else on earth." He scuffed the dirt with the toe of his boot. "It's where fantasy and reality slam into each other head on, and the result is a *five*-ring circus. There's the performing animals—that's the actors and directors and cameramen and costume designers and makeup people— and then there's the trainers, the people with the money who crack the whip and make the animals perform."

"Do I detect a note of bitterness, Mr. Director?"

He looked at her with a wry smile. "Yeah, I guess. Look, you've got ten times the talent of your sister. Daphne photographs like an angel, but she can't hit her marks."

"Hit her marks?"

"I'm trying to do something new and different. I'm moving the camera around as the actors move around. For that to work, they have to stop or turn at marks chalked on the stage floor. To be at the right place when the camera gets there. Otherwise you might just as well plant the camera on a tripod up in front of the stage, yell 'action,' and turn the crank until someone falls down or the camera runs out of film."

"Your idea sounds so interesting!"

"Yeah, but Alan hates it."

"Why?"

"It takes an actor who can hit his marks and a dolly grip and focus puller who can hit their marks. It all takes a lot of time to set up the moves, and time is money."

She asked what a dolly grip and a focus puller were. She asked a dozen other questions, and this time the door to the banquet room remained open for a long time. Then she asked him a question that slammed it shut again.

"So, do you plan to get married some day?"

"Well, sure," he said quickly, but he heard the pain in his

own voice. "When I find the right . . ."

"Oh. If you don't want to talk about it . . ."

"No, it's all right. Allison, uh, she's a contract player for Segal Studios. Does a lot of secondary roles, makes good money, and . . . well, she didn't want to interrupt her career for family and motherhood." That wasn't exactly what she'd said, but it would do for now.

"But eventually . . ."

"Sure," he said. "I'm not in a big hurry right now, but I'd like to find someone, make sure she was someone I could live with for the rest of my life, before we start a family."

Megan rose abruptly. "More coffee?"

He looked at her, surprised. "Yeah. Sure. Thanks."

Megan kept her back to Steamer as she knelt in front of the fire. She lifted the enameled coffeepot from the cast-iron grate and poured, using her actions to conceal her misery. She'd known, of course, that he wasn't married. She'd read in her movie magazines that he was one of the most eligible bachelors in Hollywood, but she'd still needed to hear him confirm it.

But *why*, for Pete's sake? What good did that knowledge do her? She was married, but, worst of all, she would never be able to give him what he wanted—a family. All the potions and notions Doc Byrne had given her had done no damned good. Well, never mind; she still had to be friendly, get to the point where she could confess to him and beg him to see that she got a light sentence.

She handed him his mug. "So how did you get from . . . where was it? Afton? To Hollywood."

He nodded. "Yeah, Afton. Well, Mom taught drama in high school before she married Dad. She had a big box of play scripts, and, after Dad died in a stampede, I read all of them. I made a stage, maybe three feet wide and two feet deep, and sort of performed those plays with wooden figures I carved out of pine, with pasted-on faces cut from magazines, and miniature tables and chairs and horses and dogs." He blushed slightly. "Sort of like a dollhouse. And I played all the parts."

She clapped quietly. "That's a wonderful story."

He nodded. "Thanks. Now it's your turn. Tell me about you."

Megan's misery became acute. He was going to probe into her life, looking for evidence, and she would probably slip and tell him something that would get them all thrown in jail. Well, that was what she wanted, wasn't it? She wanted to get him on her side and gain his sympathy.

"I don't know where to start."

"Then it's best to start at the beginning."

Where had it all begun? Yes, with The Scandal that had destroyed her father's career in the bank, leaving them poor as church mice. Then the rich, handsome young man came to town soon after that, and how romantic it was when he courted her. How wonderful Fiona was to her after the wedding, and what a great opportunity she and Terry had to run the ranch when his parents were gone. But she could see Steamer wasn't buying a single one of her lies.

He nodded. "See, you did know where to start." He smiled, rather weakly, she thought. "Sounds like you've got a nice future all mapped out for yourself."

Oh God, what does that mean? Is he warning me? Telling me I have no future? Now what do I tell him?

"Uh, mostly."

"Mostly?"

"Well, Terry and I, we've been trying to . . . to make a baby." She could feel herself blushing furiously. Why was she telling him this? "Seems like I can't get pregnant. I've been to Doctor Byrne, but nothing seems to help." She was about to babble on but slammed a lid on it. He didn't need to know every damned detail.

"I see." He stared into the fire until she thought perhaps he'd fallen asleep. At last he said, "We could—" He jumped up. "We could get to sleep, is what we could do. Long day tomorrow."

She nodded, picking up her autoharp case, and he helped her to her feet. They walked slowly in the direction of the sleeping tents.

"So, uh, sleep well," he said.

"You, too." She smiled, keeping up the pretense. "See you in the morning."

She had moved two yards in the direction of her tent when she heard him calling her name. She stopped and turned back. "Yes?"

"I know some folks down in California who have . . . adopted children. Worked out real well for them."

"Oh. Well, good night."

Had they been more alert to the noises of the night all around them, they might have heard the faint noise of a human bumping into a nearby tree. After they entered their tents, Junior detached himself from concealment and tiptoed away. Every word Megan and Steamer said had carried to him clearly on the cold, silent night air.

CHAPTER 20

Sunday Morning, June 21

Tommy tiptoed through the woods, darting his flashlight about to chase away bears. The urge in his bowels had driven him from his sleeping bag and out into the pre-dawn light in search of the blue tent.

When he reached it, he was thrown into turmoil. The odor of poop rising from the pit and the flies now buzzing around inside repelled him. He decided a spot in the woods would be just fine, and silently thanked his mom for reminding him to pocket a length of toilet tissue from their cabin at the ranch for emergencies. This was sure an emergency!

He crept nervously along the faint path to the latrines and then into a small clearing. The shadows seemed to move. Besides, the idea that he might get lost was unsettling, even if he could see the camp. He quickly dropped his pants and evacuated his bowels.

He was enjoying the first pleasures of relief when a twig snapped in the shadows somewhere behind him. He froze, his heart thudding; there was another crack and the sound of feet thumping on the ground. He looked over his shoulder and from the corner of his eye saw a black thing moving behind him. It stopped, looked at him, and said, *"Boo!"*

He lost his balance and sat down but quickly leapt up with a strangled cry and froze in terror a second time. He could not run, for his feet were hobbled by his pants. The black thing made a noise like laughter and thumped off. He began to cry.

After a while, he started to clean himself, but he was shaking with cold and humiliation. He dropped the toilet paper, tore it, dropped some more, and succeeded in smearing himself badly. He was wondering how long it would take him to die when he heard footsteps again and looked up in renewed misery.

Steamer stood a few feet away, watching with a slight smile. "Looks like you've got yourself a real problem there," he said gently. Tommy's sobs slowly turned to laughter. "And it looks like you could use some help," Steamer continued. He pulled a red bandana from his pocket. "Here, use this."

Tommy stood quietly, his heart rate slowing, while Steamer helped him clean himself. Neither of them noticed as a black form moved from the latrines toward camp, paused, and then moved on. Together they scraped a hole in the ground and buried the excrement and the bandana.

"What happened?" Steamer asked.

As they made their way back to camp, Tommy explained. When he finished, Steamer chuckled. "That must have been Paul."

"Oh. I hate him."

"Why?"

"He's always making jokes, but they're mean jokes."

"I see. Well, best you stay away from him, yes?"

"Okay." Tommy hung his head. "You won't tell anyone, will you?"

"No, if you promise me you'll use the latrine from now on." Tommy nodded agreement. "Okay, go get washed up. And the next time, if you absolutely have to shit in the woods, dig a pit. And take your pants all the way off."

Pia was certain the emotions warring inside her would split her into two quivering halves. *Damn men anyway.* When Tommaso had returned to their tent, the stench coming from him woke her long before she was ready to get up. He'd been frightened and reluctant to tell her but finally confessed.

Now the early morning sun warmed her as she watched. The cast and crew were setting up the day's shoot, moving about in what appeared to be a chaotic frenzy. Yet under Steamer's focused, controlled direction, the shots were getting checked off on Esse's script.

Admit it, she thought. *You're in love with him. He's strong and protective, and Tommaso worships him—but he's also the enemy.* Yes, things were going well this morning—but that was because Miss Gorgeous Cow With Blonde Hair was sober. If—no, when—Daphne started drinking, Steamer would go back to doing take after take after take, and the rate of production would slow down.

Uncle's last cigarette burn, the one at the bottom of the cross, itched intolerably. She turned away, loosened the cuff of her shirt, and scratched.

And damn Paul Marshall too, for frightening Tommaso. She'd considered killing him, but after the fiasco when she'd shot the calf, she no longer had any confidence in her pistol. And he was the only one who could keep the production on track. She could feel one of her violent headaches coming on.

She'd been watching the shoot with care, hoping to see Steamer doing something wrong that she could use to pressure Alan into disciplining him. Everyone was in a good mood, however. F-Stop, the cameraman; Esse and Paul; Katrina, the wardrobe mistress; Fayrene, the makeup girl, and even the men moving gear around were all bound into a smoothly functioning team.

Steamer called for an end to the morning shoot and walked toward her. He was smiling, his even teeth white against his tanned face. "So, Pia, did you enjoy watching?"

She managed an answering smile. "Yes, fascinating, Steamer. I think everything went well?"

"Indeed it did."

"I've got dozens of questions I'd love to ask you. Could we eat lunch together?"

"Ah, sorry. Megan wants to show me a place down the trail where we could shoot this afternoon. But you go eat. We'll be back in ten minutes."

Pia's headache pounced with savage intensity as she watched Steamer and Megan disappear down the trail.

Megan had awakened with words like "today is the day," "just do it," "get it over with," and "just tell him" recycling endlessly through her mind. She rolled out of her sleeping bag exhausted from lack of sleep. Outside, the ground was soggy from the heavy rain last night, but at least the sun was shining.

At breakfast, she'd gathered her courage and told Steamer about a place down the trail where she thought he might want to film. A strange look had crossed his face, but he agreed to look. Now the morning shoot was over. He said something to Pia, who turned away and scowled fiercely at Megan before heading for the dining tent. As Steamer walked toward her, Megan felt her heart begin to flutter.

"Shall we go look at your spot?" Steamer asked.

They walked along the trail in silence. A crow cawed somewhere; she could hear squirrels chattering and the rustle of small birds in the brush. When they were far enough from the camp she was sure no one would see them, she stopped.

Steamer looked around slowly. "This is the place you were talking about?" She nodded. "Well, I don't think it will work all that well, but thank you anyway."

"That's not . . . that's not why I asked you to . . ." She could feel her heart pumping double time, and suddenly words gushed out like muddy floodwater rushing past huge rocks.

"Oh, Steamer! I . . . I've been so frightened ever since . . ." She stopped, watching him closely for a sign of sympathy.

He moved closer and touched her arm. "What is it, Megan? I've never seen you like this. Frightened of what?"

"They . . . they're going to kill me!"

"Whoa! Slow down here. Who? What in hell are you talking about?"

"It was last Saturday, at the movies." She told him about Gertie and what she'd overheard when she listened in on phone conversations. "So what it is, is I'd rather go to jail than be killed by the mob."

Steamer took off his hat and fanned himself while he shook his head. "You lost me way back there somewhere. Come on, sit down, slow down, and tell me everything."

"I don't want to sit. I'll never get up if I do." She looked around. They were in plain sight from the trail. "Let's move over there, where people can't see us."

When they were standing in the shade of the pines, out of sight, Steamer said, "Now, what's going on?"

"At first I felt like I was being disloyal, to my family, you know. I mean, I knew about their business, but I thought there wasn't that much, and if I said anything, they'd get in trouble with the law, and—"

Steamer made a slow down gesture with his hands. "Wasn't that much *what*?"

Megan could feel a major meltdown threatening to overwhelm her, and she gathered her courage. "Liquor."

"That's what I thought. I just needed to have you confirm it. Go on."

"Then I saw—in the barn I mean—I saw they've made a kind of platform that can lower from the rafters. It's camouflaged with old furniture and stuff, but there's cases and cases of whiskey hidden behind it."

"Is that all?"

She felt the terrible fear and tension of the last week begin to melt. "No. Before that, Sally—that's Sally Mann, you know?"

"I have absolutely no idea who Sally Mann is. But go on."

"Oh. She's head of the WCTU here. She told me she'd contacted the Prohibition Unit and that they were going to send an undercover agent into town to investigate."

"And did they?"

"You ought to know," she snapped.

He fanned her with his hat. "Your brain must be getting overheated, Megan. Why in hell would I know?"

"Uh, well, Tuesday, when you were helping me dry the dishes, remember?" He nodded. "I told you about the rumor that was going around, that a lawman had arrived. And you said, 'But Prohibition *is* the law. You might want to be careful what you do.' "

"So, maybe I did. So what?"

Her emotions were threatening to erupt again. "I thought . . . I thought you were warning me."

"Me? Warn you? Why?"

"Because I thought you—"

"What?"

"Never mind." She was about to resume when she heard noise behind them in the forest. A quick scan revealed nothing.

"Is there more?"

"Uh, yes, at the railroad station, the day you all arrived? That's when Buddy told us about you."

He laughed, shaking his head. "Told you *what* about me? And who is Buddy?"

"He's the town drunk." She told him what Buddy had said: that Steamer was the lawman who was coming because he'd played a lawman, which was the perfect disguise, and how the sheriff had confirmed it.

He stared at her for a long moment, then started laughing. "And you think I'm a real lawman, right?" She nodded. "And you're going to take the word of a drunk?" He was staring at her in disbelief.

The last of her courage was evaporating. "Damn it, Steamer! I want to confess to you!" She knew she was shouting but didn't care.

He drew back a step. "Wait a minute. So, if I'm a lawman, and you confess to me, then I might be able to get you a reduced sentence, right?"

She nodded, empty now of all emotion.

He held her by both shoulders and shook her very gently. "Megan. I am not a lawman. Look at me." She lifted her gaze to him. "Let me repeat that. I. Am. Not. A. Lawman. I have absolutely no connection with the Bureau of Revenue or any of their sub-departments. Yes, Buddy's right, I did play a sheriff in one movie, but I'm an actor and a director."

Megan had one last card to play, the one she'd saved until the last. "I know where they keep their records. I've seen Terry lock them in a file cabinet. I know where the key is."

"So what? I know *nothing* about law enforcement. What would I do with them? I suggest you tell the sheriff."

Her fear and anxiety vanished. Relief and hope surged into her to take their place. She swayed closer to him, ready for his embrace.

"Hey! You two! Steamer, Megan!"

They whirled apart, turned. Junior was walking toward them through the pines. "Betty says you better come eat or she'll throw it to the pigs."

Steamer had been filled with joy when he finally understood why Megan had shunned him. He was equally overwhelmed with terror when the full impact of everything she had said forced its way past his bliss.

Megan was trapped in a dangerous, ugly situation. He would be, too, if he allowed his heart to rule his head. Her husband and her in-laws were obviously involved in a large-scale smuggling operation, violating the laws of Prohibition, and a friend involved with the WCTU had called for an undercover agent to come to town to investigate. Megan had been warned of a threat on her life, probably from whatever mob was supplying the booze.

She did not love Terry, but did she love *him*? They'd been about to kiss when Junior blundered onto the scene; that might have been a partial answer. Now that he was thinking clearly, he knew a kiss would have been foolish—God alone knew what Junior might have seen and gossiped about. He desperately needed to talk to Megan, to understand everything, to plan, and to be certain.

He forced his attention back to the scene around him. Lunch was over, and silence had descended over the cook tent as food worked its soothing magic. Work would start again soon, but he could see no one wanted to be the first to rise and leave. Alan, Paul, and Pia were sitting together and talking. Something in their behavior alerted him. He watched them more closely, hoping they wouldn't notice. Heads together, talking in low voices, they glanced quickly up and away when they saw he was watching them. Yes, they were talking about him. Paul was trying to convince Alan of something, and Pia was backing him. Alan was uneasy and worried by whatever Pia was saying.

Alan gestured for him to come over. "We were just talking about a change in the shooting plans for this afternoon, Steamer. Daphne is not feeling at all well."

And I'm to blame for working her too hard, is that it? And now she's drunk? "I'm sorry to hear that. So what am I supposed to shoot?"

Paul said, "You won't have to do anything, Steamer. Alan and I were going to take F-Stop and the camera and just go out and shoot some stuff. The camp, Betty and Joellen working, the wranglers working with the horses, stuff like that. We may shoot some stuff of Pia, too. You can take the afternoon off."

And talk to Megan. Suddenly Steamer didn't give a damn whether the footage they shot would cut with the rest of the film. "Whatever. Have a good time."

Junior had hot-footed it back to camp with Megan's shouted words echoing in his mind. *Holy shit, she was going to confess to the lawman,* he thought. That was something Fiona needed to know pronto. He threw his saddle on Champion and was cinching it down when Pa's voice startled him.

"Going somewhere, son?"

He gritted his teeth and turned to face his father. "Uh, yeah. I just want to, ah, go for a little ride. Relax a bit."

"It's Sunday."

Resentment burned through Junior. When the hell was Pa going to stop riding herd on him? He clamped down on the angry words ready to spring from his mouth. No need to antagonize him. "I've already said my prayers this morning, Pa. I don't think God is going to care if I go for a little ride."

His pa stared at him, his lips twitching. "Is someone going on that little ride with you?"

Junior looked at him, puzzled. "No. I just want to get away, have a little time to myself."

"You're not planning to take that blonde floozy with you?"

"Blonde . . ." Junior knew his face was betraying him.

His pa pounced. "Yes, her. I saw you at breakfast, making goo-goo eyes at her. And her all smiles and nodding and agreeing to whatever plan it was you was proposing."

Junior gathered his courage. It was time to settle things with Pa. "So what if I was?"

Pa stomped closer. "How many times do I have to tell you? I won't have you fornicating with women like that. She's not one of our kind. I won't have you having no kind of an encounter with a woman outside of our church."

At last Junior had Pa where he wanted him. The triumph he knew was coming was sweet. "Don't you think maybe you oughta practice what you preach, Pa?"

His pa's face darkened. "How dare you?" he said with a snarl.

"Tell you what, Pa. Let's you and me pray over it. Tonight."

His pa fell back a step, his mouth open. Junior swung into the saddle and urged Champion into a trot. A hundred yards along the trail to the river he passed Megan and Steamer. They had bath towels over their shoulders, and Steamer was carrying one of them fancy fly-fishing rods.

CHAPTER 21

Sunday Afternoon, June 21

Megan's emotions rose and fell in response to her surroundings. If she walked in the shade, gloom descended; if she crossed into a patch of sunlight, her spirits soared until she was light-headed with joy. In the shade she thought she heard something following her; in the sun the forest stretched away empty and silent on all sides. Steamer had parted company with her ten minutes ago. "I'll go upriver a ways and fish for a while, so you can have privacy. Enjoy your bath," he'd said.

She'd stopped to fetch a bathing suit from her duffel bag. Joellen had told her about a place where a back eddy had made a deep pool close to the riverbank. She could get really clean all over. Then, as she was walking away, she'd heard Betty ask Joellen if she thought Megan had seen Steamer's equipment.

She turned right and trudged through masses of foliage. Betty's comment kept whispering through the background of her thoughts. Had Betty and Joellen really seen Steamer's "equipment"? If they hadn't, how would they know . . . It was ridiculous; no man's thing was as long as his legs. It was all in good fun, and they'd been teasing her. But if they were, how did they know how Megan felt about him . . . *Oh God, was it that obvious?*

Far overhead a hawk screamed. She gazed up into the cloudless blue, saw it fold its wings and plummet downward. She laughed out loud. The hawk was free to choose its own path in life; didn't she have the same right? So what if her love for Steamer was obvious? Steamer was an honest, law-abiding man. A life with him would be stable and secure; they had a lot of interests in common.

Then another thought ambushed her like a gang of desperados. What if it wasn't her who couldn't get pregnant; what if there was something wrong with Terry? What if she got pregnant by Steamer? Oh, that was so totally foolish. She wasn't going to have sex with Steamer. She plunged on through the brush as if it would scratch the confusion out of her mind.

She was hot and tired when she saw Steamer far upstream. She waved. He waved back. Had he caught anything? *Curiosity killed the cat, but satisfaction brought it back.* When she reached him, he smiled at her, and his smile sizzled all the way down to her toes.

"I thought you were going to take a bath," he said.

"I've got plenty of time. Just thought I'd see if you've caught anything first. Mind if I watch?"

"As long as you don't scare the fish."

"Oh, phooey! How could I do that?"

"Make a loud noise."

"I thought that was just something fishermen said to keep women quiet."

"It is."

She glared at him. He struggled to keep a straight face and finally laughed. "I don't think fish can hear." He reeled in his line and moved upstream a few yards, looking all around carefully. "I wonder, though. Do you think fish have emotions? Do you think a boy fish falls in love with a beautiful girl fish and wants to take her home and keep her forever?"

Her heart did a cartwheel. He might as well have hooked her with that tiny little fly, for when he moved upstream again, she followed. Megan watched as he drew back his shoulder, upper arm, then his forearm, drawing the fly back toward him across the water. When only his wrist was left to raise, he did so with a sweep and a snap that lifted the fly smoothly off the water and sent the line arching gracefully behind him. Just before the line and fly rod pointed straight back, he reversed his motion, sweeping the line over his head. The fly floated to a landing on the surface. After another cast, he reeled in and moved upstream and cast again.

"How many times do you have to do that?" she asked.

"Until we're far enough away from camp."

After a moment, she reminded herself to breathe again. "You mean, far enough away so I have privacy. To take a bath."

"That's one thing you could do."

"But suppose someone sees us—I mean, *me*?"

"Most everyone on this trip is polite enough to respect our—I mean, *your* privacy." He reeled in and began to walk upstream.

"Are you just going to walk away?" When he only glanced back with a smile, she followed, resenting the warring emotions that made her feet contradict her mind.

Steamer grinned back at her over his shoulder but kept on walking. Megan scuffed through the willows behind him, listening to the gurgle of the stream. He stopped and began casting again. When she reached him, she saw that they were screened on all sides from the view of the camp. A back eddy of the river had carved an oval hole in the riverbank. If they were in that hole, the heavy growth of willows along the bank would screen them from any view except directly overhead. The sun warmed a small beach of fine, white sand at the north end.

She stopped beside him and lay on her stomach on the soft grass at the edge. "What kind of fish are they?"

"Mostly Dolly Varden trout."

"I had no idea there were so many." She lay silent for a moment, studying the trout swirling lazily in the back eddy. "I'm a fish, too."

He stopped casting and put his rod down. "Oh? What kind?"

"A goldfish. Sally Mann has a large bowl of them in her parlor." She tossed a small water-smoothed stone from hand to hand. "Damn!" She hurled the stone into the river. "I'm an expensive goldfish in a bowl, and so is everyone else at the ranch. We're all swimming around and around, doing exactly the same thing every day, but the monotony doesn't seem to bother anyone else."

He kneeled beside her. "Sounds like you're saying you're trapped."

"How brilliant of you." She glared briefly at him, then dropped her gaze to the ground and began yanking at blades of grass. "I'm sorry. I'm not angry at you. I'm angry at . . . everything. What happened this morning was like—Well, it was as if I've been swimming frantically, desperately tearing through the water, slamming into the sides of the bowl, then suddenly instead of hitting the glass, I'm lying on the floor, gasping for air.

"Then, a while back, I saw a hawk flying free, way high up, and I realized I have a chance to become a bird."

He said, "Um," kneeled beside her, and massaged her shoulders. His fingers, strong and warm, found and kneaded the sore places in her shoulders, then her upper back, and then her lower back. A new and different sort of pleasure moved downward with his hands, something she'd never felt with Terry.

His hands moved lower, and the kneading motion became a slow, caressing movement. She wanted him to continue, but she didn't. She needed time to think and rolled away from him.

"I need a little time to . . . uh . . . take a bath." She saw disappointment beginning to flood over him. "First."

He smiled and rose. "You're going to take a bath in your

swimsuit, of course."

"Of course. I'm not some camp follower who can just jump into the creek nude."

"I'll go upstream a little way. Call me when you need your back washed."

Megan blushed, then sat on a log and began to undress. She pulled off her boots and socks, then stopped to look around. There was not another human being in sight. Far away, down the meadow, tiny horses grazed; she could occasionally hear the faint melodic clinking of their bells.

She listened intently, trying to hear something else. Was something moving behind her? The silence invaded her ears, and she decided there was no sound but the separate and distinct sounds of the river and the horse bells.

She unbuckled her belt and pulled her shirt out of her waist overalls. She began to unbutton them when something moved in the willows behind her. She stopped and stared at the spot, but there was nothing there—until she turned away.

"Steamer!"

He looked up and waved, and she waved more urgently. She shouted his name again. He came walking rapidly. "What is it?"

"Something moved. Over there."

"There's nothing here that will harm you, darling."

The word "darling" blew all the remaining doubts from her mind. She smiled at him. "But I did see something. Really."

"Yes, you did. There's a magpie over there." He came closer, and they watched the large black-and-white bird searching for food.

"I supposed Joellen would bathe nude."

"So what's all this nonsense about Joellen?"

"Never mind."

"At least Joellen wouldn't be afraid to go in the water."

"I'm not afraid!" She kept a smile from showing. "I suppose

you had a bath together yesterday."

"And I suppose she'd be fun to take a bath with. But I don't want to bathe with Joellen. And if you stopped supposing, we might get somewhere."

And then she knew it was time. This was the only place they had, and he was challenging her to put up or shut up. Well, all right, but first she was going to get even with him for walking off and leaving her. She walked to the edge of the river and looked at him helplessly. "There's mud on the bottom."

He moved closer to the edge and peered over. "It will feel good squishing up between your toes."

She giggled. "But what if there are things in the mud?"

"For crying out tears, woman. There's nothing in the mud that will harm you."

She leaned over and peered into the water. "Well, what's that?" She pointed.

"What?" He moved closer to look. She sidled behind him, took a deep breath, and pushed.

He came to the surface with a shout. "You stinker!"

"That's what you get for walking off and leaving me."

Steamer climbed onto the bank, and Megan got ready to run, but he only began removing his clothes.

"What—what are you doing?"

"I have to dry my clothes, don't I?"

He pulled off the canvas shoes he used for wading, then his pants and shirt; finally, his undershirt and underpants. His body was lean and firm, and his equipment—well, it was normal. She turned away, blushing. He was so open about it, so natural.

He spread his wet clothes on the dead tree and walked slowly toward her, and because he walked slowly, she did not run. He took the placket of her shirt in his fingers, gathering the material tighter and tighter until she was in his arms. He kissed her, caressing her mouth with his tongue, and slid her shirt down over her shoulder. His hands moved slowly, sliding down her back and around to her front. He unbuttoned her pants and slid them off, and his fingers caressed her private place. She was starting to melt when he scooped her up.

He looked down at her. "Like I said, I don't want to take a bath with Joellen. Might be fun to take one with you."

Her eyes popped open. "Steamer! No!" He dropped her in. She surfaced with a shriek. "Oh, shit, it's cold!"

"Well, I'll be damned. A four-letter word from the lady."

He came down to the small sandy beach and held his hands out to her. When she was standing beside him, he rubbed the bar of soap over her body and began washing her, building up a soft, fragrant lather. His hands moved slowly, massaging her, pulling her to him. When he slid inside her she wasn't ready yet, but he didn't begin thrusting. Instead he slid his hands down her buttocks and pressed her against him, released her, pressed, released, pressed, released, massaging her buttocks in slow circles. She threw her arms around his neck and tried to wrap her legs around his waist, but the soap made her slip until he bent his knees and lowered them ever so carefully to the beach, staying inside her. Megan forgot to complain about the sand on her back.

Far overhead, the hawk screeched.

CHAPTER 22

Sunday Evening, June 21

Junior kneeled on the riverbank behind the willows, trembling. Now he'd spilled his seed on the ground, and it was all the fault of that whore, Megan.

He realized he was breathing like a winded horse. Had they heard him? He made a small gap in the willows and peered out. No, they seemed to be asleep in each other's arms. It was time for him to get out of here.

He crawled backwards out of his hiding place as silently as he could. He needed to pull up his overalls, but he couldn't do that without standing up. Now they dragged on the ground, catching on willow stubs. He yanked at them in frustration. The resulting snap sounded like the crack of doom. He froze, expecting a shout from the sand, but heard nothing. He wanted to leap to his feet and shout and curse, but he knew he had to remain silent. He backed the rest of the way out of concealment as quietly as a mouse.

When he could no longer see the river and judged that the gurgle of the water would mask any sounds, he stood and pulled up his overalls. Champ was still tied where he had left him, well off the trail. A nosebag of grain had guaranteed his silence. He removed the canvas bag, threw his saddle on, cinched it down, and climbed aboard. He held the gelding to a slow walk as he headed back to camp.

Anger assaulted him with a double-bitted axe. Pa stood on

one side, chopping at him about not having sex until he was married. But the evidence his pa had fornicated with Jasmine was in his saddlebags. Besides, he'd watched animals doing it all his life: stallions covering mares, dogs fucking bitches, boars fucking sows—and they didn't have to be married, did they?

Megan hacked at him on the other side. She had refused him, chased him out of her bathroom with her bath brush, yelling at him about how she was married. And there she'd been, rutting on the beach like a bitch in heat. Had God done anything to her?

Champ whinnied in protest as Junior yanked him to a halt. He grabbed at the thought that had just slithered through his mind and dragged it back to where he could look at it again. When he had, he came to the same conclusion: God had done nothing to Megan or to Steamer.

What else had his pa lied about? He patted Champ on the neck to apologize, then urged him to a trot. He detoured around camp and headed on down the trail toward the town of Kelly on the banks of the Gros Ventre River.

The town of Kelly had a post office, a dance hall, a hotel, a garage, a mercantile store, a cafe, a population of five hundred, and a telephone. The phone was located in the Kelly Koffe Kup, which was crowded with lunchtime customers when Junior walked in. It had been a long ride in from camp. He'd get back after dark, but it was worth it.

He headed for the phone on the back wall but was brought up short when a voice called his name from the booth he had just passed. He turned to look. Guil Huff sat with two other ranchers Junior did not know, thick china coffee mugs in front of them.

"Where you going in such a rush, son?" Mr. Huff asked.

"Morning, Mr. Huff." Junior hated to stop to chew the fat

224

with him, but knew he'd best be polite. Mr. Huff was one of the valley's most important citizens, and getting on his bad side was not a good idea. "I need to use the telephone. Got to call back to the ranch."

Mr. Huff nodded. "Hear tell you've packed a bunch of dudes out there back of Rattlesnake Canyon."

"Right." Junior removed his hat, turning it round and round by the brim. "Bunch of folks from Hollywood."

One of the men Junior did not know spoke. "Sheep Mountain's going to slide one day, you know." Junior looked at him in puzzlement, looked to Mr. Huff for help.

"You've met Uncle Billie, have you, Junior?" When he shook his head, Mr. Huff added, "Mister Beirer homesteads a ways down the canyon from me. Been all over the country back there."

Uncle Billie nodded. "That's right. Anyway, like I was saying, anywhere on that mountain, if I lay my ear to the ground, I can hear water tricklin' and runnin' underneath. It's runnin' between strata. And someday, if we have a wet enough spring, that whole mountain is going to let loose and slide."

Junior nodded along with Uncle Billie. "That's real interesting, Mr. Bierer, but if you don't mind, I really gotta make a phone call."

"What's her name?" Mr. Huff asked.

"Aw, well, no, it ain't that, it's . . ." He stopped protesting when the men all laughed again, and he excused himself and went to the phone.

He turned his back on them and gave the crank a long, hard turn. That ought to wake up whoever is on duty at the switchboard, he thought. When a voice answered, he said, "Hook me up to the Rocking Lazy F ranch. This is important."

"Yes, sir." It was Gertie on duty. He could tell from the whine in her voice.

"And Gertie?"

"Yes?"

"No listenin' in, hear me? I'll know if you're doing it, 'cause I'll hear a click on the line."

There was no reply for a couple of heartbeats, then Gertie sniffed and said, "I am a professional switchboard operator, Junior, and don't you forget it."

Fiona answered on the fourth ring—two shorts and a long. As soon as Junior identified himself, she started in, barraging him with questions. He tried to get a word in edgewise and realized he was shouting when he noticed the men in the booth looking at him curiously. He pulled his hat off and held it close to his mouth, hoping to muffle his words.

"Fiona, shut up." She squawked a protest, then was silent. "My apologies, ma'am, but I've got something important to tell you." He looked back at the booth; the men quickly looked away and went back to their own talk.

"So tell me," Fiona snapped.

"She's going to confess, is what."

Fiona gasped. "Saints preserve us! What is she going to tell him? How do you know? Tell me everything she said."

"I don't know much more than that. They didn't know I was listening in, of course, and I couldn't get no closer. But she and him, they were real cozy, nose to nose, and I heard her real clear, 'cause she shouted at him how she wanted to confess to him." Fiona was silent for so long that he asked, "You still there?"

"Shut up and let me think." She mumbled to herself for a moment and then said, "I think that accident better be a fatal accident."

"Damn it, Fiona! That's a . . . a sin. The Bible says, 'Thou shalt not—' "

"Don't tell me what's a sin and what's not a sin, young man. You haven't lived long enough to know a damn thing about sin. When you're my age, you can talk. Now just figure some way to do it."

"I can't do it, Fiona!"

Her voice broke; he could hear her trying to control her anguish. "Use your head a minute, Junior. Just think what will happen if she does that. It will destroy everything."

He could hear her controlling her sobs. "They'll throw me and TT in jail, and that will kill him. And you—what do you think they'll do to you? Kiss you on the cheek and say, 'Bless you, my son'? Even if they don't throw you in jail, the ranch will go broke, and where will you work then?"

"Uh, well, all right, I'll think about it."

"You'd better do more than think about it. Wouldn't it be better to sacrifice one lamb, rather than have all of us in jail?"

"Uh, yeah, well, okay."

"That's my good boy." The line went dead.

Junior put the earpiece back on the hook. As he left, he saw the three ranchers looking at him suspiciously. He put on a cheerful smile as he went past them and outside.

He urged Champ into a fast walk. The sun was setting, and he needed to get back to camp. He also needed to think. His conversation with Fiona churned around with memories of what he'd heard and seen today. One thought finally solidified: if he killed Megan, he wouldn't be able to fuck her.

Well, there was an easy solution to that: he had to marry her. Get rid of Terry somehow (he'd figure that out later) and bring her into the kingdom of heaven. Then she'd have to obey him, and he'd for damned sure tell her to keep her mouth shut about the booze. Everything would be all right.

★ ★ ★ ★ ★

Doodah just happened to be looking when Paul "accidentally" bumped into Tommy that night at dinner. Tommy's steak and potatoes fell into the dirt. Paul apologized, but Doodah could hear the insincerity dripping from his voice. He rose, winked at Betty, picked up the food, put it back on the plate, and handed it to Paul.

"What the hell . . . ?" Paul yowled, but Doodah just gazed steadily in his eyes.

"I seen what you did. Now you can rinse the steak off, get more spuds, and sit down and eat. Or . . ."

Paul glared back for a moment and then did as he was told. Betty put another steak on a clean plate with more potatoes and handed it to Tommy. He wolfed it down.

Ten minutes later Paul threw his plate on the ground and left the cook tent in a silent sulk. Tommy glanced at Doodah, who made a "wait a moment" motion, and Tommy sank back onto his log seat.

Another twenty minutes later Tommy was twitching with anxiety. He finally caught Doodah's eye, and Doodah nodded. Tommy dropped his blue-enameled plate and cup in the general vicinity of the wash bucket. "Think he's asleep?" he asked.

"Just you slow down, youngster. Best we make sure." Doodah turned back to the conversation he'd been having with Betty and Joellen. "I can't rightly believe that. TT wouldn't do that," he said in a low voice.

Betty put a wet plate in the drainer and pointed at it. "Dry."

He swiped at both sides and handed it to Tommy. "Put it away over there. In that packing box."

When Tommy was out of earshot, Betty leaned closer. In a low but forceful voice she said, "Doodah, if I hear one tiny little peep of gossip about this, I'll know where it came from, and I'll make you wish you'd never opened your mouth. Understand?"

Doodah drew back. "You accusing me of gossiping?"

"Damned right I am. If you let this leak out, a lot of people will get hurt. No promise, no story, and that's straight."

"Okay, okay, I promise."

Betty looked to both sides, then behind her. She picked up a stack of dry dishes and handed them to Tommy. "Here, Tommy. You put these away with the rest of them."

With Tommy again out of hearing, she went on. "Like I was saying, don't say nothing about this to Megan. You know how protective she is about her sister. If she found out, well, you'd hear the explosion a mile away."

"Yeah, yeah, go on. Get to the good part."

Betty looked at Joellen. "You tell him the rest, Jo. I gotta disappear for a minute."

Joellen uncurled herself from her place on top of some packing boxes and sat up. "Okay. This was right after Megan got hitched to Terry. Seems like Luella sweet-talked TT into going to see the pretty horses in the barn, or he talked her into it; we'll never know which. Anyways, they were gone a long time. Fiona went to take a look."

"Don't stop there!" Doodah said.

"Just a minute. Here, Tommy, put these cups away over in that other packing case, the green one."

"Aw, Doodah," he said. "Do I hafta do any more women's work? We got something important to do. He's in bed now for sure."

"Put them cups away, and then we'll go." He moved closer to Joellen. "Go on."

"Martina saw them coming back from the barn. She told me Luella was crying big crocodile tears, and Fiona was furious." Joellen stopped, a triumphant smile on her face.

"That ain't the end of the story," Doodah said with annoyance, "and don't tell me it is."

"Well, right after that, Miss Luella went off to Hollywood. Fiona put out that she was real talented and deserved to have a chance to be a big movie star."

Doodah looked down as Tommy tugged at his sleeve. "So all right already, let's go." He ruffled Tommy's hair. "Now then, Jo, where's that packing twine and a safety pin?"

Joellen jammed her hands on her hips and studied him. "You sure you want to be foolin' around out there in all that wet? Tommy could catch his death of cold."

"It won't take long. 'Sides, Tommy'll put his slicker on, right, Tommy?"

Tommy nodded, and she took a ball of string and a large, rusty safety pin from a packing box. Joellen held them out to Doodah, then broke into a grin. "I guess he deserves it, after the dirty tricks he's pulled on Tommy. Just make sure the boy don't get hurt out there in the dark."

Joellen jumped down from her perch. "Reckon I'll go along. I want to hear what Mr. Fatso does."

Five minutes later, they had left the open area around the camp and were circling through the woods to sneak up on Paul's tent. The moon was still playing hide-and-seek with the clouds, and they moved when its cold light broke through. They stopped when it went dark. Their pants legs and boots were soon soaking wet. Tommy, slicker forgotten, was saturated and shivering but, in his excitement, oblivious to both.

When they were within ten yards of Paul's tent, Doodah gestured to hunker down behind a log. "Now then, here's what we're going to do. Jo, give us a little light here."

Joellen shielded her flashlight, and Doodah fastened one end of the twine through the eye of the safety pin. "See here, Tommy, we'll tie this string in a good tight knot. Don't want it slipping out. Then I'm going to crawl over to his tent and stick this pin through the canvas. While I'm doing that, you find some resin from a pine; get a lot of it on your fingers."

"What for?" Tommy was bursting with energy, and his voice crackled with excitement.

"Shh, keep your voice down! Don't want the varmint to hear us. Just do it. You'll see in a minute."

Doodah crept to the tent as Joellen paid the twine out. Paul was not yet asleep but galumphing around inside. Doodah silently fastened the pin through the fabric at the base of the wall.

When he got back to the log, Tommy had returned with both hands sticky with pine sap. "Now what, Doodah?" he asked in a stage whisper.

"Okay, now you're going to rub that resin on the string here." He held a three-foot length of the twine taut between his hands. "That's right, rub it in good."

"But what for?"

"See, as soon as he puts out his light, then you're going to pull that string tight and stroke it with the other hand. It'll be just like a fiddle string. The vibration goes along the string to the pin. It's going to sound like something scratching at his tent, trying to get in, only he won't be able to see anything. That pin is damn near invisible inside, and he's not likely to find it."

"Keen!" Tommy whispered. "I hope he goes to bed soon."

Paul shone his light in a full circle around the interior of his tent. Everything was finally laid out in perfect order: sleeping bag and pad all made up, duffel bag arranged, boots standing next to it, and clothes laid out. Satisfied, he heaved himself into the sleeping bag. He turned off his light and put it down beside his Colt .32 Pocket Automatic pistol. He lay back, shut his eyes, and crossed his hands over his chest.

He was just drifting off to sleep when something scratched frantically at the tent. His eyes popped open, and he stared into the darkness, his heart pounding. The noise came again a few moments later, and he sat bolt upright, grabbed his flashlight, and stabbed the beam around. There was nothing there.

It's probably just some goddamned rat or something, he thought. The noise had stopped; whatever had been making it must have been frightened away by the light. He switched it off and sank into the comfort of his bed.

The noise, when it came again, was even more frantic and insistent. It sounded as if the damned thing was trying to chew through the tent. At this thought, adrenaline shot through his system as if from a fire hose. He sat up with a shout of dismay, grabbed his light and pistol, and leapt from his sleeping bag.

He stood rigid in the middle of the tent, gasping for air. When the probing beam of the light revealed nothing inside, he gingerly lifted the sleeping bag and peered under it. There was still nothing there. He lifted his boots with his fingertips and shone the light into them. Nothing there as well. He lifted his clothing, shifted the duffel bag, and looked inside. Convinced at last that no animal was inside, he once again crawled into bed.

Outside, someone sneezed violently. He sat up and listened intently. The sneeze was not repeated. He lay down again.

Tommy jammed his handkerchief over his nose and mouth and buried his face in Joellen's arms. The next sneeze was muffled enough that it did not bring a reaction from the tent.

"You'd best get yourself along to bed, young man," Joellen whispered. "You've got a cold coming on, sure as hell."

Tommy shook his head and wriggled out of her arms. "No, I'll be all right. This is too damn much fun. I'm going to fix that varmint good."

"Better not let your ma hear you using language like that,"

Doodah murmured. "Joellen's right. You should go to bed."

"Please, Doodah, just one more time, okay?"

Doodah nodded reluctantly, and they all sank down behind the log again. The light in Paul's tent went out. Soon the first snore rattled through the icy air. Tommy pulled the string tight and rubbed his resin-coated hand along it. The string thrummed, scratching at the tent wall ten yards away. The reaction from inside this time was even more spectacular: a series of gargling, gasping shouts, followed by frantic heavy breathing and a wild light show. The conspirators struggled to muffle their laughter.

The tent shook. The movement of the light indicated Paul was exiting the tent and moving around toward the back. He reached the rear just as the moon shot a brilliant beam earthward. He was naked except for his boots. Joellen doubled up, choking with laughter she could scarcely contain.

Paul moved three steps closer to their log, slashing his light along it. Joellen and Doodah pushed Tommy down behind the log and covered him with their bodies.

Paul's voice quavered as he called, "Who's there?"

When silence answered his question, the light moved away. When they felt it was safe to look again, Paul had disappeared.

In his tent, Paul crept into his sleeping bag with his boots on, shivering violently. He lay rigid, staring at the roof and praying he'd frightened away whatever it was. Everyone knew there were rats and snakes and scorpions and wild cats out here; what was supposed to be so much fun out here in the wilds?

When the scratching came again, he shot out of his sleeping bag with a scream. The noise was right under the head of his bed. He grabbed his light and his .32 pistol and ran out to the rear of the tent. A long, thin animal's tail stuck out from under the edge of the tent.

"Gotcha, you son of a bitch!" He thrust the pistol forward and fired once. It was still moving! He fired twice and whirled at a sound behind him. There, behind the log, he spotted movement! It was getting away. He fired again, three times, waited expectantly.

A human voice boomed out from behind the log. "Goddamn it, you stupid bastard, you damn near hit Tommy!"

Had a wasps' nest been flung into every tent, the reaction would not have been more frantic. A buzzing crew of film people and trail hands was soon swarming around the log, stinging the air with questions. The flying words were angry, frightened, or curious, according to the mood of the questioner.

"Shut up!" Parley's voice, toughened from years of shouting orders over a cattle drive, shocked them into silence. His head swiveled from side to side until his gaze landed on Doodah. "All right, Mr. Cummings, what's going on?"

In answer, Doodah lifted the resin-coated string into view. Parley's light followed it to the connection with Paul's tent, back to Doodah, then to Paul.

"You all right, Mr. Marshal?" When Paul nodded a faint reply, Parley continued, "As you can see, the boys have been playing a little joke on you."

Doodah tightened the string and rubbed it. Paul watched, covering his genitals with both hands. A moment later the full impact of the lights playing over his nude body galvanized him into action. "That's a rotten damn trick!" he shouted.

Parley strode toward him, holding out his hand. "Give me that damned pop gun before you hurt someone with it." Paul handed him the pistol and fled into his tent.

Pia swooped through the night and folded Tommy in her arms, turning him away from the scene. She glared at Doodah. "How could you do this to an innocent child?"

Doodah glanced at his feet. "Ma'am, we were only helping

Tommy get revenge. That fat slob deserved it. He scared Tommy something awful."

"What are you talking about?"

Tommy pulled his head from his mother's protective embrace. "Remember, Mom, I told you. He scared me so bad I sat in my own shit!"

"Tommaso, I will not have you using four-letter words."

"But Mom, he—"

"And look at you! You're filthy dirty, and you're soaking wet." Tommy sneezed violently. "And you're getting a cold, too."

Pia hustled him off through the dark. The field of battle soon cleared of contestants and spectators; explanations, sniggers, and questions, then more questions and laughter, passed from Doodah and Joellen to the rest of the camp.

A half hour later, the bottom dropped out of the rain clouds. In the morning the campsite was a mud bog.

CHAPTER 23

Monday Morning, June 22

Megan had been awakened from a restless sleep by a brilliant shaft of light creeping under the tent she shared with Luella. She dressed quickly. Her sister was snoring heavily as she strolled through the warm sunlight to the cook tent.

Inside, the odors of bacon and coffee greeted her. She accepted a tin cup of the strong black brew from Joellen and wandered around examining things. When the rain began last night, the film crew had moved their equipment under the shelter of the tent. It was now crowded with boxes, crates, and bags of all sorts.

She heard footsteps squelching in the mud outside. Steamer ducked under the tent flap and smiled at her. It was as if she were back on the riverbank again, lying satiated in his arms. He came to her, and, as they moved behind a stack of boxes, she noticed Pia enter the tent. The expression on Pia's face might have scared Megan if she had seen it, but there was no space in her being for anyone but Steamer.

They were not completely hidden from view, but she did not care. Their kiss sent waves of pleasure rumbling through her. She wanted it to last and last, but the pleasant sensations were soon overwhelmed by the terror that had haunted her sleep.

"Steamer, stop!" She pushed him away.

"What is it?" he asked, hurt and worry in his voice.

"Oh, Steamer, I love you so! I never in a million years would have thought it could be like this. I want to be with you forever, but—" She buried her face in his shirt. He stroked her hair gently.

"What is it, Megan?"

"I'm so frightened. Let's get out of here, now. Just saddle up and get the hell out."

He raised her face, searched her eyes. "Right *now*?"

"Yes!" She nodded vigorously. "Yes, now. Oh, Steamer, you have no idea what I've been living with. It's Fiona. I've got to get away from her. She's responsible for the smuggling operation that's bringing all the booze into town. I have no idea how it got started, but she and TT are up to their eyeballs in shit."

Steamer smiled at her. "Another four-letter word from the lady."

She thumped him on the chest. "Don't! That's not funny, damn it. She and TT and Terry and God knows who else, they're all tied to the mob like Siamese twins. Me, too, don't you see?"

He drew back a bit with a grim look on his face. "Yeah, yeah. It doesn't matter that you've never had anything to do with it. If they think you know something about it—and you do—they might kill you to keep you from talking."

"Not *might*. They will. I told you Gertie was listening in. She likes to gossip, and she heard someone saying they were going to kill us. All of us."

"Okay, you're right. We do have to get you out of this mess, but not right now." She stared at him in disbelief. "Look, if we ride out now, what do you think that will say to them?"

"I'd look guilty, is what you're saying."

"Right. And what do you think your husband would do? And your mother-in-law? Are they going to just roll over and play dead?"

"No. They'd do anything to keep me from leaving." She nodded. "Okay, but what do we do?"

"We're safe here for now. We've got another week to ten days before we finish filming and have to head back. That will give us time to make a plan."

Megan wiped her eyes on her sleeve. "We could make a better plan if we weren't hungry."

He laughed. "Right. Let's go see what Joellen and Betty have whomped up for us."

As they moved from the semi-concealment of the boxes, Megan saw Pia examining herself with great care in a hand mirror.

"Good morning, Pia."

Pia plucked one hair from her eyebrow, then shifted her gaze in the mirror to look at Megan. "Good morning, Mrs. Foxworth."

Pia's emotions had been bubbling like a witches' cauldron ever since Megan and Steamer had ducked behind the boxes. Steamer had turned her down for a *contadina*, a farm girl.

She examined herself again, searching for flaws. But her nose was straight, her skin smooth and soft, and her dark hair cut in the latest mode from Hollywood. Her teeth were white and even, and her eyes were large and luminous. The pot of anger and jealousy inside her threatened to boil over. Pia yanked it from the flames; it would do her no good to dump it on them now.

She wanted, suddenly and desperately, to escape, to run and hide where Uncle would never find her. But she knew he would always find her. That man on the train, he was surely in Jackson Hole by now, sniffing around and asking questions about her. Uncle would never forgive her for delaying the production. Throwing a tantrum now would be like throwing gasoline on a fire.

She had made a major tactical error by coming on the trip. Now she was trapped here with no reasonable way to get back and report to Uncle. Even if she tried to ride out now, she'd never find her way back to town. Plus Tommaso was coughing and sneezing in their tent, and his forehead was hot to her touch.

The memory of Uncle's cigarette sizzling on her arm made her wince. No, she'd have to find another solution—and the solution was to turn the screws down on Alan. She found him sitting next to Bettina. They were talking quietly together as they ate. She rose and made her way through the crowd and stood looking down at them with her hands folded in front of her. At last Bettina looked up.

"Good morning, Bettina. Good morning, Alan." He sopped up the last of his egg yolk with his toast and nodded at her.

"May I sit with you for a moment?" Pia did not wait for an invitation but sank down onto the log on the other side of Alan. "So, Alan. What are we doing today?"

"*We*, Mrs. Donatelli?" Bettina asked, eyeing Pia over her coffee mug. "Do you have some sort of proprietary interest in this film?"

Alarm flooded over Pia at Bettina's use of the words "proprietary interest." She remembered they could have several meanings, such as did she have a *personal* interest, or did she have a *monetary* interest. It made no difference exactly what Bettina had meant; it was clear she was suspicious.

Pia covered up with an innocent smile and a gush of sugary words. "Oh, Mrs. Segal, I'm just so fascinated with all this, I feel as if I'm a part of it. I know I'm really not, but now that I've been here, I'm just so anxious to see how everything turns out."

Bettina smiled blandly at her. "Yes, of course." She turned to her husband. "Well, dear, what *are* you doing today?"

Alan laughed a fake-jovial laugh. "I am planning to get a lot of film shot today. Same thing everyone else is planning."

"Oh, that's wonderful." Pia paused long enough to indicate she was going to change the subject, but not long enough for Alan to grab hold of the conversation. "All this riding around in the outdoors is so exciting, isn't it? You must miss your sons. I'm sure they'd enjoy being here if they weren't so busy in Italy."

Alan charged back into the conversation as if she had not changed the subject. "So you see, Pia, you can just relax and enjoy a day in camp while we're out filming."

"Please, don't sentence me to jail, Alan! I do so want to go with you to watch the filming. I'm just so fascinated by it."

"I'll tell you what." He nodded as if in agreement with himself and continued. "Today would be a good day to get some shots of you jumping."

She was about to reply when Parley strode up to them. "Mr. Segal, best you go out shooting right now. I don't trust this weather to hold. You'll want to get back to camp in plenty of time. Mornin', Miss Pia. Say, maybe you'd like to ride out with me, help me round up some strays we've got running around back here?"

Pia smiled a quick, hard smile that did nothing to disarm Parley. "Thank you so much, Mr. Frampton, but Alan has asked me to go with them. To do some filming of me jumping."

Alan rose. "All right, everyone. Let's get to work."

Junior could feel the anger boiling through his veins like tiny little bubbles of white-hot fury. The problem was, it was doing nothing to keep him warm. His fingers were stiff and numb, and when his hand slipped and slammed into the pack saddle, the pain was intense. He could feel Pa's fancy beaded gloves inside his shirt. If he could put them on, his hands would be warm—but he wasn't ready for Pa to know about them just yet.

Where in hell had this freaky cold air come from? Here it was June, summer supposedly, and the camp was a bog of icy mud. Damn them all anyway, beginning with Alan. What a damned fool he was for wanting to go off shooting somewhere else this afternoon. Now Junior had to pack up the camera gear.

He finished checking Betsy's halter and was moving on to Patch, the next pack animal, when he stopped. Something was not right. There was no weak link in the lead rope between Betsy and Patch. There should have been a loop of binder twine between the two lead ropes. That way if one pack animal got hung up, or spooked and bolted, the twine would break and the animal ahead would not get dragged down. He'd have to get the twine from Betty and fix it.

He moved on to the next set of pannies and started hanging them on the pack saddle. He could tell that Jennifer, the mare, was as angry as he was about the stupidity of moving just one mile.

Pa didn't yap at the horses about fornicating. Animals just did it naturally, and so why was he was not supposed to do it? God hadn't punished Steamer or Megan, and what the hell had they been doing if it wasn't fornicating? He stopped working abruptly, stunned by his next thought. Here he'd been so damned worried about what God *would* do to him that he hadn't paid any attention to what He *hadn't done:* He hadn't punished Pa or him for fornicating with Jasmine.

He pursued this chain of thought as he moved on to the next pack animal. He heaved the load up onto the saddle, covered it with a manty, and tied it down with a diamond hitch. God hadn't punished his pa or him for fucking a whore, and God hadn't punished Steamer for fucking Megan beside the river. Did that make Megan a whore?

Damned if that wasn't the answer: all women were whores.

He felt his anger and frustration lift and fly away like an eagle soaring high in the sky. Daphne had all but agreed to ride out with him to their hunting cabin after breakfast, and then Alan had thrown shit over everything by dragging Daphne off to be filmed. Never mind. They could ride out tonight just as well. He smiled with relief and anticipation.

"What's that shit-eating grin all about, son?"

Fear stabbed him, then vanished. He had Pa's number now. He wasn't going to be afraid of him any longer. "Shitty weather coming," he replied.

Pa gave him an odd look and glanced up at the clouds overhead. "Most likely. Now get this show on the road." He started to walk away.

"Hey, Pa! Wait a minute." Pa turned back, frowned at him. "You didn't put . . . I mean, I didn't see a weak link between Betsy and Patch."

"I know. We don't have time to fix it."

"But Pa, what if—"

"You're only going a mile. I want to get ahead of that damn film crew. Couple of horses need shoeing." When Pa used that tone of voice, there was no arguing with him.

After a while they started moving down the trail. Trouble was coming; Junior could feel it in his bones.

That night Megan listened to the rain slamming down outside. The rain made it highly unlikely that anyone would come looking for her, so she snuggled deeper into Steamer's embrace. Her body and soul were still vibrating with a deep, resonant note that filled her with hope and tranquility.

Thanks to Luella, the shoot that afternoon had been a disaster. So when the rain had started again that night, Megan hesitated about one half second before deciding that Luella could damned well sleep by herself for one night. After gulping dinner, she and Steamer needed no words; they simply went to Steamer's tent as if it was the most natural thing in the world. Once cocooned in the warmth of his blanket roll, they made love to the howl of the wind, the gurgle of rainwater rushing around the tent in little channels, and the occasional flash of lightning.

A few die-hards were still up. Megan could hear drunken laughter and exuberant voices still emanating from the cook tent. Among the loudest was Luella. Megan could always tell the state of her sister's inebriation: the more she drank, the more her voice became hard and brassy, until she sounded like a bugle blowing the call to charge.

Steamer seemed to know she was thinking about her sister. He rolled onto his back and asked, "What happened this afternoon with Daphne?"

Megan watched the candlelight flicker on his face for a moment. "Uh, well, it started to rain on the way back from the shoot. She didn't have her rain gear tied on the back of her saddle, so she persuaded Junior to stop and dig it out of her duffel bag. Which was on a pack mule."

He rolled over onto one elbow and stroked her cheek. "And then?"

"My idiot sister flapped her slicker around like she was shaking out a rug. So what do you think happened next?"

He laughed. "The mule was real cool, calm, and collected and just stood there and watched?"

"Of course it did!" She kissed him. "And her duffel bag and a bunch of others sort of jumped off the pack saddle and threw themselves over the side of the trail." She kissed him again. "Junior has a splendid vocabulary of cuss words. Very imaginative, very colorful. Didn't help that it was getting dark, either. Took almost an hour to get everything loaded and strapped down again."

Steamer was silent for a long while. Megan was wondering why when he turned and looked directly at her. "Megan, booze is destroying your sister."

She nodded slowly. "I guess I'm beginning to see that. I haven't seen her for, what? Three, four years now? And she doesn't write, and she's always busy when we try to telephone. What's going on with her down there?"

"Her drinking has become worse the past year, year and a half." He continued, telling her about the deterioration he'd witnessed. He told her about how Daphne had gradually become a liability on the set, despite her great photogenic quality. "Alan refuses to see it," he said. "He's, ah, involved with her."

Megan sat up with a sharp intake of breath and stared at him. "Oh, God, what a mess!" She lay down again and gazed at the roof of the tent. "I suppose I should have guessed. Oh, Steamer, what am I to do with her?"

"Well, she's not the only person in Hollywood with a drinking problem." He reached for her hand and held it. "There's a hospital in Santa Barbara that specializes in treating people like Daphne. They've developed some sort of new way of helping them. As soon as we get back, we can get her admitted."

"We?"

He leaned over, looking at her with a big smile. "I'll be glad to help you, Megan."

"Thank you. Good idea. But . . ."

She could see panic and disappointment flood across his face as he asked, "But what?"

"I've dragged you into such a terrible mess. It won't be easy. Fiona will fight us tooth and claw. She knows I know too much about . . . about what's going on at the ranch. I'm scared, Steamer. They won't just let me walk away."

"Shhh. No one is going to hurt you." He cradled her face in

his calloused hands. "They'd have to get over my dead body to get at you."

She thrust herself into his arms, laughing and realizing that there was an edge of hysteria in her laugh. "They won't have a chance to hurt us. We are going to be devout cowards and run and hide where they can never find us."

"All right. We can work it out; I know we can."

Then they were quiet, listening to the rain dripping off the pines onto the tent. The noise in the cook tent was diminishing, and they were drifting off to sleep when Megan shook him.

"Huh! What?"

"Listen."

"I don't hear anything."

"That's just it. No rain."

Steamer pulled the tent flap aside, and brilliant moonlight shone through. "You're right." He kissed her. "Now go to sleep."

She did, as did he, so they did not hear squelching footsteps and a high-pitched giggle as two people passed by outside.

Junior walked on tiptoe—not that there was much chance anyone would hear them. The picket line was a hundred yards from camp, to keep the smell of horse shit and the horse flies from annoying the guests.

He settled Daphne on a dry spot and walked with great care to the picket line, where five horses stood motionless. The majority of the horses had been hobbled and turned out to pasture. Doodah, Shorty, and Curly had picketed their mounts so they could ride out in the morning, round up the rest of the herd, and drive them back to camp.

Before moonrise and while all the others were eating dinner, Junior had added his stud horse, Champion, and Peaches, Daphne's mare, to the picket line. He'd stashed their saddles and bridles close by. Now he plucked the canvas cover off their tack and picked up the bridle for Champion. He whickered softly as he bridled him and swung his saddle onto his back. He was tightening the cinch on Peaches a few minutes later when a sucking noise made him look around.

"Going somewhere, son?" Pa pulled his other boot from the mud and stepped closer, shoving his hands deep into his hip pockets. His face was carved from frozen granite. Junior searched for a flicker of warmth, a hint of understanding, but Pa's face didn't change. Junior saw him glance at Daphne's horse, saddled and waiting.

He ransacked his mind for a way out, knew at last there was one, and only one, way out: to stand up and be counted among the men. "Yes, matter of fact. Me and Miss Devine, we're going for a little moonlight ride."

"Were you now." Pa moved closer with a slow, steady tread. His voice was frighteningly calm. "I do believe I've told you that I won't have you fornicating outside the bonds of holy matrimony, especially not with whores like that blonde floozy." He walked closer, until he was two feet away. "I have, haven't I?"

Junior backed off a pace. "You have. Yes, indeed, you have." He sucked in a giant breath and let it out. "The one person you don't seem to have told is yourself."

It seemed to him that tiny little cracks appeared in the rock slab of his pa's face. He was silent an unbearably long time, rocking back and forth on his heels. Finally he said, "And what in hell does that mean?"

Junior extracted Pa's beaded gloves from inside his shirt and held them out. "Thought you might like to have these back."

Junior would remember much later that in the brilliant, icy light of the moon, he could see and hear the cracks in his father widening and deepening like a frost-split boulder. He'd remember how he'd seen them running down his chest and legs.

"Where did . . . ?"

"In Jasmine's room."

Pa's fist shot out like the piston on a steam engine, catching Junior under the ribs. Pain exploded through him, and he stumbled back. Pa came after him. Another blow slammed into his ribs, and he felt one crack. "Pa! Stop! You're hurting me."

Pa moved forward again, and something went by Junior in a blur. He saw Daphne hurl herself at Pa, flailing at him, but Pa threw her aside like a wet dishrag and came on again, knocking Junior to the ground. Pa was drawing one booted foot back to kick when Daphne staggered to her feet and into Pa, throwing him off balance and knocking him down. They rolled in a tangle of arms and legs in the mud. Junior rose, grabbed his father, and rolled him off Daphne. Then Junior dropped with both knees onto his father's gut. Pa gasped for breath, and the fight went out of him.

Junior stood, pulling Daphne to him and sheltering her in his arms.

Pa got to his feet and stood, weaving slightly. "God will punish you for this."

"There ain't no God, Pa."

"How dare you blaspheme."

"If God was up there, he would have punished you long ago for what you've done to Ma all these years."

Pa started to move toward him, but Junior closed the distance between them in two quick strides. He shoved his fist in Pa's face. "You hit me again, and, by God, I'll kill you."

"You little worm. Get the hell out of my life, and don't ever show your face in this valley again."

Junior laughed hysterically. "If there is a God, may He strike you dead with His lightning."

Pa said nothing, only turned and walked away. Junior turned to Daphne. "Can you ride?"

"All I want to do is get as far away from here as I can. If I fall off, tie me on."

An hour later, they were in the warmth and shelter of the hunting cabin. Junior built a fire in the woodstove, opened a can of beef stew, and put it on to warm. He pumped up a bucket of water, and, when it was hot, they took turns cleaning the mud and blood from each other. Daphne taped his ribs; they ate and lay down together.

CHAPTER 24

Tuesday Morning, June 23

Megan had awakened very early and left Steamer sleeping. People were already giving them knowing looks or glancing quickly away with a little smile as they passed. There was no point in adding grist to the gossip mill. The news would reach Fiona soon enough.

She sipped her coffee and gazed out beneath the flap of the cook tent. Off to the north dark clouds were an omen of more rain, or perhaps even snow, to come. It was the strangest weather for June she'd ever experienced.

The thud of heavy boots in the mud outside made her look up. Parley stomped under the shelter of the tent. His face matched the clouds to the north.

"Good morning, Parley," she said.

He stopped as if he'd slammed into a granite wall. "You!" he snarled.

She drew back in alarm. "What's . . . what is it?"

He closed the space between them like a freight locomotive. She feared he was going to shout at her, but with Betty and Jo-ellen chattering like squirrels as they prepared breakfast, he leaned over her and kept his voice low. It was more threatening than if he had shouted.

"Seems like Junior and your sister went off for a little ride last night."

"Ride? I don't understand."

He looked to both sides, seeming to realize that Betty and Jo-ellen were watching curiously. He moved closer yet and dropped his voice again. "What's not to understand, since it's all your fault?"

Megan scooted back and tried to rise, but he jabbed a finger at her, nailing her to the packing back she sat on. "Yes, you! You and all the others like you with the morals of a mink, sashaying around in your skimpy clothes, tempting a man to abandon his faith!"

"Wait one damned minute!" Megan rose and forced Parley to back off a foot or two. He blinked in surprise. "Are you telling me they haven't come back yet?"

She watched his jaw tighten until she thought she'd hear his teeth crack. She could see Betty and Joellen looking at something behind her but did not dare turn around.

Parley leaned closer, his face contorted with fury. "Don't play the innocent little girl with me. You know damn good and well what that whore of a sister has done to my son."

She was now certain he was going to hit her and backed away—and into someone. She thought her heart would stop from fear until she realized the man behind her was Doodah.

He pulled her gently away from Parley, sheltering her, then stood smiling at him as if he were no more than a puppy. "Now then, Mr. Frampton," he began. "I do believe this would be a good time for you to just go on about your business. Unless, of course, you'd like to tell everyone all about how you drink jas-mine tea."

Megan would ask Doodah later what that was all about, but right now she was too amazed at the effect this skinny old geezer had on Parley, who turned ashen, slowly retreated, and left the tent.

"You all right now, Megan?" Doodah asked.

250

"Yes, okay, I'll be fine. Thanks for . . . whatever it was you did."

Doodah chuckled. "All bullies have a weak spot. That's why they're bullies. Now how about we get some flapjacks and eggs?"

As she and Doodah ate, questions kept popping into her mind only to be displaced by fear. She'd seen Parley castrating calves with a dirty knife, then branding them as if they were made of stone while they bawled in pain when the red-hot iron sizzled on their hide.

Should she tell Steamer what had happened? He'd defend her, she was certain of that, but he'd be no match for Parley. Steamer might have been born on a ranch, but he was now civilized, educated, and sophisticated. Parley would not kill him; he'd simply cripple him for life.

Doodah might have been reading her thoughts. He'd gotten up to bring her more coffee, but, as she held out her mug, he did not pour. She looked up into his weathered face.

"You take good care of Stan, you hear?" She nodded, and he poured. "He don't belong here no more. Cowboying is a hard, dirty, exhausting job. He could do it at one time, but he's a city boy now. When we get back, you dump Terry and make your life with Stan, you hear me?"

"I hear you, Uncle Doodah. And thank you."

Pia watched Alan hold a long Havana cigar next to his ear as he rolled it between his fingers.

"Why do you do that?"

He fired the cigar with a wooden match, puffing huge clouds of smoke before he answered. "To tell if it's still fresh. If it makes a crackling noise, it's too dry."

"I see." Pia shuddered inwardly, glad that Uncle smoked only cigarettes. The burn from a cigar would be three times as big

251

and far more painful. "But tell me. You haven't said a word about . . ."

Alan had ordered Steamer to shoot a screen test of her this morning. Neither man had said much after it was done. At lunch she had alternated between extremes. She'd be sure on one hand that she had failed, and then sure on the other that she had passed, as they said here, "with flying colors." Now she was suspicious that Alan was delaying telling her just to make her uncomfortable.

"About what, Pia?" Steamer had come up behind them and now plopped down on the log beside her.

"Oh, Steamer! You know what I'm talking about."

Alan faced her directly and said, "I'll tell you, Pia. You are going to be Segal Studios' next star. A bright, shining star in the firmament of Hollywood."

It was as if a granite slab had suddenly been lifted from her, a weight she had not until now realized she was carrying. If she were a star, Uncle would not dare touch her.

"Is this true, Steamer? Was I that good?"

He nodded, but there was a lack of enthusiasm in the gesture that immediately cut the cream off the top of her happiness. Why was he responding that way?

"Yes, damn it, you were," Alan said. "And not only that, but all those shots of you jumping, they were great, too. We'll be able to use them, and it's going to be a great film."

She could sense Steamer's agitation even before he spoke. "Damn it, Alan, how are we supposed to cut shots of Pia jumping on a flat saddle in jodhpurs into a story about a pioneer woman in 1870 whose husband is killed by cattle rustlers?"

"Oh, don't be such a worrywart, Steamer." Alan's tone was hearty and jovial, yet carried a hint of uncertainty. "Simple, Steamer. Esse will rewrite the script."

Steamer guffawed loudly, shot to his feet, and stared at Alan in disbelief. "Well, good luck. I'll want to meet the magician who can stitch those two stories into a seamless whole." With a final shake of his head, he walked off.

Pia's happiness began to curdle. *Was Steamer right?* Aloud she said, "So, Alan, tell me. Is the film going to make a lot of money?"

"Of course it is. We're getting great stuff out here. Steamer's just a director; he doesn't understand. The audience doesn't want a fancy story. All they want is a spectacle. And believe me, what we're shooting is spectacular."

"So. That is good news, yes? It means you'll be able to make a payment on your loan very soon, yes?"

He patted her arm as if she were a dog. "Pia, you just don't understand. There's still months and months of work before the film can be released and in theaters. For the love of God, back off! I'm doing my best. You'll get your money, I promise."

Now what was she supposed to do? If she obeyed Uncle and enforced collection of the loan, Segal Studios would certainly go broke. That would mean she'd lose her chance of stardom and the freedom from Uncle that being a star would bring her.

How much did Alan owe right now? She sorted through her memories and came up with a sum. She could make a payment out of her own money. It would leave her with only a very tiny cushion against disaster, but she'd do it. As soon as they got back to civilization, she'd lie about receiving money from Alan. It would buy her enough time.

She realized Alan was waiting for some sort of response. "Very well. Just do remember that your sons are still in Italy. We know where they are at all times."

He took a step toward her, and she shrank back from the look on his face. For the first time since she'd met him, a tremor of fear went through her. He'd gained courage somewhere, somehow.

He gave her a sardonic look. "And how do you plan to get back to town to tell your people? It's three days' ride either that way"—he gestured east—"or that way." He pointed west along the trail. "How will you eat and sleep? And protect Tommy from being attacked by a cougar when you are all alone?"

Chagrin bit into her, but she'd be damned before she'd let him see how deeply humiliated, infuriated, and exasperated she was—as much with herself as with him. She had rushed her fences again and been thrown. So she said, "A cougar? Is this a mountain lion?"

He nodded. She forced herself to smile and turned away to conceal her movements from people in camp. She took her .25 pistol from her coat pocket. "Then I would use this," she said and jabbed him in the ribs with it.

Alan glanced down, blanched slightly, and then sneered. "You don't expect that mouse gun to kill a cougar, do you?"

She concealed her dismay. "Of course. I am a very good shot, and I will let it get close. Now. When we return to civilization, I will send a cable to my people." *And a check to Uncle.* "Perhaps this good news will persuade them to be lenient."

She saw his gaze shift to something behind her and turned to look. Parley was stamping in their direction, wearing a scowl that turned quickly into a smile when he saw they were watching him.

"Mr. Segal. Miss Donatelli." Parley tipped his Stetson to her and turned back to Alan. "Just wondering if you had any plans for this afternoon."

"More of the same, Parley. More of the same," Alan said.

"I thought I might suggest something."

"Go ahead, Mr. Frampton," Pia said.

"If we ride out a little ways, there's a guy named Guil Huff who's got a nice spread down past Rattlesnake Canyon in the valley right next to the Gros Ventre River. Log cabin, barn, corral, horses, and steers, all that stuff. Could be a good place to film."

Alan frowned. "I don't think that's such a hot idea. We're on a roll. Might as well stay here. Won't waste so much time that way."

Parley stuck his hands in his hip pockets, looking somewhere between them. "Guil, he might let us put up in his barn for the night."

"Oh, Alan, that sounds like such a good idea. I'm so tired of sleeping in a tent," Pia said.

"Ah, well . . ." Alan scowled. "All right; I'll buy it. Steamer is going to squawk about it but never mind. Good idea, Parley."

"All right. I'm going to send Doodah and the girls on ahead with the chuck wagon. That way when we get there, they'll be all set up and waiting."

"And I'll tell everyone to pack," Alan said.

When she was alone, Pia allowed her emotions to surface. She'd won! Alan was completely under her control. She was pondering how she would kill Uncle when it struck her: of course! She wouldn't have to do it herself. Alan was going to make her a big star, and then she could afford to hire an assassin to do it. She walked to her tent smiling to herself.

Megan had seen Alan and Pia with their heads together. She wondered briefly what sort of plot they were hatching, but she was too deeply immersed in her own happiness to pay attention. She went back to gathering her belongings and packing.

She was, at last, going to escape from Fiona's talons. It was amazing how her life had turned upside down in just one day. Sure, when they got back to the Rocking Lazy F, there was going to be a huge dustup. Terry and Fiona and TT would lean on her to stay, and Terry would whine. But Steamer would stand by her, and she'd divorce Terry. She was going to have both: a career and a happy marriage.

Her rainbow dreams blinked out as a storm of icy reality hit her. She was being utterly, totally, and completely foolish. She was still entangled in the family spider web and still under a death threat from mysterious strangers. No one was going to let her merely waltz out and wave good-bye. She had to out-fox them all somehow.

Suddenly she realized: just because Steamer was *not* a Prohi didn't mean a real agent or agents weren't coming to town. Sally Mann was so dead set against alcohol that Megan had no doubt Sally had contacted Washington and stirred them into action.

What did she know that she could use as a weapon? She knew about the booze in the barn—but the minute Fiona got wind of anything wrong, those bottles would stampede into the backcountry never to be seen again. Many of their guests knew about the bottles, but they would lie to save their own hides.

Then Megan knew: she'd go to the file cabinet! She didn't know exactly what was on the papers Terry had put in there, but they had to be important if he was locking them away. When the film crew returned to the dude ranch, she'd find an opportunity to sneak a peek at those papers.

She folded the last of her clothing into her duffel bag and strapped it closed. They'd be moving out soon. She went to look for Steamer.

Steamer was sweating and cursing in what was called "The Black Hole." A tent made of layers of black canvas, it was just big enough to accommodate the camera magazines and one man. It was light tight and practically airtight. F-Stop had begged him to unload the last reel of film from the morning shoot; he'd already done six and was tiring of the task.

Steamer now appreciated how hard F-Stop worked to unload

each reel of film and transfer it to its metal container. He extracted the film from the camera, fumbling in the dark. He put it in the can and seated the lid firmly. He threw open the double flap of the tent and exited, grateful for the fresh, cool air. He sealed the can with tape and labeled it with the date and place it had been exposed.

He looked up as a shadow fell across the can. Megan smiled down at him. "So, I guess we're going to be able to finish shooting down at Guil's place."

"Yep. Now, where is it?"

"What?"

He sorted through the cans of film waiting to be packed onto a mule. "There it is." He pulled one can from the pile. "Your screen test. I just want to keep it close by me. For good luck."

"Oh, Steamer, I love you so much." His face clouded over again. "We will be able to . . . to be together, won't we? Every time I think about the future, I get scared."

"Absolutely. I guarantee it." A loud neigh made him turn. "Looks like we're about ready to move out."

Megan moved around the campsite, watching it return to wilderness. She felt overwhelmed with happiness. Even the dark clouds massing to the west and the cold did not dampen her mood. In two hours, she'd be warm and comfortable in Guil's barn, and she and Steamer could start to plan their future.

Now she mentally ticked off names as riders and their mounts gradually moved out. Doodah, Betty, and Joellen had left an hour ago with the chuck wagon. Shorty and Manuel, leading pack mules with their duffel bags, followed them. Parley rode at the head of the second group like a victorious army general. Behind him, Alan, Esse, F-Stop, and Marlene rode in a cluster, shouting ideas back and forth. Freddy Denys and Sandor Kalman followed close behind, their saddlebags bulging with exposed film. Last in line had been Curly leading pack mules.

Who was left? She looked around. Tommy's cold had gotten worse. He had a hacking cough and sneezed violently every few minutes. Bettina and Eric Winchester, the hairdresser, were helping Pia pack their saddlebags. Katrina and Fayrene were gossiping, as usual, until the last minute came to mount up. Miguel folded the two tents and prepared to pack them on a mule. The tents would not be needed at Guil's and had been left as the last thing to be packed up.

Where in hell were Junior and her sister? Megan scanned the area, hoping to see them riding in from wherever that hunting cabin was. Not seeing them, she heard the telltale clinking noise of a horse with a loose shoe and turned. Steamer was approaching, leading Splotch.

"Loose shoe?"

Steamed nodded. "I tried to pull it off, but it's not quite loose enough. Just have to hope it holds on until we get to the barn."

"Okay." She nodded. "What do you say we move out?"

He gathered her in his arms and gave her a long, passionate kiss. He broke off. "Junior and Daphne?"

She shrugged. "They'll find us. Whenever."

"So go get Nevada and mount up. I'll help Tommy and Pia get mounted."

CHAPTER 25

Tuesday Afternoon, June 23

Fiona tensed every muscle in her body to hold her fear under control; it helped keep her from screaming at TT as well. She really loved the damned old fool. They'd been together for thirty years, good times and bad. But damn it, why couldn't he lay off the booze? He'd forgotten everything she'd told him.

"Damn it, TT! I told you!"

TT pushed and pulled at the wheelchair's rims, agitatedly moving his chair back and forth a half inch each time. "Aw, now, Fiona, I'm real sorry. Seems like recently I just have trouble remembering things. Tell me again."

"Maybe if you laid off the booze for a while, it would help."

He hung his head. "Yeah, well, I'll try, but the pain in my leg, you know, it gets so bad and the only thing—"

"Glen May came by last night. To pick up the check Alan left for him, to pay for the band, okay?" TT nodded. "And he said to me, he said, 'You sure have a gold mine in that daughter-in-law of yours.'"

TT rocked his chair back and forth. "I guess I'd have to say I agree with him. So what?"

Fiona wanted to scream with exasperation but controlled her anger. "Junior, ah—you remember we agreed that Junior was supposed to make sure Megan had . . . ah, an accident, right? You remember that?" He nodded, head hanging.

"That was Sunday afternoon, and this is Tuesday morning, a

day and a half since he called in from Kelly. So what if he's done it already?"

TT raised his head and focused on her. She could see he was struggling to remember. "Yeah, if she's scarred up, she won't look good for the movies."

Fiona sat down close to his wheelchair, took his hands in hers, and gazed directly at him. "I've been a damn fool." She choked back a sob. "I'm so damn jealous of her. She's young and beautiful, and I'm not anymore and . . ."

TT leaned his head against hers. "You'll always be beautiful to me, Fiona."

"Oh, God, TT, I want to go home!" She wiped her eyes on the sleeve of her blouse. "I'm so scared and tired of all this. Let's just get the hell out of here."

"Can't, old girl. They'd find us no matter where we went."

"Well, what the hell do we do? Remember, Junior said that Megan was going to confess to Steamer."

Something registered in his eyes, and the look of confusion left his face. "Oh, yeah. Shit, now I remember. Oh, double shit. We gotta do something." Then TT started working out their problem. "Seems to me the first thing to do is call Junior off. I'll tell Terry to ride out and tell Junior that his Ma wants him, that she's in the hospital. He'll do anything for her."

"Good idea. But what about Megan?"

TT nodded slowly for a moment. "Remember that Megan was going to stay home, not go out with them. It wasn't until we told her we needed the money she would bring in that she decided to go."

Fiona clutched TT's arm. "Oh! I was so angry at her, I didn't pay attention. What did you have in mind?"

"Get her home, loosen up on her, let her go to the movies as much as she wants, and sing and play. Maybe that would keep her home."

Fiona felt a bit of hope. "That might work. If she hasn't fallen in love with that Steamer person."

TT nodded, a grim smile on his face. "Right. I'll go find Terry."

A timid tapping at the office door shut off the rest of her worries. "What is it?"

It was one of the kitchen maids. "Miz Foxworth, there's a gennamum here as wants to speak with you."

"Thank you, Mary." Fiona rose and opened the door—and clutched the doorjamb in terror. The stranger who stood there was a lawman. She knew it; her instincts about such things had been honed by years of encounters with such men.

"Mrs. Foxworth?" Fiona managed to nod. "My name is Raymond Drago." He was holding out a leather wallet with a shiny badge. "I'm with the Prohibition Unit of the federal government."

Steamer saw the bulbous shapes on the slopes of Sheep Mountain come into view slowly as the Hollywood folks rode down Rattlesnake Canyon. When he first caught sight of them, Steamer was amused and expected the boulders to bah or bleat like real sheep. Then, as Splotch jogged along, he had thought about the warmth and shelter that lay ahead in Guil Huff's barn. He'd gone back to his thoughts about Megan.

Vestiges of their riverbank encounter still oscillated through his body. As thrilling as that experience had been, something even more exciting and non-physical had sprung up between them. This was resonating beyond the mere physiology of sex. He was as excited about the future as he had ever been. He glanced at his watch: it showed him it was four fifteen.

He knew how he felt about Paul: suspicious and uneasy. After firing wildly into the darkness on Friday night, Paul had come whining to him, begging him to get his pistol back from Parley.

When Steamer refused, Paul had threatened to kill him.

A strange noise made him look up. Sheep Mountain was falling on him! Except it had to be an illusion, since mountains don't fall on people. It was a hallucination brought on by fatigue, by the cold, and by the rain that somehow kept slithering under his saddle slicker to soak into his determination to be a good sport.

But Splotch pricked his ears forward, and his gait became a nervous jolt as the ground shook, and a rumbling screech overrode the burble of the river below. Steamer stroked the horse's neck, spoke soothingly to him, and looked again at the mass of rock billowing a thousand feet above the narrow trail. The movement was no illusion.

He wanted time to think. He wanted time to be terrified. But Splotch was jolting in a nervous frenzy beneath him. Behind him, Megan made an explosive, terrified noise halfway between a shout and a scream. He turned back in his saddle. Her face told him she, too, was trying to decide whether this was a horror or a hoax. He wanted to go to her, but he was powerless as Splotch and Nevada were now lurching and rearing in panic. They could do nothing but hang on and watch.

On the narrow trail below, horses were neighing and humans were screaming, but the sounds were soon submerged beneath the shrieking roar of the mountain. Parley and eight riders behind him were in the direct path of the landslide. Trapped by the raging Gros Ventre River on their left, and with Curly and Miguel and the pack mules behind, they were trying to drive their horses up the near-vertical canyon wall to the north.

Some had turned their horses around but could not pass the knot of riders behind them, who were also fighting to turn their panic-stricken mounts. Some managed to stay on; others were thrown to the ground, leaving their horses to run, heads high, eyes wide, and riderless. Two horses plunged into the river, unseating their riders, who struggled to swim against the icy current. Steamer could see mouths open; he knew those mouths were shouting orders or yelling in terror, but the noise of the monstrous wave of rock, earth, and trees continued to drown mere human sounds.

Movement along the trail on the opposite side of the river caught Steamer's eye. He registered a brief image of Guil Huff frantically spurring his horse northward, before the horror of the slide claimed his full attention once again. The leading edge of the landslide reached the bottom of the canyon. It surged up the north wall like an ocean wave breaking on a steep shore. Parley and the riders with him vanished beneath it.

A second front of the wave ran toward the next clump of riders. By now the dust billowing up from the slide obscured Steamer's view. He saw a truck-sized boulder bounce through the air and graze someone; boulder, rider, and horse disappeared in a slough of mud. The mass of earth stopped moving soon afterwards, and Steamer thought he saw three humans again.

He waited for the wave to retreat and leave its cargo on the shore of the canyon like toddlers on a beach, but the mountain remained squelching contentedly as it settled into the swollen river. A final dusting of boulders settled into place like powdered sugar on a cake.

It was over.

The hiss of the rain returned, but something was wrong. Then it came to him that his body was locked in a giant vise. As he forced himself to relax, the sights and sounds of the real world began to penetrate once again. An odd sound behind him resolved itself into the clatter of someone talking.

Megan was shaking and sobbing, talking to herself and to the mountain. Making certain Splotch was under control, Steamer dismounted with care, went to her, and helped her slide from the saddle. She babbled feverishly, but nothing made sense. After a while she stopped and shivered in his arms for a long time. When at last she calmed down, he wiped her face with his bandana.

She stared at him, fighting for words. "What do we do now?"

"Well, this is as good an excuse as any to go home, I guess."

"Stop it! Stop it! How can you be so flippant? People are dead down there!"

"Sorry," he mumbled. "I don't . . . I can't . . ."

The word "dead" finally penetrated the wall of disbelief he had erected. He was, suddenly and unexpectedly, ice cold. His vision blurred and wavered. He sank to the ground, unable to control the convulsive trembling turning his legs and arms to mush. Megan collapsed beside him; they clung to each other for a long time.

At last Steamer got himself under control. Supporting Megan on one arm and leading their horses with the other, they went down to join the other survivors.

Fiona had, at the sight of Raymond Drago's shiny badge, come within an inch of vomiting with terror, but she managed to do little more than collapse into her chair and swallow hard.

"Prohibition Unit?" she gasped. "What do you want with us?"

"My job is to enforce the law under Volstead Act of 1919. May I sit down?"

Fiona sprang up and dragged a chair from the back of the office. As she and the agent sat, she glanced at TT. He was holding one finger to his lips as if pondering the mysteries of the universe, but she knew he meant to keep calm.

"I take it you do know what the Volstead Act is?" Fiona nodded vigorously. "Prohibits the sale and consumption of alcoholic beverages. With a few exceptions, of course," he added.

"We know what the law is," TT said in a croaking voice. "We obey the law here in Wyoming."

Drago nodded. "I'm sure you do. I'm not here about that, however." He pulled a photograph from his briefcase and showed it to Fiona and then TT. Fiona felt a small measure of hope begin to creep up on her. It was of Pia.

"I'm looking for this woman," Drago continued. "Your sheriff told me she is a visitor to your lovely ranch."

"Yes, she is," Fiona said. "Uh, why are you looking for her?"

"All I can tell you is that she is wanted for questioning in connection with . . . well, never mind that. She is here, isn't she?"

Fiona felt hope rising to an even higher level. Maybe he wasn't going to search the ranch after all. "She's not here right now."

"I see. Rather, I don't. Did she go somewhere else?"

"She has gone off into the backcountry." Fiona told him how Pia had inserted herself into the moviemakers' company and then ridden out with them on their trip in search of virgin scenery.

Drago leaned back with a frown and nodded to himself. "That's what the sheriff said. Just checking to make sure." He rose. "Okay. I need to go to the telegraph office again. So long."

He shook TT's hand and departed. Fiona and TT waited five minutes in silence, occasionally glancing at each other in disbelief. When Fiona was sure he had gone, relief flooded through her.

"Go get Terry. He's got to find Junior and bring him back in here right now."

TT nodded and started to wheel his chair out but then stopped. "You know what, old girl? Something's wrong here."

"What in hell are you talking about?"

"I've seen too damn many lawmen's badges to be fooled."

265

H. Lee Pratt

"And?"

"That badge of his looked to me like a cheap fake."

266

CHAPTER 26

Tuesday Evening, June 23

Twelve riders had gathered a hundred yards from the base of the slide. Those who still had horses had dismounted and were holding their lead ropes; the horses stood quietly, heads down. No one said much. Some limped, some bled, some stared, and some sobbed. As Megan and Steamer joined them, Steamer sensed an undercurrent of hysteria ready to boil to the surface.

Something ugly seethed to the surface of his own mind. He was angry with Parley for dying. Now there was no one to take charge and lead them safely out of the wilderness. With a muttered curse, he climbed on a rock, stuck two fingers in his mouth and whistled. Heads turned in his direction. As they realized someone was making noises like a leader, they snuggled up to him like puppies.

"Anyone seen Parley?" Steamer called. He'd seen Parley vanish; did he expect him to materialize from beneath the avalanche?

Fayrene pointed at the slide. "Under that."

"Just checking." Steamer could see an eruption of some powerful emotion working its way up from deep inside her.

Seconds later it splattered him. "How come you don't ask about Freddy?" she shouted. "He's under there, too! What the hell do you mean, 'just checking'? How can you be so damn thoughtless?"

Steamer wanted to melt into his boots and vanish. "Sorry,"

he mumbled. "I wasn't thinking." He made an effort to shrug off the mantle of leadership they were throwing over his shoulders.

"Where's Junior?" he asked. Then he remembered, and the thought that Junior and Daphne might be fucking in warm, dry comfort brought with it a blast of anger. Had he been a fire-breathing dragon he would have flown to the cabin and charbroiled Junior.

"Can we get to the hunting cabin?" Steamer asked Miguel.

"Don't know where it is," Miguel answered. "Me an' Manuel, we jus' start working for Parley this summer."

Steamer saw he was grimacing, holding his arm against his side. "Arm broken?"

"Jus' bruised bad. It'll be okay."

"How do we get out of here?"

Miguel shook his head. "I not rode this trail before." He looked east. "I theenk same way we came."

Bettina was soaking wet and shivering violently. She jerked her chin at the landslide. "Can't we climb over that? I've got to find Alan. He's down there somewhere."

Everyone turned to look at the mass of earth blocking their route to civilization. Behind it, the patch of lighter grey that marked the position of the sun had moved closer to the horizon. Steamer studied the gigantic mass of boulders and mud. Splintered pine trees stuck out of the mass like bones from a compound fracture.

"No way we could get the horses over that rubble. And we'd have a long way to walk, even if we could."

Fayrene's voice was gritty with despair. "What do we do about everyone . . . under that? Freddy . . . his body . . ." She choked back tears.

Steamer jammed his hands in his pockets and tried to think clearly. What were their options? He turned to Miguel. "All the food was with Doodah and the girls. Any way they can get back to us?" *Assuming they're still alive.*

"*Creo que no es possible.*" Miguel spat a gob of chewing tobacco at the slide. "Guil's place ees back up the trail from the slide. I don' theenk they can go past the slide."

"*Ehi!* We could swim out," Pia said. She was clutching Tommy closely to her, shaking so violently that Tommy was squirming to get away from her.

"That water is ice cold," Steamer replied. "You'd be too numb to keep your head above water within ten minutes. Besides, we have no idea how long before the dam might break."

"But . . . we must do something," she wailed. "Anything would be better than standing here doing nothing."

Steamer whistled on his fingers. "All right, listen up, everyone! It will be dark soon. Best thing we can do is make camp for the night and ride out tomorrow." He looked back up the trail. "Miguel?"

"*Si?*"

Steamer pointed back up the trail. "Get up there on that little bench under those pines and get a fire going, okay?"

Miguel nodded and started off.

"Megan, you go with Eric and see if you can't round up some of the horses that bolted." She remained silent for a long time. He shook her arm to snap her out of it. "You all right?"

Megan seemed to be clawing herself up from a deep chasm of pain and grief. "Damned well better had be, hadn't I?" Her voice was steady and calm. "Come on, Eric."

Fayrene's contralto voice rose over the quiet gurgle of the river. "What the hell are we doing standing around? I saw Freddy . . . after . . . afterward. He may still be up there. I'm going to look for him."

Steamer hesitated. Clambering over the slide was going to be extremely dangerous, but if there was any chance of finding a survivor, the try would be worth it. "Okay, I'll go help you look. Be damned careful."

As they rode toward the base of the slide, Steamer heard a horse behind him. Katrina was trotting to catch up with them, and Steamer remembered he had seen Sandor again after the slide had knocked him from his horse. He glanced back as he heard another horse and saw Bettina trotting to catch up.

As they approached the slide's base, Steamer sensed something wrong that threatened them. There was something he should understand but did not. The mass of the slide awed him. He swept his gaze from side to side and from top to bottom as they approached the slide. The dam was about half a mile wide and over two hundred-fifty feet high.

Then he understood. It *was* a dam. He looked eastward along the gorge. The river, no longer rain-swollen and furious, was quietly swelling into an ever-widening pool of muddy water. It had risen a foot already.

"The river!" he yelled as he dismounted. "It's rising fast. We can't stay long." He started up the face of the slide.

Fayrene and Katrina nodded, quickly dismounted, and followed him up the broken face of the dam. Rocks and boulders shifted beneath them, and their feet sank into soft spots as they climbed, searching and calling, toward the top. Bettina followed close behind him.

Steamer clambered past trees still firmly rooted, as if nothing had changed. Breathless and sure that he was slipping back two steps for every three he ascended, he stopped for a brief rest. He saw Fayrene kneeling in the dirt a little way above him. She seemed to be praying.

Freddy's body was seized to the waist in the grip of the earth, his face in a puddle of mud. Steamer bent beside Fayrene and prayed that the rock that had smashed his skull to strawberry pudding had killed him before his nose and mouth had been imprisoned in the mud.

Methodically, Fayrene began to dig her husband's body from the earth. Steamer worked beside her, throwing rocks aside and pawing at the earth until the two of them were able to lift the body free of the imprisoning muck.

When Steamer bent to help carry it, Fayrene stopped him. "I've always taken care of Freddy. I'd prefer to do it myself now."

She lifted his body with great tenderness and began to pick her way down the slope, carrying her husband's body as if it were no more than a blanket roll. Steamer watched her down the slope until he heard someone yelling. He turned to see Bettina straining to move a large boulder. A man's leg protruded from beneath it from the knee down. He recognized Alan's fancy ostrich-skin boot.

"Help me. He may still be alive," Bettina gasped, straining, red-faced, against the boulder.

A need to reclaim one life, to strike back in fury against the mountain, motivated Steamer to heave against the boulder even as a rational portion of his mind told him the man was surely dead. And, yet, perhaps there was an air pocket under there. Together they pushed at the giant rock, but the loose earth of the slope prevented them from gaining enough leverage to move it. At last Steamer stopped, but Bettina shouted at him to keep pushing.

Steamer touched her gently. "It's no use, Bettina. He must be dead."

"No!" The despair in her voice chilled him. "Alan! Oh, Alan!" She strained for a moment longer to move the boulder, then stopped and seized the leg sticking from the ground. She pulled once, pulled twice and fell over backward clutching the leg in her arms as it came free of the earth.

271

There was a beat as she stared at the thing in silence. A deep, guttural scream burst from her. She flung the leg away, vomited, threw herself facedown on the ground and wept in a savage roar that made Steamer's skin crawl.

She stopped sobbing almost as abruptly as she had started, sat up, and wiped her face with a dainty handkerchief. As Steamer knelt beside her, she began to slap the dirt from her clothes. At last she turned to him. "Bring me Alan's leg."

"What . . . what are you going to do with it?"

"You think I'm some kind of lily-livered socialite, don't you? Well, my old man was a drunk and an oil-field roustabout, and I pulled myself out of the gutter and learned enough about society to marry Alan. But I haven't forgotten how to survive." The anger left her face, to be replaced by determination. "I may not be able to bury all of Alan, but at least I can sing the Kaddish for him."

Steamer wrapped the bit of trouser leg that remained around the end of the stump and brought the naked thing to Bettina. "Don't look at the end. Want me to carry it?"

Bettina shifted on the wounded earth until she rested on her hands and knees; she tried to stand. When she fell back, Steamer bent to help her, but she pushed his hand away and staggered to her feet. She reached for the leg but at the last moment drew back.

"Yes, please, you carry him."

Steamer tucked the leg under his right arm. The world around him contracted suddenly, and he felt as if he were isolated safely on a tiny island. He sucked cold, wet air into his lungs until reality of fear, anxiety, pain, and fatigue returned.

He and Bettina started down, hopscotching from boulder to rock, sliding and stumbling on loose earth and shale. The sound of voices made him look up. Katrina sat beside Sandor, holding his hand and chatting with him in a cheerful voice. When they reached her, she looked up at them with a happy smile.

"I found him alive! Isn't that wonderful? He thinks he's going to die, but that's ridiculous. Everything is going to be just fine! As soon as the pack string gets back, we're going to take him right down to the hospital and get him patched up as good as new. Isn't that right, Sandy?"

Steamer knelt beside Sandor. Katrina continued to babble as he examined the injured man, and he almost told her to shut up before he realized she was trying to drive away the demon of fear.

Sandor opened his eyes. "Leave me here, Steamer." His voice was mushy.

"Oh, Sandy, do stop!" Katrina clapped her hands softly, as if to get a child's attention. "We're going to get you to a hospital in just a few hours."

Sandor shook his head. "Used to take a packet of crackers, crush them up inside the wrapping before dumping them on my chili. No mess that way." He tried to smile but grimaced with pain instead. "That's me, just a packet of crumbled crackers."

Steamer cursed silently. "Don't be an idiot. We'll get you out of here. Listen, can you feel pain anywhere?"

"Understand. I can feel my fingers, toes." Sandor was breathing in shallow gasps. "Guess some ribs are broken, and one leg. It's not that though. It's my guts. Big rock fell on my stomach. Leave me. I'm going to die."

Steamer examined Sandor, ignoring his protests. His left leg was broken in two places. Using Sandor's belt and his own, he tied his left leg to his right to immobilize it, then pulled his jacket and shirt away. The skin over his stomach was abraded and discolored. Steamer buttoned his shirt and jacket around him as tightly as he could.

Fayrene stood a few feet away, head down and shoulders

slumped as she stared at her husband's corpse.

"Hey, Fayrene, give me a hand." When she reached him, Steamer said, "We have to move him. Remember how to make a chair to carry a person?"

She nodded, and they tried to raise Sandor to a sitting position as gently as possible, but he fainted with a moan of pain. As Bettina and Katrina held him into a sitting position, Steamer and Fayrene knelt on either side of him. On their signal, the women lifted Sandor off the ground, and they clasped hands on arms beneath him to form a seat. Bettina carried Alan's leg under one arm as she steadied Sandor with the other, and they descended.

Steamer flexed his right hand, wondering what had happened to it. His left arm hurt, as well, and as he massaged it clumsily with his cramped hand, he wondered where the pain came from. His feet were made of ice cubes, and it was dark and noisy around him.

Then he realized they had carried Sandor to the bottom of the slope and waded through the edge of the Gros Ventre River. It was no longer a river but a muddy, frigid lake covering the trail. He staggered with fatigue. The noise around him resolved itself into individual voices, and the panic and pain behind those voices brought him back to reality. Fayrene came down from the slide with her husband's body in her arms. The sun was only a faint ember buried in an ash of ugly grey clouds. It would be fully dark in an hour.

They laid Sandor gently in front of the fire. Steamer stood near it, shivering violently as it began to warm him. *Now what?* He glanced around in the fading light and counted: twelve survivors. Plus there were Junior and Daphne, unless they'd decided to ride back to the ranch for some reason. Doodah, Joellen, Betty, Shorty, and Manuel—where were they? Had they escaped the slide?

"What do we do now?" Bettina asked.

Steamer scanned the survivors slowly. They were all exhausted, and many had serious cuts and bruises. "I think we'd best stay put for the night," he said. "I see Lew has a big fire going."

"But we can't all sleep next to the fire!" Pia said with exasperation.

"*Senor* Steamer?"

"Yes, Miguel?"

"I bring two tents down with me on pack mules. And the sleeping bags. We not need them down at Meester Huff place, so I bring them out last."

Steamer felt some of the tension leave him. "That's a damn lucky break, Miguel. Let's fetch them and get them pitched."

Terry had ridden to Kelly, pissing and moaning all the way about Ma sending him out in the cold and the rain to replace Junior. He hitched his horse outside the Kelly Koffee Kup and went in. Something hot to drink and a piece of apple pie would go a long way toward making him feel better.

Martha, the short-order cook, banged a slab of apple pie with cheddar cheese and a mug of java down in front of him. "So, Terry, what are you doing so far from home this time of day?"

When he had explained his mission, she looked at him, shaking her head slowly. "What's the matter with you people in Jackson? Didn't you feel it?"

"Feel what?"

"The landslide. The whole goddamned side of Sheep Mountain just slid into the river. The concussion knocked dishes off the shelf here." She poured more coffee. "Where are your people camped?"

"Supposed to be out at Leidy Lake."

"No way you're gonna get there. There's a big lake filling up behind the slide. The trail is blocked."

"No shit!"

"No shit. 'Course, your folks will be safe up there. No way the lake is going to rise that high. But it's going to take a week to cut a new trail around that mess out there." With a cackle of laughter, she added, "You can't get there from here."

"In that case, I need to use your phone. To call Ma and tell her."

"Phone line is down."

"No shit?"

"That's the second time you've said that."

Terry hated to eat dinner after he'd had dessert, but there was no sense in riding home in the dark on an empty stomach. "What's good for dinner?"

"Chicken pot pie."

"Sounds good. And more coffee, please."

CHAPTER 27

Tuesday Night, June 23

Megan ached with fatigue, and her eyes weren't working properly. She tried to focus on the sleeve of her jacket. At first she thought the smudge was dirt, but the spot was white. She nudged it with one finger. A heavy flake of spring snow melted under her touch. She lifted her head. Fat soggy flakes were tumbling down one by one to vanish as they touched the ground.

One memory rotated around and around in her mind: lying with Steamer on the sandy riverbank, replete with love. But another part of her feared bitter disappointment might be lurking just beyond the edge of conscious thought. She was doomed to return to her goldfish bowl. Only this time, the bowl would be made of milk glass, and she would not even be able to see out.

She hammered the last tent peg into the hard ground. Her arms ached, and her hands were raw from handling the rough canvas. Steamer sank to his knees beside her. "How are you doing?" she asked.

He shrugged. "As well as can be expected." They got to their feet and went out to stand in front of the roaring fire, turning around like chickens on a spit. He looked at the survivors huddled silently around the fire. "These people haven't got enough wilderness knowledge between them to fill a thimble."

A faint smile touched her lips. "We'll just have to do our best, won't we?"

He hugged her once again, quickly. Megan had just started to warm herself when Paul rolled up to them.

"Well, now what?" he demanded.

"I think the best thing we can do is try to get some sleep, Paul."

"Sleep? We gotta get out of here, get something to eat."

"And how do you propose to do that?"

Paul appeared temporarily baffled but seconds later was blustering again. "That way!" he said, pointing toward the slide.

"Can't get the horses over it," Steamer said. "Of course, if you want to walk over it, you go right ahead."

"Damn right, I will." Paul turned and stomped away from the light of the fire. Megan silently counted the seconds. By the time she reached thirty, Paul walked back into the light.

"So we go out that way," he snarled, jerking his chin in the direction of the trail. "The horses can go up there, can't they?"

"Makes no difference whether they can or not," Megan replied. "Sandor is seriously injured, can't walk or ride. Tommy has a bad cold; this weather could turn it into pneumonia. Most everyone else is so damn tired, they can't move. We can't move tonight."

"But—"

"No 'buts,' damn it. Junior and Daphne are still missing. I'm not moving until my sister gets back. And we need to build a litter for Sandor. And Tommy needs a night's sleep."

"Well, uh, uh . . ."

"I suggest you find a spot in one of the tents and try to get some sleep. We'll move out tomorrow morning. If they haven't sent a rescue party out by then."

Scowling fiercely, Paul backed away and went into a tent. Soon the rest of the survivors had huddled together under canvas. Steamer delegated a rotating watch to keep the fire going, and together he and Megan went into the tent and huddled side by side in their sleeping bags. The cold coming up from the ground made Megan's hip ache.

As she was drifting into an uneasy sleep, a crackling sound roused her. Paul pulled a candy bar from his coat pocket and surreptitiously unwrapped it. He devoured it in two bites, crumpled the wrapper, and tossed it away.

Fiona's nightmare had become progressively more terrifying. Now that damned Prohi, Raymond Drago, was coming toward her with the revolver in his hand pointed at her heart. She put up her hands to protect herself, but it did no good. He fired three times.

She awoke in a cold sweat. The shots came again. Her heart rate slowed as she realized someone was knocking at her cabin door.

A voice outside said, "Ma?"

She got out of bed and pulled on her wool bathrobe, leaving TT snoring. She unlatched the front door. Terry stood there shivering.

She stared at him. "What in hell are you doing home? I sent you out to replace Junior."

Terry pushed his way in and closed the door behind him. "Can't get there."

"What do you mean? What happened?"

"I got out to Kelly, stopped for pie and coffee. You won't believe it. There was a big landslide out there. Sheep Mountain let go and slid into the river. The trail is blocked. Ain't no way anyone can get out to Leidy Lake."

"Stop saying 'ain't.' You know better. Now tell me all about it."

Terry sank into a leather armchair. "The landslide blocked the river. Now there's a lake covering the trail."

Fiona sat in the other chair. "Oh, my God."

"It's a huge slide, Ma. Better hope and pray no one was caught in it. They'd be buried under two hundred feet of mud and rock."

Fiona felt a little glow of hope. If Megan and that lawman, Steamer, had been in the way of the landslide, all her problems would be solved. "Where exactly is the slide?"

"About two miles west of where Horsetail Creek runs into the Gros Ventre."

"Do you think any of our people might have been caught in it?"

"No one knows anything right now." Terry looked at her with sudden alarm. "Shit! What if they did? We'd better get up a rescue party."

"Slow down. Let's think a minute." A vision of Megan buried under tons of rock made her feel guilty. Yes, she wanted Megan out of the way, but not like that.

"No, I don't think that's a good idea," she said. "They were scheduled to be up at Leidy Lake today. That's a long way back of Kelly. And even if the trail is blocked, Parley and the film crew can take care of themselves. They have a ton of food, lots of gear. And they can always ride out on Slate Fork Trail."

"Yeah, I guess you're right. We can wait until morning and see what the situation is then."

CHAPTER 28

Wednesday Morning, June 24

Night crept by like an assassin and murdered Megan's dreams. She huddled in the homogenous mass of bodies and tried to think of anything but where she was. If she fell asleep, she fell into a nightmare; if she awoke, she awoke into a nightmare. It continued like that until daylight stabbed her between the eyes, demanding she face reality.

Sitting up was a slow and painful process. She went outside. Reality was somber grey; the muted forest was green and white. Snow decorated the tent like vanilla icing applied by a drunken baker. The fire had burned low. She realized someone else was also standing near the fire and forced her eyes to focus. Paul was chewing on something. When he saw her watching him, his chubby face took on a guilty look.

Anger twisted her guts, and her stomach growled in protest. How dare he not share his food? She'd seen him pigging out on candy bars ever since he arrived at the Rocking Lazy F. Should she try to remonstrate with him?

She heard a noise behind her. Steamer emerged from the tent and put his arm around her. At this, Paul peeled more of the wrapper back, took a deliberate bite, and smirked at them, chocolate oozing from the corners of his mouth.

No, this was probably not a good time to talk to Paul about sharing. Megan turned herself into Steamer's arms, and, as they hugged, hope began to rise in her again. The people back in

Jackson must realize by now that they were in danger.

Reluctantly she broke away from Steamer's arms. "We ought to build up that fire, get people moving."

"Right," he replied. "I'll take care of the fire. You wake up the sleepy heads."

Megan pulled the tent flap aside and went in. Pia was staring into empty space and rocking Tommaso in a slow rhythm. He was breathing heavily through his mouth with a rasping sound, but Pia seemed unaware of him.

"Pia?" Megan shook her foot. "Time to get on the road."

Pia's eyes lost their glazed look. "It's gone, isn't it?"

"Gone? What's gone?"

"The film. My screen test. It's under all that rock out there."

"So what?" Megan snapped. "That's the least of our worries."

"You don't understand." Pia began to weep. "I was counting on that for . . . for our future. So Tommaso and I could escape from—" She wiped her eyes. "Never mind. Come on, Tommaso, wake up."

On her hands and knees, Megan went about rousing the others.

Sandor lay with his head in Katrina's lap; his shirt had fallen away over his stomach. A huge purple-green bruise covered most of his stomach's surface.

"Sandor can't walk," Katrina said, "or ride."

"Don't worry. We'll make a litter for him."

"Do we have to move? Can't we wait until someone comes to rescue us?" she asked.

"I don't know, Katrina. No one knows we're here. We're supposed to be at Leidy Lake. Besides, it's only half a day since the slide. It may take a while for people to realize we're in danger. What's more, they are all going to be focused on their own problems, like saving their livestock and crops from this storm.

They won't have much time to think about us."

Katrina nodded, got to her feet, and left the tent. Megan crawled around and urged the others to wake. She shook them violently when they failed to respond and drove them out into the light of day.

Then she joined the survivors standing in a circle around the fire. She could see her own feelings of despair and helplessness mirrored in the eyes staring dully back at her. It would be all too easy to creep back into the tent and go to sleep—perhaps forever.

"Listen up, everyone!" She clapped her hands, a painful act in the cold. "We can't stay here. We've got to move out."

"Why?" Eric demanded angrily. "Why can't we just wait for rescue?"

"Because." Megan wasn't sure herself that she was right. Maybe a rescue effort was under way, maybe not. She repeated what she had said to Katrina. "And, besides all that, we'll feel better taking action. If we sit here all day, we'll be prey to every hobgoblin our minds can throw at us. So get ready to move out."

"Metal," Bettina said in a startled voice.

"What does that mean?"

"Our canteens are metal," Bettina replied. "We can put them on the coals at the edge of the fire and heat the water in them."

"Why?" Paul snarled.

"Drinking hot water will put heat inside us."

"Hey!" Lew said. "There were wild gooseberries all along the trail yesterday. I'll bet we'll find some around here if we look."

"Good idea, Lew. Take Eric and Fayrene with you."

"I'll go, too!" Paul shouted.

"I'd rather you would . . ." It was too late. Paul was already striding off along the trail. Lew, Eric, and Fayrene hurried to catch up with him.

Steamer hugged her. "Good thinking, darling. I'm going to get Miguel to help me build a litter for Sandor, then we'll round up the horses, get saddled up, and get ready to move out when the berry pickers return."

Megan nodded and poured some hot water into her cup; she drank it slowly. Something white landed on her hand. She lifted her head. Fat soggy flakes were tumbling down one by one, to vanish as they touched the ground. She could almost count them as they fell. She sat down. Just for a minute. She'd feel better with a short rest.

Steamer watched as Megan sat. She looked as if she were asleep, and he walked over to her intending to wake her. Instead he sank down next to her. Improvising a litter for Sandor had been more difficult than he had anticipated. His bottom had no sooner touched the log than he heard boots thumping on the ground behind him.

"Hey, Steamer, want some gooseberries?"

He roused himself and looked up. Lew, Eric, Fayrene, and Paul had returned. The rest of the survivors were crowding around them, eagerly reaching for the berries they held in their hats.

"Hold on, everyone," he said as he got to his feet. "Don't grab. We need to share and share alike."

The delicious scent of the berries rising from the hats of the pickers made saliva squirt into his mouth. He had managed to ignore the hunger pangs gnawing at his belly, but now they reminded him hunger would be the one thing that could destroy them. They couldn't fight over food. How could he make it fair?

"Bettina?" Alan's wife looked up. "Why don't you divvy up the berries? Give everyone a small handful until they run out."

"Right." Bettina came forward. "Okay, gather around, every-one."

As she started to parcel out the tart, green berries, Lew said, "Paul doesn't get any."

"Why not?"

"Because," Lew said, "he ate two handfulls for every one he put in his hat."

Paul's face turned purple. "Like hell I did!"

"I saw him, too," Fayrene added. "He went off by himself, turned his back on us, and thought we weren't looking. He's had his share already."

"That's a damn lie!" Paul shouted.

Fayrene walked close to Paul and touched his jacket. "Take a look. His clothes are all covered with berry juice, and his hands and face are sticky because he was gobbling them down as fast as he could."

Steamer ran a finger down the front of Paul's jacket. It was damp and sticky. "All right, Paul, you've had enough. What's more, Megan and I saw you eating a candy bar this morning. Now just back on out of here."

Paul's anger was slow to surface through the layers of fat encasing him. When it did, he slowly lowered his hat to the ground at Steamer's feet—then he rose quickly and slammed both hands upward under Steamer's ribs, knocking the air out of his lungs.

Steamer backed off, struggling to breathe again, but Paul came after him. "Don't you tell me what to do, Steamer. I've had enough of you interfering in my life. You think you're such a hot-shot director, you mess up all my production plans with your fancy camera moves. Well, I've had enough. Get out of my way, and stay out of my way."

"Come on, Paul. This is not the time to talk about old grievances. We need to work together to get home safely."

Paul took one giant stride, and once again both of his hands shot out and slammed into Steamer under his ribs. Steamer felt as if a charging bull had rammed him. He fell back, tripped on the uneven ground, and landed on his left elbow. Pain lanced through his arm, leaving it feeling numb. Lew and Eric got between him and Paul, who stalked away muttering obscenities. Steamer staggered to his feet and stepped on something soft and squishy. He glanced down. He'd planted his boot in Paul's hat, mashing the berries.

Megan clutched his arm. "Are you all right?"

"I'll be okay. I think. Here, can't let these berries go to waste." He held the hat out to her.

Megan took it and stared at the mess inside. The odor rising from the hat was unbelievably tempting, and she tried her best to eat slowly. In the end she gulped down her portion and then licked her hands and fingers to get at the last remnants of nourishment. She never gave a thought to what might have been on Steamer's boot.

A faint sound impinged on her thoughts. She strained to separate it from the sound of the wind. A faint clip-clop of horses' hooves emerged from the silently drifting snow. She strained to see as the pace of the hoofbeats picked up, accelerated to a gallop, and came closer.

Junior and Champion materialized from the snow, followed at a little distance by Daphne. She was bouncing in her saddle, clinging desperately to the horn. Junior yanked his horse to a sliding stop and stared around with his mouth hanging open for a long time. At last he focused on those staring back at him.

"Oh, shee-it," he said as he dismounted. "What happened?"

"You didn't feel the landslide?"

"Ooh, I did!" Daphne's eyes were as big as cow pies. "I tried to tell him something was wrong, but he—" Daphne glanced at Megan, who saw a guilty look creep up her face. Junior ignored her and looked around with increasing bewilderment. "Where's Pa?"

Nobody said anything.

"Come on, where's Pa?"

"I'm so sorry, Junior," Megan said. "They . . . he . . . they were right there."

"Right where? What the hell are you talking about?"

"Right in the leading edge of the . . . he's under that." Megan nodded towards the mass of the slide. "Freddy was, too, but we found his body. Sandor is alive, but it doesn't look good for him. Curly may have escaped. The last I saw him, he was way behind the others."

"Pa's underneath that?" Junior frowned. "Where?"

Megan pointed at the slide. "And Alan. And Esse, and F-Stop, and Marlene. And . . ." She couldn't remember who else had been crushed to death.

"Damn it, don't just point. Show me."

"There's nothing to see. They didn't have a chance."

"I want to see!"

"Your father is dead." Megan took Junior's arm, shaking it gently for emphasis. "He's at the bottom, under all that."

"You saw it? Then show me." He seized Megan's arm and dragged her along behind him as he strode toward the slide, his boots thumping an angry cadence in the slush.

Junior slowed his walk as he and Megan approached the base of the slide. He looked at the new lake; he looked at the raw scar where Sheep Mountain had been. He looked at the corpse of the mountain and stabbed a finger at it. "Under that?"

Megan nodded.

Junior sat down heavily on a boulder, leaning his forearms on his knees, and hung his head. Megan watched for a moment, then sank to her knees beside him and placed both hands on his arm. He was sobbing violently but almost silently.

"I don't think he suffered," she said. "It was over in an instant."

Junior looked up and swabbed at his eyes. "You're sure? There ain't no chance he got away?"

She shook her head emphatically. "They disappeared just like that." She snapped her fingers.

At the sound, he jerked away and, after a horror-stricken look, twisted again with silent anguish. "He can't be gone. It just ain't possible."

"It was horrible."

He gasped, breathing out convulsively, until Megan wondered if he would ever breathe in again. Then he sucked in a giant breath and howled, a cry of anguish so powerful, Megan shuddered with alarm. He clutched himself tightly as if to control the violent spasms racking his body. Each spasm was accompanied by a loud moan that vibrated in his throat.

After five minutes he calmed down. He glanced at Megan. "Thanks," he mumbled.

"Come on." Megan tried to pull him to his feet. "Let's go back to the fire."

He pushed her hand away. "Not yet. Just leave me a while. I got to say good-bye to Pa. In my own way. You understand?"

Megan nodded and went back to join the others. Daphne sidled up to her with a mournful expression. Megan waited for her to say something, but she only hung her head and blushed more.

"Well?" Megan knew she sounded exasperated but didn't care.

"Well, gee, we felt something shaking us, but we didn't pay any attention because we were . . . I mean Junior said it was because we were . . . well, he meant that we were so, um, compatible that all the shaking was just us. And besides, the cot was real wobbly, and he said not to worry, and . . ." She began to sob.

Anger ripped into Megan. She slapped Luella, who choked

on a sob but stopped crying.

She felt Steamer put his arms around her, hug her tightly. "That won't help, Megan. Let's get her into a tent."

She felt strength and courage flowing back into her. "All right." She hugged her sister, led her inside a tent, and made her lie down. The ground under the tent felt like ice.

"I'm sorry, Luella. You lie down now, try to sleep." Luella collapsed in a heap and curled up in a ball. Megan left her and went out again to stand next to Steamer.

"I just . . . I couldn't bear her histrionics any longer." She searched his face. "Are you all right? Paul hurt you, didn't he?"

Steamer grimaced. "I'm as well as can be expected after being hit by a Mack truck." He moved his left arm in a circle. "My elbow is sore, but I don't think anything is broken. I'll be all right."

At the sound of approaching footsteps, Megan looked up. Junior was striding toward them.

"Shee-it, what a mess." Junior shoved his hands into his hip pockets. "I could sure use something to eat. Where . . ." His head jerked left and right "Where's Doodah? And the girls?"

"They aren't here."

"Where in hell are they? What happened?"

"What happened is, Alan decided to ride out early." In a few words she told him about the plan to shelter in Guil's barn until the storm cleared and then to shoot scenes at his ranch. She told him how Doodah, Betty, Joellen, and Manuel had ridden out ahead to set up camp. "My guess is, they made it out and turned up the trail before the slide. They're probably safe now. If Guil's place isn't under water, that is."

"Yeah." He rocked uncertainly on the heels of his boots, looking around and nodding to himself.

"Okay, tell you what. There's some corn meal and jerky back up at the hunting cabin. I'll ride back up and get it. We can make mush with it, and the jerky will add flavor." He turned to go but then turned back. "Where's Daph?"

"What do you mean?"

"Just that. I want her to go with me."

"No! She's exhausted, Junior. She's asleep in the women's tent. She can't go now."

"Like hell she can't." He whirled, strode to the tent, and stormed through the door flap. Megan plunged after him. He was shaking her sister roughly, urging her to wake up, but Luella did not stir. Megan dropped quickly to her side and listened. Daphne was breathing slowly and quietly.

Megan shot to her feet and hit Junior in the gut. "Leave her alone! Stop bothering her and get the hell out!"

Junior backed away and out of the tent. "Okay, but I'll be back to save her. She's gonna help me destroy the evil infecting our town."

"What in hell are you talking about?"

"Don't play innocent with me, Mrs. Foxworth. You know damn good and well what's going on at the ranch."

Fiona glared at TT across the scarred pine surface of her desk. Late afternoon sunlight made the frosted glass of the office door glow orange. TT was sober, quiet, and scared. She didn't blame him. A dull ache of fear had settled into her bones and wouldn't leave.

"You sure he won't be suspicious about that platform?" she demanded.

"Goddamn it, Fiona, how in hell can I predict what might go through his mind? You've been out there. You've inspected it. I think it looks pretty ordinary."

"This guy Drago seems like a pretty sharp scythe," Fiona said with a moan. "He could just chop us down like wheat."

TT leaned forward in his wheelchair. "Old girl, we just gotta

290

play it calm, cool, and collected. If we—" A loud triple knock rattled the glass in the door frame.

"Who—" Fiona cleared the phlegm that suddenly clogged her throat. "Who, ah, is it?"

"Sheriff Goodman. And Agent Drago."

"Come in," Fiona squeaked. The door whooshed open, bringing a blast of cold air and the hulking presence of the two lawmen.

After they exchanged a minimum of polite noises, the sheriff said, "Agent Drago is still looking for that Donatelli woman. You had any news about them film people?"

Before she could answer, TT demanded, "Have you checked out his bona fides, Sheriff? Is he really an agent? And why is he bothering our guest?"

The sheriff turned to look down at TT in his chair. Fiona thought he looked rather uneasy. "Of course I have. You telling me I don't know my business, TT?"

TT shrank away from him. "No, no, 'course not, Sheriff. But why is he interested in her? She seems like a real nice lady, and she has her kid with her."

Agent Drago smiled a crocodile smile at TT. "Well now, you see, Mr. Foxworth, of course I can't give you details, and it's really none of your business . . . but I can tell you that she's involved with a gang of bootleggers. She's wanted for questioning."

"Well, she's not here." TT glared back at Drago. "She's out there."

Drago looked at TT for a long moment, then nodded slowly and precisely. "So you haven't heard anything from them. Do you think the slide might have hit them?"

"Oh! My God, I hope not." Fiona said. "They were supposed to be out at Leidy Lake by now. That producer, Mr. Segal, said it sounded like an ideal location. He was planning to do most of his shooting there."

"How do I get there?"

"Can't get there from here," Fiona said. "That damn landslide has blocked the main trail along the river."

"The main trail, huh? Which means there is another trail."

"Right," TT said. "I reckon the best thing you could do would be to drive out to Parley's base camp, see if they might be there. Maybe they decided to go back there after the slide. If they aren't there, you can come on back and ride out on Slate Creek Trail up to Leidy Lake tomorrow. It's a lot longer and rougher trail, but . . ."

Fiona saw the sheriff's hands clenching and unclenching at his side. She hadn't seen him on a horse in months. The most dangerous critter he'd ridden recently had been his office swivel chair.

Drago smiled. "Why, thank you, Mr. Foxworth. That's a good idea." He paused, frowned, and rubbed his chin. "Would you have any horses we could rent? Day after tomorrow?"

"Of course," Fiona said. "And there won't be any charge, Mr. Drago. We do all we can to cooperate with law enforcement. That old devil rum is ruining this country."

CHAPTER 29

Thursday Morning, June 25

The next morning Megan noticed the cold striking up at her through the summer-weight sleeping bag. Her body was scrunched up as tightly as a bale of hay, and her elbows, hips, and knees were made of knotted baling wire. She was sure she would never get the stiffness untied. She should spur herself out of her sleeping bag and get up, but a herd of worries milled about in the corral of her thoughts.

Junior had ridden off into the night, promising to return with food from the hunting cabin. Would he really return, or had he ridden out on some back trail? And how was Luella supposed to help him destroy the evil infecting Jackson Hole? She'd asked him what that meant. He'd leaned closer, his icy gaze boring into her, and said, "You know damn well what I'm talking about."

She was ashamed now that she had pretended to be innocent. Yes, she *did* know damned well what Junior was talking about, and it was time for her to admit that her in-laws were smuggling huge quantities of booze into the ranch and do something about it.

She twisted violently in her sleeping bag. Next to her, Steamer grunted with annoyance and was soon snoring again. At this reminder of his presence in her life, her fears of Junior diminished. His father had died a horrible death, and he would be too consumed with grief to bother her or Luella.

Her thoughts meandered back to the ranch, Fiona, and her file cabinet. Would Fiona and TT be foolish enough to keep incriminating records in it? Well, of course they would! Fiona had Megan under her thumb, didn't she? Except that she was damned well going to go back and get into those files and steal anything that would protect her, Luella, and Steamer.

Someone was making odd whimpering noises. Megan opened her eyes. Luella, who was sleeping on the other side of Steamer, was sitting up. Her face was beaded with sweat. She was shivering, and her gaze was on something outside the tent. She waved her arms as if pushing something away. Megan leaned over Steamer and touched Luella on her forehead.

"No!" she cried, jerking away from Megan's hand. "Please, TT . . . no . . . don't make me suck . . ."

Her cry woke Steamer, and he rose up on one elbow and watched Luella for a moment. "Looks to me as if she's having the DTs."

"DTs? What's that?"

"Delirium tremens. It's a withdrawal reaction when someone physically dependent on alcohol suddenly stops drinking."

"But isn't that good? I mean, that she's stopped drinking."

Steamer hugged her. "The problem is, the DTs can be fatal if not managed properly by a doctor."

"Oh, Steamer! What am I going to do?"

"First we get her to a hospital in town. After that, long-term care in Santa Barbara."

"How come you know so much about alcoholism?"

"Never mind." His face darkened. "I'll tell you later. We'll probably need to tie her on to her saddle to keep her from falling off."

Steamer's fingers were clumsy and aching from the cold. It had taken him an hour to find enough spare rope, but he'd finally lashed up a sort of net that would keep Daphne on her saddle no matter what. Peaches had stood uncomplaining while he adjusted the saddle on her.

With the last knot tied, he stepped back to view his handiwork—and swayed on his feet as exhaustion swamped him. All he wanted to do was lie down and curl up into a tight little ball and die. He clung to the saddle and sucked in huge breaths of cold air.

He tried for a while to think about the future, but the harder he tried, the more it fled from him, shrieking with laughter. He gave up. He had only one option right now: survive.

The sound of a horse moving uneasily somewhere down the picket line made him look up. Paul's horse, Jingles, had her head up and was shifting nervously. Steamer moved to where he could see. Paul was rummaging in his saddlebag. He removed a candy bar, stripped it naked, and gulped it down.

As Steamer approached, Paul looked up with a smirk. "Good morning, Steamer."

He opened his mouth to say something, shut it, and gazed deeply into Paul's eyes. Paul steadied for a moment. His gaze wavered, returned, wandered around, and finally dropped. Steamer walked off without looking back. He was freezing cold.

He was warming himself at the fire when he heard the clop of horses' hooves approaching. When Junior and Champion appeared throughout the trees, they were greeted with a cheer.

"Mornin', everyone." A large sack was tied on behind his saddle. Junior dismounted, released it, and handed it to Bettina. "Time for breakfast."

An hour later, the large iron pot on the fire was issuing mouthwatering smells. The survivors gathered around as Bettina ladled out portions of corn meal mush flavored with beef jerky. It tasted better than any T-bone steak Steamer had ever eaten. He was scraping the last bit out of his bowl with his finger when Paul rolled to a stop in front of him.

"More food."

"You've had your fair share. Just like everyone else."

Paul poked him in the chest with his spoon. "Cook more."

"I don't believe that would be a good thing to do. We all agreed we need to save some for tonight."

"I didn't." Which was true. Paul had remained silent when they'd discussed the rationing.

"Nevertheless, you get no more. And you know why, and I know why." Paul glared at him and turned away. Steamer relaxed and moved away to put his bowl in the wash bucket.

Then suddenly, from the corner of his eye, he saw Paul charging at him. Paul's boot slammed into the thigh of Steamer's right leg, and he crumpled to the ground. Paul kicked him again, screaming profanities at him. Steamer rolled out of the way in desperation as Paul came after him. People were screaming and grabbing at Paul when the Colt .45 boomed.

Steamer looked up to see Paul stare down at his feet, then up at Junior pointing the six-gun at his crotch.

"The next one will go in your balls. Now back off." He shoved the Colt in its holster. "You all get packed up. Time to move out."

Steamer got to his knees and then to his feet as Megan rushed to his side. "Are you all right?"

He could tell his thigh was going to be mighty sore. It had felt as if a Brahma bull had rammed him. "It'll be a bit sore, but I'll be fine."

In another hour the meager remains of the corn meal, the cooking pot, the tents, and the sleeping bags had all been loaded aboard the pack mules. Steamer and Megan had lashed Daphne on to her saddle, and the riders had all mounted. One saddle remained empty. Champion stood quietly, tied to a tree.

Steamer stood in his stirrups and looked around. "Now where in hell is Junior?"

Megan dismounted. "I think I know where he is. I'll go get him."

"Megan, be—" He was going to say, "be careful," but she was already out of hearing.

Junior's behavior worried him. At times he was quite rational. At others he behaved as if he'd been eating locoweed. Steamer thought he might have shown some grief at his father's death, but at camp he was as emotional as a dead cow in the snow. On top of that, he was badgering Megan about "getting rid of the evil infecting our town." Steamer presumed he meant liquor, but how was Junior involved with the smuggling?

When Megan found him, Junior's eyes were bloodshot and red-rimmed. His face was haggard. He was staring at the slide, rocking back and forth on his knees almost imperceptibly.

Sympathy rolled through her. She moved closer, kneeled beside him, and touched his arm. Junior continued to stare, not registering her presence. "Junior?"

"What is it?" he said in a low, clear voice. "I can hear you."

She pulled back, startled. She had assumed he was submerged in a bog of misery out of which she would have to dig him. "I'm . . . I'm sorry about your father. You must miss him terribly."

He turned to her with infinite slowness, his eyes slag heaps of misery. "It's my fault," he whispered.

She felt her skin crawl. "Your . . . how can it be your fault?"

He leapt to his feet like a tormented animal, stared at her in anguish, whirled, and stalked off into the snow.

She plunged after him. "Junior?" When he did not answer, she touched his arm again and then shook it. "Spit it out, whatever it is. It will fester and rot inside if you don't."

"Pa and me, we were . . . we were having an awful fight," he began. He jammed his hands in his pockets and kicked at a stone.

"Children and their parents *do* sometimes fight. What was it about?"

"It was about, well, about . . . women." He emphasized the last word in an odd manner but said nothing more.

"Somehow that doesn't surprise me." When he frowned suspiciously at her, she continued, "Go on. What about *women*?"

"Pa kept telling me I hadn't ought to, well, shouldn't, um, fornicate with Daphne." Megan nodded. "He kept saying it's against God's will."

"But you did anyway."

"So did he!" Junior's voice cracked like breaking ice.

"What?! He was, ah, fornicating with my sister?"

"No, I didn't mean that! Although I 'spect he damn well would have if I hadn't got there first. No, that's what made me so damn angry. He was . . . well, he was sneaking into town and . . ."

"Let's see. Your dad had a *girlfriend* in town?"

"Yeah, something like that. He was such a damn . . ."

"Hypocrite?" He nodded violently. "And?"

"It wasn't fair!"

"And?"

"And I . . . I called down. I mean, I told him God would punish him."

"You did what?"

"After I . . . with Daphne . . . he saw us. He came out of the darkness and told me he wasn't going to stand it anymore. That's when I said it."

"Said what?"

" 'May God strike you dead with his lightning.' "

"May God strike . . . you asked God to kill your father?"

Junior shuffled his feet in the snow. He nodded. "I told you it was my fault."

Megan blew out the breath she had been holding. "You can't really believe that, can you?"

"Believe what?"

"That you have that kind of power over God?"

He drew back as if she had slapped him. As he stared at her, she added, "That must scare the shit out of you."

He found his voice at last. "What do you mean?"

"Wondering if someone out there is praying for *you* to die."

"Nobody would—" He snapped his mouth shut with an audible clack of his teeth. He turned away abruptly and examined the sky, the mass of the slide, and the snow-covered ground as if he could suck meaning from the air and rocks.

When he turned back, his face was peaceful. He looked at her with narrowed eyes, bobbing his head several times with large, definitive nods. "God is merciful," he said.

Megan shivered. "He may be, but he's no kind of God I'd want to worship."

He grabbed her arm and yanked her around to face him. "You will learn."

"About . . . about what?"

"I prayed to God for guidance, but He did not answer me."

Megan at first thought he was staring at her, but he was gazing at something far beyond her. Megan shivered, but not from the cold. She tried to pull away.

Junior tightened his grip. "Do you understand? I thought maybe He had deserted me, but then I realized that His message to me is that He is relying on me and trusting me to do His work on earth. And you will help me."

"Yes, yes, I understand." She pulled her arm free. "Now let's mount up and head out."

CHAPTER 30

Thursday Afternoon, June 25

Megan wanted to fall asleep in the saddle, drift off into dreamland, and wake up safe and sound at the ranch. She'd heard Doodah could do it. One time he'd fallen asleep leading a pack string back to base camp. Parley had opened a gate in the trail, and Doodah and the mules rode straight on through and three miles down the trail before he woke up.

The morning had passed in silence save for the clop of hooves, the creak of saddles, and the occasional human voice. All sound had been muffled by the softly falling snow. It wasn't unusual for snow to fall this late in the year, but not this much. *It's summer, damn it.* Megan sighed. She'd have to complain to the weatherman when she got back to town.

She opened her eyes. Ahead, Pretty Girl's brown rump was disappearing in the snow. A while ago they'd taken a short break to drink water, stretch, and walk around a bit. As a result, the order of their march had changed, and she turned to see who was galloping up behind her.

Paul reined Jingles to a stop behind her. "Get out of my way!" he shouted.

"Slow down, Paul. This trail is too narrow."

"I don't give a damn. I'm hungry, and I want to get to town and get something to eat."

"We've only got another half day to ride. We'll be at base camp tonight. There'll be food there."

300

"Tonight! Get out of my way." He slammed his spurs into Jingles, who grunted in pain and plunged into the woods above the trail. Megan thought Jingles would fall and break a leg, but Paul drove her through and back onto the trail at a gallop.

Five minutes after Paul had vanished into the snow, a hideous noise reached her ears. Shouts and screams, curses and crashes, terrified whinnies, the crack of branches, and the rattling of stone mingled in a torrent of sound. It faded away to a trickle and then stopped.

Megan urged Nevada ahead as fast as she dared on the narrow, slippery trail. Moments later she came out of the woods and gasped with surprise.

It took her a while to sort out what she was seeing. Ahead, a huge chunk of the trail had vanished. It looked as if it had been sliced away from the cliff rising on the right and dropped into the canyon on the west side. She saw Junior and Miguel standing at the edge, staring down into the gulf. She didn't see the pack mules.

She dismounted and gazed downward. At the bottom, a hundred feet below, Pretty Girl, Sue-Sue, Danny, and Pin Head still kicked, struggled, and screamed as they tried to get to their feet. The tents and sleeping bags had burst from their bindings and were scattered around the giant boulders at the bottom of the narrow canyon. The cold, clean scent of freshly cut rock still lingered in the air.

"What . . . ?" The rest of the words would not come out. She could only stare at Junior, Miguel, and Paul.

Junior pulled his gaze from the disaster at the bottom. He whirled on Paul. "You stupid fool!"

Paul cringed and tried to back away as Junior advanced on him, throwing an explanation back over his shoulder to Megan. "Damned stupid fool came busting up behind Pretty Girl and spooked her bad. She went over, dragged the others over with her."

Junior reached Paul and grabbed his shirtfront. "Now look what you've done, you asshole." He drew his arm back to punch Paul in the face, but Megan flung herself at him and dragged at his arm.

"Stop it!" She thrust Junior away and stood between them. "If we start fighting, it will destroy us all. We need all the hands we have just to get out of this mess."

Junior glared at her and then relaxed. "Yeah, all right. A fat lot of good he'll do us." He stabbed a finger at Paul. "You damn well do what I tell you from now on, 'cause if you fuck up again, you're going to be hamburger. And you owe me for them mules. Fifty dollars each."

The balance of the survivors rode out of the snow, dismounted, and clustered around Megan, Paul, and Junior. Megan ignored their gasps of dismay and demands for answers and reassurance. "Now what?" she asked Junior.

The screams of the injured mules were still echoing up from the canyon. His face was contorted with pain, and she realized he was grieving for the animals. "Gotta put them out of their misery," he whispered.

"How are you going to do that? You can't get down there."

He studied the situation for a moment and then nodded. "Yes, I can."

Five minutes later, he had removed the picket line rope from his saddle and tied it to a stout pine near the edge of the slide. He tossed the end downward, then passed the rope under his bottom to control his descent. With both hands on it, he walked backward down the steep hill. As he went, his feet sent loose shale down on the mules, who kicked and struggled anew.

When he reached the bottom, Megan saw him stagger and stumble over boulders, broken pack saddles, and ripped sleeping bags. Then the deep boom of the .45 carried up to the survivors, and at last the four mules were silent.

He stood a moment gazing at the carcasses, then cupped his hands around his mouth and called out. Most of his words vanished in the wind and snow. Finally she understood that he was going to tie the sleeping bags to the end of the rope, and they should haul them up when he gestured. Megan waved to show she understood.

An hour later the gear had all been pulled up, followed by Junior. A vast silence descended on the survivors, who stood gazing in despair at the ripped, soggy bags, at each other, and at the snow drifting through the darkening sky.

The color of Megan's thoughts matched the color of sky, and she was grateful when Steamer wrapped her in his arms and stroked her hair. His embrace kept her from collapsing with despair. Was it only a few days ago Gertie had whispered to her that "they" were coming to kill her? She burrowed deeper into Steamer's arms, thinking of who "they" might be. Almost certainly, they had to be the people who supplied TT and Fiona with the illegal Irish whiskey. But what had her in-laws done to merit such a dire threat? Those ledgers locked in Fiona's file cabinet had to contain an answer. She extracted herself from Steamer's embrace. She *would* get back to the ranch and steal them.

Junior distributed the sleeping bags. The riders tied them behind their saddles, turned their horses around, and plodded back the way they had come.

As the survivors were riding to their appointment with disaster, Sheriff Goodman and Agent Drago had motored to Parley's base camp. Now they climbed from the comfort of the sheriff's car and wandered around the deserted corrals and storage sheds.

"Well, it's obvious they aren't here," Drago said. "Might as well go home."

"Not so fast." The sheriff watched as Drago picked his way around the mud, stepping from dry spot to dry spot. "I want to have a look around."

"Well, hurry up." Drago looked at the corral with a sneer. "This place stinks."

The sheriff turned away so Drago would not see him smile. *Who the hell did he think he was, this city boy, giving him orders?* "Just hang loose for a while. I'll be right back." He walked behind the corral and up the trail a ways, turned off into the woods, and lit a cigarette.

He'd almost reached the end of his smoke when Drago's voice quavered through the pines. "Sheriff! Where are you? Hey? Come on, let's go. Sheriff?" Goodman dropped the remains of his smoke on the soggy ground and nodded with satisfaction. Drago just might be a little more cooperative from now on.

He walked back to the camp. "Sorry. I was just checking their tracks. Wanted to see how long ago they were here."

Drago stuck his hands in his trouser pockets with a nonchalant air. "And what did you find out?"

"I reckon they must have made it to Leidy Lake. Let's see." He looked up at the sky and counted on his fingers. "Yep, I do believe they would have made it to the lake before the slide."

"Well, all right. Let's go—What was that noise?"

"What noise?" The sheriff didn't want to admit that as of late his hearing had gotten worse. "I didn't hear anything."

"There! Sounded like a shot . . . three more."

The sheriff cocked his head to one side and held his hand behind his ear. "Probably just some rocks sliding, what with all this rain."

"No. Rocks don't go 'bang' four times in a row."

Pia huddled in her sleeping bag, consumed with misery. Her hands were filthy and sticky with dried gooseberry juice. The cross on her arm ached with the cold, and her face was as stiff as pine bark.

She had no idea what her face looked like. She fumbled for her saddlebags and took out her compact. What she saw in the mirror terrified her. A streak of grey about six millimeters high ran along the front of her hairline from ear to ear. Oh God. If Uncle thought she was getting old, he'd discard her like a used corncob.

Beside her, Tommaso coughed a great gargling cough and spat a glob of green phlegm on the ground. Would they reach a hospital in time to save his life? *If* they survived this night, which she was now beginning to believe they might, thanks to Steamer. The party had ridden back to the same campsite they'd left that morning and made their last pot of mush. Steamer, Lew, and Eric had built a lean-to shelter large enough to keep the snow off all the survivors.

The sun looked like a coal glowing under a coating of ash-grey sky when Bettina lay down next to Pia. Steamer and Megan crept under the shelter and lay down on her other side. At the sight of the two of them cuddling together, an icicle of anger stabbed Pia. Steamer belonged to her! She touched the .25 Colt riding securely in her waist pouch. Could she find some way to shoot Megan? No, Megan had been kind to her. There was a better way. She'd go to Hollywood, become an actress, and seduce Steamer away from Megan.

"Bettina?"

Bettina rolled onto her side and faced Pia. "What is it, Pia?"

"I, um, I was wondering when we'll be able to shoot another screen test."

Bettina stared at her in surprise, then rolled onto her back. "I'm not sure that will be possible, Pia."

Anxiety clawed at Pia. "But . . . I *must* have a role. Somehow. I must make money."

Bettina sighed deeply. "With Alan gone, I don't see how the studio can survive, Pia. I suppose I can recommend you to another studio."

The anguish started from somewhere deep in Pia's being, heated by despair and pain and loss, and erupted in a geyser of hot tears. She felt Steamer and Megan move closer to her. Beside her, Tommaso squirmed with discomfort.

Steamer's voice reached her through the tears. "What is it, Pia? What's wrong?"

In answer she pulled her left arm from her sleeping bag, drew back her shirtsleeve, and rolled her inner forearm into view. She heard three gasps of surprise and murmurs of consolation.

"My God, Pia," Megan said. "How did you burn yourself?"

Pia swiped at the tears now washing some of the sticky juice from her face. "I didn't. Uncle did it."

"Uncle who?" Bettina asked.

"He's my . . . protector."

"He's your protector?" Steamer asked. "And he did this to you? Some protector."

Bettina sat up. "Maybe you'd better tell us about it."

So she did and felt another geyser of hot pain. She told them about Uncle burning her arm with his cigarette to punish her for disobedience and then rewarding her with another jumper. She told them how she'd come to Hollywood, as his enforcer, to demand payment from Alan for the loan Uncle had made him. She explained that he'd ordered her to travel with the crew to make sure the movie was finished. Finally she told them how she needed to make money so she could hire her own assassin to kill Uncle and save herself and Tommaso.

When she stopped Bettina stared at her open-mouthed. "What a mess. But there's still one thing I don't understand. You said your 'uncle' is in Italy. How can he reach you here?"

"Oh." Pia swiped the backs of her wrists across her cheeks. "There is a man following me. He's Uncle's agent. I saw him on the train in a coach car. He was sent to make sure I don't fail, and, if I do, to bring me back to Uncle."

They asked her more questions, talking more loudly in their curiosity and excitement, until someone yelled at them to shut up and go to sleep.

"All right, go to sleep everyone," Bettina said. "I'll figure something out in the morning."

Pia lay back and rolled over to face away from them. She didn't want them to hear her crying, so she muffled her sobs in her sleeping bag. Her body ached to have Steamer hold her in his arms; he would protect her forever.

She dug her fingernails into her palm to stop herself from thinking of Steamer. He was in love with Megan, and she had the chance of a Chinaman in hell of capturing him. She pulled Tommaso closer to her. He would have to be her little man. How could Bettina possibly save them?

Steamer, Megan, and Bettina were silent for a while. Steamer had started to snore gently until Megan sat bolt upright with a cry of alarm.

"Megan! What is it?" Steamer pulled her to him and held her close.

"Pia's uncle's man! He's probably the man who's coming to kill us."

"Kill you? Who? Why?"

"Gertie listens in on telephone calls. Don't tell anyone she does it, because she'd get in trouble. But just a while ago she heard someone saying they were coming to the ranch to kill us."

"Why, for God's sake?"

Pia sat up. "Because TT is behind in his payments."

Megan lifted her head from Steamer's shoulder. "How do you know that?" Pia could hear the incredulity in her voice.

"I just told you," Pia snapped. "Where do you think the liquor comes from? How do you think Uncle can afford to buy the best jumping horses in the world for me and Rolls Royces and yachts for himself?"

"But why would he kill us? Then we wouldn't be able to sell the booze even if we wanted to."

"He probably wouldn't kill TT or Fiona," Pia said. "He would threaten to kill *you*, to force TT to sell the ranch to him. It's an old trick: send your local dealers more than they can sell, then demand their house or their business in payment."

Fiona huddled in her swivel chair, wrapped in a blanket, and listened to the night. What with the snow piled up outside, there was little to hear. TT had gone to bed, nursing a bottle as usual.

She didn't know where in the hell the sheriff and that nasty man, Drago, were. They should have returned from Parley's base camp long ago. Maybe they'd reached the film crew out at Leidy Lake. If so, they might have stayed overnight with them.

Terry had gone to town, and, besides, it was too late to send him out for a look-see. She levered herself reluctantly out of her chair. *Time for bed.*

She reached for the doorknob just as a knock sounded. It scared the shit out of her. "Who is it?"

"Sheriff Goodman."

She unlocked the door, and the sheriff heaved his hulk through it, shaking snow from his Stetson. "Evening, Fiona. Thought I might find you awake."

"What did you find out?" she demanded.

"Cool off, Fiona. It's mighty damned cold out there."

"Oh, yeah. I expect you could use something to warm you

308

up?" She opened the bottom drawer of her file cabinet. She took out the bottle hidden there and poured two glasses.

The sheriff downed his in one gulp and smacked his lips. "Now that's mighty good stuff, Fiona."

She took the hint and poured another. "Now then. Where in hell are they?"

"Well now, we drove out to Parley's base camp, but they weren't there." He held out his glass. "So then we went on over to Slate Creek Trail." He sipped the whiskey.

"And?"

"Trail was blocked. Big slide. Creek was running real deep."

Fiona sagged back. "So, in short, no news."

"That's the long and the short of it."

Fiona rocked for a moment. "Now what?"

The sheriff finished the last of his whiskey. "I'll take another shot at finding them in the morning." He stood and put on his hat. "You know that agent, Drago? I'm beginning to think he's not what he says he is."

Fiona clutched her chest. "Not . . . then what is he?"

"Thought you might know." He opened the door but turned back to her with a smirk. "Just a warning, is all."

CHAPTER 31

Friday Morning, June 26

Megan knew it was a nightmare, but no matter how hard she tried, she could not escape. She was hemmed in on all sides by a heavy mass, and Agent Drago was stabbing her with an ice pick. The flashlight in his other hand shone in her eyes.

Consciousness arrived slowly. She cracked one eye open. The sun shone into her eyes through the chinks in the lean-to. The heavy mass resolved itself into the bodies of the other survivors packed tightly together for warmth. Agent Drago was nowhere to be seen, but her conversation last night with Pia came back to her. Drago was going to kill her to force TT to sell the ranch to "Uncle." And he'd kill her with an ice pick in the heart.

If she did not force herself to get up and get moving, she would probably die of exposure and starvation. Of course, if she did somehow return to the ranch, she'd probably die anyway. At least she was going to die fighting.

She pried herself out of the mass of bodies and crawled on her hands and knees from beneath the lean-to. The snow had stopped, and the sun peeked through occasional holes in the cloud cover. She stirred the fire to life and added some more wood.

"Megan?" Bettina had come up behind her.

"Good morning, Bettina."

"Is Daphne a natural blonde?"

"What?! This is a hell of a time to pry into . . . why?"

310

"If Pia and Tommy had blond hair, that man who is after her might not recognize them."

"Oh! What a great idea. But . . . he'll be looking for the two of them. If Tommy is with her . . ."

"Let's go talk to Pia."

Pia stared at Bettina. "Bleach my hair?"

"And Tommy's," Bettina replied. "No. Listen to me. We can pass you off as Marlene, who was blonde. Fayrene will also make you up to have facial injuries—bandages and stitches and so on."

Pia felt some of her fear diminish. It might work. "But . . . he'll be looking for *two* of us. He knows we're traveling together. Just bleaching Tommaso's hair won't fool him."

"Does he know what Tommy looks like?"

"I don't know. Uncle may have given him a photo."

"Then you'll have to separate. I will—"

"No! I can't be without Tommaso. He's the only thing that matters in my life. I can't live without him."

"Make sense, Pia!" Bettina shook her hard. "If he sees the two of you traveling together, he'll know for sure."

"But, how . . . who would take care of him? How would he get to safety?"

Megan said, "We're going to ask Charity Palmerson to pretend that Tommy is her son and travel to Los Angeles with us on the train. After that, Bettina will take care of Tommy until you can find a safe haven."

Anguish twisted Pia's insides once again. Safe haven? Where could she ever hide that Uncle would not find her? How could she become a blonde, like that common floozy Daphne? How could she leave her son in the care of another woman, especially an American woman? But what alternative did she have? She nodded.

"If I know anything about my sister," Megan said, "she will have insisted that Fayrene have hair bleach with her at all times."

An hour later Pia was no longer recognizable. Her hair was now nearly white, and a dirty bandage covered half her face. Fayrene had gone a little heavy with the peroxide, but Megan had no sympathy for Pia's complaints.

The survivors had eaten their breakfast of hot water and were finally on the trail again. Beneath her, Nevada plodded along, head down. She wondered what he was thinking about, or did horses even think? Behind her came Peaches with Luella lashed in her saddle. Megan did not really need the lead rope. Most of the horses were old hands on the trail and followed each other nose to tail out of long habit.

Junior rode at the head of the pack, leading the way. Close behind him rode Paul, jabbing his heels into Jingles as he recited the menus of all the many banquets he'd attended. It puzzled her that Junior put up with Paul, but he was buried in his own thoughts. The time was coming, she suspected, when Junior would emerge from his cocoon of misery. When he did, would he be rational or in another of his crazy moods?

Behind Luella, Eric and Miguel carried Sandor on the makeshift litter. Katrina walked close behind, occasionally crooning words of encouragement to her husband. Behind them, Bettina and Fayrene rode with Tommy between them, and Bettina told him stories about Hollywood and child movie stars. She was probably priming him for his next role in life.

Ahead, the land flattened out somewhat. Megan could see riders bunching up and stopping, and, as the trail widened, Steamer came up behind her.

"What's going on?" he asked

"I can't see. They're stopped up ahead for some reason."

"I'll go see."

Steamer stared helplessly at Slate Creek. A torrent of muddy water tumbled down the creek bed with a gargling roar. In calm water, they might have swum the horses across; in this liquid hurricane, they would be lucky to cross without the horses drowning or breaking a leg. The peril to humans was something else.

He sensed the mass of the other survivors gathering behind him: a dark, angry, voracious force that threatened to shove him into the maelstrom. He dismounted. Around him the others got off their horses, and Eric and Miguel lowered Sandor's litter to the ground with moans of relief. After eating a tiny portion of cornmeal mush washed down with hot water, they had drawn straws to see who would ride and who would walk. A long straw had given Steamer the dubious privilege of riding the first hour. He'd pay for the luxury later when it came his turn to carry Sandor's litter.

Beside him, Bettina asked, "Can we go around it?"

Steamer turned to Junior for an answer. Junior's gaze was on something in another time and space. "No."

"But we've got to get across," Pia cried. She was hugging Tommy tightly to her side. "Tommaso is very sick. I must get him to a hospital, or he will die."

Junior turned to her very slowly, his face an empty mask. "God in his infinite wisdom will decide who shall live and who shall die."

Steamer resisted the urge to kick him in the ass. Junior had grown increasingly weird since the slide and his father's death. His manner had turned cold and distant, and his focus was on some inner torment.

Still, Steamer could not resist a sarcastic tone as he said, "While you and the Lord are deciding matters of life and death, could one of you tell me if there is any way we can get around this?"

"No."

"That's no damned help." Steamer walked closer to the edge of the creek and looked upstream and down. "Get me that picket-line rope."

Junior's eyes racked focus back to the present. "What for?"

"Never damn mind!" Steamer said with a snarl. "Just get it for me."

Five minutes later Steamer had secured the rope tightly under his armpits with a bowline knot. Upstream, Junior and Miguel held the other end, ready to pay it out as needed. He hesitated on the bank of the creek that was now undercut by the raging waters. Megan held him tight for a moment.

"Are the matches safe?" she asked.

They'd made a plan. He would put a dozen phosphorous matches in his waterproof match case and secure it in his shirt pocket. His first task on reaching the other side would be to gather wood and build a fire. He second would be to tie the picket line to a stout tree on the other side. Each person and horse would then be attached to the line to prevent them from being washed away as they crossed the raging stream.

He patted his shirt pocket. "Safe as they'll ever be. See you on the other side. We've got a lot to do together, darling."

Steamer inched carefully down the bank but fell the last few feet into the churning water. It was liquid ice. He'd have only a few moments before the cold drained his strength. As he struggled to swim, he used the force of the water against the restraining line to swing him like a pendulum across the creek. He fought his way over boulders, slamming into them and dropping into holes over his head.

At last his feet touched the other side. He crawled up the bank and collapsed in a heap, gasping for air. If only he could sleep for a century. He saw Megan gesturing for him to get up. He waved back, then took the line to a stout pine and tied it firmly around the trunk.

By the time he had gathered enough wood to start a fire, he was shivering so violently, he felt as if his bones would shake right out of his skin. As he built the pyramid of kindling, his clumsy hands kept knocking it down, and he had to start over several times.

At last he had a base of leaves, small twigs, and, finally, larger branches. Halfway measures would not do. It had to be right the first time. Numbness was shutting down his body more rapidly now. The fire was essential if they were to survive.

He knelt beside the kindling. He was aware that some of the others had crossed and were watching him. "Don't just stand there!" he shouted. "More wood. Dry wood. Hurry!"

They scattered, and he focused all his attention on the kindling and the strike-anywhere matches that he now unwrapped with great care. He picked up a small rock and scratched the first match across it. It sparked, smoldered, and went out. *Damn.* The rock was wet. He unwrapped another match and examined it. It seemed dry enough. He rubbed his thumb on the skin of his forearm until he felt that it might be dry, and then he scratched his thumbnail across the bright blue tip of the match. Flame spurted, held, and ate its way back along the wooden shaft. He held it to the leaves at the bottom. They smoldered, smoked, and went out.

Two matches later, the leaves had dried out enough to burn. He watched the flame creep up the twigs, wrap itself around them, and begin climbing to the next level. He blew gently at the base of the flames and fed more small branches in one at a time. *Why wasn't the fire warm?* It was only when he put his finger directly in the flame that he understood how numb he had become.

Shouts and the piercing neigh of a horse in agony made him look up. As he rose, his body betrayed him, and he nearly pitched into the fire, but someone grabbed his arm. Megan stood beside him, wet and shaking. He put his arms around her and held her tightly until the noise behind them forced him to break away.

Midnight lay on his side, kicking and thrashing in the water. He was attached to the picket line by his lead rope, which was all that kept him from being swept downstream.

Where was Pia? Her newly blonde hair bobbed to the surface as she rose and fought to swim against the current. Steamer lunged down the bank into the icy water and managed to grab her arm as she swept by. He pulled her from the creek and laid her beside the fire.

An hour later everyone was safely across. The fire had been built so high that Megan was sure it could be seen on the moon. Never mind: it threw out heat like an open gate to hell. Steamer, Miguel, Eric, and Junior had thrown together another lean-to shelter. They were once again huddled in a tight mass: warm, dry, and totally exhausted.

CHAPTER 32

Friday Afternoon, June 26

The sun had crossed over into afternoon during the survivors' struggle to cross the raging creek, build the fire, and build the lean-to. Nightfall was but two hours away—but hunger was not. Hunger was here, now, clawing at Megan like an insane animal trying to escape from her guts. There'd been no question of moving on tonight. Hunger would not kill them for a few days yet, but cold and fatigue would. With the shelter of the lean-to and the warmth from the fire, they could regain enough energy to move on tomorrow.

"I'm *hungry!*" Paul's anguished howl shattered the quiet.

"So's everyone else," Junior yelled. "Now shut up!"

Paul rose and stalked over to Junior. "Why don't we eat that horse?" he demanded, jabbing a finger at Midnight's corpse lying in the creek.

It took Junior one angry stride to reach Paul, grab his shirt collar, and smack him across the face. "Don't even think about that. What the hell are you, some kinda cannibal? That would be like . . . like eating dead humans, hear me?"

"But, but—"

"Button your lip!" Junior pushed him away. "We'll be home in a day or two. Besides, you've got enough lard on you to survive a month. Go sit down."

Paul sagged to a seat.

For a long time Megan heard nothing but the crackle of the

fire and occasional murmurs from the survivors. She was staring into the flames, her mind vacant, when she had the feeling
someone was staring at her. She pulled her gaze from the fire—
and directly into Junior's eyes. He was indeed staring at her,
nodding rhythmically, with a faint smile on his lips.

She felt her body tying itself in knots despite the warmth of
the fire as a memory of talking with him yesterday afternoon
sprang at her, leaving her weak with fear. Had he really called
on God to strike his father dead, and did he really believe God
had granted his wish? No wonder he had such a crazy look in
his eyes. He was carrying a terrible contradiction within his
soul. Then he had told her she was to help him rid the town of
the evil infecting it. How was she supposed to do that?

In her musings, she heard a sound. At first she thought she
was hearing things. Was it someone playing a bugle? Was it the
cavalry coming to the rescue? Hardly. As far as anyone down in
Jackson Hole knew, they were safe and sound. But wouldn't
someone have noticed the landslide by now? Why should a
rescue party not be on the way? The sound repeated. Sighing,
Megan realized it was only an elk bugling. She slumped with
disappointment—until she noticed Junior had got quickly to his
feet and was listening intently. He whirled and came over to
her.

"Let's go!"

"Go? Where? Are you crazy?"

"Hear that? Elk we can eat. We're going to bag one."

She pulled away. "I'm exhausted. Leave me alone."

He grabbed he arm. "The Lord has sent you to me. He means
for you to help me bring His cleansing fire down upon the
evildoers in our town."

Megan felt a paralysis sliding over her, a feeling quite different from the numbness of the cold. All willpower and self-
control had been sucked from her, leaving her prey to an outside

force that was dictating every move. Should she scream, run, and push Junior into the fire?

She glanced at Steamer. He was huddled in a tight ball beside the fire, sound asleep. It would be selfish to wake him—or any of the others, for that matter.

She rose. It was better to keep Junior where she could watch him. They stalked through the lengthening shadows. In the distance she could hear the faint crackle of brush as the elk herd browsed. Occasionally she caught sight of a dark patch of brown moving through the pines. Junior held the Colt .45 cradled against his chest. He'd fired one shot at Paul's feet and shot the four mules who'd gone off the trail. So he had one shot left. They would have to be very close to the animal to guarantee a kill.

The herd was moving east. Junior bent, picked up a handful of dust, and let it dribble from his fingers. The wind was from the northeast; it was very faint, but strong enough to carry their scent to the elk if they got upwind of them. Junior stopped, turned back, and pulled Megan close to him. "We're going to move east a ways, get a little bit ahead of them. That way we can set up a good, steady shot when they move into range."

Ten minutes later they had crept into position behind a large deadfall. The trunk would provide a good rest on which to steady the Colt. The herd grazed slowly toward them as the faint breeze held steady out of the north.

Junior leaned closer. "You're sure an uppity little thing," he whispered. "Damned if I know why Fiona wanted me to mess up that pretty face of yours. I like my woman to be pretty, so I'm just going to have to disobey her. And after I take care of my business at the ranch, I'll have time to teach you some manners."

Later she would marvel that she had found the courage, but at the time, the words bolted from her mouth before she realized she was going to say them. "What business at the ranch?"

"Shit, Megan. Stop pretending you don't know."

A landslide of emotions fell on her, crushing her with the same suddenness and blind indifference as the boulders that had snuffed out the life of her friends. Yes, she did know, and it was time to face the truth: alcohol was ravaging her family. She had been playing nice and pretending everything was just perfect in her and Terry's marriage. She had looked the other way and gone to the movies.

She felt as if she might explode with rage and frustration. How could she feel joy at the same time? But she did—and if she did explode, she'd go hungry. The elk were almost in range.

"You're right. No more pretending."

A cow elk was grazing just ten yards from them. Junior turned away and, with extreme caution, eased back the hammer on the Colt. The elk looked up, startled, and stopped. Megan held absolutely still, and the cow began grazing forward again.

In the deep afternoon light, the muzzle blast was like a Klieg light. When the smoke cleared, the elk lay dead three yards away.

An hour later the smell of roasting meat drifted through the night. The elk had been butchered in record time, hacked apart with hunting knives and the camp hatchet. Now two haunches, skewered on pine branches, dripped fat into the fire.

The promise of food had created a new sense of hope in the survivors, and they sat close to the fire and to each other, staring avidly at the dripping meat. A murmur of conversation arose above the sound of the fire, and an occasional laugh sparkled through the icy air.

Megan and Steamer leaned against each other, holding hands. He turned his head closer to her and said, "I do believe we're going to make it out of this mess."

She smiled up at him. "Yes, we'll probably make it out of the woods, but we've still got to get out of town. That man, Drago, is going to be looking for Pia and Tommy, and if he thinks we had anything to do with helping her escape . . ."

"She sure looks different with blonde hair."

Megan nodded. "Yes, but she's dead set against leaving without Tommy, and Drago would be sure to look beneath the makeup if they were together."

"From the victorious tone of your voice, I gather you've thought of a solution."

She squeezed his hands. "We're going to ask Charity Palmerson to pretend Tommy is her son, Bertie's, brother, Corkie, and travel to Los Angeles with us."

"Not a bad idea. But what about you? Do you think Fiona is just going to let you walk out?"

"When she discovers her secret ledger is gone, she'll have no choice."

He gave her a questioning look, and she told him about the account books locked in the bottom drawer of Fiona's file cabinet. "At least I'm pretty sure they contain incriminating evidence."

"That's a good bet. If she catches you . . ."

"She won't. I'll kiss up to her, pretend I'm going to stay. Then I'll steal them and put them in my safe-deposit box at the bank. With a note to the manager to open the box if anything happens to me."

Steamer watched as the roasted elk haunches were laid out on logs and chopped into portions. Eager hands seized them, and soon people were ripping off bites of steaming meat with their teeth. They ate fiercely, heedless of the fat and juices smearing their hands, their faces, and their clothing. Soon there was little left but a few shreds of charred flesh. Steamer helped spit the forelegs and put them in position over the fire.

As the hot food reached his stomach, he realized it was more powerful than the most potent sleeping medicine. A lovely warmth spread over his limbs, and he soon felt more relaxed and comfortable that he had in days. His eyelids dropped like a fire curtain at a theater, and then they popped open as pain stabbed his right calf. Paul was drawing his foot back for another kick, but Steamer rolled out of the way and jumped to his feet.

"What the hell are you doing!"

"You haven't been watching me, Steamer. I've been playing my most successful role, and you've been asleep."

Steamer stared at him, still befuddled with sleep. "Role?"

"As Emperor Nero. Now watch me."

Paul reclined beside the fire, lying back along a log as if it were a divan. He lifted a huge chunk of elk and gnawed on it, making moaning noises of pleasure and slurping at the meat. Steamer watched in disgust.

"Hey! Steamer! Don't you think I'm funny?" Steamer shook his head and turned away, but Paul continued, "Hey! Look at me, Steamer. The audience roared with laughter when they saw me in this scene. Tell me I'm funny."

"Sorry, Mr. Buckingham, but I've got other things to think about."

"You don't think I'm funny?" Paul's face crumpled, and he burst into sobs.

Paul stopped abruptly. Steamer watched as he rummaged in his saddlebags and heard him grunt with satisfaction. When he came back, Paul carried one of Betty's knives: a boning knife with a narrow but ridged blade, seven inches long, honed to fine edge and set in a hefty wooden handle.

Steamer backed away slowly. "Well, now, I'm glad you found that missing knife, Mr. Buckingham. I'm sure Betty will be glad to get it back."

"Don't try to sweet-talk me, Mr. Important Director. It's time I put an end to your shit. Permanently. I'm going to gut you like a pig."

The blade glittered in the firelight as Paul slashed. Steamer sucked in his belly, thrust his hips to the rear, and pushed his hands overhead. The knife ripped his shirt. He felt a ribbon of pain streak across his abdomen.

He could hear the shouts and screams of the other survivors, and he could see blurred forms milling around trying to stop the attack. He was aware of Megan as she lashed out, kicking Paul solidly on his thigh.

Paul swiveled and thrust the knife at her. "You're next, lady. Stay there until I come back for you."

The delay gave Steamer a chance to whip off his leather jacket and wrap it around his left arm. It would give him some shielding.

He was aware the camp was in an uproar, but the need to focus on Paul's movements drove the sounds and movements of the others out of his mind. Paul was advancing now, slashing the knife horizontally back and forth in short strokes. Each time Steamer tried to dodge left or right, he felt people jumping away as Paul cut him off with surprising speed. Steamer estimated he was nearing the edge of the steep drop-off into the turbulent creek.

Paul slashed at him again. He barely had time to block the blow with his jacket-wrapped arm. He whirled, hoping to entangle the knife in the jacket, and felt the knife's point stab into his forearm. The force of the move ripped the jacket away. Paul shook it off the knife and came at him again.

Steamer kept backing up, dodging from side to side as he did. He glanced quickly over his shoulder. The drop-off was barely three yards away. Behind Paul, he saw Megan advancing with a flaming branch in her hands. The direction of his gaze tipped Paul off. He turned. Megan swung the blazing branch like a baseball bat. For the first time, Steamer saw fear on the man's face.

"Drop the knife, Mr. Buckingham." He forced his voice to a soothing, reasonable pitch. "Let's try to patch things up when we're all feeling better tomorrow."

"Fuck you, Steamer. You ruined my career, and you're going to pay for it." He stepped in, thrust the knife, and screamed in rage as Megan jabbed the burning branch at him. He swiveled and thrust at her, but the length of the branch kept him away.

He pivoted back toward Steamer and rushed, slashing and stabbing ferociously. Steamer ducked and weaved violently as the pain of his wounds sucked at the last of his strength. He felt sure the edge was no more than a yard away. If Paul didn't sink the knife into him, his own clumsy weakness would soon drop him over the edge.

"Jump, you bastard, jump!" Paul's voice was filled with glee. He stopped, straddle-legged, two feet away from Steamer. "Which is it going to be, the knife or the creek?"

Steamer saw Megan run up behind Paul. She swung the fiery branch up between his legs. A look of terror bolted across his face, followed by a scream of agony. As Megan continued to twist the branch into his crotch, he danced a comic polka to escape—and danced off the edge.

CHAPTER 33

Saturday Morning, June 27

Steamer's eyelids were made of granite and kept falling, no matter how hard he struggled to lift them. He raised his chin and peered down the trail. He could see no low-hanging branches ahead that would sweep him off his saddle. Maybe he could close his eyes, just for a moment. The rhythmic clip-clop of the horses' hooves reminded him of the grandfather clock his mother had brought with her from the East. He could hear it now: ticktock, ticktock.

Then something hard and cold slammed him in the back. That was funny. If he'd run into a branch, he would have felt the pain on his front. What had hit him on the back? He forced his eyelids to rise.

Splotch was looking down at him. Steamer could see, between the horse's ears, patches of blue sky beginning to show through the clouds. He'd fallen off, for chrissake.

"Hey, Steamer, you all right?"

He sat up. Eric stood a few feet away from him, holding one end of the litter on which Sandor lay. Miguel held the other end, and now they lowered it to the ground. Fayrene, who had been walking beside the litter, sank to her knees and resumed her soft crooning to Sandor. Steamer could not make out the words, but they sounded as if they might be a part of an ancient African ritual.

"I'm going to have to be all right, right?" He smiled, knowing

325

the expression looked phony to them. "Just give me a hand back on."

He mounted. "Thanks. Are *you* all right?" He could see bloodstains on the handles of the litter.

"Like you said, Steamer, we're going to have to be, right?"

He nodded and gently urged Splotch into a walk. Far ahead he could see Junior and Miguel, followed by Megan, followed by Daphne on Peaches. After they had eaten the last of the elk for breakfast, Daphne's DTs had lessened somewhat, and she had not had to be tied on her saddle. She was still living in her own dream world, singing and waving her arms as she occasionally muttered something about TT.

Just ahead of Steamer was Bettina, who rode along with Pia and Tommy. She was talking forcefully to Pia, calling her Marlene and reminding Tommy not to call her Mom. Tommy's cold had gotten better, but he still had a hacking cough and could barely talk.

The next time Steamer looked ahead, he saw that Junior, Miguel, Megan, and Daphne had disappeared in the clouds still hanging over the trail. He poked his heels into Splotch, who changed from a slow walk to a walk.

Two minutes later he reached a fork in the trail. The leading riders were nowhere in sight. He listened hard and heard faintly, to the right, hooves tapping on hard rock. He looked right, left, and back right, frowning. Something was wrong, but the low-hanging clouds disoriented him.

"Hey!" he bellowed. "Slow down! Wait up!"

In response he heard the sound of hooves stop, and he jabbed his heels into Splotch. A moment later he had ridden out into the sunlight—and realized what was wrong.

Junior had turned back and now rode up to him, scowling. "What's the matter, Steamer? Getting a little saddle sore? I don't know about you, but I want to get back to base camp. Now."

Steamer nodded slowly. "That's a really good idea, but you're not going to get to camp that way."

"You don't like the way I'm sitting my horse, is that it? Or maybe I'm not dressed right, like one of you movie cowboys?"

Steamer tried to put a lid on the laughter bubbling up from deep inside like a geyser, but it spewed out anyway. "No. It's just that you are going the wrong way—I mean, the wrong direction—to get to base camp."

Junior's face hardened. "Really? I'm on the wrong trail?"

"Yes."

"And how would you know that, Mr. Movie Director?"

"Mount Leidy is on our left."

Junior jerked upright in his saddle, stared at the snow-capped, ten thousand foot peak of the mountain.

"We're riding west," Steamer added. "Camp is east from the fork."

"And how would a dude like you know where east and west is?"

"I had a look at a map before we left. Just to get oriented."

"A map?" Junior sneered and turned to Megan. "Come on, let's go. This drugstore cowboy don't know his ass from his elbow."

He turned Champion back toward the west and moved off. "Come on, I said. Might as well get used to obeying me."

Steamer watched as Megan sat, her head turning first to him, back to Junior, and then back to him. "Are you sure, Steamer?"

"Absolutely."

Megan rode closer and spoke in a low voice. "He's really gone off the rails, Steamer. I don't know where he gets this idea that I'm his wife, but he's just been getting crazier and crazier. He's scaring the hell out of me."

"Okay, let's just ride on out of here."

"Right. Luella, follow us."

They had ridden some distance back to the fork when Steamer heard the sound of galloping hooves behind them and a shout from Junior.

He galloped up to them and hauled Champion to a stop. "The Lord just revealed to me that I was going the wrong way. But that don't matter no more, because now I know what God wants me to do before we can be married." He rode slowly past Steamer, nodding at him as he went past. "I'm sure glad I didn't do what Fiona wanted."

They all rode down toward the fork where the rest of the survivors were waiting with bewildered looks on their faces.

Megan felt a change in Nevada's walk, and she could hear the steady rhythm of his hooves increasing. The horse knew his home corral was not far away. She lifted her head and glanced around. She'd seen that particular boulder on the way out, hadn't she?

The pines along the west side of the trail were festooned with a string of tiny lights formed as the sun made rainbows from the water drops clinging to the needles. She saw, through the branches, that the sky to the west was empty of clouds and shone a brilliant blue over the snow-capped Teton Range. The air, scented with pine, was growing warmer.

Ahead, a line appeared through the trees. The line was too straight to be natural. As she rode closer, it resolved into the roofline of the storage shed at base camp. The realization that soon they would be back in civilization came crashing down on her. One ordeal was ending, and another was about to begin.

The first thing she would have to come to terms with was Paul's death. After he had been swept downstream in the raging creek, not a single person had moved to save him. Later, they all agreed to tell the same tale: that he had gone crazy and stumbled into the fire and then thrown himself in the water to douse the flames. But what if his body was recovered, and the coroner found burns in his crotch and nowhere else? Was she supposed to feel guilty for saving Steamer's life? No; she knew Paul's last agonized screams would remain with her all her life, but she'd done the right thing. She would face the press and the law without guilt.

But how was she supposed to face Fiona and Terry? Yesterday, just before he shot the elk, Junior had said, "Damned if I know why Fiona wanted me to mess up that pretty face of yours."

Understanding had crept into her mind like a root slowly penetrating a rock. She hated herself for thinking this way, but she'd been forced to conclude that Fiona had bribed Junior to injure her somehow. Fiona had instructed him to cut her face or burn it so that she would be ugly and unable to be in the movies.

Now, like that root-riven rock, she was of two different minds. One side of her wanted to flee without even passing through Jackson Hole. She wanted to sneak away in the night and never set foot on the ranch again. The other side of her knew that she had an obligation to all the survivors. She owed it to them to pull the fangs from Fiona, TT, and Terry before they had a chance to poison the future.

Nevada's pace quickened to a trot. A few heartbeats later, she saw the corrals and sheds of Parley's base camp through the trees. Suddenly all she wanted was a huge meal, a hot bath, and a good night's sleep. The future would wait until tomorrow.

A half hour later the exhausted riders had dismounted and had walked, limped, or been carried to Parley's red, stake-sided truck. Megan was helping Daphne climb in when the sound of a car approaching made her turn. The sheriff's new black-and-

white, with a chrome-plated siren mounted on the roof, pulled
to a stop.

She was glad Steamer was standing beside her as both doors
flew open and Sheriff Goodman and Agent Drago jumped out.
Megan stifled a bitter laugh as they approached and heads swiveled in all directions with expressions of bafflement and anger.

"Well, you sure took your own sweet time getting here,
Sheriff," Megan said.

He shoved his hands in the hip pockets of his waist overalls
and glared at her. "We didn't . . . I mean, where in hell have
you been? What the fuck happened? Where's Parley?" He walked
toward the red truck and looked at the survivors huddled in the
back. "Where is everybody?"

"There was a landslide, Sheriff. Maybe you've heard about
it?"

"Yes, we . . . goddamnit, Mrs. Foxworth, don't play games
with me. Where the hell is Parley? And the others?"

While Megan and Steamer took turns condensing three days
of hell into a five-minute recital, Agent Drago walked to the
truck and scrutinized the passengers. Megan held her breath
until he came striding back to her.

"Where is Mrs. Donatelli? Pia?"

Megan looked him in the eye and said the line she'd been
practicing. "She was killed, Mr. Drago. In the slide."

"What about her son? Tommaso?"

Megan bowed her head and sniffled. "He was such a nice,
polite boy."

"*Merda!*" His black eyes bored holes in her lie. She felt
Steamer put his arm around her. "Who is that kid in the truck?"

"Oh. That's Corkie Palmerson. Did you meet Charity Palmerson at the Rocking Lazy F?" She was about to add more
details but kept silent. More details would only give him more
to be suspicious about.

He glared at her a moment longer and then turned to the sheriff. "I need to get back to town. Immediately. To cable my superiors. For further instructions."

"Whoa there, Drago. These folks have just been through hell. I have to see if they require any help right now."

Drago sneered at him. "It seems they have transportation. The best thing you could do for them would be to go now and notify the hospital. They won't be prepared for such an emergency."

Megan watched as the sheriff measured Drago's words, his face clouded with doubt. "Well. Uh, that might be a good idea. That be all right with you, Mrs. Foxworth?"

"Steamer can drive the truck. Can't you, Steamer?"

He nodded. "We'll be right behind you, Sheriff."

"Hey! Wait up!" Junior strode up to them. "Can I get a ride into town with you, Sheriff? I got some urgent business."

The sheriff was nodding when Steamer asked, "What about the horses, Junior?"

He turned slowly to Steamer. "What *about* the horses?"

"I expect they're hungry."

"Miguel will feed them."

"And what about Miguel?"

Comprehension dawned slowly on Junior. "Oh. There's a couple cans of stew in the shed, and a stove. He can bunk down in there. He'll be all right. Let's go, Sheriff."

The three men got into the black-and-white and drove off, splattering mud on Megan and Steamer. The sheriff did not turn on the siren, not on these deserted back roads, but Megan was sure he would once they hit the highway.

She climbed into the front seat with Steamer. He leaned over and kissed her. "You sure just stepped in shit, Megan."

What in hell was he talking about? "How?"

"That little lie you told Drago. About Tommy being Charity's

331

son Corkie."

"Oh, my God! You mean, if he gets to Charity first?" He nodded. "Well, let's go!"

Steamer turned the ignition switch. The starter whirred—and whirred and whirred. He stopped, waited, and turned it again. Nothing happened. He turned the switch off.

"Don't stop! Keep trying."

"We'll just run the battery down. What with all this rain, the distributor cap has probably gotten damp. I'll have to dry it off." He jumped down and lifted the hood. For several minutes, as Megan's anxiety rose, he did something she could not see.

The hood slammed down. He got in and said, "Cross your fingers." Once again he twisted the key—and the engine coughed into life.

CHAPTER 34

Saturday Afternoon, June 27

The ride back to town had taken what seemed like hours, and Megan was frantic with worry by the time they pulled up in front of the hospital. She scanned the waiting crowd: Drago was not there, but the sheriff was. He'd alerted not only the hospital but, by the looks of it, the entire population.

She got out and joined Steamer at the rear of the truck. She helped him open the back and put the loading ramp in place. The crowd pressed closer, gawking at the survivors stumbling out of the truck. Between watching frantically for Drago, answering questions, and helping her friends into the hospital, she was as busy as a one-armed wallpaper hanger. She saw Gertie hovering at the back of the crowd and waved a quick hello as she escorted Daphne toward the entrance.

Inside, the odor of carbolic acid disinfectant battled against the smell of disease. An orderly and a nurse ignored her as they rushed toward the entrance. "Hey!" she called, but they continued. She was looking for someone else to help when she heard a voice behind her.

"Megan!" It was Doc Byrne. He strode closer, grasped her upper arms, and looked deeply into her eyes. "Are you all right?" She nodded. She felt like hell, but she wasn't ready to admit it yet. Doc continued, "The sheriff blew into town an hour ago with the news." He released her arms, stood back a bit, and looked her up and down. "What in hell happened out there?"

Her shoulders slumped. "I'll tell you the whole story later, Doc. Right now . . . did you see anyone else with the sheriff? Was that Agent Drago with him? What about Junior Frampton?"

"I wasn't here when they arrived." His gaze shifted to look behind her. "What's the matter with Luella?"

Megan pulled her sister closer. "That's more to talk about later. Right now, I need you to get her into a private room and have someone watch her to make sure she doesn't run away."

Doc frowned at her. "I can't just do that without knowing what her problem is."

Megan looked around. No one was nearby. "Her problem comes out of a bottle. Now can we please talk about it later? And please trust me?"

Doc nodded slowly. "Being as it's you, Megan." He waved at a passing nurse. "Take Miss Devine to room three and stay with her until I get back. Understand? Do not leave her."

After the nurse had led Luella off, his mouth twitched into a smile. "Any other special requests?"

"Yes, as a matter of fact. Come over here." Steamer was helping the orderly wheel a stretcher through the doors. On it Pia— now Marlene—slept deeply.

"This is Marlene Reis. She's one of the film crew. Whatever you do, don't take her bandages off in public. Steamer will wheel her to the back entrance."

"Damn it, Megan, you're asking me to violate my professional ethics! What in hell is wrong here?"

"A hell of a lot. We need to get her to the ranch. You can treat her there. In private."

"I just can't do that, Megan. I need these people here at the hospital, where I have facilities to treat them."

"Please! Trust me. If she stays here, she may die here."

"You'd better have a good story to tell, Megan." Doc Byrne

sighed heavily. "All right. But I can't leave. How are you going to get her to the ranch?"

"I saw Gertie outside when we arrived. She can drive us."

"All right. What about the rest of your group?"

"Sandor Kalman probably has serious internal injuries. His wife, Katrina, is with him. Ah, Eric and others from the film crew have minor wounds that will need bandaging. After that they'll need a good meal and some sleep. The boy who's with Bettina Segal . . . log him in as Bertram Palmerson. He's Charity's son. Bettina will need attention too, but she's a real trouper. She'll be all right."

Before he could object, she turned away. "Come on, Steamer. You wheel Marlene to the back entrance. If anyone asks, tell them she has to go to the hospital in Cheyenne. Then go find Gertie and have her bring her car around. I'm going to say good-bye to Luella."

Megan knocked on the door of room three and walked in. Luella, thank God, was asleep. As she turned to leave, a voice behind the screen separating the beds quavered, "Is that you, Megan?"

Maybelle Frampton, Parley's wife, sat up straighter when she saw Megan. She was wan and rail-thin. Her right arm was in a sling, and a large bandage covered her left cheek.

"Maybelle! Are you—Well, I guess maybe that's a foolish question." She moved closer and held the older woman's hand. "What happened?"

"Oh, I slipped and fell. In the kitchen." As Megan frowned in disbelief, she added, "On soapy water."

"I'm sorry to hear that, Maybelle."

She ducked her head. "I heard . . . I heard Parley died. Is it true?"

"Yes."

Maybelle lifted her head, and a faint smile flickered across her lips. "How did he die? Did he suffer?"

"No, I think it was all over in seconds for him." Privately she thought Parley's death had been agonizing and terrifying, but there was no need to tell his widow that.

Maybelle stared at nothing for a long time until Megan asked her, "Are you going to be all right?"

Her gaze snapped back to Megan. "Oh, yes . . . I mean, I'll miss him . . . but then, he is with *his* God."

"I can't stay any longer, Maybelle. You let me know if I can do anything for you, all right?"

Megan would never forget Maybelle's tiny smile of peace and victory.

As Steamer wheeled the gurney toward the rear entrance, his emotions seemed like a river full of logs floating down to a sawmill. Each one was bigger than the next, and they were all slamming and banging into each other in the raging currents of his mind.

But one log was more important than the others: Megan. He had to stop her from floating into the sawmill of her family and being slashed into lumber. Then there was Agent Drago, and it mattered little whether he was a Prohibition agent or an agent of Pia's mysterious "uncle." Either way, he was a threat to her. But there was nothing Steamer could do just now. He was going to have to deal with each day, each minute, as it came at him.

Outside, Gertie's old rattletrap car stood next to the sheriff's shiny, new patrol car. He lifted Pia's inert form and carried her to the car. Gertie opened the rear door, and Steamer laid her on the seat. As he did, Pia awoke with a gasp, terror shining in her eyes. When she saw who it was, she pulled his head down and kissed him with a long, hungry kiss.

He broke away. "We have to get you away from here, right now, *Marlene.*" She closed her eyes with a little whimper and lay back on the cushion.

He shut the rear door just as Megan exited the hospital. She took a few steps, saw the patrol car, and halted with her hand to her mouth.

"Oh, shit!" She walked to the black-and-white and gave the right front fender a vicious kick. "Steamer, the sheriff is talking to Doc Byrne right now, but he's planning on coming out to the ranch soon. We've got to delay him!"

"Yeah? How?"

She stood beside him, kicking a tire. "Hey! What about that distributor thing? Like when you fixed the truck at base camp?"

"Yes! We need a bucket of water." He searched quickly along the rear of the hospital and found a hose bib but no container of any kind. Then the solution hit him. "If you see him coming, do anything to distract him."

He lifted the hood of the patrol car and unsnapped the clips that held the cap on the distributor. He turned on the hose, took in a huge mouthful of water, ran back to the car, and spewed the water inside the distributor and distributor cap. He clipped the cap in place and slammed the hood shut, then got into the front seat of Gertie's car. Megan got in back with Pia. She cradled Pia's blonde head in her lap, and Gertie started the engine. She backed out, braked, and put the car in first gear.

As they drove off, Steamer saw the sheriff emerge from the hospital with Drago close behind.

CHAPTER 35

Saturday Afternoon, June 27

Steamer waited anxiously, watching the play of emotions across Charity Palmerson's face. He'd given her a rushed, highly condensed version of the disaster at Rattlesnake Canyon, followed by an equally abbreviated version of what they wanted her to do.

"Well, Steamer, that's the most amazing story I've ever heard. Of course, we'll help. Bertie loves play-acting. So do I, as a matter of fact." She paused and then exclaimed, "Oh! But Drago has seen me with only one boy. How do we explain that I now have two?"

"*Corkie* snuck away and went out on the trail ride without you knowing about it. Someone told you he'd done it, and you've been frantic and angry for days. He's a wild one, does this all the time. In fact, he'd vanished several times before he snuck away on the ride."

"Okay, I guess that will work. For a while, anyway. Until Drago has time to think it through."

"He'll be coming to check up on you," Steamer said. "We arranged a small delay, but the sheriff has probably figured it out by now, and he'll be bringing Drago along anytime now."

"Oh! We'd better talk to the boys right now."

Fifteen minutes later, Steamer had the boys enlisted as actors in an elaborate fantasy. It involved cowboys and Indians, the US cavalry, and spies. The boys were to play outlaw brothers sworn to protect their secret identity. Corkie was to have a severe cold and be unable to talk; Bertie would speak for him.

"Now, bath time. Both of you. Into the tub."

"Aw, Mom, not now!" Bertie said.

"Your *brother* Corkie has been out on a long, secret mission. You need a hiding place to talk about what he found out. You can talk privately in the bathroom without the spies overhearing you."

Charity stripped the boys, and they climbed into the tub. She worked up a good lather with the bath brush and soap and left them, closing the door.

Steamer said, "If Drago finds me here, it will make him suspicious. Can you handle him alone if I leave?"

"You're right, and I can handle it. Shoo."

Five minutes after Steamer had exited the back door of the cabin, a knock rattled the front door. "Who is it?" Charity called.

"Sheriff Goodman. And Agent Drago."

She opened the door, prepared to be charming and disarming, but the anger engraved on their faces made her heart hammer in her chest. She fell back, flustered. "Good evening, Sheriff, Agent Drago. Is something wrong?"

Drago pushed through the opening and stalked around the living room, looking in every corner.

"Hey, you! Drago!" she shouted.

He jerked as if a mule had kicked him. "Are you talking to me, lady?"

"I certainly am. Who do you think you are, bursting in here like a . . . a charging bull and invading my privacy?"

He stalked toward her, shoved his hands in his hip pockets, and stared down at her with a snarl. "I am an agent of the Prohibition Agency, and I'm searching for a criminal. And if you fail to cooperate, I'll arrest you as an accomplice."

Sheriff Goodman moved beside her. "Come on, Drago, you'll

catch more flies with honey than you will with vinegar. Calm down and be polite to the lady."

"All right, all right. I'm looking for that woman, Pia Donatelli. And her son. Have you seen them?"

"Why would I have anything to do with her, Agent? She's not really my class."

The sound of boyish giggles and loud splashing carried through the bathroom door.

"Who's in there?" Drago snarled.

"Just my sons, having their evening bath."

Drago yanked the door open and strode in. The boys stopped their play and looked at him in surprise. "Who are you?" he asked.

"I'm Bert Palmerson." Charity could see he was frightened.

Drago ignored him and turned to Corkie. "And who are you?"

"He's my brother, Corkie," Bertie said. "He has a bad cold and can't talk."

Drago focused on Corkie, who promptly coughed a deep, hacking cough. As Drago glared at him, waiting for a response, Bertie asked, "Hey, Mr. Agent, do you want to see a hurricane?"

With that Bertie seized the bath brush and began flailing at the water, splashing soapy suds out of the tub. Tommy joined him enthusiastically. A large wave landed on Drago's trousers and boots.

Charity thought he was going to hit the boys, but he backed off with a snarl. "You need to teach these brats some manners."

Megan had separated reluctantly from Steamer, but they had agreed that he would talk to Charity while she confronted her in-laws and her husband.

Dealing with Fiona had been easier than she expected it to be. After Megan had satisfied her curiosity about the disaster, Fiona quickly switched the conversation to Pia and Tommy.

Megan was forced to tell her the truth. Fiona's first sight of "Corkie" would have blown their cover story.

Fiona rocked back in her office chair. Her lips twitched as she digested what Megan had told her. "Okay, we'll play along, won't we, TT?"

His wheelchair made agitated little squeaks as he wheeled it back and forth. "So this Drago guy, you say he's a Prohi?"

"Yes. He has information that Pia is working with someone here who is smuggling large quantities of liquor into town. He has a warrant from the agency to search for it. And now I need a bath, some food, and a good night's sleep."

Terry had been surprisingly solicitous. He had heated a large batch of water for her, and now Megan sank into the tub and let it soak the aches from her bones. Not only that, he'd also gone off to the kitchen to fix her soup and a sandwich.

The bathroom door bumped open, and Terry came in, carrying a tray. He set it on top of the laundry hamper full of her filthy clothing and brought her a mug of hot chicken soup. She sipped it slowly, afraid that if she gulped it down she'd toss it right back up.

He now pulled the stool closer and sat with the sandwich on a plate on his lap. "You ready for some solid food?"

She nodded, and he handed her one sandwich half. "You sure look real tired, Megan. Guess you must have had a rough time out there. Can you tell me a little about it?"

"In a minute." The second half of the sandwich quickly followed the first, and a comforting warmth spread through Megan's aching body. She handed him the empty plate. "Now. I can talk a bit."

Which she did. He listened quietly and asked a few questions while his gaze roamed over the soapy water covering her body. When she ran down and stopped, he shook his head in wonder.

"You sure been through hell, Megan. But I'm going to make it up to you."

"That's nice, Terry."

"No, I really mean it. I'm going to buy you a new gas stove so you won't have to burn wood."

His gaze had focused on where her breasts would be if the soapsuds weren't concealing them. Oh, God, that expression meant he was going to want "special treatment" tonight. She could scarcely bear the thought, not after that glorious experience on the riverbank with Steamer.

"Not only that. I'm going to hire a local girl, someone to help you out."

"That's nice, Terry."

His gaze was still hog-tied to her breasts. She might as well get it over with. He'd get suspicious if she refused him. She looked down coyly and gently swirled the suds away, exposing her breasts. His expression froze for a second before he gulped and spluttered and tore his gaze away. He rose, knocking the stool over, and handed her a towel.

"Uh, you get a good night's sleep. We don't want you to be sick. And I'm thinking it'd be a good idea if we started over. From, like, the beginning. You know?"

She could scarcely believe what she was hearing. She dried herself as Terry gathered the plate and cup.

"I got work to do, but you go ahead and get into bed. I won't wake you when I come in." He left, closing the door behind him.

The familiar comfort of her mattress and pillow and the warmth of the comforter felt sinfully luxurious. Megan wanted to think about Terry's behavior and the future, but her thoughts were rapidly disintegrating into fog. She'd just been through hell and was battered mentally and physically. Had everything that had happened to her been an illusion? Had she made a snap judgment about her love for Steamer? Shouldn't she stay with Terry, try to work their marriage out, and make sure she was choosing the right path?

Megan awoke with her heart pounding, staring into stygian darkness. Where was she? A two-tone snore from beside her ended her disorientation. The moon was down, which meant dawn was not far away.

She crept out of bed. The odor of whiskey told her Terry was not likely to waken, but she moved quietly anyway, sliding her feet into her slippers and pulling on her wool bathrobe.

Fiona, TT, and Terry had all done their best to pretend they weren't the least bit worried about Agent Drago and his search warrant. Megan hadn't decided what she believed about Drago, but it made no difference. She was trapped between a bull and a cow, and she didn't want to be the one who got screwed.

Fiona had also done a very good imitation of a mother hen, settling down over her to keep her warm and protected. Either the law or the mob was about to come down on them, and Fiona was making sure Megan was still sharing their nest when it happened. For now she had to play nice with her family, until Fiona's ledgers were locked in her safe-deposit box.

She tiptoed through the yard by starlight and made her way to Fiona's office. It was even darker than her bedroom had been, and she could barely make out the bulk of the file cabinet. She felt around on Fiona's desk until her fingers touched the box of phosphorous matches kept there for lighting the lamp, but she didn't dare do that. She might drop the glass as she lit the wick or, worse, knock over the lighted lamp. She struck a match and held it high until she located the brass jar where Fiona hid the key.

With the drawer unlocked, she felt around for the ledger. There were two! Why hadn't she remembered? She struck another match. When she finally found the correct ledger, the match was burning her fingers. She dropped it, then pushed the account book down over it and ground it into the floor. She dropped the key in her pocket and padded quietly out the door.

Back in her bedroom she hid the ledger under her dirty clothing in the laundry hamper. Now all she had to do was smuggle it out of the ranch tomorrow.

CHAPTER 36

Sunday Morning, June 28

The loud rapping on her door jolted Megan out of a dreamless sleep, leaving her groggy and disoriented. "Terry? Go see who's at the door," she mumbled.

The rapping repeated, louder. She flung one arm out to poke Terry. His side of the bed was empty. She threw the covers off and went to the door. Fiona stood outside, a cup of coffee and a doughnut in hand. The angry frown on her face was instantly replaced by a sticky sweet smile.

"Morning, Megan. We need you to come to the living room soon as you can. Got a lot of people from the press here." Her smile wavered. "Seems like you're some kind of heroine."

Megan took the coffee and pastry. "What time is it?"

"Past ten. Now hurry."

She dressed and ate. She wanted to think about what she could tell the press and what she had to conceal, but her mind was still full of moldy hay this morning.

She ran through details in her mind. Tommy was now Charity's son, Corkie. At least he was if Steamer had persuaded her to take on the job. Pia was now Marlene Reis from Hollywood. She was in the women's bunkhouse; the guest rooms in the lodge were full. And what about . . . With a suddenness that surprised her, she collapsed into a chair and hugged her knees tightly. What about all those who had died? She swallowed hard. Eight human beings had died a horrifying death and been entombed under tons of rock.

But she had survived. Was she supposed to feel guilty for being alive? Should she stay with Terry, try to work things out, atone for being here, live an apology, and stop planning for the future? No, damn it. Even if she wanted to, there was no way she could return to the past. She had changed irrevocably and was already living in the future.

But to insure that future, she had to get that ledger into her safe-deposit box at the bank. She rose, swallowed the last of her doughnut and coffee, brushed her hair, and stepped out the door.

The atmosphere in the living room of the Rocking Lazy F was like a bomb with its fuse ready to be lit. Guests were clumped in family groups, whispering to one another with occasional restrained glances at the newsmen who had invaded their home away from home. Sissy and Susie were reading, but not reading, a movie magazine; they were ready to devour the real live gossip that had landed so unexpectedly on their doorstep. Three men and a woman, obviously reporters, were talking quietly with two photographers. Steamer stood at the back of the room, watching.

Megan's appearance lit the fuse. The guests fell silent, the reporters shouted questions all at once, and the photographers rushed forward. She was blinded by brilliant flashes. When she could see again, Agent Drago and Sheriff Goodman had appeared behind the reporters. Drago was reading from a telegram. She could see the yellow sheet of paper shaking in his hand. He was blinking rapidly, his shoulders tight under his jacket. He crumpled the telegram, threw it on the floor, and jammed his hands under his armpits.

She had no more time to wonder what was spooking him as the reporters crowded closer. At some point during the ordeal,

Steamer and Bettina came to stand by her side, and for what seemed an eternity they answered questions. How many were dead, and how did they die? Who were they? Now that it was all over, how did they feel?

Megan knew she would not feel regret over Parley's death, but she suspected the horror of it would give her nightmares for many months to come. Curly Martin and Manuel Rodriguez, Miguel's twin brother, had been warm and wonderful people. She'd miss the opportunity of getting to know them better.

"Thank you, ma'am. Now I understand four of Mr. Frampton's crew are still missing?"

The memory of the fake gunfight between Steamer and his Uncle Doodah lifted the burden of the past few days. She knew, she just knew, that Doodah, Betty, Joellen, and the new hand, Shorty Alvorsen, were alive.

"We have reason to believe they made it up the river to Guil Huff's ranch before the slide would have hit them."

Another reporter spoke up. "Mrs. Segal?"

Megan watched with admiration as Bettina handled the storm of questions with regal dignity. Yes, Segal Studios had been dealt a near-crippling blow with the death of so many valuable employees. No, the movie they had come to shoot would never be finished, but somehow she was going to continue making movies as the most suitable way to honor her dead husband.

"There's been a rumor that Mr. Buckingham, Paul Buckingham, died under suspicious circumstances on the ride out," the woman asked. "Can you tell us about that, Mrs. Foxworth?"

It was the question she'd been dreading. "He wasn't killed; he died. That is, he killed himself." They'd agreed to the story to protect Steamer. "Mr. Buckingham was, shall we say, a bit crazed by hunger. He was rampaging around, trying to grab more food, when he stumbled and fell into the fire. He then jumped into the creek. The current was too strong for him and carried him away downstream. He obviously must have drowned."

"You didn't try to save him?"

"None of us had enough strength left. Anyone who'd tried to rescue him would have drowned as well. Ten minutes in that ice-cold water and you'd be paralyzed."

"What are your plans, Mrs. Foxworth?"

"Why, of course, I'm going to stay right here in Jackson, with my husband and my wonderful in-laws, Fiona and TT."

"What about you, Mrs. Segal? And you, Mr. Daniels?"

"Mr. Daniels and I," Bettina said, "plan to return to Los Angeles on the train today. I'm sure you understand that we need to get home to arrange a suitable tribute to Alan."

Megan had been aware that as the press conference wore on, Drago had become more and more agitated, whispering to Sheriff Goodman at the back of the room.

Now he shoved his way through the reporters and photographers. "That's enough!" he shouted. The news people fell back in surprise and confusion. "There's a criminal investigation going on here," he continued, glaring around at them. "I'm still searching for a suspect. No more questions, do you hear me? Out! Everyone out!"

Sheriff Goodman stepped up beside Drago. "Come on, cool down. These people have been through hell. You can come back later when they're more rested. And when you have a warrant."

As the sheriff guided Drago out of the living room, Megan thought she saw him roll his eyes at her.

Throughout the press conference, Steamer had been walking on hot coals, certain that Drago had selected Megan as the target of his frustration. His anger at her had saturated the atmosphere of the press conference. And yet, behind all anger lies fear. What had terrified him?

As the crowd dispersed, Steamer noticed the yellow telegram Drago had crumpled and thrown away. He strolled over and, as if annoyed at seeing trash, bent over and picked it up.

In his room he smoothed it out and studied it. It was coded in four-letter groups. He was about to toss it out when one word at the end caught his attention: *ciao*. He recognized it: for his Italian friends it meant both hello and good-bye. It was a sort of universal greeting, but why would someone in the Prohibition Bureau use Italian? Maybe the sender was hoping it would be mistaken for a code word. It was pretty good evidence that Drago was what Pia said he was—an agent for her "uncle," the mobster.

Deciding that he'd look for someone in Los Angeles who might be able to decode the message, he folded it with care, put it in his briefcase, and continued packing. Bettina had made arrangements for her private railcar to be attached to the train from Victor. In the noise and confusion at the end of the press conference, Megan had managed to pass a few words to him: "Don't worry. No matter what I say or do, trust me. I'll be at the train." The last he saw of her, she was playing the dutiful daughter-in-law with Fiona.

He hoisted his suitcases and carried them to the front entrance of the Rocking Lazy F. Several families who were leaving on the same train gathered around the touring car as Terry loaded their luggage. Fiona was glad-handing the departing guests, urging them to return next season.

Steamer dawdled, pretending to check the straps on his luggage. Where was Megan? Wasn't she going to come say good-bye and maybe pass a secret message to him? She'd ignored him and treated him like a stranger. He knew she had to fool Fiona and Terry, but would she really let him leave with no last word?

Then he saw her coming from the direction of the kitchen

and carrying a large wicker basket. Daphne trailed behind her, head down, moving with tiny, tottering steps.

"Goodbye, Steamer." Megan clamped the basket to her left hip and shook hands. He could see Fiona watching her like a cat watching a mouse hole. "That was sure some kind of adventure, wasn't it? Can't thank you enough for all you did to help. Now you come back up sometime and visit, you hear?" Her hand trembled slightly as he held it. She squeezed his firmly, quickly, twice. "Have a good trip home."

She turned away just as Fiona came up behind her and reached for the basket. "Let me take that for you, Megan. I need you to get on over to Sally's and get veggies for dinner."

"You let me carry it, Mother Foxworth." Megan shifted the basket to her right hip, keeping it away from Fiona. She leaned closer and hugged her. "I don't want you to make your arthritis worse."

"Come on, Luella." Megan took her sister by the arm and towed her away. "Gertie is waiting for us."

Steamer watched her move off, towing Daphne behind her. A moment of doubt nearly drove him to his knees. Megan had been so cool and brisk as she said good-bye. Was she really going to join him on the train? Of course, she was. Thinking any other way was madness. She'd been cool because Fiona had been watching her every move and listening to her every word. She loved him. She would be there.

The squeak of TT's wheelchair behind him made him turn. The old man was wheeling up to him, a grin on his face. "Hey, Steamer! Got good news. A rider just came into town, rode in the long way around. Doodah and the girls are safe, up at Guil's place. Thought you'd like to know."

"Thanks, TT. Damn right I want to know. You tell Uncle Doodah that I'll be back as soon as I can to see him, okay?"

★ ★ ★ ★ ★

The closer Gertie's car got to Jackson, the more Megan's body seemed to grow heavy, defying her to move. As they passed Isaiah's Grocery she saw Frank, his pants drooping as usual, sweeping the front porch with lackadaisical strokes of his broom.

A memory jolted her of stepping on a dead rat and whirling around and into Steamer's arms. What if that had not happened? What if she'd never met him? She'd be going back to the ranch, not to Hollywood. She'd be going back to Terry and his demands for "special treatment" and to Fiona and a huge pile of dirty dishes every day.

You got yourself into that mess. Yes, she had. She'd been so anxious to please everyone that she'd pleased no one and had allowed her mother to push her into marrying Terry. It was time for her to grow a backbone.

"We're here, Megan." Gertie was looking at her with concern.

They were parked in front of the bank. Megan removed the ledger from the basket. "Take care of Luella, will you? I won't be long."

Inside the bank she approached the desk of the manager, Bill Swanson. He was a dour, lanky Swede who had replaced her father as manager after he'd been caught embezzling. Little wonder she had never gotten along with him.

He looked up with his normal gloomy smile. "Good morning, Mrs. Foxworth. Is there something I can do for you?"

She pulled her safe-deposit box key from her purse and held it up. "I need to put something in my box."

"Very well." He rose and led her back to the vault. They inserted their keys into the dual locks and pulled out the box. Megan placed Fiona's ledger in it.

"Now, Mr. Swanson, you need to know something."

"What's that, Mrs. Foxworth?" He closed the door and gave

351

her back her key.

"If I'm killed or crippled for life, or if anything bad happens to Fiona, or TT, or Terry, you are to open my box and take that ledger to the Prohibition Agency."

He drew back, a look of alarm darting across his face. "Why?"

"None of your business."

"That's an unusual request. I'm going to have to have you put it in writing, Mrs. Foxworth."

"I don't have . . ." She looked at the clock on the wall. There was still time for her to get to Victor before the train departed. She scrawled a hasty note of instructions and handed it to him. "I think that will cover it, Bill."

His mouth twitched with displeasure at her use of his first name. "I'll put this in your file."

Megan stepped outside—and stopped abruptly. Gertie's car was empty. *Where in hell were Luella and Gertie?*

She dashed to one end of the street and looked up and down the cross street. She saw nothing. Frantic now, she ran toward the other end, hearing voices raised in argument as she neared the cross street.

Gertie was clutching at Junior, who was holding Luella away from him. They were all talking at once. Luella was pleading with Junior to buy her a little drink. Gertie was pleading with Junior to let her go. Junior was shaking Gertie off as he might shoo away a fly, and he was scowling at Luella.

"Ain't no way I'm going to buy you a drink, you foolish woman. How many times do I have to tell you, alcohol is the devil's drink."

"Luella!" Megan slowed as she reached Junior. "Thank you for taking care of her, Junior. I appreciate it, but now we have to go. Gertie, get Luella back in your car. I'll be there in just a moment."

Junior shoved Luella away and turned to Megan. "Where are you all off to in such a rush?"

"Uh, to Sally's. Fiona's in a hurry for us to buy some vegetables. See you later."

"Yes, you will. I've got some business to take care of, but soon as that's done, I'll be back so we can be married. Now don't you go away."

CHAPTER 37

Sunday Afternoon, June 28

Pia hunkered down in the wheelchair, fondling her .25 Colt under the blanket. She had to fight the urge to look around and search for Tommaso in the crowd surging about the train platform. Bettina had warned her not to do that. Drago would be there. Drago would notice and would be suspicious.

The wheelchair bumped over the rough planks of the platform as Bettina pushed it toward the train. A half-dozen women in dowdy garments waved placards denouncing the evil of alcohol. The arriving passengers looked dazed at the blast of martial music that greeted them as they descended the steps.

No wonder, Pia thought, *the band is terrible.* The sour notes from the trumpet player alternated only occasionally with sweet ones. The fat man played the tuba as if he'd rather be at home asleep. The drummer thumped his bass drum with a rhythm that wasn't.

None of this helped Pia's anxiety one bit. She'd been hiding in the maid's bunkhouse at the Rocking Lazy F, pretending to be ill and praying that Drago would not search there. Then, before dawn, Tommaso—no, she must remember that he was not even Tommy anymore; he was Corkie—had come to say good-bye. Charity and Bertie had been drilling him on proper pronunciation of English words. He'd been so proud of himself at his accomplishments. She was happy for him yet, at the same time, chagrined by the change in him. He was already an American.

Damn Uncle to hell! If he were standing before her now, she would shoot him dead. *The hell with all the witnesses.* She ground her teeth. She was going to have to play their game if she ever wanted to see her son again.

"Good morning, Marlene."

Steamer stood beside her chair. He'd spoken her new name quite loudly, obviously to remind her. Behind him, she could see the sheriff and Drago getting out of the sheriff's patrol car.

"Mornin', Mr. Daniels." She tried to imitate Betty's drawl. "Is . . . ?" She scanned the crowd on the platform.

He shook his head with an almost imperceptible movement. "We've got ten minutes before the train leaves." He turned away. She could see his gaze sweeping the station, looking for Megan.

"Now you remember not to strain your voice," he added.

She nodded. He meant that she was to keep her mouth shut. Her accent would betray her, but with any luck her appearance would not. Early this morning Fayrene had added more fake blood, stitches, and bandages. She looked like a blonde victim of a massacre.

Her disguise was going to be put to the test very soon. Drago was walking slowly through the crowd of departing passengers, scanning them minutely.

Behind him, Charity was herding "her boys" through the crowd. It was proving difficult. Someone had outfitted them with real western clothes and new lassos, and both boys were twirling their ropes with enthusiasm. They were drawing irritated stares from some and bemused smiles from others.

Pia dragged her attention from the boys. Drago was getting closer. She tightened her grip on the pistol.

Drago slowed, came closer, and gazed at her. A memory of

the calf she'd shot rose in her mind: it had simply bawled and run away, proving that the .25 was not a real man killer. But still, she could shoot Drago in the eye if he touched her.

"Morning, ma'am. And who are you?" he asked.

She was lifting the pistol to clear the blanket when Corkie and Bertie ran behind him, their whirling lariats slapping into his legs. He turned from her with a snarl. "Goddammit, keep your brats away from me! And teach them some manners!" he shouted.

Charity smiled seductively at him as she shooed the boys away. "Oh, now, Mr. Drago, boys will be boys." She slid her hand under his arm and gazed up at him. "Why don't you tell me a little about your work? It's so important, keeping alcohol from destroying our country. And you could help us get aboard, if you would be so kind."

With an annoyed glance behind him, he escorted Charity and the boys to the train. Pia drew a deep breath and blew it out slowly. Perhaps she could begin to hope.

Steamer returned. "The conductor said we can get you into Mrs. Segal's private car now, Marlene." She felt the chair begin to move.

"Stop!"

Gertie's car slowed abruptly and stopped as she jammed on the brakes. "What's wrong?"

"Nothing," Megan replied. "Well, no, that's a lie." She got out and walked to the edge of the road. They were at the crest of the last ridge, from which she could look back and see Jackson Hole. The town and fields were bathed in warm afternoon light that emphasized the green of the fields and the snow capping the Teton Range. Behind the mountains the sky was a deep cyan. She could hear Luella singing to herself in the back seat.

Gertie came to stand beside her. "Having second thoughts?"

"No. Yes. No." She drew Gertie closer and hugged her. "It's just that . . . I'm wondering if I'll ever see all this again. It's the only thing I've ever known, all my life, and . . . Not like Luella, who's been to Hollywood."

"Are you sure this is what you want to do?"

"No, I'm not. But I've burned all my bridges behind me and sown the land with salt."

"What does that mean?"

"I left some damaging evidence behind."

"God, I wish I had your courage, Megan."

"That didn't take courage. Where I really had to be brave was admitting to myself that everything was all my fault."

"We'd better get on the way. Don't want to miss the train. You can tell me about it as we drive."

As the car rolled down the backside of the mountains toward Victor, Megan said, "I always had a tendency to conform, Gertie. To do everything everyone expected of me, to please everyone all the time. I married Terry to please Mom. Then I found out what was really going on at the ranch, and I buried myself in my dreams of being a big movie star, just like Luella."

"My name is Daphne Divine."

Megan swiveled to look at her sister and smiled. "Right. From now on, you will always be divine. And my kid sister. And I'm going to take care of you."

As they pulled to a stop at the depot, Megan could see TT and Fiona greeting a dozen incoming guests. They all looked stiff, uncomfortable, and bewildered by the fresh air and sunshine. Well, a month at the Rocking Lazy F would turn them into dudes and dudines, and they'd go home with memories to last a lifetime.

Steamer was helping "Marlene" up the boarding stairs at Bettina's private railcar. She disappeared into the shadows of the interior, and Steamer turned with an anxious look on his face. The moment he saw her, his face broke into a huge smile. He waved.

She waved back and pointed to Luella. She made motions that he was to come and get Luella and take her to the train.

A gaggle of guests was still flapping around on the platform, searching for luggage and trying to control their excited children. Megan started to thread her way through them—and came face to face with Fiona. The shock and surprise on her face were rewards in themselves.

"Megan? What . . . are you doing here?"

"I'm leaving, Fiona."

Fiona seized Megan's arm and turned her away from the train. The old bird had claws like an eagle. "What the hell do you think you're doing, missy?" She turned to TT, who had been squeaking along behind her in his chair. "TT? Help me. She's talking nonsense. Get her into the car."

Megan yanked her arm free. "I've got a present for you, Fiona." She reached into the right front pocket of her waist overalls, but the key was not there. Her heart slammed. She dug into the left front pocket—and found the key. She held it out to Fiona, who stared at it in horror and then grabbed for it.

Megan snatched it out of reach. "I've locked the ledger in my safe-deposit box at the bank. And I've left written instructions that if anything bad happens to me, or to you, or TT or Terry, the manager is to turn it over to the Prohibition Agency. Good-bye, Fiona. I'll make arrangements in Hollywood to divorce Terry."

Steamer put his arm around her. "Time to go, Megan." He followed her to the stairs and helped her aboard the private car and then out to the observation platform. They stood for a long time, arm in arm, watching Victor dwindle to a smudge on the horizon.

Steamer had at last allowed himself to be lulled into a reverie by the clickety-clack of iron wheels on iron rails. Megan dozed with her head on his shoulder. Bettina sat across from them. Her gaze pointed at a book, but she didn't seem to be reading.

She lifted her head. "Hey, cowboy, you look as if a cow just shit on your blanket roll."

Steamer laughed. "I didn't think you were reading." He shifted to a more comfortable position, and Megan sighed and snuggled closer. "I was just thinking of Paul."

"Want to tell me about it?"

"I keep seeing him jumping into the river, over and over. I feel like shit about his death."

"Go on."

"I've been wondering. Do you think that if I'd listened to his ideas, tried to work more closely with him, maybe . . ."

"I'm not sure, Steamer." Bettina sipped her coffee. "Would the two of you have avoided the conflict that led to his death? I don't know."

"Oh. Would you mind if I told you something?"

Bettina shook her head.

"Okay. I lied about how my dad died. It wasn't a stampede that killed him. It was booze. Mom worked so hard after that to feed us. If Uncle Doodah hadn't been able to help once in a while . . . well, we might not have made it.

"Then, because she was so busy, she left me to play by myself most of the time. That's how I got the idea I was sufficient unto myself. So what I'm realizing is that I've been a loner working in an industry that requires cooperation. So I guess what I'm asking is, do you think I can make it, back in Hollywood? Can I support Megan and myself?"

Bettina nodded slowly. "Yes, I believe you can. Now." She put her cup in the saucer very gently. "But not with Segal Studios."

"Why . . . not?"

"I don't know how I can keep the studio running. I've also faced some nasty truths, Steamer. Such as, Alan was operating on borrowed money, and, yes, I know what you told me about what Megan did . . . and that may protect me for a while.

"But even if the mob never comes after me again, without the film we were shooting up there, I have nothing to fall back on, no product to release."

They sat a long time watching the scenery passing. Steamer broke the silence. "I was thinking about going back to ranching, but Doodah was right. I've changed too much to do that. So. I could sell the ranch. It'd bring in a good wad of cash. Do you think we could work together, keep the studio going?"

Bettina looked down, and he could see she was controlling tears. After a while she pulled out her handkerchief and wiped her eyes. "We can only try. And if I can sell the mansion, we could be partners, okay?"

They shook hands.

EPILOGUE

A headline from *The Santa Barbara Daily News*, Monday, June 29, 1925:

EARTHQUAKE SPREADS DEATH. INJURED FILL HOSPITALS. OTHER CITIES SAFE IS WORD

From the pages of *The Wyoming State Tribune:*

JACKSON, Wyo., July 7.—A valuable property was destroyed Tuesday night when an unknown person or persons fired a fusillade of shots into the barn on the Rocking Lazy F ranch. TT Foxworth, owner of the popular dude ranch, stated that he had stored a large quantity of lamp oil in the barn and that the shots must somehow have ignited it. In addition, the family had stored a quantity of wooden furniture there, which added fuel to the conflagration. The barn burned to the ground.

JACKSON, Wyo., Friday, July 8.—Agents of the Prohibition Agency conducted a surprise raid on the Rocking Lazy F ranch yesterday. TT Foxworth and his wife, Fiona, both expressed shock and surprise at the raid, stating that the agency had obviously been misinformed about the presence of illegal liquor on the property of the popular dude ranch. No arrests were made due to a lack of evidence.

JACKSON, Wyo., Monday, August 15.—Sheriff Joe Goodman is investigating the death of Parley Frampton, Jr., known to his friends as Junior. The cause of death appears to have been an accident. He was found dead in the south forty of the Frampton spread. He had been run over and sliced to death by a harrow while plowing the field alone. Sheriff Goodman stated that the controls of the tractor appeared to be defective, as the clutch appears to have engaged while Frampton was making an adjustment to the harrow.

Suspicion was aroused when wounds on the body indicated that Frampton was run over more than once. Sheriff Goodman denounced rumors that the death was connected to the presence of whiskey smugglers operating in the area.

Anyone who may have witnessed the accident or has any knowledge of it is urged to contact the sheriff's office.

From "Births and Deaths" in *The Santa Barbara Daily News*, 1926:

Born: To Stanley and Megan Daniels, a baby boy, 8 lbs 2 oz, on March 15th, at St. Francis Hospital.

A postcard from a tourist to a friend, May, 1930, postmarked in Jackson, Wyoming:

Dear Madge,

You'll never believe what happened to me! I met a real *town drunk* the other day! His name was Terry, and he was cadging drinks from us in a bar. He had some outrageous story about a landslide that he would tell us for the price of a shot of whiskey! Of course I refused to listen.

Having a wonderful time. Wish you were here.

Love,
Clare

News article from *The Hollywood Reporter,* February 27, 1942:

The remains of Daphne Divine, known for her many glamour roles in the 1920s, have just been found. Miss Divine vanished from St. Francis Hospital on June 30, 1925, one day after the devastating earthquake in Santa Barbara. She was said to be recovering from nervous exhaustion brought on by overwork and stress, according to Miss Divine's sister, Megan Daniels. Mrs. Daniels made the identification based on jewelry found near the remains.

"My sister was never without that gold and turquoise bracelet. It was given to her by an admirer, and she was passionately attached to it. A prayer book was also found under her body," Mrs. Daniels said.

ABOUT THE AUTHOR

H. Lee Pratt was born in New York City in 1930 and grew up in Arizona and California. After graduating from San Diego State University with a degree in telecommunications and film, Lee served with the US Army in Korea.

Lee was a keen adventurer and world traveler. The backcountry of the west, however, held a very special place in his heart, and he was energized and renewed by its natural splendor.

Megan's Song was inspired by Lee's many horseback pack trips into these remote, beautiful areas.

He lived in Santa Barbara with his wife, Connie, until his death in 2016.

The employees of Five Star Publishing hope you have enjoyed this book.

Our Five Star novels explore little-known chapters from America's history, stories told from unique perspectives that will entertain a broad range of readers.

Other Five Star books are available at your local library, bookstore, all major book distributors, and directly from Five Star/Gale.

Connect with Five Star Publishing

Visit us on Facebook:
  https://www.facebook.com/FiveStarCengage

Email:
  FiveStar@cengage.com

For information about titles and placing orders:
  (800) 223-1244
  gale.orders@cengage.com

To share your comments, write to us:
  Five Star Publishing
  Attn: Publisher
  10 Water St., Suite 310
  Waterville, ME 04901